LITTLE JEW ON THE SOUL TRAIN

Rae Sikora

Plant Peace Daily

CONTENTS

Title Page
Swimming With Sharks   1
Karina   13
Dirty Laundry   18
Karina   35
What Makes Grass Grow   37
Karina   52
Animal House   55
Karina   61
Concave Breasts and Gousters   64
Karina   72
Eight Signs Your Child Might Be Retarded   75
Karina   90
No Fucking Storm   93
Karina   100
The Soul Train   101
Karina   120
Your Test Results Are Positive   123
Karina   135
Eating Tongue   137

Karina	145
Beautiful Tush	148
Karina	176
Down to Earth	177
Karina	198
Get the Jew Off the Bus!	202
Karina	216
Surprise Flight	219
Karina	236
The Book of Etiquette	240
Karina	252
Truck Driving Woman	255
Karina	271
One Way Ticket	274
Karina	287
Serial Monogamist	291
Karina	327
Little Bruce the Guru	331
Karina	340
Acknowledgement	343

SWIMMING WITH SHARKS

Pessy had to close the thick wool winter coat over her enormous belly with one of her scarves. She was over 9 months pregnant and the bump was like an oblong watermelon bulging painfully under the tight skin. She had done everything Olga had told her to do, so she wouldn't get pregnant. Pessy had used the diaphragm and jelly the doctor had given her, said no to her husband as often as she could without getting him angry, and she had been drinking the awful bitter tea that Olga had made for her. Then, when she did become pregnant, she had been doing everything Olga suggested to make sure she gave birth to a boy. She avoided strawberries and any reddish vegetables and she had eaten more cucumbers and pickled capers than she cared to remember. Now, she was getting back on the train to ride the hour to the city so she could ask Olga what she could do to make this baby finally come. She was over three weeks late and the doctor would do surgery if she didn't go into labor by the coming week.

Pessy was careful to not drink all morning so she would hopefully avoid having to use the small bumpy disgusting piss scented train bathroom. She lied to Lazer and told him she was going to her friend Fran's house. He didn't believe in tea leaf readers and thought Olga was a waste of money and time. Unlike Lazer, Pessy believed in the same trusted people her own mother had turned to in times of need or wanting clarity. Pessy refused to see the many times Olga had given bad advice or was totally wrong about what would happen. She had total faith in her.

So Pessy waddled to the station and got on the 9 am express train to Chicago.

By the time she reached Olga's apartment, she had to shuffle-run straight to the bathroom. She had called Olga yesterday and asked if she could please give her advice over the phone. Olga insisted that it had to be in person if the leaves were going to be accurate.

Pessy sat at Olga's little table with the stained lace cloth and drank the tea that was waiting for her as soon as she came out of the bathroom. Olga didn't speak. She sat with her eyes closed across from Pessy and listened to her sipping on the tea. Finally when she heard Pessy put the purple flowered teacup back in its saucer, she opened her eyes.

-"All of it? Every drop?"
-"Yes, I drank all of it, Olga"
-"Good"
Olga grabbed the cup with her crooked arthritic fingers and long red nails.
-"I see the problem. This little boy has changed his mind about coming here to earth. He agreed to come here some time ago and now he can feel how painful life is here. He knows things are not easy in your life and he feels all your sadness and stress and does not want to be part of your life."
-But Olga, of course it is difficult. I never wanted another child. I did everything you and the doctor told me to do so I wouldn't get pregnant. We can't afford another child. We are already struggling. Lazer is angry at me for letting myself get pregnant.
-"Dear Dear Pessy, there is nothing I can do to make this child come out against his will. You have to make your home a place he is not afraid to live in. You have to relax yourself and accept this baby as a gift. Lazer can be as angry as he wants to, but it

is also his fault that you are pregnant. Lazer should be wearing a sheath or get surgery if he doesn't want more babies." Olga looked back into the cup of leaves. "This little boy is going to have a hard time once he is born and you will have many challenges from him. This world will not be an easy place for him to be. I am going to give you a little bag of special herbs you will wear around your neck and put under your pillow at night. It will help you relax and maybe the baby will relax and hopefully want to come out. Have you been wearing your ribbon?"

Olga was talking about the red ribbon that all the Russian women wore safety pinned to their bras to keep away the evil eye and any curses. It was safety pinned to Pessy's bra then and every day of her life. Every Russian baby had one pinned to their underclothes from their birth. Pessy would not ever leave the house without the ribbon secured to her by her mother when she was a child and now she pinned it on by herself as an adult.

"Olga, of course I have my ribbon."

Pessy pulled her blouse down enough for Olga to see it.

-"Pessy, I am going to give you a thicker one made of real India silk. You must wear it day and night. Only take it off very briefly when you bathe. You must be very careful in these next days."

Pessy let Olga pin the bigger ribbon on her bra and took the little cloth bag of herbs that Olga had made for her. After using the bathroom one more time, she paid Olga and walked the two blocks to the train.

She rode the hour back to Kenosha thinking about Olga's words. She had to find a way to relax about this baby.

Kenosha was a strange town. Set right between the industrial towns of Chicago and Milwaukee, it had all the industry and crime of those cities, but none of the culture. Like all the small industrial towns on Lake Michigan's shores, the lake was part of the manufacturing world, but not loved as a lake should be. Ships came in on it, industrial waste was spilled into it, but no one walked the shores admiring it like they do with an ocean shore. Kenosha was named for a native, Chippewa word, for pike. Pike are the fish that used to live in the lakes. And the Chippewa tribe was run off, slaughtered or enslaved to take over the land there. Just like the new developments called The Oaks or Willow Run that contain no oaks or willows after the bulldozing, Kenosha did not have one native resident. The town was a mix of Mexican immigrants and blacks working in the factories and whites who either worked in the factories as management or as factory workers. The factories were the only place the races could be found side by side. Outside of the factory they lived in different worlds.

Four days after her trip to Olga, Pessy woke up early and the pain in her abdomen was so intense Lazer loaded her into the turquoise Rambler station wagon and rushed her to the hospital. The floorboards of the car were rusted through. Pessy had put cookie sheets over the huge holes months ago, but the cold spring wind still blew up through the floor mats and made her legs cramp. The pain was
unbearable.
Dr. Bergen was there to meet them.
-"Pessy, it is time. We are going to have to go in for the baby."

What seemed like a minute later, Pessy woke up in her hospital bed in stiff bleachy sheets and was handed a giant fat-covered baby with a little ponytail and a pink ribbon in her hair.
-"There must be some mistake, nurse. My baby is a boy."
The two nurses laughed.
-"No Mrs. Lebowitz, there is no mistake. This is your little girl."
-"But, I just had this baby, mine couldn't be this big with hair."
-"Yep, she weighs 10 pounds and has a full head of hair, but she

is yours for sure."

Pessy was confused. Could Olga have been that wrong? And, all those cucumbers and pickles and capers. Lazer came in a few minutes later. He looked stunned.
-"Pessy, the doctor told me....another girl? I thought it was going to be a boy? Oy."

Pessy and Lazer examined the baby to make sure it was really a girl. Her 10 pounds of fat made her look like a little mini Michelin tire guy. Rolls of fat that looked like she had tight rubber bands up and down her legs. Her eyes were slanted from the fat and she looked like an Asian or Eskimo baby. Pessy pulled up the fat of the baby's belly, hoping to see that it was a boy with a tiny feckie, but it was indeed a girl.

They were going to name the boy baby Lou after Lazer's father. Now that they had a girl, they decided to name her Lucy.
Two days later they brought Lucy home to her older brother and sister and her grandparents. The very first month at the house, in the bedroom, she rocked the crib on wheels until it got wedged in the doorway and the door had to be removed to get to her. Pessy's first thought was what Olga had said about the baby not wanting to be born. She was sure that the door incident was no accident. She was pretty sure Lucy was trying to get some space, and if she could have, she would have screamed, "Let me back into the womb!! I didn't know what I was getting into here!" She was nicknamed The Watermelon by all their friends before she was even born because she looked like one in Pessy's belly. Pessy was sure The Watermelon was late coming out because she was trying her hardest to delay the inevitable. She had no interest in going from the warm, swimmy, fairly safe home inside a mom body to the unpredictable noisy chaotic world just a few inches away on the other side of some muscle and belly fat and skin.

Lucy's brother Ronny was three years older than her and her sister Karen was six years older than her. Karen, Ronny, and Lucy must have seemed like good choices when your names are Pessy and Lazer. Lucy was quickly nicknamed Lulu and then Lu. She would rarely be called Lucy by anyone except the first day of the school year with every new teacher.

As soon as Lucy was old enough to understand words, her family told her she was dropped by parachute from a plane coming from Alaska, and that's why her eyes were slanted like an Eskimo girl's. She had floated down to their backyard and they decided to keep her. They told Lucy this wacky story so many times that she believed it was true. In kindergarten, she told her teacher, Miss Moretti and the kids at school that she was dropped by parachute down to her temporary family, but had actually been born in Alaska and would probably be returned there one day to her original Eskimo family. Miss Moretti called Lucy's parents and told them that she was a liar and that they should control her wild imagination. She told them it was best if they nipped this in the bud early on. Lazer and Pessy sort of threw Lucy under the bus and didn't tell Miss Moretti that they were the originators of that story. Even if they had fessed up, Lucy was never going to be in Miss Moretti's good graces. Miss Moretti was one of the many Italian Catholics in Kenosha and they all seemed to hate Jews.

Lu got an education early on in how much people hated Jews. The first winter in school, Lu walked to the kindergarten building at Sunnyside Elementary School one morning and arrived before the doors opened. There were three identical outside doors with ramps to the three kindergarten classrooms, but only two rooms were in use. Lu curled up near the door in a deep snow drift and fell asleep. When she woke up, no one was around. Lu got up and realized she was sleeping at the one door that was never used. She looked in the windows and saw that the kids were all inside. She had totally slept through all of them arriving and they must have not seen her in the huge drift by the third door. When she came through the door and explained where she had been, Miss Moretti, slapped her for lying about being at the third door. Lu offered to show her the round place where she had fallen asleep and the snow had melted under her. But Miss Moretti just slapped her again and kept saying she wanted to know where she was for the hour she was not there. Finally, she pinned a note to Lu's jacket that said: "Lu was an hour late for school and will not tell the truth about where she was for that hour. She is not welcome back until she tells the truth." Miss Moretti called Pessy at work to come pick Lu up at the school office. While Lu waited in front of the secretary's desk at the office, Mr. Johnson, the principal, gave her a lecture about lying. Lazer and Pessy spoke to the principal that week about Miss Moretti's reputation for hating Jews and asked that Lu be given a chance in the other kindergarten class. Lu was switched to Miss Mitchell's kindergarten class and was treated like the other kids in the class. That was all it took for her to fall in love with Miss Mitchell. She was Lu's first teacher crush. Lu stared at her like rescue dogs stare at the first caring person in their lives.

Lu was always tired in the morning. She rarely slept through the night. She was afraid to fall asleep. Each night would start with Lu on all fours rocking and rhythmically banging her forehead into the solid maple headboard of her bed. Sleep meant a world almost as terrifying as the day world and she would have the same two nightmares every night. In the first one, women with long red fingernails and red lipstick would come after Lu and corner her in the fenced area behind the batter's mound in a baseball field. Then they would pick at her face with their sharp nails. This dream sprang from her anxiety about her two aunts, Lenore and Esther, who would take Lu places alone and try to pick the black mole off her cheek. They told Lu not to tell anyone and said the mole was there because of a curse someone had put on her. It was a real life nightmare. To Lu, their long red nails looked and felt like claws. They would make Lu's face bleed, but they never got the mole to go away. After the torture session, usually on a park bench, Lenore would buy Lu toys to keep her from telling anyone what they were doing. Lu tried to hate all the toys, but the stuffed powder blue dog that looked just like a real dog, other than the color, was like a security blanket she clung to for years.

Every night after the baseball field and long nails dream came an even more horrifying one where Lu would be walking on a thin concrete wall between two giant swimming pools far below her. One had clear turquoise water, and the other one had murky water with sharks biting at the surface. Every night Lu fell into the one with the sharks. Just before hitting the sharks, she would wake up when she fell out of bed and peed all over herself. Nights were long and scary. Lazer snored like a fire-breathing dragon all night, the hallway was dark, and Lu was too afraid to walk to the bathroom. She was positive there was a whole gaggle of long-armed-slimy kid-eating monsters under her bed who would grab her ankles if she dared to put her feet on the floor. Lu became expert at leaping into her bed from 4 feet out. Her monster fears only grew bigger when her brother entertained himself by hiding under the bed and grabbing her feet as she came by. Ronny also loved parking himself in the bedroom closet and when the lights went out, opening the noisy door and sliding across the floor, one-legged Quasimodo style making drooling and grunting sounds. Lu would scream that kind of scream that makes horror films popular. Her parents could have made a lot of money recording those screams and selling them to Hollywood. Pessy would run in when she heard the scream and wash Lu and change her into dry pajamas. This happened every night and Pessy never got angry at Lu.

Lu was never a good nap taker. She slept when she wasn't

supposed to (like at synagogue) and was awake when she was supposed to be napping. In kindergarten, there were dark blue foam nap mats with the kid's names written on the end with marker on tape. They would roll them out in a special order at naptime. Lu loved the Flesh twins, Wendy and Cindy. Cindy Flesh's nap mat was next to Lu's in Miss Moretti's class and Lu had to leave her when she got transferred next door to Miss Mitchell's room. Lu cried when she left Cindy. But, moments later she realized, she was getting Wendy Flesh in her new class and got happy again. At naptime, Wendy's mat was just a few inches from where Lu's feet were. Lu would spend the whole naptime twirling Wendy's long hair in her toes and massaging her head with her feet until Miss Mitchell would come over and ask Lu to please keep to herself.
But Lu just couldn't do it and would dive her toes right back into Wendy's hair when Miss Mitchell walked away. Wendy would keep her eyes closed and either giggle or moan. If Lu stopped for even a moment, Wendy would take her foot in her hand and push it back into her hair. Miss Mitchell tried putting socks on Lu's feet to make her stop, but the socks would come off and Lu was back at it. Finally, she let Lu and Wendy have their ritual and gave up on making Lu sleep.

Miss Mitchell showed Lu that some people would be nice to her even though her family was Jewish. But, Miss Moretti taught Lu a more important lesson. Lu learned from her what it feels like to be hated because of a group you are born into that you have no control over. It is Miss Moretti who helped steer Lu toward working in animal rights and all social justice work. As she grew up, Lu did not want any individual to suffer because of their race, religion, gender or species. So as scary and difficult as that time in her class was, it was a great lesson for Lu in empathy and compassion from someone who did not have those qualities.

Lu was a girl on the move and the fat melted off her from constant running, playing, skipping, biking and climbing through life and her eyes unslanted by 2nd grade.

Jews are often seen as, or see themselves as, the ultimate victims. Woody Allen plays the paranoid victim Jew in so many of his films. A pretty accurate caricature of the tribe. Like each kid in a family handles the same situation differently, each culture handles their challenges differently. Most Jews choose to stay together as much as possible and they are always watching their backs, worried that at any moment they will be hauled away in some nasty train and separated from family and gassed. Even if not conscious, the fear is in our bones.... some of us more than others. African Americans or relocated Africans in any country worry about the same thing. "Someone will fuck with my family and separate us and not see us as fellow humans." It is the same story knit into their bones, but with a totally different reaction in their life choices.

For most of her years at school, Lu was the only Jew in the whole school because Ronny and Karen were so much older. Back then she didn't know that people hated Jews. She only began to get a clue when she was not allowed on the lawns of certain neighbors. At 5 years old she stepped on the corner of one family's lawn and the father, Ricardo, came out shirtless with huge oiled muscles (he liked bodybuilding in their basement with a mirrored wall to watch himself) and told Lu to get her "Jew foot" off his lawn. Lu pulled her foot off the grass but still didn't really understand what that meant. His kids seemed as confused as Lu, but after that they stopped playing with her or talking to her. They wouldn't even look in Lu's direction.

Venturing out into the world of school and other kids was like a second shocking exit from the womb for Lu. Definitely frying pan into the fire.

One winter day, Lu was walking home from kindergarten and

a group of kids pushed her down in the snow and kicked and hit her all over her body. They tore her coat and threw her mittens and hat into the salted and greasy black winter street. One kid pulled out big clumps of her hair. The whole time they were yelling, "You goddamn little kike" and "Go back where you came from fucking kike!" and "Die Kike!" Lu thought they were saying kite. It wasn't until years later, thinking back on the incident, she realized that there were cars with adults actually driving by and not stopping to help. Lu was so obsessed with why they were calling her a kite, that she forgot to notice what was really happening. Once the kids were done with her, and walked away laughing, Lu stayed still for a long time looking up at the sky until she couldn't hear their voices anymore. She crawled over to her hat and mittens in the street. The pink hat had been run over a few times by cars and was covered in dirt and salt and ice chunks. She hobbled home in her torn winter coat and filthy wool hat. The salt burned the places on her scalp that were raw and red where the tall blonde boy had pulled out her hair. When Lu came through the door into the kitchen, she ran to her mom. Pessy grabbed her close and sobbed those big heaving kind of tears, squeezing Lu the whole time. When Lu told her what the kids were saying, Pessy explained that they were saying kike, not kite. Lazer and Pessy forbid the word "nigger" in their house. So, Lu had to think for a minute when Pessy explained that kike is the word for Jews like the n-word is for blacks. She cleaned Lu up and then cried even harder when she saw the red raw scalp blotches where they had torn out clumps of her hair. When Pessy wanted to call the school and tell them what happened Lu begged her not to. She knew it would only make things worse. In the next few days, Lu knew her mom had done something about it, but Lu never asked. When she told Lazer about the incident, Pessy had to make the attack sound less severe than it was because Lazer would have wanted to punish the kids himself and that would not have gone well. Those kids mostly stayed away from Lu after that, like she had a contagious disease or was invisible. Lu liked the idea of being invisible. Maybe it should have felt lonely, but by then she was starting to lose her happy kid personality and she preferred to be left alone. Maybe in other languages there is a word for that part of us that describes it better. It is like moving backwards toward that place in the womb where your sense doors are not taking much in. Just floating around in that liquid and being formed. Pessy helped Lu do her hair each day with colorful hair clips in a way that would hide the pink bald spots until the hair grew back. Pessy worried that those spots would just scar and the hair wouldn't grow back, so she rubbed cream on them everyday until the hair finally grew in.

KARINA

I met Lu when she was in her 40's. She had been a visiting presenter in a college course I had on social justice issues. She told that story to the class. I am so glad I recorded her so I could write up the details later. The year after I had class with her, I graduated and got a job as a journalist for a weekly entertainment guide in Scranton. I knew from that day Lu came to our class that at some point I wanted to interview her and get more of her story. It was years later when I focused on getting that story and finally tracked her down. It took some major digging to find her current information. I called her probably twelve times before she answered her phone. I reminded her who I was and told her I had been trying to reach her for some time. She told me she still had a landline and didn't even have an answering machine. I asked if I could interview her. Lu couldn't understand why I would want to do that and she sure didn't think it needed to be in person. Her response was, "Hey why don't we just do it right now? Ask me the questions you want to ask right now on the phone." While I wasn't sure what I would do with the interview once I had done it, I WAS sure I wanted to do it in person. This was not just about writing the story, there was something about Lu that made me want to have more time with her. You could say I was compelled, maybe even a little obsessed about digging deeper in this. She had told the story about Pessy and the tealeaf reader and about kindergarten and the incident with the pink hat, and I was sure there was more to her story that I should record. I asked her if I could come to her place in New Mexico and interview her. I was pretty sure it would take many days and I would record the whole thing. She told me she would think about it and call me back. When she called me back, three days later, she sounded less than enthusiastic.

She calmly shared that she was a bit of a hermit and that it would not be that easy to get to her place. The nearest airport was more than two hours away and to get to her house you had to canoe across the Rio Grande River and hike a rough trail. She also said she would not want me to stay there at the house since it was not really set up for guests. I could tell she thought I would say "nevermind" and give up on the whole idea. But, I didn't. Instead I asked her when she would be willing to have me come for at least a week. I told her I would get a motel room and a rental car. We made plans for a week at the end of January. Somehow I imagined New Mexico as desert and sunny and hot all the time, so I didn't pack right. When I arrived in Albuquerque, it was snowing and 25 degrees. I just hoped it would be warmer when I got to Embudo where Lu lived. I was chatting with the rental car woman and she told me it would be much colder and snowier in the north where I was headed. The rental car person and Lu had both told me I should have 4 wheel drive for the rental car, but I chose not to spend the extra money and I went for the cheapest compact car. I drove the two hours north on roads that were still covered in ice and snow and I had no cell phone reception for that last half hour of the drive on the worst section of road. How was this going to work? Lu told me to call her when I was close and she would canoe over to pick me up. I hoped I would have reception as I got close, but no such luck. I turned around and drove back to the south until I had reception again. There was nothing on that road but high rock walls on one side of me and the Rio Grande flowing on the other side of me. Not a house or a business where I could stop and ask to use the phone. The few houses I saw were on a tiny strip of earth between the road and the river and they didn't look occupied. I was too scared to stop and check. When I finally got reception, I told Lu what had happened and that I had to now turn around again and get back to the place she told me to park. She laughed, "I told you it isn't easy to get here. I'll see you soon." I drove north again and barely found the little turn off and steep icy way down to her parking spot. The rental car lost all traction and I was sliding sideways out of control down the driveway. I couldn't breathe. All I could picture was the car ending up in the river with

me in it. I quickly rolled down the windows so I could get out of the car and swim to the surface if I needed to. I had zero control of that car. At the bottom of the driveway, Lu must have put down the sand that finally gave me some control and I was able to put on the brakes. I didn't even realize that I had started crying and by the time Lu got to the car, my head was resting on the steering wheel and I was shaking uncontrollably. I felt a hand on my shoulder and looked up to see Lu. She was wearing a big winter scarf wrapped around her head and neck and a major winter jacket. I was in a city style rain jacket. I made a note to myself to ask more questions and do more research for any future stories in new locations. Lu looked concerned and that somehow made me relax a bit. She was there for me. "Karina, are you ok? That was quite a slide down the hill. Must be some shitty traction on this rental. I see you didn't go for the four-wheel-drive I suggested" I assured her I was now ok. I parked and grabbed my equipment bag and we climbed down some rocks to the place she had tied the canoe. It wasn't far across the river, but it looked impossible to me. The water was churning and there were giant chunks of ice floating by. She helped me into the boat and told me to just keep my body low and sit in the front and she would paddle us across. The ice chunks were smashing against the side of the canoe, but Lu was just calmly paddling across and chatting with me over the sound of the ice hitting. I held the sides of the canoe like my life was on the line. We bumped into the little dock on the other side and she held onto the dock while I climbed out. There were three adorable dogs sitting next to the dock. They sniffed me and then focused completely on Lu. The snow was so deep that I just stayed in that spot on the dock until Lu had finished tying off the canoe on the bank. The dogs were obviously familiar with the whole routine and once the canoe was secured, they went to Lu for head rubs and then ran up the path. Lu looked down at my shoes, which were really nothing more than light summer slip-ons, and reached into a huge metal box near the dock and pulled out big rubber work boots.
"Put these on and you will be fine. Let me take your bag. We will hike slowly since you aren't used to the altitude. It will take you a bit to adjust." She was right. Within 5 minutes of walking with her,

I was out of breath. And her idea of walking slowly, was my idea of hoofing it, I could barely keep up.

While we were hiking to her house, Lu asked me how many days I thought the interviews would take. I gave her my best estimate, "As long as it takes and as long as you are willing to let me keep recording you. I can always change my flight. But, maybe five days?"

She didn't look delighted with that answer. "Hmmm, you may want to leave earlier. This might not be as interesting as you have imagined. Anyway, as long as you are here, I am going to give you some warm sensible clothes to wear and you can use my truck to go back and forth to the motel. That car is useless on these roads. What motel are you staying at?" When I told her the name of the motel, The Katchina, she shook her head and told me that it was even further north and would be a rough ride even with her truck. We got to her little house and I was in awe. The place looked like an adobe hobbit house with colorful mosaic and clay inside and out. The sun was shining on it and when we got in the door, the floors and the whole place were toasty warm and she told me that was just from solar gain from the sun. The dogs had gotten there well before us and were already soaking up the heat from the warm tiles. I looked around and saw the dog door they had used. Lu introduced me to each dog. Noodles was the big goofy hairy one. Olive was the little sweet black shiny one. And Pip was the medium one who seemed to be in charge. Noodles couldn't keep her nose out of my crotch when we got in the door. Lu came to the rescue, "Noodles, go lay down." Immediately Noodles went back to her sun soaking buddies. There was music playing and I immediately recognized it as one of my favorite Bach cello pieces. Lu showed me around the house and made us tea and we sat in the attached greenhouse in cozy big soft chairs to start our first interview. I was so happy to be warm and to be with her. "Lu, thanks so much for being open to doing this and thank you for being so welcoming. I know you like your space and privacy, so I really appreciate this. Sorry I didn't come prepared for the weather. I thought New Mexico was hot and sunny year round."

She gave me a warm smile, "It's good to have you here. I should have warned you about the weather. I didn't think I would remember you from all the students I've spoken to, but I totally remember you and those oceany eyes and that accent of yours. New Mexico is sunny and warm year round in the southern part of the state. But up here it is called high desert and it goes from hot and sunny summers to freezing ass, but sunny, winters. But, don't worry, I have plenty of warm gear for you and we are about the same size. I will set you up."

I felt totally cared for. It is hard to describe the feeling right then. Like having solid ground under my feet and that there was nothing to worry about. For the first time in what felt like a very long time, I wasn't thinking about work or deadlines or things I needed to take care of. It was just peaceful. I looked past Lu and the bright red tomatoes growing on the plants behind her in the kitchen greenhouse and the sky was the deepest blue I had ever seen. Even in my hometown in Sweden, the skies were never that blue. I clipped a microphone to Lu's sweater, started my recorder and the interview I had anticipated for so long was beginning.

DIRTY LAUNDRY

"Lu, I am going to record all of our conversations, so you don't need to talk slow or keep anything short. Just share everything that comes to mind when I ask you questions or even if I am not asking you a question and something pops into your head. Don't edit anything out for my comfort or cut anything short, just share anything that YOU are comfortable sharing. OK? If one answer runs into another topic or memory, just go with it."

"Sure, that works. But, I also want to say that if at any point you think it is boring or you wonder what the heck you were thinking coming all this way for this mundane crap, then be honest, and we can stop the process and just go hiking or snowshoeing or skiing and drop the whole interview idea, ok?"

"I don't think that will happen, but I promise to be honest."

"I never asked you what you want to do with the material you get in the interview."

"I honestly have no idea, Lu. I have been compelled to do this since I heard the story you told in class about being Jewish in a non-Jewish town. But, I really don't know what I will do with it. I will figure that out and let you know at some point and make sure you are ok with my sharing it publicly."

"Ha, there is nothing about me or my life that I wouldn't share publicly. So I am guessing it will all be fine. Oh, and I think we should have a time limit. I don't like sitting for long. So, maybe maximum one hour and then a break to go hiking with the dogs?"

"We can check in at one hour and see if we want to stop there, does that work?"

"Sure, that works."

"Great...then, let's get rolling."

"Lu, if someone were to write a book about you, what would be a good title?"

"Hmmm, the first title that comes to mind is *Looking for Love in All the Wrong Places* or *Looking for Love for All the Wrong Reasons*. But I think a better title would be *Little Jew on the Soul Train.*"

"I love all those titles. Tell me why *Looking for Love in All the Wrong Places.*"

"I have had so many quick little intimate relationships and made so many bad choices in love and lust. I thought lust was love. I couldn't even list everyone I have had sex or a relationship with. I could describe it like this….imagine you are skydiving and you are brave enough to take the leap out of the plane without thinking about it. Then, like halfway to the ground you become aware of what you have done and you want to change your mind and wish you hadn't taken the leap and the panic fills your whole body and now you are trapped. That is how relationships have been for me. A sort of 'I want this, I want the closeness and the cozy escape from the world.' But, then suddenly I would panic and run. I am a bolter. Always have been. I have had relationships with both men and women. I have stayed too long with the ones who were not healthy for me and bolted too quickly from the most amazing people. That is a big regret. I can think of four right off the top of my head who I should have committed to for life. They were absolutely perfect for me. But I threw them away."

"Oh, I am so sorry. Regrets suck and relationships are hard to navigate. I sure have never figured out love relationships. I will ask you more about your relationships later. And, what about Little Jew on the Soul Train? What's that about?"

"I was this little Jew who grew up in a town and a house that I didn't feel safe in. There was probably no place in the whole world I would have felt at ease. It was just my nature. The human world was not my comfort zone. Well, it really still isn't. My first safety and the first place I felt like I could breathe was in the Black community. It was a sort of wild place for me to be before I discovered true wilderness. I was supported and embraced and shaped by African Americans. So I guess that title is kind of about my soul's path… so the Soul Train is not just about the television black soul version of American Bandstand, which my family watched every day…..it is also about my soul and my path being shaped from decades of bouncing over the tracks of life. The whole thing is kind of ironic because I felt the most comfortable in the black community, but it was also the place that any outsider would have said was the least safe place an innocent kid like me could be. I don't know if reincarnation is just a made up myth or if it is the truth of our lives. Do you believe in reincarnation?"

"I don't know. I think, like you, I am open to it being a possibility, but I can't know for sure, so I just think of it as an idea of something that might be what we go through in life."

"Exactly, same for me. The thing is that I have never been able to work out why the black community always felt more familiar than the white family I was born into. I have read extensive true accounts of what African slaves went through when brought to this country. I am drawn to those stories like nothing else I read. And the intensity of a living being taken as property and what was done to them haunts me all the time. I manage to go through my days not thinking about it, but when

I sleep at night, my dreams are filled with the horror stories of slavery and I wake up in a sweat or crying. My guard is down when I am asleep and these things can surface. The thing is in these dreams, I am always the slave. I can feel every aspect of being that person. I feel the freezing cold air around me when I am curled up like a dog sleeping at the door of the teen-age girl who owns me because she was given her own slave as a gift when she turned 11. I can feel the pain of being whipped across my back because I stole a little piece of soap from the master's house. I really mean I can feel all of it in my body when I am the slave in the dream. I feel the temperature, and textures of what I touch and the earth under my bare feet and sometimes my head itches because we are not allowed to wash when we want to and I have woken up from the dream scratching my head.

Years ago when I lived in Minnesota, I had Kenyan friends who were speaking Swahili to each other about a month into our friendship. I chimed in, in English, and answered what one of them asked. They all stopped talking and stared at me. They asked how I knew what they were talking about. I was confused, because I thought it was all in English. They told me the whole conversation had been in Swahili. None of us knew what to make of it, but I understood most of what they said when they spoke their home language. The day after that weird moment, I was at work and a guy name Rick, who was a co-worker, came into work and said he wanted to tell me something. He said, "You know how we have wondered why we are so close and comfortable with each other? Well, yesterday, I had a session with a past life regression guide and she told me that I was your wife in Kenya and we lived a long happy life there in one of my past lives." I don't know what I think of all that New Age stuff and the things that this woman was telling Rick. But I do know that on the day I was understanding a long Swahili conversation between my Kenyan friends and thinking they were speaking English, Rick was being told I was a Kenyan man in my past and that he was my wife. I still don't know what to make of it all. But I stay open minded about past lives and other reincarnation ideas because I assume that what we are aware of as humans is just the tip of the iceberg. There is so much we don't have a clue about and never will."

"OK, that is a crazy story. Just a weird mystery. But it gave me goosebumps when you were telling it. If there is reincarnation and we have past lives, I wonder if you and I knew each other before, in other lives."

"If there is such a thing as past lives, I am guessing we did know each other in some way, because I am very comfortable with you in my home and that is not the norm for me."

"That makes me happy. I am so glad to hear that. Lu, will you be comfortable if I ask you some questions that will be like airing your dirty laundry. I always loved that expression in the USA. I am from Sweden and we don't have that expression. The closest we would have is smutsig byk, which translates to dirty laundry, but it doesn't have the same use as here."

"I always liked that expression, too. People say "Don't air your dirty laundry". But I don't feel like that. I would guess that most of the people in my family would say not to air it and most of my friends would say, "air it". The thing about dirty laundry is that we ALL have it. Everyone has a hamper full of stuff that is not tidy or stain-free. Everyone has some stinky stuff. I figure that when people hide the dirty laundry, it makes people who have a bunch of it, meaning everyone, feel like they are bad or weird or messed up in some way. I am not saying that our whole identity should be the challenges and craziness of our past. And I know that some people spend most of their time wallowing in their wounds and the dysfunction of their past and that is who they keep presenting to the world. I just think it is a good idea to be real, to be truthful with each other and to stop choosing what we share based on how people will react. There is no one in my story who is better or worse than anyone else. Just a bunch of humans who wake up each day and try to figure out the best way to dance on this spinning blue and green ball called Earth. Lester, who raped me while his girlfriend was 30 minutes away in Milwaukee watching TV, is no worse than anyone else in my life story. It is all the grist that came together to make the dough that baked into me. And I am still baking.

You are going to wonder why black people are my favorite people, my first family. What almost killed me and what saved me are the same thing.

I dove into my black community like a dog who has never known freedom runs into barbed wire fences and cactus. Happy, joyful, free and careless. Blissfully ignorant to the dangers that surrounded me.

If I tell you all the stories, you will sometimes think some of my black family were mean and violent with me. But you have to hear what's underneath that. They are the ones who helped me become a somebody, a personality. They dug something deep out of me behind all my fears and my wanting to leave earth. They found the person who could live in this body of mine and could dance and sing and feel things. A few tried to beat it out of me, but I understood that. I understood wanting to beat the person who looks like the ones who have kept you down your whole life. The whites who stole your people from their home and brought them to this foreign place and then made them into property and took away who they could be, took away all possibility. So, ironically, those same people took me away from a situation where I could not be who I was and helped me find that somebody deep down inside. Laughter in humans is like a dog who is feeling safe enough to roll on his back and let his belly be exposed. I lost my laughter as a child. I lost my laughter in a home that didn't allow crying or weakness or anything that was about feeling what was deep inside and expressing it. I thought my core was dead, my joy was gone. And then it came alive again.

So I hope you understand that there are no villains in my story. I think sometimes we see the world as the victims and the villains. I have seen that most of the villains were once victims. And they are all great teachers."

"That is such a beautiful way to put it. I think I am one of the people who sees victims and villains. It's hard not to sometimes. Well, I will work on that and try to catch myself. Lu, tell me about what your family was like when you were born. I want to hear it all. In class you told the story of getting beat up for being Jewish in a town with few Jews. It sounded awful. Did things ever get any easier?"

"Some things got easier and some didn't. I was a tough kid who had to just keep getting tougher. But I really feel like most of the empathy I can find for those around me, human and non-human, came from those early days of getting beat up and judged. I learned that I never wanted to be the cause of someone else's suffering. I am sure I caused a lot of suffering unknowingly in my life, but I really wanted to work on trying not to whenever possible."

"I love that you can look back and see a positive from it, a gift. What was your home life like then? Was your family more an outdoor family or more intellectual?"

"Ha, we were neither. We were more of a hard working family who liked to eat. I don't remember having any books at our house other than The World Book Encyclopedia and the phone book. Maybe we did have others, but I don't remember them. I think of intellectual families as being surrounded by bookshelves that were overflowing with well-read books. Those families would sit around after dinner and read and the father would be smoking a pipe. We were not that family. All I know is that when I started reading, I wanted to read everything. I was a voracious reader of cereal boxes, milk and juice bottles, Philadelphia cream cheese wrappers, Jiffy cake mix, Bisquick, weed killer, Welch's grape jelly jars, dog biscuit boxes, toothpaste tubes, hemorrhoid cream (always in our refrigerator), soup cans, and anything else with words that I could get my hands on. I memorized all the packages in our house...knew every word ...sadly I still remember all the words. It is taking up valuable brain space. Like, the Crest toothpaste tube words: "Crest has been shown to be an effective decay-preventive when used in a conscientiously applied program of oral hygiene". Even though I haven't used that kind of toothpaste since I was living with my parents decades ago, it is imprinted in my crowded brain. I had no idea what those words meant, but I loved saying them. I would chant it a lot, not caring or noticing if anyone was around. My brother kept telling me I needed to shut up... that I needed to stop mumbling the toothpaste and hemorrhoid tube words all the time if I wanted to have any friends and not keep being a weirdo.

Reading billboards and the ever-changing signs outside stores pretty much kept me in fresh reading material all the time. Some stick in your head for life. The ones that I turned into jingles, really stuck. Making up songs and jingles was a constant fun distraction for me. I still have the jingle, "Pan-fried baby beef livers tonight" pop into my head unrequested at least once a week. Strange jingle for a vegan to have stuck in her brain, eh? It came from a sign outside Pop's Home-Cooking restaurant. They had a guy who came out with a long stick and put words, one letter at a time, on the tall sign in the parking lot. For years I was jealous of his job and aspired to get there one day. I thought his only job was making words with giant letters.

Our town eventually got a summer book mobile that drove around like a library on wheels. I would check out so many books that the stack would be over my head when I carried them and I had to look around the side of them so I wouldn't fall on my face. My eyes were bigger than my brain speed and

I never got to all of them before their due date. This was a greedy little theme in my life with all things. If I love it, more is better and it is best to have reserves on hand. On the rare occasion that we went out to eat, I would order enough for a 300 pound truck driver and have to take the leftovers home for me and the dog. My dad would tell me my eyes were bigger than my stomach, but it wouldn't stop me from my leftovers insurance policy. The bookmobile had a little paper chart shaped like an ice cream cone for each kid. When you read a book, you got another color layer of paper ice cream on your paper cone on their wall. The ones with the most layers of paper ice cream would be displayed in the bookmobile wall. This seemed realistically like my one chance at fame. With that as my goal, I would return my pile of books and lie to the librarian, telling her I had read all of them, just to get more colors on my cone chart. I think that was third grade and it was the last time that anyone saw even a hint of my being competitive or wanting fame. I wasn't built for competition. Pretty much didn't give a shit who won. Still don't. Later when I joined swim teams, I had better times in practices than in meets. I couldn't find a part of me that cared who came in first place.

Even after the bookmobile arrived, I kept reading the giant box of Kotex that sat on the floor in front of the toilet and the little box of Tampons (that I pronounced, "tampoons"). It eventually dawned on me that I didn't actually know what those things were in the boxes.

I learned at a very young age to send letters and address envelopes and stick a stamp on the envelope. I would send for ridiculous things from magazines and get into trouble. I remember the stamp collector stamps that were only a dime. I was 7 years old and put the dime in the envelope and mailed it off. Didn't tell a soul. The stamps came and there was a bill for a lot of money that came with them. When I showed Pessy the bill, she made me send the stamps back and made me promise to stop mailing things without showing her first. I did send the stamps back with her help, but I didn't ask her about the mailings that came after that. I tried to make sure they were really free things I was sending for. The very best thing I ever got in the mail after sending away for it, was the Mutual of Omaha Wild Kingdom Map of the World. It was gigantic and I would unfold it on the living room carpet and watch Wild Kingdom on television while holding my finger on the place on the map where Marlin Perkins was being filmed. That map must have been at least 4 feet across. We were only allowed to watch one television show per day. So we would carefully study the TV Guide and each of us kids would choose a show. Wild Kingdom was my Sunday pick every week. But, I would dilly dally in the hallway during Karen and Ronny's shows, too. I got little snippets of other shows."

"I can totally picture you as a kid doing those things. Would you say your family was wealthy or poor? Were you more of a working class family? Why weren't there many books in your house?"

"I know more about that now than I did back then. I guess we were working class. I wonder how many young kids know if they are rich or poor, upper class or middle or lower. Maybe they all know on some level, but I don't think I ever knew. Lazer and Pessy never fought about money…at least not in front of us kids. And, we always had the most yummy food and a warm house in winter. So, I figured we were very rich. I didn't know that Pessy sewed all of our clothes because we couldn't afford new clothes. I figured we were just too special for that store bought stuff. We would drive to the city and go to the Sav-A-Lot department store and show her clothes we liked in the store. Then she would get fabric and sew us something close to our favorites. It usually worked out ok until the year she decided she could crochet my winter clothes. The first debut was the mohair dress. I went to school looking like a giant turquoise sheep with pom poms hanging off my arms. I got bullied so bad that day that I had to be sent home from school early to escape the kids "baa baa " sheep calling at me and pushing me around. There were signs that we were not wealthy people, but I didn't see them. Pessy worked fulltime at Sears Roebuck department store and that would have been a give away that we were not wealthy during the stay-at-home mom era. But she loved her job, so I figured that is why she worked. Our house could have been an obvious clue, too, but I never suspected it was small or that it could be any other way. The place was tiny with shared bedrooms. We had one small bathroom for a family of five, and I would sit on the pink and grey formica counter with boomerang shapes in it and watch the show: My mom bathing was one of my favorites. She would lift each of her enormous breasts to wash underneath them. My dad shaving with a can of shaving cream or the cup and brush like my grandfather used was a total treat. I loved the scraping sound of the razor going over his stiff whiskers and the way he had to jut his jaw out real far making a Dudley DoRight cartoon face to shave his neck. Anyone peeing was totally fascinating and I was bummed to be told to leave when it was time for someone to poo. I was sure I was missing out on something. It was non-stop entertainment in there. Some rare moments I would have the bathroom all to myself and would pull my mom's nylon stockings out of the pink quilted hamper, put them over my entire head, look in the mirror, and then slowly raise the stocking to create ugly gangster faces with my eyelashes up on my forehead. I would just lose it laughing until I had to pee.

You asked why we didn't have books around...and I really don't know. I know that my father graduated as a mechanical engineer and my mom didn't get her high school diploma until she went back to school at 40 years old. I am guessing they didn't have time to read, but I also know that Lazer thought that reading anything but current events was a waste of time and wouldn't help us succeed in the world. If we were reading anything but Time Magazine or the newspaper, he would tell us to go do something productive. But I also know that he kept his stash of Playboy magazines hidden in a drawer next to their bed. He always said to Pessy it was for the great articles, not the pictures. The moment Pessy and Lazer left us with any baby sitter or on our own, Ronny and I would run to the Playboy magazines and look at all the pictures. I am guessing we were both getting the same thrill from them."

"You playing with the stocking in the bathroom is hilarious. And I can just picture you and your brother looking at the Playboy magazines together. I love that. Did you know your grandparents? Were they born in the USA?"

"I knew three of them. None of them were born in the states. They were Russian and Polish and sent over as teens to save their lives. Stuck on a boat heading to a place where they didn't speak the language and had no one to depend on."

"I can't imagine that. It was hard enough for me coming to America as an adult and adjusting, and I came by choice and I had learned English in our Swedish schools. Tell me about each of the grandparents. We call the mother's mother mormor and the mother's father morfar. Then we have the words for our father's parents, farmor and farfar. But in English, you don't have a way to tell whose parents it is, which I think is confusing."

"That makes so much sense. Wish we had words that made it clear. We come from people like Malka, Pessy's mom. So in Sweden, she would be my Mormor. Malka was mostly blind and still knew the price of everything at the grocery stores in town. She would take the bus an extra half hour to save 50 cents on Miracle Whip. One day I walked into her apartment and her cotton white hair was sticking straight up like Eraserhead and felt hard like wax lips.
I said, "Gram, what's going on with your hair?"
She said, "I used a new shampoo. I like it. It smells good."

I took her hand, "Gram, show me the shampoo."
Grammy Malka walked me to the shower and picked up the bottle. It was Turtle Wax for cars.
I told her, "Gram, this is not shampoo, it is car wax. You can't use this on your hair."
Gram yanked the bottle out of my hand and shouted, "You can't tell me what shampoo to use."
I said, "Gram, you should ask for help in the grocery, you can't see the labels."
She shouted, "I don't need anybody's help."
She was a wild card. She would do the rounds to each of the department stores in her city, Chicago, and put a dime in the shopping bag dispensers and then take an armload of bags. She was an undeveloped criminal. In a different life with the mafia, she would have been a real asset. One closet in her apartment was dedicated to her shopping bag collection. I think it was people like Malka who gave Jews a bad name. The cheap Jew stereotype could have been created on just her life alone.
One day she walked into the deli for a loaf of bread. The price had gone up a nickel. When she found out the new price, she threw the bread on the counter and shouted, "You got the bread and I got the money", before she grabbed my hand and we stormed out the door. It wasn't until we were a block away that I told her I had a barrel dill pickle in my hand that we hadn't paid for and she just said "Good, enjoy."

In the end, it was her stubbornness and blindness that killed her. She refused to use potholders, insisting that dish towels were good enough. Pulling cookies out of the oven one day, the dish towel caught fire on the oven element and burned her entire apartment and most of the building down with her inside. They tried to save her, but her skin was like black patent leather and her old body couldn't pull through. She died on a hospital bed with a stainless steel half barrel covering her from her neck to her knees and her back resting on wet blue antibiotic gauze cushions. She had been through a tough life. She worked factory jobs and did double time as a cleaning woman in people's homes who treated her horribly. Her husband died young of lung cancer from continuous cigarette smoking and she ended up a single mom with four kids and a lot to handle. It made her tough. A four foot ten muscular thing that you wouldn't want to cross.

Zade was my dad's dad. So you would say "farfar" in Swedish. He came to Ellis Island from Russia as a teen and was given three choices: He could be a tailor, a butcher or a barber and get training for free. He was shipped off to Chicago and began training as a tailor. But then he saw that the boys who were barber trainees had more money to gamble in the pool hall and found out they got tip money. He went to the authorities and convinced them he wanted to change up and be a barber. He was a beautiful guy, inside and out. Wouldn't speak a bad word about anyone. But he had a gambling habit that made his wife Zelda, my bubbie, crazy angry. So, in Sweden she would be my farmor, father's mother. She worked two factory jobs and he gambled the money away. They struggled all the time with money. Zade took loans out from the Jewish mafia and almost got the family killed more than once because he couldn't pay up. We kids didn't know how serious his gambling addiction was, so we would go along with it when he was taking care of us and took us to the horse-racing track. If he hadn't gotten us long bags filled with dyed red pistacios every time, no one would have been the wiser. But Zade would bring us home at the end of the day looking like we were sporting a bad red lipstick job and our fingers covered in red dye. We would help him place bets. We loved to bet our birthdays or any dates we liked. Fourth race, horse number 16 for an April 16th birthday. Zelda would yell at Zade about gambling all the money away. Some days, he would make a little money and other days he would have lost all their money.

Zelda was strong and beautiful, but angry much of the time. Now, as an adult, I understand why. Her fingers were often burned from the cookie factory she worked in. They had to pack hot cookies into boxes and there was a lot of pressure to work fast. If they had to go to the bathroom, it couldn't be on their own terms, just during specific break times. In every family, it seems, there is the parent who has to be tough and discipline and keep some order and the other parent who gets to just enjoy the kids and the house and they are thought of as the "good guy". Zade was the good guy and Zelda was the tough one. Just like Pessy was the good guy and Lazer was the tough one. If I had decided to have children, I think I would have been the tough one. But, who knows until you are faced with it.

We just were not one of those intellectual families. And I think that got passed down through the grandparents who were all working immigrants. I could have a whole dictionary of the words we used for things that my parents and grandparents were not comfortable talking about directly. For example, you definitely couldn't say vagina or penis like more intellectual families did. Those were called feckie for penis and schmungie for vagina. And Pessy wouldn't say condom, she would say "condo" and then giggle. My grandmothers asked me if I had "gotten my sickness" which meant: did I get my period yet. The only time they came close to "The Talk" was when we were watching the movie called Never on a Sunday on television and I went to the refrigerator to get something to drink and Lazer followed me and asked me if I knew what a prostitute was. I was 12 years old. We didn't look at each other and I answered him while still staring into the fridge. "Yep, I know what a prostitute is." "OK, that's good". End of discussion.

Getting my period was a shocker to everyone it seemed. We were on a road trip in Arizona. Ronny must have been about 16 and I was about 13. Lazer and Pessy dropped us off at a horseback-riding place. There were kids about our age who led the rides and they talked with fake cowboy accents and wore western cowboy clothes, even though most were from Michigan and Wisconsin suburbs. They took about 10 of us out at a time on a painfully slow and boring bouncy clomping loop around the ranch. It was over an hour and when we were just about back to the barns, I felt wetness between my legs and on the saddle. Ronny was next to me on his horse called "Sparky". I remember that because Sparky was probably the slowest of the horses and definitely needed re-naming. I showed Ronny the blood on my saddle and he freaked out. He started screaming his lungs out, yelling for help. "My sister is hurt, she's bleeding! Somebody help!" All the young fake cowpokes came running from the barns and our ride leader came over and looked down and without a word did an about face with her horse and started laughing. The other kids all did the same thing. At the same, our parents who were standing at the barn waiting to pick us up, came running. I can barely remember what happened next, except that Pessy whispered something to Ronny and he slid off his horse and wouldn't look at me, or anyone. I slid off my bloody saddle and we all left with our heads hung down. My best shorts were blood soaked. It took me a little while, but I finally registered in my slow brain what was happening. Pessy put a few maps and magazines on the car seat and a plastic bag under them and told me to sit on that so I wouldn't ruin the car upholstery. But she didn't look me in the eye and she didn't say a word about what was really happening. Lazer stopped at a pharmacy and Pessy ran in and came out with a paper bag a few minutes later. At our motel room she handed me the bag and told me, "Go in the bathroom, lock the door and figure it out." In the bag there was a box of tampons and a jar of Vaseline. I sat on the toilet and studied the instructions diagram for a long time and then I tried to find the hole to put the tampon in. It took me well over an hour of trial and error before I found the spot and managed to get it in. The whole time I could hear them watching TV in the motel room and talking about me. "What is taking her so long?" "I need to get in there to pee" "Why don't you go help her?" "No she needs to figure it out on her own" and all this with periodic knocks from Ronny shouting at me to "hurry up in there". So strange that something that is so part of life is kept behind closed doors."

"OK, that is crazy. In Sweden we talk about those things more directly. At least in my family. We learned a lot about bodies from being naked in the sauna at our summer house. And we could ask about anything and get a straight answer from our parents."

"That sounds way too sensible and kind."

KARINA

We both had a good laugh and then decided to take a break and go for a short hike with Lu's dogs. The dogs knew we were about to hike, just from the boots we were putting on. They got all riled up and started wrestling with each other and barking their heads off. Lu gave me perfect thick hiking boots and then handed me snowshoes. You would think that being from Sweden I would know how to use snowshoes, but I had never been snowshoeing. Just outside the front door, Lu showed me how to strap on the snowshoes and we started up the path to a ridge. When Lu pointed up to where we were going, I couldn't imagine me making it. Like she had read my mind, Lu said, "We will just go as far as you are comfortable going. Just be honest if it gets to be too much."

Lu asked me questions about my life the whole way up the ridge. I had to give short breathless answers because the altitude and the weight of the snowshoes and all the effort to get through the deep snow were kicking my butt. What I would eventually come to realize is that sitting down, I would be recording everything about Lu's life... but hiking, she would be learning all about my life and I would learn more details about hers. The sharing was on a different, more comfortable, level when we hiked. I decided then that I should bring my recorder on any future walks or hikes, but have the mic clipped to my jacket. Still with no idea how I would use any of this.

We sat on boulders in the sun at the top of the ridge and I was surprised how warm I felt even in the cold wind. That was the moment I can look back on and know that I was starting to fall in love with New Mexico. The smell of burning pinon wood from Lu's neighbor's fireplace kept us company most of the way up the ridge and I had

never smelled anything so perfect.
Back at Lu's house, I took a moment to lie down on the rug with the dogs in the sun. Olive was the sweetest little thing and spooned right into my belly and chest. Four hours later, I woke up, still on the rug and heard Lu in the kitchen making something. It smelled like chicken, but I knew that Lu didn't have any meat in the house. I got up and realized it was already dark outside. Lu laughed when I got to the kitchen, "You and the dogs had a good work out. You passed out about two minutes into petting them on the rug."
I felt terrible, and told her, "I'm so sorry. We didn't even get back to recording and now it's dark. I better get to my motel. I'm really sorry."
Lu smiled big and warm, "I am not going to make you go back across the river and drive the awful road in the dark. I made up the sofa for you and dinner is almost ready. I have anything you need. Pajamas, towels, new toothbrush, just let me know what you need. I put some stuff on the table in there."
I put on the sweatpants and sweatshirt Lu left for me and we ate creamy garbanzo stew in front of the kiva fireplace. It really was heavenly. There was some music playing I didn't recognize, like soft East Indian chanting. We sat there with the dogs snoring and we didn't talk at all. Just ate and watched the fire. It was the longest I had ever been silent with another person. That would have usually made me so uncomfortable. But, it felt completely natural.

I got up and started to take Lu's dish from her, but she said, "You just relax. I am happy to clean up." While she was doing the dishes, I fell asleep again, slouched down in the comfy chair. I haven't slept this much in years. My life was so tightly wound and scheduled, I could barely fit in sleeping more than a few hours each night. I didn't know whether to feel guilty or relieved.

WHAT MAKES GRASS GROW

"Yesterday we ended with you talking about the tampon incident and getting your period on the horse. That was just so nuts. So, aside from not talking about things like that in your family, it sounds like there was a lot to figure out and navigate on your own. The Jewish thing was probably one of the most difficult, right? Were there other issues with being a Jewish kid in a non-Jewish community?"

"I think some of the issues might have been related to the Jewish thing and some were just that I was a strange little kid. I didn't know that I was a strange kid. If any kid who is a bit "different" could figure out how to be normal and fit in, I think they would. I was just me doing what I do. It may have related to the Jewish thing, since that limited the options for kids to play with in the neighborhood. I learned to entertain myself.
I would press hard on my eyes and see little "movies". One of my favorites was the one where I could see what made grass and other plants grow. I remember coming into the kitchen and the whole family was there at the pink Formica table. I told them that I knew what made grass grow. Then I explained how it grows from the bottom, not the top and that there is a liquid and a gas that moves up through it and pushes it taller. I thought they would be so happy to know this and that they would be grateful for their genius kid and sister. Instead, they looked at me with totally blank stares and my sister told me

not to share things like that. "What is wrong with you? Keep that stuff to yourself", she said.

So, from then on, I did. Or, at least most of the time. When I didn't see the movies behind my eyelids, I saw red swastikas floating around. I kept that to myself and sort of assumed that is what everyone saw behind their eyelids. I didn't connect it to the continuous education we got on the horrors of the holocaust and how important it was to never let it happen again. I really just assumed that most people would see floating red swastikas when they pressed on their eyelids.

In my elementary school years, all my best non-dog buddies were in their 70s and 80s. Again, must have been because the kid's my age were mostly instructed to stay clear of the Jew family. My closest friends were the neighborhood old folks who I loved being with and my grandfather, Zade. Eighty-year-old Mrs. Bryant across the street gave me my first waffle iron and taught me to make cream puffs when I was about 7 years old. The Sulskis were an old Eastern European couple who lived behind us and I could cut through the raspberry bushes in our yard to go hang out with them at their house. They fed me a lot of food and showed me old photos of their family and let me look at their stereograph picture cards. The strange photos would go all 3D when I looked through the special stereograph holder with goggles. Have you ever seen one of those?"

"I think so. I think I may have seen one at an old neighbor's cottage next to our summer house. I don't remember it that well."

"I have one in the shed. I will pull it out tomorrow so you can check it out. I have about 100 photo cards for it. You will love it."

"That is so cool. I can't wait to see it."

"Anyway, Mrs. Sulski would rock me in her lap and tell me stories while my head drifted between her giant plump waist length breasts. She always wore a white apron. Her house and clothes smelled like rotten cabbage and bread baking in the oven and her fat rough hands smelled like ivory soap. I have always had a canine nose. Super sensitive sniffer. So, most of my memories are smells or food. Mr. Sulski was always grabbing his wife's butt and squeezing it when he thought I wasn't looking. She talked about food and he talked about the old country.

Grandma Bortnik lived next to the Sulskis. She wasn't our grandma, but she told us to call her that. Her husband had been dead a long time, but she always talked about him or to him like he was there with us. She taught me to make real yeast bread because she was shocked that a 7-year-old girl didn't know how to make bread. She would say, "Come Saturday...we make bread and I give you cool drinks." I was better at eating the warm bread smothered in butter and honey than I was at making the bread, but she kept trying. My loaves would've made great strong building materials. After weeks of trying to teach me, I remember her having a long talk with her dead husband with me sitting right there. "Ivan, I have done what I could. I taught her everything I know. Let's just hope one day she can make nice bread. Do you think I should stop trying to teach her for now?" Then there was a long pause when Ivan must have been answering her. "OK, this will be our last day trying. I will just let her eat." Ivan must have communicated from the beyond that it was hopeless to try to teach me. Grandma Bortnik told me she married Ivan because their families arranged the marriage, but she was happy about it without really knowing him because she would get the name Bortnik which means beekeeper. She said it was nicer than her family's name, but she would never tell me what that name was.

Our family would go every week to the only synagogue in the area. It was an old one in Kenosha that was really small and smelled like cherry scented urinal perfume cakes and mothballs. At synagogue, after the service, there was food served in the basement and there was always a tea lady serving everyone tea and coffee. The volunteer job rotated between the Haddassah women...they are a Jewish women's group at every temple. When the tea lady was distracted, I would scoop up all the lemon slices and take them to a corner of the hall to eat. The other kids were going for cookies and cakes and I was addicted to the lemons. One woman, Mrs. Klein, was way too sharp and caught me stealing lemons quite a few times. She would shout loud enough to make everyone turn toward the commotion, but I never turned back or returned the lemons. After eating lemons, I liked either hiding in the coatroom and rubbing my face on all the soft mink coats or hanging out with the oldsters like Sparky Blum and the other guys smoking cigars. Couldn't hang out with the ladies...I always hated the smell of strong perfume...so the guys, who were more fun anyway, would surround me in a cloud of cigar smoke and ask me questions that made them laugh when I answered them."

"What kind of questions would they ask you?"

"Hmmm, I don't really remember the questions. I remember not understanding a lot of what they asked, so I would just make up an answer. Oh, actually I do remember when they asked me what I would be when I grow up. I was very specific about that. I told them I would be a veterinarian after going to vet school in Ames, Iowa. I had talked to our veterinarian about how to do what he did. And I do remember one of them asking me who I was going to marry. I answered that I wasn't getting married because I would be too busy being a veterinarian and any husband would just get in the way. I was probably six years old, but I remember them just howling with laughter at that answer which didn't seem funny at all to me."

"I love that you gave them that answer at 6 years old. Did people in your town have a way to know you were Jewish? How would they

even know?"

"There were lots of ways to know. Do you know what Chanukah is?"

"A little bit....but I never really had it explained to me."

"It is this Jewish holiday which comes around Christmas time, so at some point the Jewish families had to start giving gifts to keep their kids happy. It was really not a significant holiday until it had to compete with Christmas. It is celebrating a miracle when the Jews had to flee for their lives and the oil in the lamp lasted 8 days even though there was only enough oil for one day. I think that is the gist of it. Anyway, it was a mixed time for me as a kid. On the one hand I loved the greasy food, the songs, the chocolate coins (called gelt), the candle lighting every night, the presents and playing dreidel, which is a spinning top game. On the other hand, it was the time of year when everyone was reminded we were different than everyone else in the neighborhood. Pessy is an artist through and through and she would put dye into liquid glass wax and paint a Chanukah mural on our giant living room picture window. The local paper would photograph our family posed with the mural and put it in the news. This meant that the kids who loved to use the little Jew girl as a piñata, (you can beat on it, but no candy comes out), would be reminded that it was time to help me remember that I was not welcome in the neighborhood or at the school. One kid, David Anderson made me lick the rusty metal on the swing set in Tot's Park a block from our house. He made me do it until he said I could stop. If I stopped before I got permission from him, he would kick me hard on my legs or stomach while the other boys held my arms behind my back. The boys would make a human fence around me so I couldn't run. I had to lean over the bar and lick the rust until it would nearly choke me. Then he and the other boys would laugh when he finally told me I could stop and I would stand there and wait for him to say I could go. One time he made me suck on the metal swing chain while he chanted "Jews suck, Jews suck" and his friends joined the chant. So many things I couldn't share with Pessy and Lazer because I knew it would break their hearts.

Sunnyside Elementary sounds cheery, but it wasn't. I have many more awful memories than sweet ones. The school janitor, Bernard, made a giant blue motorized dreidel. Every year for the Christmas assembly, I had to stand next to the groaning spinning thing that was four times my size, and sing Chanukah songs by myself. It was their idea of being inclusive, but every year it just reminded the tough kids that the weird little Jew exists and they would beat the crap out of me when I tried to walk home after the assembly. Sometimes, I would wait in the bathroom or in any empty classroom for a long time after school, hoping that all the kids were long gone. But, they had a lot of patience when it came to waiting for me to come out the door. I couldn't escape them.

One Chanukah, I got a little hand crank printing press from Lazer and Pessy. It came with individual letters on little rubber squares and a little tweezers for placing the letters on the printing wheel. I decided to have a neighborhood newsletter. I named it Lu View. I can't remember how I came up with that, but I thought it was really clever and I was sure I would have lots of subscribers. Since I didn't have any friends my age except Jeannie Ray next door, I mostly wrote about the old people I was friends with, the wonderful garbage men, the milkman, and a dab of Jeannie and her 5 brothers from next door mixed in. Oh, and I included animals in the neighborhood. It was very labor intensive to put one rubber letter at a time onto the printing wheel, so I kept to the essence of the news. "Mrs. Bryant made 12 cream puffs today. I ate three." "Jeannie Ray can eat a whole onion raw, like an apple." "The frogs in the swamp laid their eggs that are hanging off floating sticks like jelly." "Mrs. Sulski's cabbages are huge this year and she is making sauerkraut this week." "Carl the milkman parked in front of our driveway and my dad had to leave for work and screamed at Carl." "The garbage men, Dick and Rob, got new blue uniforms with their names on them." "The Griffiths let me climb their sour cherry tree and eat all the cherries I wanted." Each story was one sentence long. I included all of the most fascinating news and I didn't charge for subscriptions. I delivered to about 10 homes and considered the whole thing a great success. Lazer asked me to leave any of our family news out of the paper, and I mostly did. I was always especially interested in what was going on next door at the Ray's house since they weren't Jewish and everything looked and smelled different over there. You know, different foods and different products. For example, non-Jews use Pine Sol to clean floors and Jews use Spic N Span. Jews make brisket and non-Jews make pot roast. Non-Jews eat turnips and Jews eat broccoli covered in cheese sauce or potatoes, onions and carrots. I did have one feature story that read, "Mystery solved: Pot roast is the same thing as brisket." That gives you an idea about how irresistibly compelling the newsletter was. I was really fascinated by the difference in Jewish houses and non-Jewish houses. Maybe it is different nowadays. Maybe everybody eats the same stuff and uses the same stuff to clean. The Ray's house had things like country style curtains with tie-backs and a big light fixture made from what was supposed to look like an old west wagon wheel. They had soft red plaid furniture with pillows. We had big thick shiny gold curtains that you couldn't have tied back even with truck bungees. And our turquoise sparkly sofas and chairs were covered in zippered thick clear plastic that eventually turned yellow with age. The softness below the plastic was such a tease and the cracked and ripped plastic would grab and tear at our sticky thighs if we wore shorts. We had Mediterranean style lights on gold chains with lots of colored glass and a replica statue of a horned Moses. My brother and I were home alone playing frisbee in the living room one day, and the Moses fell and broke. Ronny and I were completely freaked out because we thought it was some expensive original work of art. We somehow thought we were rich people with original artwork in our house. Since we always had a lot of great food around, I am guessing Ronny and I equated that with being upper class. We thought our two bedroom, one bath little brick house was a castle. We tried to glue Moses back together before my mom got home from work. It took all of one day before she noticed the lopsided Moses with thick glue spots oozing all over his plaster body. Her reaction made us pretty certain that it was indeed an original and very expensive work of art. She cried in her bedroom and we felt horrible. I now know that the statue was made out of cast plaster and was pretty worthless in the art world or even at a thrift store, but to Pessy it was priceless. Oh, Ronny and I had another friend close to our age. Bobby Crane. He was really my brother's friend and I shared him. Looking back, I figure Bobby was gay, but I am not sure how that all turned out for him. He was weird and unpopular like me and Ronny and we liked that. He played the tuba and lived in a house like ours that was right next to our backyard. He had a nice family who didn't hate Jews. With one hop over the chain link fence, we could be in his yard. He was big and I don't think he hopped the fence or hopped anything. When my brother got his Morse code flashlights with little louvers so you could signal a long distance, he gave one to Bobby and we could talk to him all night. We tried to memorize the Morse code, but the back of our lights had the whole alphabet for us as cheat sheets. I absolutely loved the whole dot dot dash secret alphabet."

"That is so hilarious that you thought the horned Moses was the original. So great. I wonder where Bobby is today. All these people you knew as a kid...I am guessing the older ones are long gone, but the kids would sure be fun to track down. Do you think you would ever do that?"

"Probably not. Well, not most of them. But I think I may try to track down one of my best friends, Muna, since I haven't been in touch for over 30 years. Oh and maybe one other friend. Oh, don't get me started on that sentimental stuff. It is not my thing, but talking to you may inspire me to find a few of them."

"I hope you do find them. You will have to let me know what you discover. What was your parent's relationship like? Which one were you closest with?"

Lazer and Pessy were stormy. Left brain engineer meets right brain artist. When they met, he liked her breasts, but had another girlfriend. It was Zade, Lazer's dad who chose Pessy as the one Lazer would marry. Back then it was arranged marriages and you didn't marry for love. In the modern world, nowadays, Lazer and Pessy would have been divorced within a year. As it was, they talked about leaving each other and getting a divorce on a regular basis and we kids all hoped they would. We hated living in a war zone home. One time when we were all pretty young, they talked so seriously about getting a divorce that we were sure it was happening. We hooped and hollered and danced around excited that it was really going forward. All three of us told everyone the good news at school. We told the kids and our teachers. News spread quickly in Kenosha and I am guessing all the kids went home and told their parents and the phone lines were smoking that night. Not to mention we all had party lines. That meant you could pick up the phone any time and listen to the conversations of people in other homes.

The next day when my parents got home from work, they were livid. Lazer shouted at us, "Why the hell did you tell the kids and teachers that we are getting divorced?" Ronny looked up at them pretty innocently and said, "Aren't you?"

Lazer softened a little bit, "No, that is just how adults talk. It doesn't mean anything."

Pessy looked really sad. Not sure if she was sad that they

weren't getting a divorce or sad that all her co-workers thought she was getting divorced or sad because her kids wished she would get a divorce.

In the fifties there was still a strong stigma attached to divorced families. It is probably best that they didn't get divorced because we kids would have been ostracized even more in the community. I knew one divorced family and those kids were not treated well by other kids. They ended up moving away because the father hung himself about a year after the divorce. We all knew which house he hung himself in and Ronny and I would go there and try to see in the windows. We were hoping to see the rope or some other exciting thing.

Maybe Lazer and Pessy's life would have been easier if they had stayed around their families in Chicago and had the support. But, Lazer took the family to Wisconsin for a job offer and left everyone and everything familiar behind. It must have been hard on them. And, maybe their life was never meant to be peaceful. While Lazer was all logic, Pessy was more of a free spirit. I was visiting them once and noticed that all Pessy's bras had a little red ribbon safety pinned to them. I asked her what they were for and she told me that they keep her from being cursed. She said if someone gave her the evil eye, the ribbon would protect her. Pessy was shocked I didn't remember that all of our underwear as kids had a piece of red thread sewn to it to protect us. I sort of remembered, but I must have thought it came with our underwear and didn't think about it. She also went to tealeaf readers and fortune-tellers and even had the tealeaf reader interpret the tea leaves in a cup she had her dog, Winky, drink from. Logical people are not nearly as entertaining as the right brain people. Pessy was constant entertainment.

Lazer and Pessy never did do projects well together. Even small teamwork was hard for them. On our vacations, Pessy was supposed to be the map-reader. But, that was not her forte and on one particular trip we were speeding down the highway in Tennessee and she was wrestling with the giant paper map when it flew right out the open window. You have probably never seen a paper travel map. They were huge once you unfolded them and you could never re-fold them the original way. Some families might have laughed about the map flying out the window, but our family had to deal with a full day of fighting and stress from it. After that, Ronny took over as official map-reader for our trips.

One year, Lazer and Pessy took a trip to New Orleans without the kids. They left us at home with a giant German woman named Gurda Ziegler who we didn't know. I have no idea where they found her. Maybe in the Pennywise paper? Gurda cooked strange fart smelling cabbage-y foods and wanted us to sit on her lap and sleep in bed with her even though we were not babies. She creeped us out and even in our own house we had to maneuver our little lives to avoid her. New Orleans got Lazer and Pessy all excited about everything French revival or fake French or Cajun anything. After they got home with no gifts for the kids, except a jar of hot pepper sauce, they announced that they had a gift coming in the mail for the whole family to enjoy. About a week later a box came in the mail with a giant wallpaper mural for the wall of our kitchen. It was a cheesy watercolor scene from the French Quarter. It would make the whole wall look like we were gazing out from our bougainvillea-covered wrought iron balcony onto the rooftops of the city. I am guessing that back then it was not thought of as tacky, it was probably high fashion for homes along with avocado colored appliances and turquoise Naugahyde furniture covered in plastic. So the wallpaper was a perfect fit for us. They started putting up the wallpaper mural in the morning and at midnight they were still swearing at each other as they each took a hypodermic needle full of water and a squeegee to each of the thousands of bubbles that had formed under the mural. We kids knew to stay clear of them when there was a house project. For three kids who were pretty much constantly eating or playing, it was not easy to avoid the kitchen the whole day and night of the French Quarter fiasco. We were hungry, but we weren't masochists, we stayed clear of them. It was raining outside or we might have stayed at the swamp we loved all day. Instead we mostly camped out in Ronny's room with the dog and even watched a few forbidden television shows without them noticing. I felt like a hero that day for racing into the kitchen, grabbing a box of Liv-a-Snaps dog treats, Ritz crackers and a giant box of Velveeta cheese food and running back to my brother's room to feed us. I forgot to get a knife so we pinched squishy bits of Velveeta off the big block and sandwiched them between crackers and ate triumphantly. Later when we were thirsty, I raced in there again and grabbed the jar of Tang and a glass and we made drinks in the bathroom sink, stirring with our fingers. It was like those soldiers in the war movies who venture out of the trenches, running real low to avoid gunfire. I was the brave soldier heading into the kitchen. It is weird that I can forget major events in my life, but I remember every moment of that day like it just happened.

Lazer could do projects on his own with just a little swearing. When it was just our mom, Pessy, doing a project, there was no swearing. The two of them together would turn into a shit storm. Pessy on her own just focused in and got the job done. She was also the one who didn't mind a mess, as long as we were having fun. She had us finger painting from the time we were babies and cutting our own linoleum block prints before we were old enough to safely handle the carving tools.

Every year she sewed incredible custom costumes for us for Halloween and Purim. We got used to always winning the prizes at any celebration for the best costumes. It was expected.
I love the year that I went to the Purim celebration at the synagogue dressed as a hamantash. The bad guy in the Purim

story was named Haman and we all had noise makers and would go crazy loud whenever the rabbi would say Haman during his reading. Our job was to squelch his name in the story. Haman had a triangle shaped hat and Purim cookies are called Hamantash. They are triangle shaped dough with prunes or other filling inside. My brother went as Queen Esther, complete with lipstick and tiara. He looked gorgeous in the gown Pessy sewed and I looked like my usual boyish self in my stuffed round prune costume with removable dough exterior. I could swing my arms open and reveal the big prune under the dough. My entire body was the prune with my skinny legs sticking out. Really, this woman was brilliant with the costume creation. She could have been a well-known Hollywood costume designer. Instead she had us as her models.

I was a dark-skinned kid who loved anything cowboys and Indians. I didn't understand the real history, genocide and violence of it all. None of the kids back then did. I just loved the outfits. Ronny and I pretty much always dressed as cowboys in everyday life. Red cowboy boots, holster, braided lasso design shirt, cowboy hat....the works. But, my fascination moved toward the Native American culture and my mom honored my passion with a third grade Halloween outfit that won awards at every community event. I told her I wanted to be a squaw with a cradleboard and a papoose on my back. Without hesitation, she turned me into the most authentic Native woman she could. She colored a baby doll brown to match my suntanned skin and the papoose was complete. A totally unconfident socially nervous kid, was turned into a confident beautiful Native American princess. I was strutting my stuff, happy to have a baby strapped to my back in a perfect cradleboard replica that Pessy made from an old broken laundry basket.

I can totally appreciate what Lazer gave us. While Pessy gave us creativity and freedom, Lazer gave us practical life skills like playing sports, swimming and fixing everything that needed repair. Ronny was always good with electrical and mechanical stuff. Me and Karen were good at those things, too, but we weren't as passionate about it as Ronny. Put a screwdriver in that boy's hands, even as a toddler, and he would dismantle everything he could get his hands on including all the electrical outlets. I think Pessy and Lazer should have been more nervous about him frying himself, but they let him dismantle stuff and put it back together with wild abandon.

Pessy was the mastermind behind flooding our entire huge yard every winter for the largest skating rink in the neighborhood. She didn't care if it was practical or not. The outdoor faucets couldn't be used in the winter, so she ran a hose through a basement window and dedicated herself to evenly flooding the yard. That meant layers and layers of ice and her going out there at all hours of the night to keep the process up. The rink was popular with all the neighborhood kids, even though we weren't popular kids. The other kids would come and skate and manage to ignore us even in our own backyard. I loved skating around the huge maple trees and ducking under branches.

Lazer was the engineer and Pessy was the artist. She would have had us painting, sewing, knitting or drawing all weekend. But, Lazer balanced it out with things like teaching us how to read an electronic schematic for fixing the clothes dryer. I was aching to be outside while Ronny and I stood learning about the dryer. It felt like such an unfair thing to us back then, but I am grateful for it now that I can fix pretty much anything myself. Lazer worked for decades at a factory that made tools. So, we had every tool we needed for any job, and I still do to this day.

My relationship with the garbage men was probably the one that gave me the most laughs and the least anxiety in the human world. Years later at my 20th class reunion, Rob the retired garbage man (is that still the politically correct way to refer to them? Or is it something like waste hauler?) was the hired security guy at the door. I grabbed a bit of food and then spent the entire evening talking with him on the front stairs of the Elk's Club. It wasn't until I got home that I realized I hadn't talked to any of my classmates. I wonder what the heck made me even go to the reunion in the first place and I'm pretty sure I was just meant to reconnect with Rob the garbage man."

"What did you and Rob talk about on the steps?"

"I can't remember all that we talked about that night. I imagine we talked about the neighborhood and how I would wait by the trash bins on pick up morning just so I could hang out with them. Then I would chase them from house to house on our street on my bicycle and race them and then double back to talk to them. If he thought I was a strange little kid for being all excited about being with them, I doubt he said so. All I remember from the reunion night is us laughing and having a great time and me bringing plates of food out to him. An old retired guy and a 38 year old having a blast. I don't think I would have lasted 10 minutes if I had been inside with my classmates. I remember coming home to the dog that night, but I don't remember coming home and talking to anyone about what that reunion was like. Since I lived in another part of the country at 38 years old, I must have stayed at my folks house to go to the reunion, but I only remember coming home to my mom's dog."

KARINA

Lu doesn't like sitting for very long and within an hour or two each day she just pops up and says, "Time to hike". I have always been more of a person who just keeps working until the job is done. The idea that we are spending more time hiking than doing the interviews is so foreign to me. Normally I would have resisted and tried to convince Lu to keep going for at least another hour, but that didn't happen. Something is shifting in me and I am just able to relax into whatever we are doing. I barely recognize myself. I have lots of time to just be. In my city life, I would have kept busy with anything. I never just sat around watching birds or petting dogs or drawing. I didn't even think I had any artist or creative ability. Lu has one room that looks out over the valley and the river below and it is filled with art supplies. She told me I was welcome to be there anytime and use any supplies I want to. I wouldn't say I am at all bored here, but I feel open to anything, which is totally not like my old self. Today is the fourth day at Lu's, and while she was upstairs meditating, I wandered into that art room and sat at the giant old oak drafting table. I just picked up a pen and started drawing. I was in a different mental space than I had ever been. I wasn't thinking about time. I really wasn't thinking at all. I just kept drawing. I don't drink or do drugs, but I sort of felt drugged or something that I imagined to be like being drugged. I had no idea how long I was in there making drawings, but at some point I realized that Lu had come downstairs and was making food. It was the smell of the food that took me out of my drawing trance. I went into the kitchen and looked at the clock. I couldn't believe I had been in there drawing for over three hours. Lu was standing over the cutting board dividing up a pizza that was piled high with veggies. It smelled incredible.

She turned to me and just smiled. Over dinner I explained that I was not sure what happened and why I was in there drawing for so long. Lu looked so happy about it. She said, "That is just you settling in to a different part of your brain and heart. It's wonderful to see you relaxing into it. Linear time doesn't exist in that creative mind space." I asked Lu why she didn't have a television in her house. I am used to houses in the U.S. having at least two. She didn't hesitate to answer, "Television feels like something that numbs people's brains and sometimes their hearts. Think of all those passive hours staring at a screen that could be spent watching birds or the river or making art or playing music or helping someone. I haven't had a television since 1974 when I moved out of my parent's house. And I can't say that I have missed anything. Lazer, my dad, said to me once, "No television and no newspaper? How do you know what is going on in the world." I told him I just look out the window when I want to know what is going on in the world."
I looked past her out the window and saw the sun setting.

"Lu, I better get myself across the river and finally get to the motel. I feel terrible that I have been here three nights when you were very clear you wanted your space."

"Karina, I do love having my space, but you are very easy to have around. If you are comfortable here, I am happy to have you stay as long as we are doing the interviews. You can use my phone to call the motel and cancel altogether. They probably won't be surprised since you have called the last three nights to say you wouldn't be checking in quite yet."

I called the motel and cancelled the reservation. That was also not like me. I am not a typical Swedish person, but all of us are raised to respect other people's space and not intrude. Americans are much more bold and in each other's space. I remember walking on the beach in New Jersey with an American friend and a family was walking toward us. I veered far up toward the houses above the beach to give the family more space, and my friend, Lora, moved toward the family. She was chatting with them and I kept walking.

I came back down toward the water and Lora caught up with me. She wanted to know what was wrong and why I distanced myself from the family. I said I didn't want to be rude. She explained that it is rude to not say hello to someone you pass on the beach and I explained that in Sweden it is rude to not give them space and leave them alone. It is really knit into my bones to give people space. So, I have no idea why I was ok with calling the motel and cancelling my reservation. I had four more days before my return flight and I would be in Lu's space that whole time.

ANIMAL HOUSE

"Lu, you seem to like animals more than humans. Were you always this way? Were you just born that way?"

"I am such an animal person, that even certain parts of human language stand out for me. When you say I like animals more than humans, I want to say, "Humans ARE animals." We have separated ourselves so much from the natural world that we forget that we are animals. We mostly don't even remember that we are mammals and that our relatives are other primates and whales, dolphins and all mammals. I have been working with non-humans and our perceptions of them for so long that our speciesist ideas and language jump out at me. Here is an example. If I say to you, "Someone crossed the path" you will assume it is a human. But if I say "Something crossed the path." you will assume it is a non-human. We call other animals things. There is so much in our language and our lifestyles to keep us separate. When a news story tells about war or wildfire fatalities, it is only the human fatalities that are counted. If a human is killed on the road, it is a highway fatality, but if a non-human is killed on the road, it is called "road kill". If I called a human fatality a "road kill" I would be considered pretty unfeeling and crazy. It is rampant in our human culture to disregard other species as family and as thinking, feeling individuals. It took me over a year to get untrained from the speciesist language I used. A co-worker and I helped each other by making a pact and catching every time the other used words that were speciesist. It is so part of our culture that my computer even corrects me if I use a respectful pronoun for a non-human."

"That is so true. I never thought about it. But, what is it that woke you up to these ideas and to that animal, or non-human, connection?"

"Well, you wouldn't think someone's life could take a big turn at age five, but I think mine did. I was afraid of pretty much everything and everyone. But, I was most afraid of all non-human animals. At about 4 years-old I was forced to pet a sheep at a petting zoo. My dad made me reach out and touch the strange animal and I did this without ever looking at her or doing more than having my outstretched pointer finger graze her curly fleece. I am sure I was shaking. Back then, if I saw a dog in the neighborhood, I would go back inside for the day. Lazer was worried this fear of animals would hold me back in life. So, one evening he stopped by the dark, noisy, smelly depressing local animal shelter on his way home from work and walked into the house with the tiniest little tan and white puppy in his hand. We named her Sandy. I was terrified of her. I was told to sit in the kitchen with her on my lap that night and every night after that for about an hour until I got used to her. Sandy was a little furry bundle of torture for me and it was days before I even looked at her. I kept my eyes closed in total fear. Then it happened. I decided I would be brave and look at her. I looked in her eyes and she looked in mine. As far as I remember, it was the first time I felt deep protective love for someone other than my brother. Looking back I think it was the first time I knew that there was really someone in the world other than me. Everything changed. All my animal anxiety melted away. We became inseparable. This was a huge about-face in my life. From then on my favorite family member and favorite person on earth was Sandy. For the first time, I had a real friend who liked me as much as I liked her. I think she was Ronny's best friend, too.

I also think that growing up in a non-Jewish place and people only seeing me as part of a group and not being able to see me as a thinking, feeling individual gave me empathy for non-human animal victims or any human victims. You know how most people see animals as just a pig or just a cow or just a fish or whatever their species is and they don't see the individual in each body. That is how I felt growing up in Kenosha. It was like people could only see the little Jewish kid and not ME. This empathy for individuals and wanting to care for anyone who wasn't cared for in society started with Sandy. And that started the ball rolling. Or as Lazer put it, he created a monster. I started bringing home any animal who needed help. My bedroom was filled with cages and aquariums and creatures of every kind. The garage was filled with cages, too. Mostly of wildlife needing medical attention and I was their doctor. The ones who needed stitching, got stitched with sewing thread and needles and eventually with sterile dental floss when that appeared on the scene. I was building my compassion, but looking back as an adult, I realized that I didn't have enough empathy to understand that no animal belongs in a cage or a glass box unless they have to be there to heal up. I was supporting some nasty industries like the pet shop breeders who create hamsters and mice and rats and fishes like they are just products to make a profit on. Ronny and I started out with a few mice that a neighbor gave to us. Those few turned into a kirgillion. Same with the hamsters. I loved those mice and hamsters with a passion only matched by my love of Sandy. I will never forget when Ronny and his buddy decided that they would send one of the mice up in a model rocket and it would come down in a parachute. We went to the park and Ronny loaded one of my dear mice, named Tina, into the rocket. I cannot tell you why I thought this was harmless or that the little being wouldn't suffer. I think I just trusted Ronny to always do the right thing. I do remember being nervous, but I was there to hold her when she had parachuted down and I would take her straight home to her family. The rocket went up, but when it came back down and Ronny opened the little section with Tina, it was all blood and guts. I felt sick and sobbed uncontrollably while running home. It was my first loss of a loved one and it was my own brother who had murdered her. I was torn to pieces emotionally like Tina was physically. Pessy tried to comfort me, but there was no comforting me. It took me weeks to recover and talk to Ronny again. There are blinders that we all have to other life forms. For some people these are just thin veils and they have compassion for all life at an early age. For me it was a slow layered stripping away of seeing the life around me. It only recently evolved into understanding the inner life of trees more and more and feeling an incredibly deep connection to them. But it took decades of opening my heart and mind and eyes to what is around me. The second time I experienced the death of someone close to me was when Pessy cleaned our room and put a cage, home to two hamsters, Hairy and Mr. Grey, up on a tall dresser next to a heat register. She forgot to put the cage back down on the desk and when I came home from school I found Hairy and Mr. Grey had been killed by the heater. Now I had to live with three needless deaths that involved suffering, but even worse, I lived with two murderers I needed to forgive. Involuntary murder, but murder just the same. It took me a while to forgive Pessy and Ronny."

"That is so sad. But maybe good you started to face death at an early age, since it is so much part of life. Sandy sounds amazing. How great that you got to connect to your life's work from that little puppy ambassador. Any other memories of grade school and that time in your life?"

"I hated elementary school because it took me away from Sandy. I hated it for other reasons, too. I wanted to be outside ALL THE TIME. I spent my days at home swinging on the green metal swing set in our yard until I would fall asleep and land in the dirt. In winter, I would stay outside in my giant red snowsuit building things out of hard-packed snow until I would finally pee in my snowsuit and it would go from warm to freezing and then I would have to come in. But school puts you in a building and makes you sit in a chair and that is the opposite of what my little chimp body wanted to do. Don't you think it is strange that you spend millions and millions of minutes, and thousands of weeks and hundreds of months, and 12 years of your childhood at a place and there are only a few things you really remember? And they are odd little tidbit memories. I remember the nasty smell of hard-boiled eggs and bologna sandwiches on white bread with mayo and mustard in the gym at lunchtime. We didn't have a cafeteria and kids brought bag lunches and sat on the floor of the gym. Every time I smell hard-boiled eggs or bologna, it takes me right back to Sunnyside Elementary. My favorite sack lunch was a fluffernutter, which is marshmallow cream and peanut butter, on white bread with a Twinkie for dessert. Since I mostly packed my own lunch, I got to choose what my nutritious offerings would be. I usually packed two fluffernutters and ate one mid-morning by sneaking fingerfulls from inside my desk.

Part of feeling like we were rich was the kind of food we had. I could drink as much soda and eat all the Twinkies and chocolate cupcakes I wanted to. We had a Hostess Thrift Store that sold anything that was outdated and Pessy filled our freezer with it. Not sure you have those thrift stores in Sweden, but these places sell any products that are too old or dated to go to the supermarkets. We also had a cupboard full of Jiffy Cake Mixes. You can still find those things for like 99 cents a box. We would have lots of pretend birthdays with candles and all. I know we had food joy, but we also had a very constant relationship with Dr. Fisher, our ancient shaky dentist.

I don't remember most of my elementary school moments, but some are etched in my mind forever. One incredibly cold winter day, I saw the kids on the playground all gathered around the handicap (that's the word we used back then) ramp to the gym. I ran over in time to see Stan Stanachevski with his tongue stuck to the green metal handrail. He was crying and screaming even with his tongue all the way out of his mouth. Mr, Johnson, the dictator principal of the school came out with the school nurse and before she could say anything, Mr Johnson yanked Stan off the bar and left a huge piece of his tongue on the metal. Stan was screaming and had blood dripping down his chin onto his shirt. The nurse hurried Stan inside while Mr. Johnson roared for us all to get away from the ramp. That was the day I decided to officially hate Mr. Johnson and to start being nice to Stan. Stan talked with an accent from somewhere in Eastern Europe and the kids were mean to him. I could relate to having kids be mean, so in my mind we became friends right then. I am not sure I ever told Stan. When Mr. Johnson went back inside, I lined up with the other kids to look at Stan's bloody frozen chunk of tongue on the metal bar. I like looking at gross things, always have."

KARINA

After our session today, Lu told me to please make myself totally at home and that I could take a bath or do whatever I wanted. I had just been doing little bird baths because I had heard how precious water is in New Mexico. Lu assured me it was fine to fill the tub and soak. The tub is sunk into the ground and made of rocks and boulders from the land with lots of little mosaic bits pressed into the mortar. I ran the steamy water and climbed in while it was filling. I looked around me at the broken coffee cup handles woven into the mosaic and the other parts of cups that serve as soap holders. I have never seen so much creative beauty as I am surrounded by here. The huge plants in the bathroom surrounded my head and the sunny ridge was just outside the giant window. There is no door on the bathroom and no window coverings anywhere in the house. I am used to the city where not covering the windows means everyone can see your everything, but here there are no other humans to see in. Best bath ever. I started feeling sad that in four days I will be flying back to Scranton. That led me right into thinking about work and I could feel my body tensing up.

I closed my eyes and focused on my breath as Lu had taught me to do when my mind started racing. Lu was upstairs playing clarinet and once I calmed down, I was able to just melt into the hot water and drift with the music. I must have been in the water about an hour when someone walked in the front door and appeared at the bathroom door. He was a short muscular guy and he just stood there talking to me as if I wasn't naked in the tub. He introduced himself and said he needed either me or Lu to come help him with something. It didn't seem like an emergency because he was so calm. I sunk a little deeper in the tub so he wouldn't see my breasts. I grew up with saunas and being comfortable being naked, but not with a stranger. I had to be pretty direct with Ra because I felt like he would have just stood there while I got dressed. I told him, "If you give me a minute, I will get dressed and come help you." I had no idea where Lu was now. The clarinet had stopped, but she wasn't downstairs. I got dressed and followed this guy along a path I hadn't taken before. Turns out he digs caves. Not just holes in the earth, but massive living spaces with skylights and running water and sculpture carved into the walls and multiple rooms. We entered this cave through a tunnel and then a beautiful carved wood door. Ra told me, "I am putting a skylight up here and I need you to just pound with this pipe in the spot I have dug out, I am going up above on the hill and I will dig where I hear you pounding until I have busted through. So just keep hitting up there until you see me and the sky." I pounded with the pipe about 20 feet above me in the hole he had started up there. I just kept pounding the rhythm and not paying close attention. I was busy looking around at the amazing rooms and stairs carved into the earth. All of a sudden he busted through and a massive load of dirt fell on me. I was down on the ground and completely covered. When I looked up Ra and his dog were looking down at me. Ra just said, "Good job, thanks so much." Not, "Sorry, I forgot to warn you that you should jump out of the way when you hear me busting through." I took the path back to Lu's house and wondered what the point of my bath was. I was totally trashed. When I got back to the house, Lu was about to do her evening meditation and said I could join her. She set up a second cushion. I changed out of the filthy clothes and told Lu about Ra and the whole cave thing. She just laughed, "Glad you got to meet him. His passion is digging caves. We can hike to another one of them tomorrow." Meditating with Lu this evening my mind was agitated. A part of me is anxious to finish the interviews and get back to my regular life. Another part of me is loving this new rhythm and the lack of stress. I realized that I am afraid of getting too used to this different way of being and if I get too comfortable in it, I will be discontent when I go back home. I wanted to just get up from the cushion and do something to distract me. I started moving around a lot and trying to get *comfortable. Then I remembered that Lu said to just be with whatever thoughts came and to come back to my breath when I remembered to, but not to get upset with myself. I focused on my breath and stopped moving around. Next thing I knew, the timer was chiming and we had been sitting an hour. We slowly opened our eyes and smiled at each other. This was a good day, even in my life confusion, I knew that much.*

CONCAVE BREASTS AND GOUSTERS

"Ok lets go back to elementary school....sort of where we left off yesterday. Did you have any special friends in the school? Anyone who treated you kindly?"

"My only elementary school friend was Beth Moore. Beth had blonde hair and blue eyes and she thought I was as exotic as I thought she was. She and I naturally came together as friends because we were the most flat-chested. Well, honestly, we were concave. Sissy Lawson was just another student our age, but had breasts, and she sorted the girls out by popularity and breasts or no breasts and told us where our gym lockers would be. She assigned me and Beth a special area of the locker room she called "the boys section". The other girls would stand and stare at us while we changed into these horrible navy blue gym suits, and we tried our best to undress and dress with our bodies mostly inside our tall metal lockers. I pretty much perfected the art of undressing and dressing without showing any part of myself. (This came in very handy at summer camp). You can do a lot by wiggling your arms under your shirt. Lots of kids would meet up at the long pier on Lake Michigan. Beth and I wanted to find a boyfriend there, so we stuffed our bikini tops with tissue so we would look like there were breasts in our swimsuit bikini tops. With our first dive into the water, the tissue got soaked and when we climbed back up on the pier, the soggy tissues were oozing out of the bikini top and stuck to our ribs and bellies. Every kid, boy and girl, howled with laughter and Beth and I slinked to our bikes and rode away. We hoped those kids would just forget about the whole thing since we were the shy invisible not-popular girls. But it was good grist for teasing us for weeks. I liked that Beth's family was poor and her mom worked at JC Penny's candy counter. We got to eat all the candy we wanted. I always got a big bag of Indian corn (those yellow, orange and white triangle candies) and Beth always got round chocolates with white jimmy sprinkles on them. I would eat my candy corn one at a time and one color at a time. I always loved having treats left when everyone else had finished theirs. I am a saver. I had a bank account from when I was 5 years old. The blue faux leather covered bankbook was one of my favorite possessions. I would ride my bike to the bank and deposit my weekly allowance, even when it was only 25 cents and I was just 7 years old. The teller would stamp the deposit in my book and I watched the balance get bigger every week. At summer camp every year, we got canteen money from our parents. 10 dollars was put in my account and kept track of on the list in the little cabin that had candy and toothpaste and bug spray for sale. I never spent a dime of my canteen tab because the deal with my parents was that I could keep whatever was leftover. That canteen money went into my bank account every year. Other kids had candy all session, but I got to see $10.00 stamped into my bankbook when I got home. At the end of one summer I was riding my little powder-blue bike home from the bank and a car backed fast out of their driveway and hit me. I went flying onto the curb grass. I still don't know if the person didn't know they had hit me or if they chose to ignore the whole thing. I limped home walking my bike and had to go to the emergency room for a broken leg. I had two signatures on my cast, Ronny and Beth. I had seen popular kids with casts covered in names of friends. But, I was happy with just Ronny and Beth's names. I had crutches and for the first few weeks everybody in the house was being so nice and taking care of me. Then it wore off and they just made sure I had my crutches nearby so I could do things myself.

Some of my saver mentality wasn't so nice. My family would sometimes go to Baskin Robbins 31 Flavors and I would get a cone with vanilla ice cream. I find a good flavor or a good thing and don't like to stray from it. So, 31 flavors to choose from and I stuck with vanilla. I would sit between Ronny and Karen and slowly lick the cone just enough to keep it from dripping. When they were long done with their cones I would have most of mine. I wouldn't share mine and taunted them with slowly finishing it in front of them for the next half hour. I loved having them beg for a taste and refusing them."

"You said you went to summer camp. Could your parents afford to send all three kids to camp?"

"Oh not at all. All three of us became experts at filling out scholarship forms. Karen and Ronny would just go for one session each summer, but I would go for all three sessions and be gone much of the summer. I loved camp. I could be wild and free and away from home. Some other kids would get homesick and I couldn't understand that. I would go to them while they were in their cot crying and talk to them about not wasting this opportunity to be free. I had the option to go home between sessions, but I chose to stay at the camp and help them prep for the next session. I would scrub the kitchen with the cooks and clean toilets and organize the waterfront equipment. I loved working with the staff on those days. I thought they had all forgotten that I was just a kid. You know how kids cover their eyes and think that they are hiding and say, "You can't see me."? I sort of lived that way, thinking that my ideas about myself were what everyone else saw. So I figured the camp staff suddenly thought I was an adult. Just like I thought that everyone in the black neighborhood thought I looked just like Diana Ross. Just because I thought I did. And when I was put on the train to go visit my uncle's family in Michigan I brought my realistic looking baby doll and thought everyone on the train must be wondering how a 5 year old was already a mom. Clearly, my imaginary world was more powerful than whatever was going on around me"

"I love that you thought you looked like Diana Ross. That was a rich life inside that head of yours. I am wondering if you had any kind adults outside of your family who helped form you and guide you."

"Oh sure. Lots of them. If you look at your life like a map, you can see places where you made major turns that changed everything and you realize certain people in your life were major factors for who you became. Mr. Butts, my fourth-grade teacher, was one of those turns. He even taught us to meditate. You gotta understand that people in the USA were not talking about meditation in the 50's. This was something brand new for us kids. Each morning, he would have us close our eyes and picture a blank screen and just breathe. I could only picture an aluminum window screen, because I wasn't sure what a blank screen was. I loved those few minutes of no talking. Some kids giggled during meditation because they were uncomfortable. But I happily closed my eyes and relaxed. Mr. Butts played classical music and taught us about all the composers. I had never heard of classical music and wasn't sure what I was hearing at first. To me it sounded like layers and layers of different songs being played at the same time. It really wasn't until my 30's that I realized that my absolute favorite nourishing music was exactly what Mr. Butts had played for us. He had a separate room with musical instruments and big windows at the back of our classroom. When we misbehaved, he didn't get mad. He would just say, "Seems like you need to go back and create some music." He would keep an eye on whoever was in that magical instrument room and would come get us when we had calmed down and had time to enjoy it for a bit. It always worked. He was such a gentle loving guy. Every Friday he played his personal copy of the movie Phantom of the Opera. He had it on a giant reel of film. I don't know why he showed it every week, but we all loved it. After each weekly showing, he would show it to us high speed and in reverse. Reverse was my favorite part.

The big black mole on my face was an embarrassment, so I would keep it covered with one hand whenever I could. One afternoon, Mr. Butts told me to stay after class. When the other kids had cleared out, he sat on top of my desk. Then, in the most loving voice, he asked me, " Why do you cover your face with your hand?"
I explained, "The mole on my face makes the other kids call me names and push me around on the playground. They call me "dirt face" and "dirty Jew Face" and tell me I have a bug on my cheek." Mr. Butts pulled my hand away from my face and told me it was a "beauty mark" not a mole. He said it was beautiful. I had never heard the word beauty used for anything about me. I was shocked. I always thought I was ugly (and that mole didn't help matters).

He told me: "All the people we admire the most have something unique about them. Something special. There is an actress who I love called Honey West. She has a beauty mark like yours. It makes her special. There is another actress called Marilyn Monroe and she has a beauty mark, too. And some famous models and actresses draw a beauty mark on their face just like yours because they think it is pretty. Maybe people tease us about things that are different, but if you look at who is famous or who we admire, they are the ones with something special or new or different. When the kids tease you, it doesn't mean anything, except that you are special. Don't hide your specialness or your uniqueness. You know those same kids tease me because of my last name. And, that has been true my whole life. So, I had to learn to realize that their teasing wasn't about me at all. It was about them needing to make someone else feel like they aren't ok or cool. I even thought about changing my last name and then realized it is just a word and I can tell a lot about someone by how they treat me. So I decided to keep my name and it helped me find people who really cared about me and didn't care what my last name was." When he shared all that, my world changed. I stopped hiding my beauty mark, and I started being more confident and more myself. He launched me on my long bumpy road to self-acceptance. I am forever grateful to him. A few years back, when I was in my fifties, I wrote him a thank you letter. I remembered his address for some reason. I had been at his house once. He had all us kids to his house for a party. That address is still stuck in my head from the day I saw it written on the invitation. 504 Wells St. I knew there was little chance he was still there at that address or that he would remember me, but I sent it anyway. It turns out he still lived there. He got the letter and wrote me back. He told me it was one of the greatest gifts he had ever received. I cried grateful tears when I read his letter back to me. We stayed in touch for a bit and then for no reason we stopped writing to each other. I think we both knew it was time."

"That is so beautiful. It really shows the power of one person, one teacher or anyone, to change our lives. Maybe for better or for worse. But, I am thinking of that position that teachers have. You had a teacher who was abusive and hated Jews and you had a teacher who saw your beauty and shared it. Pretty incredible that he supported you that way."

"Yep, an absolute life changer. An angel."

"I feel like in so many of your stories, you were in danger. I don't remember ever being in danger as a kid. But, I feel like you were dancing between land mines. Did you ever feel really scared?"

"Hmmm, I am sure I did. Probably a lot. I don't remember how much I felt scared, but I do remember avoiding some people and places. Some was danger of my own choosing and some wasn't. I decided in 1st grade to call Johnny Torino my boyfriend. I would skip Girl Scouts on Tuesday nights and walk to his house and kiss him until it was time to go home. I liked to kiss him under the window to his parents' kitchen because I could see his mom at the sink above us. I didn't really know how to kiss, just pressed my lips against his, glanced up at his mom, and pressed some more. I don't know what he thought of it, but he never told me to stop. I also don't know what I was thinking. It must have been the risky danger of it all. I liked to choose my own dangerous situations instead of letting other people throw me into them, still do. I have never thought about it, but maybe it was a sort of revenge against Mrs. Torino, Johnny's mom. She told Johnny to stay away from me because our family wasn't Catholic. I had to sneak around to be with him and couldn't let his mom see me there.

Some of the danger was bigger, but I didn't realize it at the time. Maybe that internal guide that measures danger is broken in me. Remember Sissy Lawson, the one who decided where our gym lockers would be? Well, she was the most popular girl and I wanted to be in her crowd. I wanted her to like me. I wanted anyone to like me or at least think I was cool. She invited me to a party at her house one weekend when I was about 10. I thought it was because she suddenly saw my coolness or at least she couldn't see what a loser I was for a moment. I put a lot of effort into what I wore to the party and stole some of my sister's blue eye-makeup to put on my lids (That was probably a disastrous effect, but I didn't notice). It was supposed to be a sleep over and I thought there would be other girls there.

When I got there it was actually her older brother's party and her parents weren't home. She and I were the only ones our age and the only girls. The boys were all dressed in tight black clothes and clicking black heeled boots and called themselves Gousters. When I got there they were playing a "game" where they would put a lit cigarette between their forearms and see who caved sooner. They all had a lot of burn scars on their arms. They were drunk and loud and pretty fucking scary to a kid in fifth grade. But, I knew they were cool people. So, I decided to stay and be brave. Sissy told me to take a drink of alcohol and I did. Sissy told me to take a puff of her cigarette and I did, but coughed my head off. She and the Gousters all laughed. It was about then that I figured out I was not invited as a friend, but as the "watch the loser" entertainment. I started to formulate a plan to get out of there smoothly. But, before I could execute my plan, Sissy asked me to go to one of the boys and ask him how his sister's dancing lessons were going. I couldn't see any harm in that and went over and asked him.

"Hey, how are your sister's dance lessons?"

He immediately jumped up from his chair and reached into his pocket and pulled out a switchblade, snapped it open and ran after me screaming, "I'll kill you, when I catch you I'll kill you, you little bitch."

I ran to Sissy's parent's bedroom and squeezed under the giant bed. The boy's knife was swinging so close to me that I was positive I was going to die. I closed my eyes and waited for the pain of the knife slicing me. Before I got sliced, I heard Sissy's brother come in yelling at the guy to leave me alone. He was shouting, "Hey, leave her alone. She didn't know your sister's in a wheelchair. Get away from her." I took the opportunity to slide out the other side of the bed and tear ass out the front door. I didn't stop 'til I got into my parent's house and locked the door behind me. I never spoke to Sissy again after that and I stopped seeing her as "cool". I had left my overnight bag there and had no intention of going back to get it, EVER. When I told Pessy what happened, she stormed right out the door and walked the two blocks to Sissy's place. I still have no idea what happened, except that Pessy returned with the overnight bag and told me to "stay clear of that girl."

"Holy crap Lu, that is so scary. I think you just got sort of used to dangerous stuff. It was just part of your normal world."

KARINA

About an hour into today's interview session, Lu told me we were done because she had a surprise for me. We were hiking somewhere with the dogs and Lu carried a pretty big daypack. We went a completely different direction and headed straight up the massive ridge behind the house. All the snow had melted from the hot New Mexico sun and the path was dry. Well, I call it a path, but most of it was not even distinguishable as a path. For Lu it was as obvious as a well-marked state park path, for me it was just rubble. It was like walking on small red lava pieces. The dogs were amazing to watch. They raced at top speed over hills and ridges and into ravines, called arroyos here, and flew over and around cactuses but never got stuck by one. We passed rocks covered in petroglyphs. Lu casually pointed to them and kept walking, but I stopped and studied them. Beautiful white art on black and red rock. I was recording our conversation, so I had my phone camera and got amazing photos. These drawings of snakes, coyotes, suns, people, lizards were like something I have only seen in documentaries or photo books. Lu slowed down enough to be patient with me needing to stare at and photograph each one. They were so magical and I couldn't imagine what Lu's surprise would be that would be any better than those.

About an hour into our hike, Lu started climbing straight up a rock wall using her hands to pull her up. I stood with the dogs looking up at her. "Come on up," she said. I just shook my head, "There is no way I would make it up there." She told me it wasn't as steep as it looked. With shaking knees, I managed to get up to the top and we climbed into a huge hole in the wall straight into the most surreal scene. The cavedigger had been up there digging and created a maze of rooms with little carved niches in the walls filled with photos and candles and melted wax and little metal jewelry body parts. Lu lit a candle and carried it so we could see in the dark inner rooms. She explained that the cavedigger had hauled all his tools up there in a backpack and hand carved the whole thing over a few years. Then word spread about the cave and the locals would do pilgrimages to the cave to leave offerings and pray for their friends and family. Sadly, the BLM, Bureau of Land Management, owned the land and when they heard about the pilgrimages they ordered the cave digger to fill the cave back up with dirt and block the entrance. They decided it was a liability. That worked for some years, but then the locals took it upon themselves to re-dig the cave and bring it back to at least some of its original form. I asked her about the little body parts jewelry. She explained that those are called 'milagros' in Spanish. They come from Mexico and are said to help in healing the sick. So, lets say your child broke their leg, you would bring a little silver leg milagro to the cave and pray for quick healing. There were literally hundreds of these little silver body bits all over the cave. Some were covered in melted wax from candles overflowing onto them. We left the cave and I looked down at the dogs sleeping in the dirt waiting for us and it looked even more terrifying than the climb up. At least coming up I could see where to hold on to the rock. Lu assured me it would be fine and she went first and guided me down, sometimes grabbing my feet from right above her head and putting them in a more secure spot to land. Again, just having her there, so solid, made me feel like I could do this and just relax into it. That has been such a theme during this stay. Doing things I would have never done in my life and feeling strong because Lu is there to support me. We got down to the dogs and walked out to a point that had a view for miles around us. It really felt like being on top of the world. Like there was no one else on earth but us and the dogs and the ravens and hawks circling around us. We sat down and Lu pulled out containers of lunch goodies. It was a feast. I thanked her for the fabulous surprise. She laughed, "You think the cave was the surprise? That wasn't the surprise. We still have about two hours to get to the surprise." I really couldn't imagine what would top the petroglyphs and cave.

We ended lunch with brownies and hot chocolate from a thermos and continued the hike.

I wasn't keeping track of time, because the sky was impossibly deep blue and the scenery just kept getting better. I guess it must have been about two more hours, because we came around some shrubs and cactus to a place that actually had green plants and grasses and steam was rising out of an enormous pool of water. Lu didn't say anything, she just took off her clothes, put them on a rock and stepped into the pool. I stood frozen for a moment, not sure if I should turn around and give her privacy or take my clothes off and join her. Again, she laughed, "This is the surprise, come on in!" I had heard of hot springs, but somehow never pictured them in the middle of nowhere surrounded by nothing but rock and plants. Lu had thrown her clothes on the rock and I carefully folded my clothes and put them on another rock. Lu and I had a laugh about me folding the clothes so perfectly. It was one of those moments where my life before New Mexico contrasted with my time here. I could feel my previous anal type A personality getting weaker....but still trying to hold on to anything familiar.

When my foot hit the water it felt too hot and I pulled it out of the water. "It's just the contrast to the cold air, it will feel fine when you are in", Lu reassured me.

I took a deep breath and quickly got my whole body in the water. The bottom of the pool felt muddy and a bit slimy, which grossed me out at first. Then I just sank into it. When I sat the water was up to my chin, so not too deep, but deep enough to float. I floated on my back staring up at the half moon above us in the blue sky. The underwater silence and the sky transported me to some place I had never been. I don't know what to call it except 'absolute peace'. Tears were flowing down my temples into the pool. Not sad tears, just gratitude tears. This whole day has been one gift after another.

EIGHT SIGNS YOUR CHILD MIGHT BE RETARDED

"Lu, Yesterday was amazing. I have never slept so hard in my whole life. Thank you so much. I just can't imagine any other day ever topping that. That was really the high point."

"Ha, you are so young, you will have so many days that compete with yesterday. Just you wait and see."

"I hope so, but really I don't care, because that experience was enough to keep me going for the rest of my life."

Lu smiled, "Ok what do you want to ask me today?"

"Honestly, I don't have any planned questions today. I just feel like rolling with whatever comes up. But I would like to know what made you so independent and confident. You moved through the world, even as a kid, with confidence."

" Karina, I better set you straight. I was anything but confident. I was a nervous little kid with no social skills. I did lots of activities that I was forced to do by my well-meaning parents, but I would have been happier just to stay home with the dog and Ronny. Even the activities where I was surrounded by kids my age, I rarely made a single friend. Like every Saturday, from first grade on, I would put a dime in my pants pocket and 50% of my weekly allowance in the other pocket. The dime would get me on the bus that would take me downtown to the swimming lessons that my parents made me go to. I hated the KYF (Kenosha Youth Foundation) pool. It was chlorine-y and hot and mildewy and I didn't have one friend there. The showers were slimy and gave me painful planter's warts on the bottom of my feet. Before the lessons started, I would hang out in the vending machine room next to the ball clunking of the billiards tables. There in the vending room, I would engage in criminal activity with the spout of the popcorn machine. There were little paper bags you were supposed to put under there to catch your nickel's worth of popcorn. But I worked out a system to keep the popcorn coming by inserting my skinny little arm up into the dispenser. Other kids lined up for their free popcorn. They had their little paper bags and I would keep my arm up in the machine as long as I could. They would all get excited about it and thank me, but I was careful not to mistake them for friends. It was obvious, even to someone like me, that they were there for the goods, not to be close to me.

The swim lessons were always a disaster. I held the side of the pool so hard that I had blisters and calluses on my fingertips. I am no natural athlete. Any sport that other kids learn in a year, takes me five. Other kids learn it in a day, I get the hang of it in about a year.

After swim lessons, I would go into the sleazy little KYF cafeteria that smelled like ham and eggs and burned toast. I would go straight to the gum display rack and buy one package of Juicy Fruit gum from the rack between the cash register and the pie display. Then I'd put all five pieces in my mouth before I even got out the door and get to work chewing the giant wad. The place had sherbet green vinyl upholstery on swiveling round stools and my clothes smelled like lard after being in there. The only people dining were the single or widowed old men who lived in the connected rooming house. With my mouth bulging with Juicy Fruit, I would head to the Woolworth's store and buy one bright blue snow cone, toss my gum wad in the trash and suck on my snow cone while going up and down the escalator, taking any opportunity to run up the down and down the up when no one else was riding. From there, I would walk down the block with my blue lips and tongue till I got to Ruby's Deli and Tavern. Jack Rubenstein ran the place and it was a Jewish old man gambler's hang out. I sat at the bar in a cloud of cigar smoke and Jack would make me a towering corned beef sandwich with a giant kosher pickle on the side. He never charged me for eating there and he always gave me a Dr. Pepper or a red cream soda to drink. I was happy as could be. I figured that my before and after rituals for my swimming lessons were the least I deserved for putting up with something I hated.

One winter day with my dime in my pocket, I stood at the bus stop and the bus went right by me. The bus driver didn't see tiny 7 year-old me standing next to the towering snow bank on the roadside. I considered walking around for a while and then going home and pretending I had made it to the KYF for lessons. I didn't want to get yelled at for missing the bus. Instead, I braved it and went home and explained what happened. I walked slow so that no one at home would drive me to my lesson and I would be spared one week of chlorine hell. Lazer told me to figure something out by the next Saturday so I wouldn't miss my swim lessons. The next Saturday I decided to wear all red. From my hat to my red cowboy boots I was solid red. I even wore my mom's red leather evening gloves that came all the way to my armpits. I took her red rouge and made big circles on my cheeks. When I saw that bus coming, I waved my arms like a wild critter so the bus would see me. It worked and I ran into the open door of the bus, plunking my dime into the coin slot and feeling like I had done something really BIG that day. The other passengers on the bus all stared at me and whispered to each other. I had no idea they must be thinking I was a bit crazy in that outfit, I figured I was looking good and they were all talking about my amazing red outfit. Being delusional works in my favor, even now. The other kids at the KYF laughed when they saw me. I was totally unfazed by them and let them all know that I had fixed a really big problem that morning by being red.

I was a super shy kid.....so was my brother. Lazer wanted us to be assertive and strong. I was comfortable with adults but not kids. Kids scared me. One Saturday when I was little enough for my brother to be taking me around by holding my hand, my dad told us to go make some friends. He barked at us, "Go make some god damned friends. Get out of the house and find some other kids to play with. Don't come back in here until you find some friends. This is getting ridiculous. You've gotta come out of your shells." Thankfully my brother knew enough to not ask Lazer for details. We left the house with Ronny holding my hand and sat at the edge of a field where boys were playing soccer. The boys never noticed us. We just watched them. We were invisible shy kids. We sat there for a long time. Then the boys finished playing and left. Ronny took my hand and we went back home. As soon as we got in the door, I heard my dad yell from the living room. "Did you make some friends?"
"Yep", my brother replied.
"How many?" my dad asked.
"About 10", my brother answered.
"What are their names?" my dad asked.
"We didn't ask their names", my brother answered.
"Will you see them again?" my dad asked.
"I think so", my brother replied.
Mission accomplished.

My dad wanting us to be strong and assertive in the world was a noble and loving desire. But, it backfired and instead, we were nervous kids who bit our nails and picked at our scabs.

We had no social skills and horrible self-esteem with other kids. We just knew we didn't fit in with the regular kids. Pessy even put Tabasco sauce on our fingers to try to get us not to bite our nails. When that only made us into kids who liked hot foods, she tried bitter apple extract. We kept chewing our fingers bloody and to this day I love really bitter foods.

You know how some things really stick with you? They seem terrifying when they are happening and then they stay with you for your whole life as a memory. My mom bought me a blue plaid skirt with a giant gold decorative safety pin by the fringey part. Kind of like a Scottish kilt. Big fashion for kids at the time. She got it at Sav-A-Lot Department Store downtown. This was a big deal since she sewed our clothes and that would have been a breeze for her with the kilt thing. Not sure why she bought it for me. When we got home we decided it really wasn't a good fit. It would have to be returned. Lazer told my mom that I should return it by myself. I think I was in about third grade. "Don't go in the store with her Pessy. Wait in the car. She has got to learn how to do this stuff by herself." This was going to be part of my un-shy training. Pessy parked outside Sav-A-Lot. I could tell she wanted to come in and help me, but Lazer was the boss. She hugged me like I was the kid in Sophie's choice being taken away. I bravely took the box that was on my lap, with the plaid skirt wrapped in tissue inside, and walked toward the door. It felt like a death march. I walked slowly trying to rehearse what I would say. When I got to the counter where the cash register was, I froze. What was I going to say? I couldn't remember. The woman at the counter asked if she could help me.
-"I am supposed to return this." I put the box on the counter.

She opened the box and asked what was wrong with it.
Geez, I didn't expect her to ask that so I hadn't rehearsed that answer.
-"I think it is too small for me"

-"Oh, would you like to try on another size?"
This was not supposed to happen. I thought I would give them the box and they would give me money and I would be safely back in the car with my mom.
-"I don't know"
-"Well, would you like me to find a larger one?"
-"No thank-you"
-"Do you want a refund or store credit?"
(What does that mean? I had no idea what either of those was.)
-"Can I please have the money back that my mom paid for the skirt?"
-"Of course you can"
Everything took so long that Mr. Alder spotted me.

He was the manager of the Sav-A-Lot and he knew our family from the synagogue. I could see him heading my way. He was smiling like always, but I wanted nothing to do with any more conversations in there.
The woman at the cash register handed me the money and I ran out of the store and grabbed the handle of the car like it was a lifeboat and a shark was about to bite me in half. I left Mr. Alder in my wake. "Start the car mom, go! Come on let's go!" I sounded like a bank robber in a getaway car.
People who aren't shy don't understand how painful these kinds of experiences are.
The training for Ronny and I was pretty ongoing. Two of my uncles, Morrie and Aaron, were always trying new money making gigs. They got this big idea during the Beatle's heyday to create Beatle Shampoo and Beatle Hairspray. They had some artist do a drawing for the label and it was awful. You wouldn't know it was the Beatles without the name of the product in big bold letters. Their idea was to sell it door to door. In their town, Chicago, their kids peddled the stuff. But, in our town, Kenosha, it was just me and Ronny as the salespeople. It was disastrous and so painful for me and Ronny to have to go door to door. Our biggest nightmare, approach-

ing strangers. I think a few people bought them from us out of pity. That was the only shampoo we had in our house for years because they had cases of this stuff and it was the worst quality shampoo you could imagine. It smelled like low cost air freshener and turned all of our hair into bigger frizzier afros than we already had. The boxes of this stuff were in our basement and I would occasionally throw a few bottles away in the bottom of the trash so we could get to the end of our torture sooner. I had to do it little by little because we weren't allowed to waste anything.

After the Beatles fiasco, came the Lions Club disaster. Lazer had me and Ronny work the Lion's booth at the county fair. We had to take orders and serve food. We were just kids and giving change and paying attention to detail was not our thing. I am guessing they lost money on us being there. There was a training session for it and we were taught exactly what to say to each customer to get them to buy more than they intended. So, if somebody ordered a burger, we were supposed to say, "Would you like fries and a shake to go with that burger? It's a much better deal to get the whole meal." Ronny and I could not say that stuff. We would silently take their order and their money and the most we could say was "Thank you". The next enterprise was selling light bulbs door to door. It was a Lions Club thing to raise money for research for blind people. There was a major sales pitch for that job, too. And in true form, Ronny and I didn't give the pitch. Instead we would just show them the package and the brochure and say the price. We did sell some, but not enough for Lazer to keep getting us to go door to door. I would feel sick to my stomach the whole time I was doing the door to door thing. I hated it. There was about a 10-year period where, once a year, we were given UNICEF boxes from the synagogue and were supposed to go door to door to get them filled. Ronny and I would pretend to go door to door and instead go over to Bobby's place next door and we filled the box with our own pennies and nickels to make it feel heavy. The good news was that the thing was sealed until it got to the UNICEF people. So, Lazer would feel the weight of the boxes and say, "Any bills in there?" Ronny would answer, "Not sure." Then Lazer would rub our heads, "Good job you two." Shy kids can get pretty creative about working the system.

I have a good friend, Tina, who was a super shy kid, too. She told me the story of going to a party with her mom and dad and sitting on the floor in her pretty new taffeta plaid dress. The host's dog started chewing on the dress and no one was noticing but poor Tina. She was too shy to tell anyone. When her family got ready to leave she stood up and the entire bottom of her dress was gone."

"Oh no, poor Tina. That is seriously shy. But you don't seem like a shy person to me. You like a lot of quiet times, but you don't seem shy at all."

"I am definitely an introvert. I call myself a high functioning introvert. Extroverts get energized by being around a bunch of people and interacting. Introverts get drained by being with a bunch of people and the constant interaction. I get energized by alone time. I think I am probably a bit mentally ill or what I would call crazy and that makes it easier to just be on my own. I was an intense rocker for most of my life and that is probably a sign of an unstable mind, right?"

"Oh, I don't know about that. What do you mean you were a rocker?"

"The rocking only stopped in my thirties. I rocked furiously my whole life. Like this. Just forward and back all the time. It wasn't just the night rocking in my bed with my head intentionally smashing on the headboard. It was constant. My family used to say I ruined the gas mileage on the long trips in our turquoise Rambler station wagon because I rocked so violently. I rocked from Wisconsin to Florida and from California to Washington D.C. and in pretty much every state in the U.S.

Pessy worried that I was mentally retarded (Now its called "ID" or "Intellectual Disability"). In the 60s she read an article in Women's Day Magazine called "8 Signs Your Child Might Be Mentally Retarded". Rocking was at the top of the checklist. Number Two was if your child could not cross their eyes. She sat me down many times a day and begged me to follow her pointer finger from the tip of her nose to the tip of mine. I couldn't cross my eyes. Not then and not now. I saw the desperation in her attempts to get my eyes to cross so I pushed and tried to will my eyes to cross until they ached. "Try harder," she would whisper, "just keep your eyes on my finger." As hard as I tried, one eye would always wander away. To this day I wonder if I am not a mentally disabled kid who figured out how to slip through the system and then grew into an adult.

In high school, my art instructor asked why I was always rocking. I had no idea I was still rocking. Apparently, my family and friends had gotten used to it like a strange tick. I had consciously tried to stop doing it in public and thought I had succeeded.

I finally stopped rocking when my meditation teacher told me to stop in about 1990. She said, "You can't go deep meditating if you are moving around." So I made myself really stop. What is weird is that I had been rocking everyday while meditating for 6 years at that point and had no idea I was moving at all. When I stopped rocking that day in the meditation hall the mental and physical pain really kicked in. The rocking had kept me from feeling most of the pain."

"What do you think the rocking was about, why were you doing it?"

"I think it's like the animals kept as prisoners in zoos and labs and other captive situations. They literally go crazy in their situation and rock and pace. I felt trapped. Life on Earth was my prison. Rocking kept me from feeling physical and emotional pain all those years. I had to learn to deal with life and one of the best ways to deal was rocking. The other way I dealt with life was the swingset in the back yard. Those hours and hours on the swing were just a giant form of rocking. When the swingset was taken away when I was about 11 years old, I started smoking dope every day. I just didn't have the skills to easily do life on earth.

When I was about 15 I witnessed an epic fight between Lazer and Pessy. Their fights would make me feel physically sick because I wanted to protect Pessy and couldn't figure out how to do that. My face and ears would just burn hot from the emotions of it. I can't remember everything about the epic fight except that he was shouting at her about how fat she looked in a dress she had just put on to go to a funeral. All I remember is that it was the funeral of a family member she was really close to. The intensity of him shouting at her vibrated inside me and made my ears really burned hot. I just didn't have the tools to deal with that kind of tension and verbal abuse. I refused to go to the funeral and instead planned on leaving that day. I packed a bag with dog food and padded my metal bike basket with blankets for the dog to ride. I wrote a long letter to Lazer explaining why I had to leave. I basically said that I wanted him to stop abusing Pessy. As I look back I realize that I felt like I needed to do something shocking to try to make him be kinder to her and this felt like my only card to play. It was a hot summer day and within a block of the house I knew it was too hot for the dog to ride with me. I took her home and wrote another note with instructions for Ronny to take care of her. Then I rode off again. I stopped on the edge of town and stashed the bike in a storage locker at an apartment complex. That way I figured that if my family called the police the description would be for a girl on a green bike. I walked to the highway from the apartment storage and put my thumb out. This was my first hitchhiking experience, so I didn't know the protocol. First of all, you do not wear a Black Panthers tee shirt with a Black Power fist on it. And second of all, you do not just wear the thin tee shirt with no bra and nipples showing straight out saying "hello, hello". I had long braids and ripped jeans and a little Girl Scout bag, which I had forgotten to empty when I brought the dog home. So, now I was carrying a backpack filled with dog food cans and I had no dog with me. No one was stopping to pick me up on the edge of the interstate. After a long wait, I looked way up the road and saw an old man with a flat tire on his old Chevy. He was just standing there. I walked up the road to him and asked if he needed help. To this day I have no idea why the guy trusted me at all. Little hippie black power girl with no bra. But he did trust me. I told him I could change his tire and put the spare on and then he could go get the tire fixed in the next town. I jacked up the car and switched to his spare. He kept telling me I was amazing. I couldn't see that, but I liked hearing it. He asked where I was going and I told him Madison. He offered to drive me there after his tire was fixed, so we rode together to the mechanic, his tire got fixed and we drove to Madison. He dropped me off telling me to be careful. I wandered around Madison, which is a very hip college town, and saw a beautiful door in this corner building. I was staring at the door and people were going in and out of it carrying shopping bags. Above the door a sign said Food Co-op. I had no idea what that meant, but I went in and saw it was an odd looking grocery. I went to the woman at the check out and asked her if she knew of any place I could live and volunteer in exchange for rent. She told me she was the manager of the co-op and I was welcome to stay upstairs in the stock room and volunteer during the day. The other volunteers who were there that day put their heads together and within a few hours, I had a mattress on the floor up in the stock room, with clean sheets, a floor lamp, towels, and the amazing smell of herbs that were stacked next to me in boxes. It was heaven. I even had a big floor to ceiling window that let the light in.

During my days there I volunteered stocking shelves and helping customers find things. I was living there, so I volunteered more than anyone else and got to know all the stock and the routines. I was just a kid, but the manager started relying on me for letting her know what she needed to order. One of the other volunteers gave me color pencils and I would make little drawings on the back of thrown out receipts and tack them on the wooden wall at the foot of the mattress. I had hundreds of these little drawings. I am guessing they knew I was a runaway kid, but no one ever pushed me to say why I was on the run. During that time, I had no idea how much I was torturing Pessy. That was not my goal. I just wanted her life to be better and instead, I added suffering to it. I learned later that she would wait all day by the phone for a call about where I was. She finally assumed, and I guess accepted, that I was dead. They took all the photos of me they could find, and Ronny and Lazer drove all over to police stations to ask if they could help find me. Those stations must have tacked the photos on missing persons walls, because later, when I was back home, they mailed the photos back and all the teen age photos of me in the family albums have pin holes at the top. Ronny and Lazer drove right by that co-op and considered going in and decided I wouldn't be in there and it was a waste of time. If they had walked in that door, they would have found me buzzing around the store taking care of things.

After a few months, I decided that I should make my way back home so I wouldn't have to make up for missed school. I went to my sister Karen's apartment in the same town, smoked a joint and then called Lazer at work. I made a deal with him. I told him if he stopped abusing Pessy and Ronny I would come home, but if he couldn't agree to it, I would never come back. He agreed to my deal and I returned to the house. Things were better for a little while and then they went back to their old pattern. Mostly I just felt horrible for causing Pessy so much stress and worry while I was gone. That was the worst part. I had no idea that my leaving would cause her so much stress. I was so young and didn't know that people care for their kids

so much. I just felt so totally helpless in the home situation. It was hard for me to breath in that environment. I was desperate and that was the plan I came up with. If I had gone to one of my old friends in the neighborhood, like the Sulskis, they would have told me it was a bad plan and helped me figure out something else. But I didn't run the plan by anyone.
Over the years, I tried leaving earth by suicide. Not "silly teenager screaming for attention" style suicide attempts. These were well planned and solidly built for success. One involved sleeping pills and swimming to the middle of a lake, one involved ingesting Draino. And yet, each time by crazy flukes and impossible interruptions, I was foiled. I finally gave up on getting out of here early and decided I would figure this place out as best I could and stick around for a while."

"That is pretty intense. You talk about it so freely. I never even considered suicide. I am glad you didn't succeed. If you are ok talking about it, tell me about one of the impossible interruptions."

"I can tell you about the last, final attempt. I carefully collected sleeping pills. Appointments with different doctors and clinics so there would not be any suspicion. It was very calculated. It took me almost a year to collect what I thought would be enough to do the trick. I poured all the pills into a paper sack. The plan was to sit on the edge of Cedar Lake and swallow all the pills and then swim to the middle of the lake and just sleep into drowning. I was in my late twenties. I had a job as a truck driver for a produce company that delivered to food co-ops and restaurants. I was responsible to the customers, so I decided I better finish my delivery route before killing myself. I had a jug of juice and the paper bag of pills on the seat next to me in the truck. I was at the last food co-op and jumped out of the truck and pulled out the long metal ramp for wheeling the produce into the store. There was a little girl who was often there because her mom was the manager. Her name was Shana. She was a beautiful little dark skinned girl with a giant afro. I am guessing about 8 years old. I love that her name was Shana because it means beautiful in Hebrew or Yiddish. Can't remember which. So, I am up in the truck and Shana comes stomping up the ramp. She looks angry and shouts at me to sit down. Understand that this is a usually calm and sweet soft-spoken child.

I ask her "Why Shana? Why do you want me to sit?"

She pointed to an apple box on the floor of the truck and shouted, "SIT!"

I sat on the box and looked at her. The air in the truck felt strange, different. It felt a bit like I was floating above the scene watching it.

Then Shana was looking me solid in the eyes and said very calmly and in a strong direct, but not threatening way, "Don't hurt yourself."

I felt way too seen and a little freaked out.

"Shana, what are you talking about?"

"You know what I am talking about."

"No I don't"

"Yes you do. I mean it. Do NOT hurt yourself. Promise me. You can't leave the truck until you promise me."

I was completely blown away. Who was this little messenger? I could not explain it away in any logical way. It got my attention like nothing else could have. The message seemed clear. Not my time to leave the planet.

"OK Shana, I promise."

Then she smiled and seemed to go back to being that little girl I had interacted with before. She skipped down the ramp and asked if she could bring the box of mushrooms into the store.

This was our routine. She got any boxes 10 pounds or less. I handed her the mushrooms, hugged her when I got into the store with my two-wheeler load and never took those pills. That was the end of my trying to get off the planet before my time."

"*OK, that is incredible. I wonder what she would tell me if she could remember that day. Do you know where she is now?"*

"No, I have no idea where she is or how I would find her. I guess it would be pretty amazing to track her down and tell her how my life changed that day."

"It sure would. You have to let me know if you find her at some point. I would love to hear about her memory of it."

"Me too. I would love to know if she remembers it at all."

KARINA

It's late and I really want to just pass out, but I have to write about this day. Lu gave me my first lesson on crossing the river solo. We went back and forth with her in the front of the boat not paddling at all. Then, on maybe my 10th time across with her, she grabbed the big rock next to the boat and got out. I started to get out and she said, "Nope, you are ready to go solo. Head back across and then back to me." You have to understand, this is no little creek, this is the Rio Grande. Big, wide, deep, freezing cold, with huge floating ice chunks. I held onto the rock gathering up my courage. I didn't realize how much Lu in the boat had reassured me. I had been sitting on my life jacket, but decided for my solo run, I would put it on and secure it. Lu held the boat still and I put the bright orange life vest on. Come on, I thought to myself, be brave. You grew up on the Baltic Sea, riding in boats and ferries all the time. You can do this.
The dogs kept swimming back and forth with us in the icy water. I was hoping for their company, but they stayed on the rocks with Lu. I pushed off the rocks and angled the boat what I thought was perfectly. But, a huge chunk of ice hit the front of the boat and changed everything. I was aimed down river now and was being pulled at top speed away from the dock on the other side. I was panicking. My mind raced to visions of rapids and waterfalls down river and me going overboard and the boat being lost forever. I was crazy paddling against the current and picturing the boat gone and me freezing and wet when I heard a shout. Lu's voice brought me back to reality. She shouted calmly, "You've got this, just angle the way I showed you and paddle up along the shore." I couldn't look her way because I needed to just pay attention to what I was doing. After a lot of maneuvering and pushing that paddle as hard as I

could, I made it. I was paddling up river along the calmer protected shore. I grabbed the dock with my aching arms. Lu was across the river clapping for me like it was a great success. Then to my absolute horror, I realized I needed to get back across to pick up Lu. Like she read my mind, she shouted over to me, "OK, aim for that bent cottonwood tree up there and you will drift perfectly to me. You SO have this."

I made it back across doing exactly what she said. It was easy. I was amazed.

Lu tied up the boat and helped me out onto the rocks. She hugged me, "That was perfect. It is really important to have things go unexpectedly, so you know you can handle it. I couldn't have designed a better maiden solo trip for you." I felt triumphant and told her I couldn't have done it without her.

She took my hand and helped me up the rocks to her truck. The wet dogs all jumped in and Lu told me to get in. We were heading to town for a celebration meal at the little food truck, The Burrito Wagon.

Lu's kitchen is so well stocked that we haven't shopped or eaten out in days. The last time I was on that long driveway was my icy slide down in the rental car days earlier.

When we got to the Burrito Wagon, Lu told me to order a mild one. I ignored her advice and ordered a medium heat one because I thought my taste buds had adjusted to hot food in the few days I have been here. Lu just shook her head, but didn't stop me. The cook handed me my giant burrito and I bit in. Holy shit, the pain, the fire on my tongue. I threw the burrito onto the picnic table and started dabbing at my watering eyes with the napkin. The older Hispanic woman in the food truck rolled her eyes and came out the side door with a wad of wet paper napkins. She told me to open my mouth and she shoved the wet napkins in there and told me, "Hold those in your mouth, you will be fine". Then she grabbed my hot burrito, threw it in the trash and made me a mild one. Lu was laughing hard the whole time, "Sorry Karina, no sympathy. I guess every tourist needs to experience this. Wish I had a film of it. Your face was just hilarious."

Lu thanked Salina, the cook, who handed her my mild burrito. Lu tried to pay her for it, but Salina said, "No, it was good entertainment, it is on me."

From there we went to the little co-op grocery and picked up a few things. Tiniest store I have ever seen, but it had everything we needed. The guy working the checkout was so beautiful. About my age and Native American. He had two long black braids tied with string and a turquoise bead at the end of each one. He looked right into my eyes and I felt crazy butterflies in my stomach. Whew, haven't felt that in years. Lu introduced us. His name is Elan. When we got to the truck, Lu asked if I was ok because I got so quiet in there. I told her about my butterflies meeting Elan. That opened a whole discussion about me and relationships. I told Lu about the only two relationships I had ever had. One boyfriend when I was a little girl and one girlfriend in college. I just wasn't good at opening up to other people and taking chances with my heart.

We sat in the car and talked for a bit about it. Then, out of nowhere, Lu said, "I think you should cancel your return flight. You are not done here." I couldn't even respond. This is what had been gnawing at me all day, thinking I needed more time here.

Ok, enough about today. My arms are aching from the paddling and I am exhausted. Going to put Elan and thoughts about my return flight out of my mind and sleep.

NO FUCKING STORM

"Karina, tell me about your dreams last night."

"Lu, I can't remember my dreams. I was so passed out."

"Ok, try to remember them from now on. Have the intention before you go to sleep that you will remember your dreams. And then I want to hear about them."

"Sure, I will try. Alright, lets get started on recording. A few times you have mentioned meditation and I see you go to that cushion twice a day. What got you started meditating and what benefits, if any, do you get from it?"

"I had no inclination to meditate. I knew people did it and I had experienced a tiny taste of it in fourth grade with the teacher I told you about. Then, in 1984 my Australian friend, Helena, was staying with me. I heard her on the phone with a Vipassana meditation center in Massachusetts. She was asking for an application to be mailed to her for a course. This was before on-line applications. I mouthed for her to order 2 applications. One for me and one for her. I knew the place was in the Berkshires. I hadn't thought it through. I just thought we would have a fun drive to the Berkshires and a fun vacation there. It was another oops moment. She reluctantly asked for two applications, but when she got off the phone she told me that I could never do the course. It is a 10 day silent course. No writing, speaking, body language, eye contact for 10 days. Just wake at 4:00 am and meditate until 9 at night with a few breaks for rest or food. The last meal of the day is at 11 am. She explained all this to me and I just tuned it out. I was still thinking "vacation". She also explained that the main teacher, SN Goenka, was going to be at the center. He was coming from India and it was such a special thing to have him lead a course in person that there would be hundreds of people there from all over North America. Again, I tuned her out. My mind just floated with "vacation, Berkshires, hiking, road trip, fun". She really tried to explain that it would be a disaster for me. At that time I was barely sleeping because I was so busy. I would bike 15 miles a day to and from work and run at least 6 miles every evening and then go dancing most nights until at least midnight. When the day finally came to drive east, she told me to bring a tent and sleeping bag because there were no sleeping accommodations for the hundreds of meditators who were coming because of the main teacher. We drove two full days from Minneapolis to Shelburne Falls, Mass and checked in on what is called Day Zero. Then, on day one, as I was leaving my tent, the zipper broke on the door of it. We had already gone into silence and I couldn't tell anyone. I just hoped it would be ok, but it wasn't. All night mosquitos bit my face and scalp and biting ants moved into the tent and my arms were swollen and red and looking chewed up from all my scratching. I was a mess. Add to that hell that we had to meditate in a giant makeshift meditation hall that was a tent with no sides. There were too many people to fit into the tiny hall in the farmhouse that was the meditation center, so we were basically all meditating in a circus tent. I was going crazy. This was so not the vacation I dreamed of. Being woken up by a gong at 4 am and meditating all day with mosquitos biting us. I had never sat still in my life, so the agitation was growing. My back was sore, my knees were sore, I was covered in itchy bites and through all that I was supposed to sit still and observe my respiration and body sensations. I missed running and biking and dancing. I never thought I was an angry person, but I started to boil with anger. The only person you can talk to at the center is the female manager if you have something you absolutely need or at noon you can make an appointment with the teacher, SN

Goenka, you know, Mr. Big Stuff from India....the one everyone was there to see and be around. I went to the sign up sheet for a noon appointment with him. I was so angry that I tore the sheet while I was signing it. Then at noon, I waited with the other meditators who had signed up, until they finally called my name. I slammed the door as I went into the little room where he was sitting with his wife. Before I even sat down on the cushion in front of them, I started my screaming rant.
"I fucking hate this fucking place and I fucking hate you and I fucking hate the person who brought me here and I have fucking fire ants in my fucking tent and the fucking zipper broke on my fucking tent and I hate this fucking place and I am going to just fucking leave!"
Goenka's wife had no reaction, just sat there calmly... and Goenka smiled bigger and bigger as my rant went on and on. Then he calmly motioned for me to sit on the cushion in front of him.
I sat down and he quietly said, "This is a storm, it will pass. It is just a storm."
This infuriated me and I went off again. I was pointing a finger at him now and was beyond the boiling point. I was crazed.
"Buddy, this is no fucking storm. Look at my arms. Do you understand? I have fucking fire ants and mosquitos biting me every time I go to my tent and all day I sit and listen to your fucking chants while fucking mosquitos are biting me. And your fucking rules won't let me kill the mosquitos or even scratch my arms in the meditation tent. I am going fucking crazy and I can't get any fucking sleep in my fucking tent because of the fucking mosquitos and fucking fire ants!"
He was now smiling even more and very sweetly said to me, "There is one empty bed in the house, move into the house."
I was so clueless and had no idea who he was or where he lived. I didn't even register that his visit was a very rare occasion. So, I said, "Really? Move into YOUR house?"
This made him laugh so loud that he was rocking forward and

holding his stomach.

"Yes, move into MY house."

I got so happy. I was smiling and laughing with him now.

When he saw my mood change, he said, "Ahhh, storm has passed."

That stopped me in my tracks. My mood had totally flipped. And I understood the impermanence of things for just that brief moment. I looked up at him and felt nothing but love coming from him. With tears in my eyes I told him, "I can tell you are a wonderful teacher, but I don't think I am ready for what you have to teach."

This made him laugh again.

"Of course you are ready. That is why you are here. Just sit, keep practicing. Be diligent and keep practicing. And move into the house."

I thanked him and went to the tent and grabbed my stuff and moved into the house.

It was life changing. But, I am no quick study, so even now I feel like I have just begun the journey of awareness and mindfulness. I had many more encounters with Goenka over the years when he came to the USA. I serve at the centers whenever I can and I often serve at that one in Shelburne Falls. I found out that the people serving on the course where I was swearing at Goenka referred to me as the F-word woman for screaming fuck a record number of times so the whole house could hear me, in a place where there is supposed to be no swearing or yelling to a person who is revered by millions of people as a spiritual leader. Friends of mine who are long time meditators have a theory that I had to have lots of encounters with Goenka before he passed away, because I was so dense and clueless. I think they are right. I needed the biggest wake up, over and over again."

"I have heard about those 10 day Vipassana courses. People I know do them in Sweden. Are there centers all over the world?"

"There are lots of them. Most countries have at least one and many have more than one. Are you thinking of doing it?"

"It scares me a little. So maybe that means I should do it, huh? Hearing your story only scares me more."

"Maybe you should just do it...you have nothing to lose by trying a course. It shifts things in subtle ways from the very first course."

"What kind of shifts?"

"I come from pretty reactive roots. I have noticed that when I do the practice, I am less inclined to dwell on things in the past or the future and I am less reactive, more mindful. The past is gone and the future hasn't come and there is no point in getting worked up about either one. But most of us live in the past and the future much more than we visit the present moment."

"Are there other tools you have for living more in the present and being happier? You seem so content and calm."

"I am not always content and calm. But more and more I live in that place and feel a lot of gratitude and peace. I have been open to any tools that have come my way to work through this crazy human condition. If I told you the ways things fell into my lap, you would think it was magical. But, I just think that I needed a LOT of work on my inner self and those things were like lifelines I couldn't ignore. I believe that they show up all the time for everyone, but we can easily overlook them if we are not paying attention. I will give you an example.
One night I was having dinner with a few friends. When I was leaving I saw their wall of VHS tapes. That tells you how long ago it was. I think I was in my forties. There were hundreds of tapes on the shelves and all the tapes were labeled except one. It was a blue case. I reached up for it and asked if I could borrow it. The two friends looked at each other and then Lily said to me, "Why did you choose that one?"

I said, "I don't know."

She said, "Sure you can borrow it. That is a tape of the woman I work with, Byron Katie. It is her doing a process with a few folks."

I left with that tape and watched it that night. It was fascinating. I loved watching her work with people who were struggling with things in life.

As it happens, the next morning I had an appointment with a therapist I had never been to before. He was recommended by my friend Anna. I rarely went to any counselor or therapists, but there was something I had to work through. I can't even remember what it was now. In my appointment, he started doing what I had watched Byron Katie do on the tape. He was asking me the same questions she had been asking the people in the video. I asked him if he had ever heard of Byron Katie. He laughed and told me that she was his main teacher. I told him I had watched the video of her the night before. It was no accident.

Then, about a week later I got an early morning phone call from Lily. This was weird because she was not the one who usually called. It was usually her partner who called. She said to me, "I want to give you something. I would like to pay for you to go to The School for the Work. Byron Katie's 10-day school." I told her I couldn't possibly accept that because I had researched and learned that the 10 day school cost $3,000! And that was just too much to just give to someone.

Then she told me, "I want to actually make a trade. I will give you the money for the school and I want you to hike with me and help me with something. I want you to work with me on aligning my love for animals with my daily choices. I have so many inconsistencies and I need to stop supporting so much violence. We can hike while you teach me about how to make different choices. Help me find the strength to make those choices."

I was blown away by this offer and by her desire to live her values. It was really beautiful. So, three months later, I was at my first 10-day School for The Work and Lily and I had walked and talked a boatload and she was making a major effort to make compassionate choices in her life."

"You were right, that all does seem pretty magical to me. Just little chance stuff all adding up....like you being drawn to that blank VHS tape on the shelf of hundreds of them."

KARINA

Just a calm day today of interview session, hiking and food. I meditated both times with Lu, but my mind was rolling around about my return flight and Elan. I have never had anyone affect me like this. I want to pursue it and I want to run from it at the same time. It scares me. In two days I am supposed to fly back to Scranton to a job I like, but don't love. To a town I thought was home, but now feels like it was a temporary jumping off point. Just writing about it gets me all stirred up again.

THE SOUL TRAIN

"Lu, today I want to learn more about the Soul Train show you talked about. I looked up a couple of re-runs on the internet. I don't think it was ever in Sweden, but maybe it was just before my time.

"Well, our whole family loved that show and we would dance in front of it. It was our favorite music and the couples wore wild colorful outfits with big wide bell bottoms and they had some incredible dance moves. But, I think of Soul Train as so much more than the TV show. My soul's journey was on some bumpy tracks then. That time was pivotal for me. Junior High starts at about 11 years old in the USA. That is when I was plunged into the Soul Train time. Up until then, I had been at all white schools and lived in a mostly white neighborhood and the synagogue was all whites. I was surrounded by a lot of Jew hating Baptists and Jew hating Italian Catholics for my first 11 years.

I assumed things would get easier when I went to Grover Junior High. I figured that the mostly black crowd at the school would be nice to me because they weren't Italian Jew-hating Catholics or nasty Baptists. Where did I get that hopeful idea?

On Day One, the orientation assembly proved me so wrong. I had gone from being hated because I was Jewish to being hated because I was white. I was tying my shoe while sitting in the auditorium. I glanced up to my left at a girl sitting three seats away.
She glared at me and said "Whatchew lookin' at bitch?"
I gave her my most innocent smile and said, "I was just tying

my shoe"

The smile didn't work. "You gonna pay bitch."

That was my introduction to Corrine Carter. Toughest girl in the school. She had a lot of scars on her hands and her face and shoulders, so looking back, I am guessing she had to be tough to just survive whatever her life was.

Later that same day I was coming out of a stall in the girl's bathroom and she and 5 other girls were waiting. They slammed me repeatedly against the peeling silver paint wall radiator and told me not to ever look at them again. I was definitely going to give that a try. I studied each of their faces so I could remember who I wasn't supposed to look at. They left the bathroom and I waited in there, feeling the bumps on the back of my head from the radiator hits and pulling bits of silver paint out of my fuzzy hair, until I hoped the gang was well down the hall. I didn't say a word to them while they were slamming me. I was just silent. I didn't cry or beg them to stop. I just went numb. After that I decided I better try to not look at any face in the whole school, just to be safe. I became an expert on what shoes were walking in the halls of our school. And, I even started to know who was connected to which shoes. The friendly girl who wore red converse high tops, the beautiful boy I had a crush on who wore cheap no brand white tennis shoes, the totally irresistible Tony who wore black shiny boots with a little chain on the side and cleats that made him click down the hall with each step.

It wasn't easy to not look at faces because I was totally smitten with all the beautiful black and brown students I was surrounded by. I loved the tall lanky brother and sister Regina and Curtis Jefferson with their giant afros and the chunky black hair picks with black-power fist handles stuck into the back of their hair. They were the tallest kids I knew and Curtis was a star on the basketball team. Then there were the Brown brothers. Bow-legged Larry and Dougie Brown. Gorgeous and popular. Later in the year, I would be spending a lot of time at their house. With 16 kids in the family, there was no one keeping track of them, and their basement was our hang-out party paradise available 24 hours a day with zero adult supervision. I wouldn't say any of them were really my friends, but they didn't make me leave and I liked being there surrounded by the smells and the laughter and music. My guess is none of them even noticed me sitting there most of the time. Dougie and Larry's mom was probably 300 pounds. She sat in a huge red recliner chair upstairs in their living room and ordered the kids around. Her arms were about the size of my waist, that is how obese she was. Her older kids were in their twenties and the youngest was just a baby. Their dad was long gone, so I wondered where the baby had come from, but I never asked. I wondered why their mom didn't go to work or ever get out of that chair. I wondered how she was able to shower or use the toilet. But, all of that just became part of normal life there. The older siblings really ran the house. Once in awhile when I would go upstairs to use the bathroom, and the mom, Yasmine, would wrangle me into doing something for her. I remember the first time she did that. She grabbed my arm as I was going by her recliner. She said, "Girl, get me a bologna thandwith with thandwith thbred." I couldn't understand what she was saying with her intense lisp. I leaned in, "What did you say?" She got all crazy with me. "Girl, you death? Wha the hell ith wrong wit you? You retharded or thumthing?" I got away from her grip and made a bologna sandwich in the kitchen. I was guessing she was trying to say "sandwich bread", so I figured I got it right. I brought it to her and she bit into it and spit it out. One of the older kids was in there by then and was laughing her ass off while Yasmine was yelling at me that I was retarded. Turns out she wanted sandwich spread which I guess is like mayonnaise. She threw the sandwich at me and had the older kid make her one, laughing the whole time. I watched their dog eat the sandwich on the carpet by my feet, mustard and all. That just taught me to stay more than an arms length away when I walked by Yasmine, but somehow she still ordered me to do stuff if she wasn't snoozing when I walked by. One time she made me rub some nasty rose scented lotion on her arms and legs because they were itching. I didn't have the nerve to tell her I was allergic to rose. I ran straight to the bathroom and scrubbed my hands after quickly rubbing it on her rolls of leg and arm fat.

A few months into that first year in junior high, a white boy grabbed me and started threatening me and held me against the locker by my neck, pushing hard and making me cough. He told me I was ugly and I stank. I had my eyes closed to try to relax and figure out what to do. I also figured a punch was coming and I didn't want to see it coming. The next moment, he was off me and an enormous black girl named Margaret had him by the shirt collar. I had learned to not look at faces, so when she held him I was looking down and saw that his feet weren't touching the ground. I looked up and she had him up against the lockers held at his neck with one hand and pressing his chest with her thick forearm. She was pointing her finger in his face with the other hand and shouting at him, "You touch her again and I will kill you. Any of y'all touch her and I will kill you." By then a small crowd had gathered for the show. She took my skinny white hand in her clammy big strong black hand and we walked down the hallway away from them. When I asked her why she helped me, she said, "I don't know why, but I like you. You tell me if anybody bother you." I had my angel. Word spread quickly in the huge school and I was never beat-up again. Margaret didn't even have to be with me. Kids just left me alone. I knew I was going to be ok when, one day, Margaret wasn't at school. She had stayed home sick. I panicked about her being out of the building and imagined I was in for a long rough day. I considered faking sick myself, and going home. But, it was a good chance to do a solo test run and I braved it. Amazingly, everyone stayed away from me. My magic protector, Margaret, surrounded me even when she wasn't physically there. I always thought of her as my black angel and after that, whenever I saw any depiction of blonde white skinned angels, it never looked right to me. I knew that the ones that protect you are big and black. With her bubble of protection around me, I was even able to start looking at people's faces and stopped staring at shoes and pants."

"I know I always wonder this, and ask you about it, but do you know where Margaret is now? It would be so great to be able to tell her what that protection meant to you."

"I have no idea where she is now or how I would find her. I am guessing she is still in Kenosha. Something tells me she would not have gotten out of there. But maybe I am wrong. She was strong and independent and that might have been enough for her to choose a path right out of that town."

"Sounds like it was a wild unsupervised place to go to school. What were the teachers and principal like?"

"I think they did their best, but the job was overwhelming. With over 40 students for every teacher, it is hard to keep things controlled. I think they just tried to make it as smooth as possible. Every Friday, our principal Mr. Martinez would bring huge pots of black-eyed peas and greens for all the kids. He was always cheery, which seemed weird at a school where all you had to do was come to class without a knife or other weapon to get a good grade. He was a Hispanic man, but the kids all said he made black-eyed peas as good as their mammas.

My first boyfriend at Grover was Junior Walker. We got together whenever we could just for kissing. I will never forget the strange day we sat in a park near the school and he leaned over to kiss me, but this time he put his tongue in my mouth. I jumped back, wiped my mouth and almost fell off the park bench. "Why'd you do that?" I shouted.
He pulled me closer and said, "You'll learn to LOVE it."

I went home that day and asked Pessy, "Mom, does Dad use his tongue when he kisses you? Does he put it right in your mouth?" My poor mother whipped around and started shouting at me, "Why are you asking me that? Who told you that boys do that?" I told her that Junior put his tongue in my mouth that day. She told me not to ever let boys do that until I was married. "But Mom, does Dad do that to you?"
She didn't skip a beat, "Of course he does, we're married!"

I can look at Grover Junior High in many ways. It was dangerous and taught me things that no little girl should be doing and it was never boring and gave me rich experiences I would never have had at the white school. I couldn't go to the white school anyway. We lived out of that district and the only other choice where we lived was to go to the private Catholic school, St Mary's, which would have been even more dangerous for me than Grover. I'm sure I would have gotten beat up by students and nuns every day there."

"What was it like going to a school in a neighborhood that wasn't at all familiar? I am guessing that all the kids and the culture were new for you?"

"It became home to me real quick. The neighborhood around Grover included lots of factories. There were also more clubs and taverns than houses. Freemans One stop record shop, Rocky's Club, Twins Tic Toc Club, and street after street of tightly packed houses with peeling paint, very little insulation, no grass in the yard, lots of broken windows and boatloads of kids.
When the loud horn would blow at lunchtime or at the end of a shift at one of the factories, hundreds of factory worker bodies would run from the factory to the taverns across the street from the entrances. My mom learned to not drive by there around those times because the traffic jam of human bodies would make us late to wherever we were going. Pessy was so

trusting and in a way oddly innocent. She dropped me off at shady taverns and clubs for wedding parties of schoolmate's older siblings. I was always the only white kid and always had full access to any alcohol, weed or speed.

One day, Pessy and I were driving past a tavern and an enormous black man in a yellow leisure suit and matching hat fell straight out of the corner swinging door and landed face first onto the ground and didn't move. I thought I recognized who it was. I was sure he had been shot since a huge river of blood was running toward the curb. She slowed down to see what was going on, but I yelled for her to keep driving. Pessy was like that. Innocent and caring. She really wanted to stop. "Lu we should help that man." "No Mom, we should get out of here and you should stop staring at it all." By then Pessy had pulled over and there was a huge crowd around the guy on the sidewalk. I recognized kids from my classes and some other folks from the neighborhood. I learned at school the next day that it was the body of a man named Dallas who was shot for no big reason or at least no reason that anybody would tell me. I knew Dallas and always thought he was about the most elegant looking man I ever saw in person. Dallas didn't actually walk. He sort of did a slide and float and wore these long coats that came to his ankles.

On a hot summer afternoon, Pessy and I went into Baskin Robbins 31 Flavors for ice cream cones. As we walked in, Leonard, one of the pimps from the neighborhood around the school, was walking out with a big-haired, high-heeled, purple-eyeshadow, red lipstick hooker on each arm. Leonard and I knew each other well and said hello to each other by name. I introduced my mom to Leonard and he kissed her hand. After they passed, Pessy said to me, "What a nice man...and his daughters are so beautiful." "Mom, those are not his daughters," was all I could say. I loved how Pessy looked at the world.

Since all three of us kids went to Grover, which was 95%

black students, we were into the music on Soul Train more than American Bandstand. At about 8 years old, I told my mom that the only man I was willing to marry was the singer, Sam Cook. She wasn't at all fazed and told me, "When you are old enough to get married, Sam Cook will probably be dead." Isn't that great that she didn't tell me I wouldn't marry him because he was famous or black or that he didn't even know who I was? She just did the math and shared it with me. My sister Karen was a good girl with good grades and she managed to keep a foot in the American Bandstand door as well as the Soul Train door. She was more heavily weighed into American Bandstand and she had lots of white friends and white boyfriends. But Pessy, my mom, was more of a Soul Train person and we knew all the songs. I think if she could have, she would have divorced my dad to marry Al Green. She melted when she saw him sing on TV. Our love of soul music didn't mean any of us had soul or that we could dance, we just thought we could.

We each have a rhythm and beat and melody inside of us. Something that makes us feel things. Some of us have more than one. It's like layers in the ocean. The classical music Mr. Butts introduced me to was my undertow, underneath it all. That was and is the music that gives me mental clarity. The next layer is that real slow back and forth that relaxes me.... that was the Jewish hymns sung on Friday nights and holidays. They have a perfect rocking rhythm. I can sing those to relax and sleep. The top layer, the predominant strong ones that are like killer waves life force is soul and RnB. My brother started this when he came home from his days at Grover Jr High and turned on Soul Train. We sang, danced, laughed and danced some more. It was our joy. You know everyone has some rhythm in them, right? Do you know yours?"

"I don't think I know mine. There are some Swedish songs I love and some pop songs I love and I do love Latin music, but I have never learned to really dance to it. I grew up with Swedish singers like Lisa

Ekdahl. I will play you some of her songs later and translate the meaning for you. They are so beautiful."

"I would love to hear her stuff. My loudest rhythm comes from my own junior high years. Marvin Gaye, Aretha, Al Green, The Temptations, The Four Tops, The Jackson Five, The Supremes, Stevie Wonder and so many others. Those rhythms give me physical power.
In college I went bowling with a group of friends one night. All my balls would go into the gutter. I didn't care. Not a competitive bone in my body and I knew I was a shitty bowler. Then someone put a bunch of coins in the jukebox and played Aretha Franklin over and over. When Aretha's Respect came on, I bowled a strike. The other kids were shocked. They had never seen me go anywhere but the gutter. They were high fiving me like crazy. Then my next turn it was another Aretha, and again a strike. And it went on like this for the whole time the soul and RnB played. Then, someone changed everything by playing some country tune and I went back to my gutter balls. My power music wasn't playing.
You can figure out your different rhythms and what music is inside you by what you choose for different tasks. If you are doing something mental, what helps you focus? If you need to relax, what do you choose? If you are running or need physical power, what music charges you up?
I like Latin music, too. But, I went years without moving my hips enough to dance to it. Maybe you should try this trick I learned. I was in Puerto Rico in my thirties and my friends Antonio and Bertha were going way up into the rainforest to a party. They let me go along. We drove up a winding road up into the mountains. At the top, I heard the music before I saw the big decrepit building. There was a huge salsa band playing and hundreds of people were dancing inside. The place was bare bones. An outhouse, but no inside bathroom, cinder block walls, flickering electric light bulbs hanging in a few spots, all the windows smashed out and no door. I was doing

what I thought was salsa dancing. I was by myself just moving the way I thought everyone was. Then an ancient woman sitting on one of the folding chairs by the wall crooked her finger a few times, telling me to come over to her. She said something like "Es doloroso verte bailar". I had no idea what that meant, so I caught Bertha's eye and had her come over to translate. Bertha cracked up. She said, "She is telling you it is painful to watch you dance." So much for fitting in. Bertha kept translating for me, "She says she can help you. She says pretend you have a pencil in your crotch aiming down and make circles on the ground with the pencil." I started drawing circles with my imaginary crotch pencil and I could feel my hips moving in ways I hadn't ever let them move. Then Bertha told me the old woman wanted me to do figure eights with the crotch pencil. The whole crotch drawing exercise went on for quite a while and then the old woman called a young guy over. She said something to him and pointed to me. Bertha translated, "She told him to take you out to the dance floor and teach you how to dance." I totally got it...the young guy moved me around like a puppet with loose hips. Got hooked on salsa from that point on. You gotta try the pencil thing, you will love it."

"OK, next time I hear latin music, I will try it. I love that pencil in the crotch trick. I keep thinking about you being so young and what your life was. It must have been strange to grow up where you had to choose your friends from the pool of kids who weren't there to take you down."

"On some level, I think all kids have to do that. Maybe I had a smaller group of kids to choose from, but being a kid is a social landmine for most, I am guessing. I like to look at life with a sort of aerial view map. What were the big turns? The 180 degree or 90 degree turns. What do you go toward and what do you turn away from? In junior high, my friends were either latino, black, canine or over 80 years-old. Teen-age years determine a lot of what we become later in life and what feeds us. The world of white teens was something I was never exposed to. I became a foreigner in that culture. If I saw a group of white boys walking toward me, I crossed the road to avoid them because I couldn't read their body language and didn't understand them. If a group of African American boys approached me, I felt no fear at all. I understood their culture and language. Through junior high and high school I stayed mostly with my familiar. Barry came into my life in high school. That added a gay white boy to my list of friends, but it definitely didn't help me understand white kid culture. The only Jewish boys I knew were my brother and my cousins. I sort of understood them, but they weren't regular wasp white boy culture either.

My first friends in Jr High were Camila and her brother, Tony. Their family came from Puerto Rico, so at our school I considered them to sort of be white like me. Tony was my boyfriend for a while and his sister Camila was my friend. I think that might have gone better if I weren't kissing her brother. One morning I got a call that froze everything. I cried for hours before telling my mom what happened. Camila's dad, Manuel, had been drinking and fell asleep with a cigarette in his hand. The mattress caught on fire and then the whole house was up in flames. Manuel had dragged himself out onto the lawn and passed out. Camila wasn't home, but Tony and his three younger siblings, including a baby, were home. Tony got himself out of the burning house and then went back in when he realized his younger siblings were still in there. He was able to grab the baby and his two younger brothers and tried to get out of the house. The flames and smoke were too much and they hid under a bed. That is where their bodies were found when firefighters finally made their way up to the second floor of the house. My heart broke for those kids and for Camila and Manuel. Manuel's life was already really difficult. His wife, Valeria, died giving birth to the baby. He worked a factory job and was raising the kids on his own. I understood why he drank after work every day. I didn't blame him for the death of the children and I never heard anyone else blame him either. Pessy took me to the funeral, but it was too much for us and we both sobbed through the ceremony and all the way home. It was the tiny baby sized coffin that shook Pessy to her core. But, it was seeing Camila sitting like an empty mannequin that tore at me. She left that day. The Camila I knew was gone. Her body remained, but her spirit left and was buried with those caskets. Our friendship was over. We never spoke about it, but we both knew that continuing a friendship meant feeling something, the loss of Tony, that neither of us wanted to. We both moved forward, not looking back. I never knew what happened to her father or her after that. It was just her and her dad after that and I am guessing they moved back to Puerto Rico to be with family."

"That is horrible. I can't imagine going to a friend's funeral at that age. I have never been to the funeral of a friend or of anyone young. Did you have other kids you were close to at that school?"

"Muna, she was my closest friend in Jr. High. I miss her. We loved each other like sisters and laughed constantly. We were pretty much always together and I know she took a lot of shit from the other students for being joined at the hip with the white girl. Muna taught me to dance. I mean, really dance. We would lock ourselves in her bedroom and I would plug in my cassette player for our tunes. I still remember that the cassette player cost me $109. That was a fortune back then, but I needed something portable to listen to music with since I was not free to play records anytime at home. Muna and I would go up to her tiny bedroom and prop a wooden chair against the door knob to keep her brothers from coming in. Then we would watch ourselves dance in the huge round cracked mirror of her dresser. She had a giant soft afro and creamy black skin with pink palms when I flipped her hands over. Again, I had no idea why she liked me. But we were two peas in a pod. I slept at her house or she slept at mine pretty much every day. Her house felt like home to me. Her mom worked full-time at a car factory and her dad stayed home because of a heart condition. He was a strange mix of loving and fun and tough and mean. But, he let me be one of his kids, so I liked the whole package. He taught me to love rubbery overcooked pork chops smothered in Tabasco sauce and he always dressed in pastel satin shirts with long silvery lapels. When Muna and I did something wrong, he punished both of us the same. I spent every Christmas at their house. Pessy and Lazer would come over there on Christmas Eve for drinks with Muna's mom and dad. I love that they would come spend time in Muna's and my world for that evening. Muna's family was dirt poor and the blankets on the beds were never enough to keep the cold draft off me, but I still loved it there. In winter we made what they called ice cream. We collected clean snow in bowls and poured evaporated milk and sugar over it and stirred it up. At our house, Muna would eat ice cream we pulled out of the freezer. Neopolitan ice cream in a rectangular wax board box. Three separate stripes of color...pink, brown and white. Muna and my family would eat the ice cream. I only liked the vanilla part and Muna only liked the chocolate part and that made us laugh because it matched our skin. We carefully, surgically removed each color with perfect precision and then, if it was just me and Muna, we put the pink ice cream on the flattened out wax board box on the floor for Sandy, my dog, to lick clean.

I know she took the time to teach me dancing because I embarrassed Muna when we went to school dances or danced at Freeman's One Stop Record Shop. Freemans had it all. A few groceries like giant pickles, white bread, mayonnaise, mustard, lunch meat, stale baked goods and candy, and all the latest 45s. There was room to dance a little and a booth with a record player where you could hear your 45 before buying it for 99 cents. Whoever was in the booth would leave the door open so the rest of us could dance to their record. I stopped noticing that I was the only white kid. I stopped noticing it everywhere. At school, at Freemans, at parties, on the basketball court, I was just another black kid. At least in my own mind. I would even see a black kid in my reflection. I remember driving home at night with my family after visiting our relatives who lived an hour away in Chicago. We did this about once a week. I would sing Supreme songs in my head and look at my reflection in the window glass. I was sure people were mistaking me for Diana Ross. It didn't help me get realistic when kids in Muna's neighborhood would ask me if I was mulatto during the summer when my skin turned brown and my hair was a ball of frizz.

Muna's dad got this big idea that me and Muna should go to charm school. He thought it would make us less tomboyish. There was one in our town called The Wendy Ward Charm School. When Muna's dad talked to my parents about it, they agreed to pay for me to go. On day one of charm school, we got our own individual make-up kits. This was a bad start for two girls who had no interest in make-up. The things were huge and included every shade of eye shadow and rouge you can imagine. It had a little mascara chunk that you add water to and swish around with a tiny brush. We had to go to charm school once a week for 3 months. Muna was the only one in the charm school who wasn't caucasian. The teacher announced that we would be doing hair lessons in week two. We got a Wendy Ward binder that covered all the important stuff and the homework. We were told that in addition to hair lessons, that week two would start with a make-up test. Muna's dad picked us up after our first session. We sat together in the back seat and looked through our binders on the way home. I noticed that all the photos and drawings of the girls in the book were skinny blondes with white skin. I slammed it shut and said nothing to Muna and her dad. I looked out the window so she couldn't see how upset I was.

On week two, my mom dropped us off. We dragged our feet and slowly walked in carrying our makeup kits and our binders.
We were hoping to be late enough to miss the makeup test.
We were the last ones there, but the test hadn't started yet. Miss Paula, the teacher, gave us instructions, "Each of you will put on makeup from your individual kit according to the instructions in your binder. I hope you practiced this past week. When you are done, raise your hand and I will come and check your work. You will get a score between one and ten, ten being a perfect makeup application job. Muna and I tried not to laugh. We couldn't even look at each other without losing it. Once that starts, there is no stopping it. I asked Muna if she wanted to do each other's makeup. Miss Paula was so busy answering the other girl's questions that she wouldn't even notice, I was sure of that. There were 30 girls in that class who all wanted to suck up to the teacher with lots of questions. Muna and I had no idea what we were doing, so we both pretty much made each other look like clowns. Not "sort of" clowns, but genuine "perform in the circus" clowns. I had used the darkest face powder in the kit, but it was still light pink on Muna's brown skin. I mixed in a dark eyeshadow to try to bring it up to the right color. I made her lips red, but got the shape wrong and it looked like she had just eaten something and smeared it all over. We held tissues to our faces to muffle our laughter and catch the laugh snot coming out of our noses. We worked hard at not looking toward each other and tried gaining our composure. When Miss Paula got to us, she was genuinely horrified. She told us to turn around in our chairs and let the whole class see us. "I have been teaching at this school for ten years and I have never seen such disrespect for what we are trying to learn here. You girls (she looked down at our names on the roster) Muna and Lu, are going to have to straighten up and do

your homework or you will never graduate. That will not look good if you want to succeed with your future dreams. Now go to the bathroom and wash your faces. Come back when you get everything off your face, but not before." Miss Paula was super pissed. We washed our faces and could finally laugh fully in the bathroom. The make-up didn't come off with the make-up remover or with soap and water. The after-washing results were as crazy as the before-washing looks. My skin just looked chapped and Muna's looked like a multi-colored rash. When we were done laughing, we went back to the classroom. There were mirrors around the entire perimeter and a swivel chair for each girl. They were all looking in the mirrors admiring their makeup when we walked in and most of them swung around to see us. We had done our best to get all the makeup off, but we still caused a buzz in the room. 30 girls laughing and snickering.

Miss Paula fumed, "Go back to your chairs. There is not time this week for you to re-do your make-up, but I expect you to try again next week. We must move on to hair now." At that, she let her gaze linger a little too long on Muna's giant afro. That fro was at least four inches out from her head. It was soft and bouncy and round.

"There are lots of different types of hair. Dry and coarse and curly hair should be worn either very long or trimmed very short and close to the scalp."

She walked straight over to Muna and started touching her hair.

"Muna, yours would be best if trimmed close to the scalp. You will never be able to grow it long enough for any of the long styles. For today, you may just want to focus on the makeup section of the binder while we focus on hairstyles. You can ask your parents if they will take you for a nice close trim or get it straightened."

Muna didn't say anything. She looked embarrassed and stared down at her binder.

When Miss Paula started to come toward me and my two

thick braids, I was too angry about how she treated Muna to let her touch my hair. She reached out toward one of the braids and I pushed her hand away.
"I will just study makeup with Muna. My hair is fine like it is, Miss Paula."
She walked away from us flustered and worked with the easy girls on setting with rollers, styling and hair-spraying their hair.

"Week three", Miss Paula announced at the end of class, "is going to be our poise lessons. We will be working on how to walk correctly and we will start our preparation for walking the runway for our first big fashion show." She asked us to please study and practice using Section Three of the binder.
"Can you see how each week's lessons correspond to the chapter in your binder?" This makes it easy for you to be completely prepared for each of our sessions. Please take this work very seriously and do your homework, we don't have much time to transform you into perfect little ladies."

On our way to my mom in the parking lot, we spun in circles and danced like clumsy ballerinas and curtsied to each other repeating over and over in fake British accents, "You are a perfect little lady."

When my mom asked how it went, I just said, "Miss Paula is an asshole. I don't want to go back."
"Don't talk like that," was all my mom said. She did not want any details on Miss Paula.
To soothe me and Muna, she took us to Baskin Robbins for a double scoop.

Halfway through our 6 month charm course, they had scheduled the first of two fashion shows. When Muna and I arrived, they told us we could pick any clothes in the department store to model. Neither of us hesitated for a moment before racing to the boy's department. We found two suits, clip-on ties, great shoes and even found cool derby looking black hats. The parents would all be in the audience watching us walk the runway. I think my dad bowed out of the whole thing, not sure what his excuse was, but I remember being jealous that he was going to be doing something else. We took our outfits to the special charm school dressing rooms and Muna and I shared one tiny space getting ready. Once we were in our outfits, Miss Paula would check us and then send us off to work on our makeup. We had been practicing the special runway walk and turn in class and Muna and I loved it and had it down. Once we were sure we both had our suits on perfectly and our hats were tilted just so, we took some time to admire ourselves in the mirror. We looked fantastic. We hugged each other and left the dressing room and looked for Miss Paula. We were sure she would be totally impressed with our outfits. Obviously we had not learned much about Miss Paula's taste in our many weeks with her. She spotted us before we saw her. When we moved toward her, she was scrunching up her face and almost ran toward us. She grabbed each of us by the shoulder of our suit coats and dragged us back toward the dressing rooms. We were carrying our own clothes and she instructed us to put them back on and give her the store's clothes when we were done. She pushed us into separate dressing rooms. I didn't realize she was waiting right there for us, so I opened the door and started to go into Muna's dressing room. Miss Paula gave a stern finger toward my dressing room and told me to get in there and shut the door. I changed back into my own jeans and t-shirt. When I opened the door with the wad of clothes from the store in my arms, she shouted at me, "Hang and fold them exactly as you found them. Now." I did it as best I could and handed her the clothes. Miss Paula snatched the clothes out of my arms and rolled her eyes. Muna slowly came out of her dressing room, looking at me and then down at the ground. Miss Paula pointed to two folding chairs and told us to sit quietly and wait for her to return.

My mom and Muna's dad were in the audience waiting for the

show to start. When Miss Paula returned through the stage door, she told us she had offered our parents a full refund if they removed us from the class immediately and took us home. "Your parents agreed and you will not be returning to Wendy Ward Charm School. Ever. I am sure you have disappointed them. I assume you have left your makeup kits in the classroom. Take nothing with you. Good luck in the future, ladies, you will certainly need it. Goodbye."

Muna and I did our happy dance in the hallway heading to the audience chairs to look for our parents. We were laughing about how she accidently called us ladies. Muna's dad and Pessy were already by the exit door waiting for us and looking pretty unhappy.

I think our parents were embarrassed. They said nothing and took us home. Separately. Muna went with her dad and I went with my mom. She wasn't angry. I think she knew that me and charm school was a match made in hell. As soon as I got in the door, I called Muna. We were both so happy to be done with Wendy Ward Charm School and Miss Paula. We were delighted to be booted from that place. And the good news was that neither of us got grounded by our parents. Muna's dad was happy to get the money back and to not have to drive us every other session. Maybe that is when my mom and Muna's dad started to understand that we just weren't going to be regular little ladies."

"I love that you two got booted from charm school. Not many of us can claim that! I don't even think we have charm schools in Sweden. I never even heard of them."

KARINA

What a day today. The morning started out with me finally making a decision to cancel my flight back to Scranton. The slightly unnerving part is that I didn't change the date to a later date…just cancelled the flight. Lu was clear with me that I was welcome to stay at her place. She told me I was the least annoying guest she's ever had and that she likes having me here. I took that as a major complement. We meditated together in the morning and then did our interview session. After that Lu told me she wanted to hike alone to get some space. I used that time alone at her house to help out a bit. I did dishes, swept floors, brought in lots of firewood and cooked a meal for when she returned. It was a simple pasta meal, but Lu was super grateful for it after her long hike. I also made the phone call I had been putting off. I called my boss and let her know I wouldn't be back by Monday and in fact I wasn't sure how long I would be gone. She surprised me by telling me that she understood needing to stick with a story until it was really complete and to just keep in touch about my return date.

Lu and I ate and then fed the dogs together. She told me I might want to take a nap because we were going out later. When I asked where we were going, she said, "African dance". I told her I didn't know how to do African dance and she just laughed at me. "Everyone in town goes and you will be just fine. They give instruction."

So, Lu told the dogs to stay home and we hiked to the river with the dogs looking pretty sad about not being included. We paddled across and drove Lu's truck to the Mission Hall in the tiny town where the co-op store is. The town has a post office, a tiny library, the co-op, a church, an art gallery, and the Mission Hall. That is it. Not even a gas station. Lu and I were just wearing sweatpants and tee shirts at the dance, but almost everyone else was in fancy brightly colored African print outfits. There were a LOT of people. All colors, shapes, sizes and ages. From little kids to people in their 80s and everyone in between. There were 6 drummers at the front of the room and we were told how to line up in rows of four people and dance to the front toward the drummers and then peel off to the back of the room and do it all again. I was paying close attention and then felt a warm hand on my back. I turned to find Elan smiling and looking right in my eyes. Then I got the butterflies in my stomach again. I looked around for Lu and couldn't find her. I wanted the anchor of her to help me. I said hello to him and then the drumming started before we could say anything else. I was grateful for the drumming until I realized that because he was standing next to me, he would be in my dancing foursome for the entire evening. I reached over to Elan and cupped my hand over his ear to tell him I had no idea what I was doing, I had never done any African dancing. He reached back over to me and cupped his hand over my ear and said, "You will do just fine, just relax into it and don't compare yourself to anyone else." The place where his hand was touching my ear was burning. This is all so foreign to me. No one has had that effect on me, ever. I got through the evening without looking like a total fool. Elan kept taking my hand and counting the steps and helping me remember what to do. There were lots of people there who were perfect at it, including Elan. I was mesmerized watching how they moved and the drumming was intense and I could feel the pounding vibrate on my sweaty breast bone. I wanted to get out of the row and just sit on the sides and watch, but that wasn't an option. Once you are in the row, you are there for the whole dance. After hours of dancing, the drumming finally stopped and all the hot, smelly, sweaty dancers were hugging each other goodbye. I was intentionally not looking toward Elan. I made small talk with the woman who had been dancing on my left. When she walked away, Elan came right over and hugged me and told me I did great. It was a really long hug. I don't come from a family of huggers, so all the hugging in the US is a bit uncomfortable mixed with enjoying it. Elan's hug was way too long for my comfort level, but I didn't push away. He took both of my

hands and said, "I hope I see you again soon."
I just smiled and went looking for Lu. In the truck heading home, she just said, "Elan, eh? He is one special man." Anyway, I am finally in bed. It is midnight and I don't feel tired.

YOUR TEST RESULTS ARE POSITIVE

"Lu, tell me more about the neighborhood you hung out in during those middle school years."

"We were legally too young to go into Rocky's Tavern. But, that didn't stop me. I loved it in there. The place was filled with black men in huge platform shoes and pastel leisure suits with big lapels and matching pastel brimmed hats. Mixed in with them were wives, girlfriends, and prostitutes with big hair, big breasts, and tons of makeup. It was all my favorite music being played so loud it vibrated in my chest. This was the era of Superfly and Shaft. Black superhero movies. Rocky's is where I found a whole different community. Muna wanted nothing to do with that world because she was a good girl. In hindsight, I wish I had just stayed in my Muna world and not ventured into my Rocky's world. In my Rocky's world, I learned about speed (white crosses and black cadillacs) and marijuana. I know now that I was just trying to find a place to be free and fit in. I was not comfortable in my parent's house or in the world and I became an escape artist. Emotionally escaping any way I could and putting myself at risk the whole time.

One of the older guys who hung around the Grover neighborhood, Lester, raped me. I didn't know I was being raped. I didn't even know the word. I thought he cared about me. I wasn't sure what love was, but he was paying a little attention to me. I didn't know I was in danger when he brought me to his house. He started pulling my clothes off me and telling me it was all ok. He was smiling and that fooled me into thinking this was something that could be good. When he pinned me down and I felt the pain between my legs I panicked. But, I didn't know what to do. I said "get off me", but he ignored me. He didn't even look at me. Then he grunted and rolled off next to me. It happened on an ice-cold waterbed and afterward I shivered on the edge of bed gripping the frame, while Lester was wrapped up in a blanket and immediately snoring. I was frozen in more ways than one. Winter wind whipped through the broken window above us and froze me physically, but I was more mentally frozen. Do I get up and run? Do I just stay still? Was I supposed to feel something? What just happened? I don't know how long I curled up there freezing. He kept snoring and eventually I made my hurting body crawl out of the bed. I gathered my clothes and dressed in the hallway and snuck out the front door. Soon, my period stopped and my belly started to grow out of my skinny body. Back then, there was no such thing as a pregnancy test you could buy in the pharmacy. Star, one of the toughest girls in the school walked up to me one day in the hall and said "Don't you know you pregnant? Whatchu doin here at school?". I hoped she was wrong and I was just getting a big belly from eating too much. I tried pounding my fists hard into my belly just in case I was pregnant. One night I stood in the hot shower and put on the hottest water I could handle and beat my fists into my burning red belly skin. I was sure it would make me not pregnant anymore. There was no internet back then to research how to get "unpregnant". All I succeeded in doing was burning my belly skin and bruising my belly and sides. I went to a Planned Parenthood clinic I heard might help me. I didn't tell anyone. I was terrified. The volunteer doctor who was on duty that day had no patience with me and yanked me into the stirrups and shoved the cold speculum into my vagina without a word. He had a lit cigar hanging from his mouth and the examination room was filled with cigar smoke. It was not like the well-run tidy clinics there are now. When I called the next day for the results of the pregnancy test, they told me it was "positive" and I was relieved. "Oh thank god," I responded in the phone to the receptionist. "Positive," she said, "means you are pregnant." After a bit of mental processing, I told her through my snotty tears and sobs, "That isn't positive". I slid to the floor next to the kitchen cabinets and cried and wailed for two hours until my mom came home from work. I told her I was pregnant and she landed next to me on the floor and we both cried until Lazer got home an hour later. He saw us there on the floor crying and shouted, "What the hell is going on here? After the day I've had, I need to come home to something like this?" Pessy blurted out "She's pregnant". Lazer grabbed me by the upper arm and dragged me out of the room, turning to Pessy saying, "Don't you move. Stay right there." He threw me on their bed and slammed the door closed. "Who is the guy? Who the hell is the father? Tell me NOW." I kept quiet. Sitting on the edge of the bed, staring at the turquoise shag carpeting in their bedroom. Lazer slapped my face so hard that I landed on the floor. I got back up on the edge of the bed. He grabbed my chin in his hand and tilted my face up to him. "You tell me who the goddamn father is so I can kill him." I couldn't tell him. I didn't want him to murder someone and I didn't want this to get any worse than it already was. I didn't know what rape was or that a crime had been committed, but I knew I just wanted the whole thing to end. Silence was my only option. Lazer slapped me more and shook me by my shoulders. "You are NOT my daughter. As long as you are pregnant you are not my daughter. Sit right there, don't move." I heard him pick up the bedroom phone and call someone about "taking care" of the situation. I didn't know what that meant.

When I told Lester I was pregnant, he disappeared, left town. Probably stayed at his girlfriend's place for a while. I don't know.

Pessy was ordered not to talk to me until I was not pregnant. He told her I was not their daughter. He told me that someone was going to take care of the situation the next day and I wouldn't be going to school. Pessy was ordered to drop me off and not talk to me until the ordeal was over with. She was crying big heaving tears and she left me at a clinic, just saying, "I will see you in a few hours". Knowing what I know now about Lazer and Pessy's love for their kids, I am guessing that was one of the toughest times of their life. The nurses and reception people were angry at me from the moment I arrived. They gave me a gown to put on and took my clothes in a bag. Then the biggest toughest nurse rolled me on my side and stabbed a huge needle into my butt cheek so hard it tore my skin. Then I was rolled onto my back again. No one would explain what was going to happen. When they wheeled my bed to the doctor, he asked what all the blood was. I told him it was from the shot. All he said was "We better just get you through this and out of here." After an awful sucking and cramping, I was wheeled back into a small room that smelled like bleach. Nurses kept coming in and looking between my legs. Hours later, one of them told me I had to be there overnight. They couldn't let me go until the bleeding stopped. The cramps were unbearable and the bloody sheets kept sticking to my skin. I had never had period cramps, so I had no idea why the cramps were so bad. After two days on crusty bloody sheets, they brought my clothes and told me my ride was there and I could go home. Pessy was in the waiting room and really broke down when she saw me. I must have looked like hell. She held me tight against her. "I couldn't come and be with you, I am so sorry." Lazer had made it clear that she was not to be with me until I was no longer pregnant.

When some of the guys I hung out with learned what happened to me, they were furious and threatened to kill Lester. A group of the older guys were like big brothers. They knew about the Lester thing and decided it was their mission to protect me from any more threats or danger. They kept apologizing for letting me down. I begged them to just leave it. No revenge and no more talking about it. I needed to move on and not think about the whole ordeal anymore. These guys were all pimps and dealers. They had a permanent motel room rental at the Beach Aire Motel on Lake Michigan. It was one of those motels where each room is a separate little cabin. They were each painted a different color. The same paint job nowadays would be seen as a gay pride thing...back then it was just considered a tacky motel. Now it would be called Shabby Chic. The little building we hung out in was Pepto Bismol pink. I was 15 years old and lived in blue jean overalls with colored tees and red converse high tops (Chuck Taylors). I biked everywhere and was a vegetarian. They were pimps and drug dealers in their twenties and thirties who drove huge Electra 224 cars that were in pastel colors to match their shoes and clothes. There was a smell in those cars that I loved. When I asked DJ what the smell was in his car, he told me it was pimp oil on the air filter. "Really, there is something you can buy called pimp oil?" He laughed hard. These guys were so good to me. No sex, no pimping me out, no shooting up drugs. I loved being at the motel. It was relaxed. There was music, T.V. and lots of laughter. When someone went out to get barbequed ribs, they would come back with everything vegetarian they could find. Coleslaw, bean salad, and rolls were mostly what they brought back for me from either Smoke Daddy or Earl's BBQ. At my parent's house, my vegetarian choice was an issue. In restaurants, Lazer would scream at me, "Eat like a normal person!!". So I stopped going out to eat with them. I wasn't being vegetarian to be different, as Lazer thought. I loved all animals and didn't want to live a life that caused them suffering. I just chose to be with people and places where who I was didn't create drama and tension. The guys at the Beach Aire were never upset with me and never criticized my choices. I felt at ease there like I never did at my folk's house."

"That is horrible. That confusion of being raped and not knowing what is going on. I'm glad you had the big brothers watching your back after that. Did that experience make it difficult to have a healthy sexual relationship later on?"

"I think it probably influenced my relationships after that. I was determined to be in control after having someone use me in that way. Some months after the rape, a friend of mine, Robert Brown, said he wanted to talk to me. He was so direct and frank about what had happened. He asked me " Have you ever had an orgasm?" I said I didn't know what that was exactly. So he told me that I could not go through life not understanding that sex should be pleasure for me. He asked me if I wanted him to give me some lessons. I know this sounds strange, but we were very honest and direct about what this was all about. He said I needed a mentor and if I didn't want to have the lessons, he understood and I could say "No" and it would be no problem. I told him I wanted the lessons. We went to his bedroom and he said, "If at any point you get uncomfortable with this, either physically or mentally, you tell me and we will stop." I was actually looking forward to having an honest experience of sex and figuring out what it could be or should be. We got undressed and just held each other for a bit. He said, "There should be some tenderness in the beginning. If there is no tenderness, then you get up and walk away. Don't let someone just bang away at your body." He rolled onto his back and told me to climb on top of him. I did that and he very gently put his penis inside of me. Then he told me to close my eyes and he did a sort of visualization. He had me imagine I was riding a horse. Within moments I had a whole body orgasm and my eyes were still closed and I was still on the horse and it was raining flowers. I had never experienced anything like that. When we were done and just lying next to each other, he said, "You can go anywhere you want to when you make love with someone. it is YOUR experience. Rape is about power and making love is about pleasure for both people. Do not ever again let someone take that from you." It was really life changing. I had a few more lessons with Robert. He helped me understand my body in a way no one else ever had. When we stopped the lessons, it was his idea. He told me I was ready for the world now. I didn't tell anyone about our lessons because I thought they would judge us and maybe even have him arrested because he was much older than me. He told me we had to stop the lessons because he wanted to just help me, not get into any relationship or attachment other than our friendship."

"OK, that is like nothing I have ever heard. I have heard of boys being taught by older women, but never a man helping a woman that way. I have been wanting to ask you if you had many white friends after connecting to the black community in such a big way?"

"I tried a few times, but it wasn't easy. I didn't really understand white culture at that point. In junior high I had a friend who went to private school because her family was wealthy. I met her accidentally through another friend and we clicked even though our worlds were very different. Marina was half-Italian and half-Jewish. Her dad was a local doctor and her mom was a born-again Christian Italian, named Mary. Mary had MS and was bed ridden. I would visit Mary each time I went to see Marina. I would bring Mary plants and other things to make her bedroom life more interesting. She couldn't even sit up so she had these weird reflective prism looking glasses that allowed her to watch the TV. The only thing she ever watched was Billy Graham, the evangelist guy. He would ask for money and she would send him boatloads of it. I got so comfortable with her that I would even change her catheter bag when it was full. It hung off the side of the bed. After years of these visits, I arrived there one day and she was really agitated. She wouldn't look toward me. She told me she had gotten a call from a friend who reported that I was hanging out with three black kids. I told her they were my school friends. I didn't know Mary was racist until that moment. She told me to never come to their house again and that I was not allowed to see their daughter. I told her that she was the first Christian I had ever been close with and that now I realized that being Christian didn't mean being kind or compassionate. After that I left and never saw her or Marina again.

Navigating the world of other humans and their ideas is such a landmine sometimes."

"That is awful. I am so sorry you went through that. But I love what you said to her. What an intense experience the whole thing was for you. A jumble of adults and kids and trying to find your footing. Did you stay in touch with your friend, Muna? Do you know where she is now?"

"Sadly, I did not stay in touch with her. I am guessing with some effort I could find her. The last time I saw her was her wedding. She had moved to Davenport, Iowa. I don't remember why she moved there, but I think it was for a job. She called me and told me that she was getting married and that I would be getting an invitation in the mail. Apparently there were going to be over 200 people at the wedding and I would be the only white person. She wanted to make sure I was ok with that. Of course I was. At the time I was living in the little cabin with no electricity and no running water. I didn't have much money for any fancy dress and I don't think I even owned a dress. So, I decided to take some fabric I had to a friend's house and sew a dress. I got a thrift store dress as a backup in case I wasn't comfortable in the hand sewn one. The last time I had sewn my own dress, it was for a cousin's black tie formal wedding and I looked like I had just come out of the jungles of Africa. I have never had any fashion sense and I thought, when I put the matching African print head wrap on, it would look fancy enough for a formal affair. I sort of thought that exotic was one option in the black tie world. It was a one shoulder thing I designed and the other shoulder was bare. I didn't have any fancy shoes, so I went barefoot. Wore a pair of my mom's high heels in the door, but couldn't really walk in them, so kicked them off as soon as I got to my seat. My sister said I walked like a man trying on heels for the first time. There were lots of problems with the whole ensemble. But, the biggest was that in the middle of a dance with my uncle, one breast came out of the top of the dress and it took a while to get the free flying breast back in. So, I was a little gun shy about wearing my own creation at a wedding. Muna's wedding was more casual, so I got to choose either dress. When I got to the big hall, I had forgotten that I was going to be the only white person and I honestly didn't notice until people started reminding me. Every person I spoke with asked me what I was doing there. Here is something I LOVE about the black community. They are honest, caring and down to earth. There is no pretense. It is something I always loved. Imagine you are the only black person walking into an event with over 200 white people. Every one of those white folks would be wondering what you were doing there, but not one would actually ask you. They would all be thinking it and none would say it. But, not in the black community. I prefer the honesty in that community. I was used to it from early on. For example, if some guy wanted to kiss you or have sex with you, there were no games about it. They would just come right out and say it. You didn't have to wonder what their intentions were. Like Snooky Belmar, for instance. He was one of the first boys to tell me what he wanted. He and I were just part of a group of friends in high school and we weren't boyfriend and girlfriend. One night at a party, he walked right up to me and said, "Come dance with me. Then I am going to kiss you and take you right back there to that bedroom and we are going to get naked together." What I love is that it gives you the option to say yes or no before things have gone too far. I love knowing just what I am dealing with. White guys might ask you to go somewhere like for a bike ride or a walk or to a party. But, even if their intention was to kiss or have sex, it would never be said directly. So, you have to figure out what to do when they start putting their hands all over you. Muna's wedding was a blast. We all danced from about 7 in the evening to 4 in the morning. Nonstop dancing and eating and a little drinking. But, no one was really drunk from drinking, mostly from dancing and sweating. That exhausted drunk feeling. Snooky was there, and we were all grown up now. We danced together most of the night. Then in that beautiful directness, when the music stopped, he took my hand, winked and we walked outside. He looked me right in the eyes and whispered, "I'm staying at Muna and Charle's house tonight. You come stay with me there and share the bed." See, there it is, direct. I could have said, "no thanks." Or, I could say what I did say back then, "Perfect". I was pretty unapologetic for my sexual openness. I remember going to dance one night at an RnB place I loved called The Union Bar. On this particular night the band was a Cajun band from New Orleans. They were called "Clifton Chenier and His Red Hot Peppers". I was wearing a tight red dress. I would bike to these places and wear pants under my dresses and then pull the pants off when I got there and dance my ass off. I didn't know it then, but I was actually quite the hottie. One of those muscular tough kind of women, but I was cuter than I knew. I thought I was ugly, but I see otherwise when I look at old photos. Apparently, the sax player could see that I was pretty hot in that red dress. I looked up at one point and realized he was copying my dancing style and we were dancing together with him on the stage and me below on the dance floor. I was dancing hard and sweating like crazy which only made the dress cling to me and show pretty much everything underneath it. At one point he wasn't playing his sax and he mouthed to me, "Do you have a car?". I mouthed back to him while doing a pedaling motion with my feet, "No, a bike." I could see where things were headed, so I left there before the last song ended. I rode home fast. But, when I got home, I thought....no wait, that is the wrong word, I didn't think at all....I decided to call him at the bar. I called the Union and asked the bartender to put the sax player on the phone. When he got to the phone, the sax player said, "Red dress?" I said, "Yep, here is my address, get a taxi." I was so damn bold when it came to feeding my hungry sex drive. His name was Caesar and he got to my place and we smoked a joint on the roof in the hot summer air and he played his sax. Then we went to my bedroom and had sex most of the night. I had totally forgotten that in the morning my landlord was coming to work on a plumbing issue and he had to walk right through the big one room studio past my bed. There was a huge beautiful black man in my bed with a saxophone at his hip. I just stood there in my robe shrugging. I brought us toast and tea in bed and Caesar told me he was married but that he would really like to see me again and stay in touch. I didn't skip a beat and told him no way. I said, "Go home to your wife and treat her better. Be really good to her. You and I had our time and it is over." The band was playing another set that night and he asked if I would be there and if he could spend the night again. I told him to just move on and stop cheating on his wife and that I was not going to be there that night and he was not welcome back at my place. But, quite honestly, it was a really wonderful night of saxophone on the roof and great sex. If he wasnt married, I would have repeated the whole thing."

"Oh god, your landlord had some stories to tell when he got home that day."

"For sure."

"Lu, I want to go back to that question about white people in your life. How old were you when you got comfortable with them?"

"It was just a long training, not really some turning point. I had a few white friends in college who decided I needed a lot of training in white culture. So, they created all these white person experiences for me. One of them, Duke, was my white music coach. He put headphones on me and made me listen to hours of white bands. I hated that music at first. But I got used to a group called YES, so Duke and a few others took me to a concert and I actually loved it. But, even to this day, I have limited knowledge of white popular culture. The same friends took me to a Grateful Dead concert and I fell asleep halfway through. Some music will come on and I am clueless that it is Bruce Springstein or other popular white music. But, I can identify any of even the most obscure soul or RnB musicians and songs. I still prefer those, but I did get more comfortable with the white culture in lots of ways. That said, give me a choice and I will choose black culture or canine culture over white human culture."

KARINA

Truthfully, I am a bit out of sorts. I barely recognize myself anymore. I feel cracked wide open. I have been doing more cooking here at Lu's and because she is vegan, I have been figuring that out and making some amazing meals without any meat or dairy or eggs. I honestly never thought that food could be this good without those things. I grew up with cheese three times a day and lots of meat. I feel the best I have ever felt physically, but mentally I am confused. Nothing is familiar here. Not the landscape, the lifestyle, the pace of our days....none of it. And despite all that, it feels more comfortable and more like home than any other place or time in my life. I have been trying to sort it out. Where does my life go from here? I have no return flight scheduled and I feel a bit lost at sea. Or, more accurately, lost at high dessert. A massage person is coming later today and giving me and Lu massages here at the house. Lu is treating me to the massage. I have never felt so cared for. And, I am nervous about the massage. I am not a touchy feely person. Well, I never have been in the past, but here I seem to have become a hugger like the rest of the people here. But, a massage, that is a whole other level of intimacy. I do not like being touched. Never have. It has been the issue with getting into a relationship. I can't get over that physical part. Saga, my best friend in Sweden, says that I must have had a traumatic birth, because not wanting physical touch is just not normal for a mammal. I have asked my mom, Monica, about it and she says I never liked being held much as a baby. I don't know what made me accept Lu's massage offer. I keep going to my discomfort zones here. The more of them I go into, the less uncomfortable I feel in them. Each time gets easier. I keep putting the massage out of my mind because it gets me into a panic. What is really crazy is that

I distract myself from the massage by daydreaming about Elan. I have never been a daydreamer and I have definitely never found comfort in thinking about a guy. Like I said, I barely recognize myself right now. Oh, then there is the dog thing. I never had a dog and never felt close to them, but the dogs have become one of my greatest comforts. I am just loving them. The little black one, Olive, is such a cuddler. She sleeps curled into my belly all night.

EATING TONGUE

"I am going to sort of switch topics here, because I keep meaning to ask you this. I know you are vegan now....but what started that and the vegetarian choice in your life?"

"I didn't expect to become a vegetarian. I didn't really know the word vegetarian when I made that choice and definitely didn't know anyone else not eating meat. I was 15 years old and loved meat. We weren't the kind of Jews who wouldn't eat pork or bacon. So, Canadian bacon, American bacon, lunchmeat, hamburgers, hot dogs...we ate all of it. I would eat the gristle from other people's steak, and drink the red juice (you know, blood) from the plate the liver thawed on and would shove as many hot dogs as I could into my mouth and then squirt in ketchup. We were at my aunt's for some kind of gathering when I was about 7. I made a sandwich with about an inch of "tongue" on it that I found on the deli tray. My brother said, "Why do you eat that stuff? It's tongue!"
"It's just called that," I said.
-"No dummy, it is TONGUE." And he pointed to his own tongue.
-"It is NOT! Mom wouldn't feed us tongue!"
-"Go ask her."
I raced into the kitchen where my mom and aunts were making more food.
-"Mom, what is tongue?"
-"It's made from a tongue."
-"Whose tongue?"
-"A cow's tongue."

-"Why do you let us eat tongue?"
-"You eat lots of different parts of cows."

That should have made me a vegetarian right then and there. But, instead, I was just a non-tongue eater. After that, I was disgusted when I watched people eat tongue. But it had no effect on my consumption of huge amounts of gristle and Canadian bacon and hot dogs. Maybe if they had been labeled as what they really were, I would have stopped eating them immediately. You couldn't really escape what "tongue" was made from. But brisket, steak, hot dogs, bacon, hamburgers were all just food names and not body parts. I did avoid chicken thighs and breasts and just stuck with drumsticks (those were not a body part, right?). If we had called them chicken legs I probably would have avoided them, too.

My friend Susie was a little older than me and could drive. She asked me to go with her to the orthodontist in Chicago. After the appointment, we went to the Chicago Red Hot Hotdogs stand. I ate two hotdogs with all the fixings. I was 15 and had no idea that would be my last meat...ever. I was a speed eater. I come from speed eaters. If you skip the chewing part, you can eat a lot of food before your stomach even realizes what just happened. I am now a chewer wannabe and manage to chew thoroughly on occasion. It usually only happens when I am eating alone or in a silent meditation course for days. Anyway, back to the life-changing day that I went to Dr. Feinstein with Susie. After the hotdogs, she wanted to go into a leather store. I had never been in a leather store. When we opened the door, the first thing that hit me was the smell. Then, the skins hanging on the walls. I thought I was whispering, "Susie, don't buy anything in here, it's dead animals." The woman behind the counter heard me and said, "Do you eat meat?" She didn't say it in a mean way. It was just a quiet question. I was silent for what felt like a long time. My brain was trying to figure out what dead animals had to do with meat. When it finally hit me, I easily said to her, "No, I don't eat meat."

Susie's head whipped toward me and she gave me the stink eye. When we walked out of the store, she asked, "Why'd you lie to her?"
"I didn't lie. I'll never eat meat again."
That was it. 15 years old and my meat eating days were over. I stopped consuming all cow, chicken, fish, sheep and pig meat. It was about a year before I met another person who was doing the same thing. That was Barry. Barry was my best bud through some of the toughest high-school years. He was the only real artist I knew and the only out gay person I knew and the only vegetarian I knew. I didn't know the word "vegetarian" until I met Barry. I had just called myself someone who didn't eat meat. So, I was not eating animals, but it had nothing to do with healthy choices. I didn't even realize that there were healthy and unhealthy food choices. I just knew there were things that tasted good and things that didn't. It was very different in those days, there just wasn't all the cultural talk about eating healthy. That means that the majority of my meals consisted of fluffernutter sandwiches (marshmallow cream and peanut butter on white bread) with a red cream soda to drink, or a grilled cheese sandwich made with American cheese on white bread, or boxed mac and cheese."

"Talking about what is healthy was always part of Swedish culture. I grew up with my grandparents pushing vegetables and going from the sauna into the icy Baltic Sea. We were all about health. American fast food and peanut butter and junk food made its way across the ocean to Sweden in about the late 80s or 90s I think. But you would have been disgusted at some of the foods we ate as kids. We regularly ate a food called "blood pudding". It is basically flour mixed with animal blood and it is sold in these ball shaped loaves. So you take it home and slice it and fry it and put strawberry jam on it. We LOVED it as kids."

"OK, that sounds completely disgusting. We had our own disgusting foods we ate, but we disguised the reality with names that made them sound yummy. I don't remember anything like blood pudding. I do remember eating pigs feet at Muna's house. That is not very well disguised. I know a lot of people think vegetarian and vegan is a diet. But for me it has always been about non-violence and loving animals. Oddly, at that vegetarian point I thought that consuming dairy was harmless to animals. I kind of thought of milk as a by-product of some sort of wonderful life that cows and goats were having. That is what I told myself. But, that all changed. Decades ago, I was renting a little cabin in rural Wisconsin from a dairy farmer. He and his family lived on the same land, but down the road from me. One day I heard a weird distressing sound from their farm and got on my bike and rode over to make sure everything was ok. When I got there, he and another guy were pushing young calves up a ramp into a truck. He explained that these were the male calves and that they were going to the veal facility. Some were so young that their umbilical cords were still wet and dangling. Their legs were shaking and they were crying out for their moms. I went around the barn and found the moms screaming and bellowing for their babies. Their mouths were wide open and they were all in a panic. Blood was coming down some of their chests from pressing against the barbed wire trying to get to their babies. The scene broke my heart. Through my tears I told my landlord that I would never again buy any dairy products. He assured me that I would get over it and the moms would get over it. I didn't want to get over it. I wanted to remember that scene. That experience made me really start exploring different foods and their impact on other species. That led me to not eating eggs, dairy, or buying any other animal products. I learned so much about the industries that I just couldn't support them. What made it a bit tough was that it was so long ago that I didn't know the word "vegan". I am sure the word was around, but I had never heard it anywhere. I had just learned the word "vegetarian". It was years before I met another vegan. And there weren't all the wonderful vegan choices you find today. I used to make my own soymilk and tofu and tempeh using dry soybeans. I fashioned an incubator out of a Styrofoam cooler with a light bulb I hung in it. My food tasted horrible. I am guessing anyone I cooked for back then is still avoiding anything vegetarian or vegan to this day. It gets old being the poster child for any group. I was the poster child for all Jews as a kid and often the only Jew in the room. I had no choice but to be generous and try to talk quietly and work hard at not being any of the stereotypes we are judged for.

Then I became the poster child for vegans in most situations. That means I couldn't get a cold, be tired, be weak, be skinny, be pale, or be anything like a hippie. I didn't do so great at the no hippie thing. I am so undomesticated that most people still consider me to be a hippie. Now I am just an old hippie.

Different experiences keep me dedicated to choosing compassion for all species and wanting to be a voice for them. Sometimes I choose the experiences and sometimes they choose me.

I was doing animal rights and non-violence education work in Israel for some years and would go there and stay with different people involved in the program. I came back to my hosts house after a training day and needed to take a walk. I was walking next to a field and three young boys were leading a huge group of goats on the hill right next to me. They were whipping the goats with sticks to hurry them along. If the goats stopped to eat, they hit them. Suddenly one of the goats gave birth while walking. She tried to stop to have the baby and was hit multiple times to keep her moving. I stopped to witness the whole thing. Her baby goat was born and the littlest of the three boys was ordered to take the goat back to the barn. The little boy grabbed the slippery little newborn goat and kept dropping it as he ran back to the barn. The mother goat was literally screaming for her baby and the baby was screaming back for his mom. The other two boys, just kept beating her with the stick to make her keep moving. It was incredibly heartbreaking to watch. And it is happening all the time around the globe. That night, as it turns out, the house I was staying in was next to that farm. The entire night I listened to the mother scream for her baby and the baby screaming back. I did not sleep at all, just cried all night. It is experiences like those that keep me dedicated to being a voice for other beings whose voices aren't heard in society.

Anyway, the vegan path became my whole path. It defined my value system and my lifestyle. It even determined my community. It still does. I have friends who are not vegan, but my closest friends share my values and live vegan lifestyles that respect all life. I know it sounds judgmental to some people. But, imagine you are working in some social justice movement. Let's say, an anti-slavery movement. Most likely, you wouldn't have really close friends who have slaves. Does that make sense?"

"Yep, that makes sense. I am starting to see a pattern in how you came to care about ALL social justice. Most of it was based on your own personal experience, not just reading about it or hearing about it in the news. You know I never really thought much about all this. I have just gotten on my career path and not looked around much at how my life choices are affecting the world around me. This is all new for me. I remember walking through the old part of Stockholm. It is called Gamla Stan. Every Saturday for a while, I would meet up with friends for lunch there. And, every Saturday, I would see this guy with a table set up and he was talking to people and handing out literature on animal rights and compassion. One day I did talk to him for a few minutes. His name was Jonas. I feel a little embarrassed now, but I was a bit confrontational. I asked him why he cared more about animals than people. Really I was just curious how someone ends up like that. His response was amazing, he said, "Caring can be very broad. It can encompass all life. Caring

for humans and non-humans and the whole earth are not mutually exclusive." Then he told me this incredible thing. He said that every year he takes ten percent of his salary and researches to find the poorest place on earth. He finds a place where people basically have nothing and are suffering and dying. He takes the ten percent in cash bills and wraps up hundreds of little packages with bits of the money and hands it out randomly on the street to people who seem to be suffering the most. He does this trip every year and repeats this ritual. He doesn't stick around to see them open it, he just spends a week handing out little bundles of cash. The year before I was talking to him, he handed out 10,000 U.S. dollars. He told me, "It means nothing to my lifestyle. I don't have to really give up anything. But, it is the most enjoyable and rewarding thing I do all year." I was really blown away by him. But, sadly, it didn't change my lifestyle in any way. I wasn't giving up ten percent of my salary and I ended up just throwing away the animal rights literature I had grabbed from his table."

"Karina, it may just have planted some seeds in you for the future. This happens a lot. People get new information and it just doesn't land on fertile ground. I have a theory that people need to hear something about three or four times, especially new information and perspectives, before they start really processing it. They have to realize it is not just isolated information, but part of an accepted and growing cultural norm. So, Jonas planted seeds that sat dormant and you will keep running into people who have similar ideals and eventually you will take the time to look at it squarely, to really think about it."

"I think that time might be now. I am starting to think that doing these interviews with you is not about something I might publish one day, but more about me developing into the person I was meant to be. I both love all I am learning here and it terrifies me because I have had such a predictable and normal life. First just a typical Swedish life and then just a typical American life...and here I am

not finding anything typical whatsoever. So, I am feeling a bit ungrounded. And at the same time, more grounded than I have ever felt. I can't make sense of it yet."

"That is so great. You are swimming in the unknown right now. It is an unsettling place to be, but it always leads to huge discoveries. Makes me happy for you.
OK, time to stop and get things ready for our massages. When she gets here do you want to go first or second? "

"I would like to go first and get it over with if that's ok."

"Perfect. I will set up the table and have it all ready for you. The massage person's name is Winona, but we all call her Winnie…. and I should tell you she is Elan's mother. He brings her here because she is blind and can't drive. So he will be hanging out while we get our massages. Usually he just goes hiking with the dogs. They love him."

KARINA

Lu dropped the bomb today that the massage person who was coming is Elan's mom, Winnie and that he would be bringing her because she is blind. My stomach flipped when I heard he would be coming here. I kind of hid upstairs until I saw Elan and Winnie arriving on the path below. The dogs were jumping all over him and he just dropped to the ground and let them give him a big slobbery greeting. He was laughing and his mom was standing there next to them laughing, too. She is a much older female version of Elan. And, just as beautiful. They both have thick dark black braids that are pretty much identical. I am guessing Winnie is probably about 60, and I think she is about the most beautiful woman I have ever seen.

I was wearing just underwear under Lu's thick robe and I was in a complete shaky panic. I heard Elan's voice downstairs and my stomach went total flipping flapping butterflies again. Winnie's voice sounded like melted butter. I decided to focus on her voice to try to calm down. But, I was still frozen in place upstairs. Lu called me downstairs and Winnie held me in a long hug. I closed my eyes so I wouldn't stare at Elan. My shakiness stopped and when I opened my eyes, Elan came over and gave me a hug. The combination of not being fully dressed and him hugging me was a bit much. As soon as he released me from the hug, I moved to the other side of the massage table so there was a barrier between us. What is wrong with me? I have never been so affected by someone. Winnie told me to be completely naked and climb onto the table face down under the blanket to begin with. She clicked a boombox and the softest female voice filled the room. Music that felt like a mix of India and church. Elan took Winnie out of the room while I got naked and climbed between the sheets on the warm table. I was physically comfortable, but mentally so uncomfortable. Completely naked. I never even sleep naked. I am more the thick flannel pajamas type. Winnie made her way back into the room and shut the door. She put her hands on my back and I could feel the heat of them through the blanket. She was chanting something in a language I didn't understand. All I know is that her hands and the chant completely calmed me. I went into what felt like a trance. Like that place between sleep and awake. When I heard Winnie's voice, I thought it had only been a few minutes, "I'm going to have you turn over." I turned over, and the next thing I knew I heard her voice again, "Very good Karina....it's been a pleasure working with you. Stay here as long as you like. When you are ready, get dressed and come to the kitchen." I thanked her and stayed for a few more minutes. I scanned my body and realized I felt no stress, no pain and even my mind was completely relaxed. This was the first time I ever felt anything like that.

When I got to the kitchen I glanced at the clock and saw it had been two hours. I had been in there two hours with Winnie for what felt like five minutes. Elan was standing there with Winnie and Lu. They all smiled at me. Elan said, "You are glowing". I went and got dressed and when I came back out, Lu and Winnie were already starting Lu's massage with the door closed. I was alone with Elan. He invited me to go for a hike with him.

We hiked in an area I had never been to before on the hikes with Lu. Up on a tall ridge, we played with our giant shadows in the sun and laughed and talked and I surprised myself at being totally relaxed with him. At one point we were sitting on a rock drinking tea, surrounded by Lu's dogs and all the neighborhood dogs who had followed us. There were eight dogs with us. We drank from Elan's thermos and the dogs all stared at him with total love eyes. I felt like joining the dogs in the whole love eyes thing. Elan is the warmest, gentlest, smartest, funniest man I have ever met. I want to just sink into him. Oh god, what is happening to me? At the same time I was thinking that, he reached over and held my cold hand in his impossibly warm hand. I looked down at his brown skin wrapped around my pale white skin. Then, like he read my mind, he said, "Yin and *yang, huh?" We hiked back down to the house. There was so much silence on the walk back down and it felt perfect. When we got to the house, Elan hugged me and whispered in my ear, "I loved our time together, Karina." It sent shivers through my whole body. He sat on a bench and said he would wait outside if I could bring Winnie out there when she was ready. That was it, I went into the house and waited until I could bring Winnie out. Sitting in the warm kitchen waiting, my mind was oddly calm, but I felt like I had just had one bite out of something delicious and my belly was asking for more. I delivered Winnie out to him when she was ready and she kissed me on the cheek while Elan looked straight in my eyes with the same sort of love eyes the dogs have for him. I sat on the bench and watched them walk toward the river. Lu came out a few minutes later and told me she'd be right back after she paddled them to Elan's car on the other side.*

I sat in the warm sun and looked at the deep blue New Mexico sky and wondered if this was what my life was going to be. Crazy thoughts. I have an apartment and a job back east. That is where my life is. Or is it? Could I have a life here? No job, no home, no community or friends. Nothing familiar. But it is all becoming familiar. In such a short time it is becoming so comfortable.

Lu came back from the river and gave me a hug. "Nice day, eh?"

"Really amazing, thanks so much, Lu"

Now, it's late... I need to sleep, but I still feel that hunger in my belly and my heart....mixed with every muscle sinking into the quilt and begging for rest.

BEAUTIFUL TUSH

"Lu, first of all, I can't thank you enough for the massage. It was truly amazing. I have never felt anything like that."

"Yep, Winnie is really the best I know. She has been doing this type of healing work for almost 40 years. I just love the whole family. They are all amazing in their own ways."

"Does she have a husband? Other kids other than Elan?"

"Sadly her husband died when he was driving across an arroyo in a huge storm. It was three years ago. The river washed the car away with him in it. He was found 20 miles downriver dead in the car. It was just awful. Since Winnie is blind, he was really her eyes. She is very independent, but she really needed him a lot. They had a love like I have never seen before. He was totally dedicated to her. His name was Wiyot, which ironically means "river name". When you see beautiful paintings around town with vibrant colors like this one and the one in the bedroom, look for his name in the corner. See it right here? He was such a gifted artist and everyone misses him and his art."

"Oh wow, so beautiful. It looks like the view from here, looking upriver. That is such a sad story. How does Winnie cope without him?"

"We all worried about that, but not for long. Elan was living up in Taos and sold his place and moved back here to live with Winnie to help her out. She didn't want him to give up his life up there, but he insisted. He had a great house. An Earthship that he built from the ground up. Totally off grid and with its own water collection. This photo is of me and the dogs up there visiting about 5 years ago. He is an artist, like his dad, and he was doing so well up there in Taos. Painting and designing amazing homes for major builders. He had a girlfriend living with him. I wasn't that crazy about her because he seemed happier when she wasn't around. She was pretty critical of him, even when other people were around. Anyway, when he decided to move back to help Winnie, he offered to have his girlfriend come with him or to stay in the Earthship. He was going to just let her live there in his beautiful house. She got really angry that he was uprooting their life, which I thought was a little extreme since Taos is only about 40 minutes from here. It's not like he was asking her to move to the other side of the world. She packed her stuff and moved back to Arizona. I always felt like he dodged a bullet there. She would have never been a loving equal partner for that amazing man."

"*What's an Earthship?*"

"It's a fantastic house built partially into the earth with big windows in front and it heats completely from the heat of the sun. All of it's systems are independent, so water and power are all right there. Water is collected on the roof and used four times before draining out to the outside gardens. I will take you to visit a few of them if you like. Elan's was really one of my favorites. It was like a brightly colored hobbit house with a huge greenhouse that produced bananas and tomatoes and greens year round. And so quiet. Not a single sound from outside could get past those walls. So, the wind could be howling outside and you would never know it inside. I visited there a lot with Winnie. I'd pick her up and we would make a day of it."

"*I would love to see one. It looks amazing in the photo.*"

"For sure, we will go sometime this week. Do you know how

long you are going to be sticking around?"

"Lu, that is something I wanted to talk to you about. I am a bit confused and not sure what to do. I am being pulled, like a strong pull, to stay in this area. You must think I am crazy. Honestly I don't even recognize myself. I am not a spontaneous decision maker. I have a life in Scranton. I have a job and friends and an apartment. But, I am a different person there and I like the person I am here more....I am not sure how to describe it....I feel more like ME here."

"Karina, I don't think you are crazy at all. New Mexico can do this to people. People either come here and feel like it is a brown dusty wasteland and nothing goes right for them or they come here and feel like they never want to leave. It welcomes people with open arms or it spits them out. You seem to be getting the open arm welcome here. I have loved watching you adjust to life here and opening up to it all. It is like watching a flower open. And, maybe this isn't my place to say, but I haven't seen Elan this happy in a long time. He is loving having you around, I can tell."

"Oh god....you have noticed us connecting. This is all so new for me. I don't even know what I would do for work or where I would live. Part of me just wants to run back to my job and home and not change anything."

"It might be a little late for that. It is not about you changing anything, it is more about everything changing YOU. I can tell you are torn about it. It would be a huge change for you, a big letting go and trusting. Let it just incubate for a few days. Try not to process it around and around in your head. Tonight when you go to sleep, write down what you would like clarity on. Take the piece of paper and read it out loud and put it under your pillow. Your dreams will give you some answers. Keep a notebook next to you and be ready to write in the middle of the night. I know it sounds woo woo new age. But, it really works. Your subconscious will work on it just because it was the last thing you focused on before sleeping."

"Ok, I will try that. Whew...let's just get into our interview. That will help me re-focus on something other than my life choices. We have talked a lot about your animal rights work. I know you also work on all social justice issues including LGBT issues. I am guessing that awareness started with your friendship with Barry in high school? Tell me more about your relationship with him."

"Barry was a potter, sculpture, painter and the most creative person I knew besides my mom, Pessy. He was my best friend in high school. He was the first gay guy I ever knew personally. When they first met, Pessy did her usual innocent question thing. Barry had thick, stretchy, ropey scars all over his neck and body. But it was the neck ones you could really see all the time. When Pessy met him she asked him what the scars were from. Barry told her about getting burned as a kid. He had a stick and he was playing with the leaf-burning barrel in his parent's backyard. His clothes caught on fire and before the flames could be put out, he was burned on most of his body. They had taken skin from parts of his body that weren't burned and grafted it on places where there was no skin left. He told Pessy the detailed story and then said, "But, Pessy, one part of my body is perfect. Do you want to see it?"
I am not sure she had time to think about it before she answered "yes".
In a moment, Barry's pants were down, and he was showing my mom his ass. "They left my ass alone. Isn't it beautiful?"
To Pessy's credit, she didn't turn away. She looked right at that smooth ass and said quietly, "That is a really beautiful tush."
That was all it took. They were friends. After school, I had a part-time job, but I would come home from my job and find Pessy and Barry knitting together on the sofa with Poppy, my mom's wiener dog. Poppy had a skin condition and always smelled like she was composting and had a continuous blizzard of white skin flaking out of her fur. But, Barry and Pessy

were like me, they could love her and see right past that dandruff and stink. I loved Barry like a best friend mixed with a brother. He could make me laugh when no one else could.

We were a bit wild and addicted to riding our bikes. One day we took a few too many white crosses, you know, speed, and got on our bikes and rode 60 miles to his grandmother's house. It was unplanned. Suddenly we were in her kitchen and she was trying to feed us everything vegetarian she could find. We were speeding so we couldn't eat a thing, you know, no appetite. She filled the table with fermented vegetables and pastries, but we only drank some juice and were out of there.

We kissed her goodbye and got on our bikes and peddled like crazy home. We had so much zippy speed energy that Barry actually busted a pedal off his bike before we made it back home. The pedal snapped right off. We called my dad to pick us up. Unaware that he had just picked up two kids flying high on speed, he just said, "Jesus Barry, you have some strength!!"

My mom doesn't have good gay-dar. So even the most obvious effeminate guy wearing a boa and glitter tights wouldn't be someone she would peg as gay. I got home one day to find Pessy, Barry, and Poppy in the living room. Pessy and Barry knitting and chatting away. I sat down next to Pessy. She asked me and Barry, "Why don't I ever see you two holding hands or being affectionate?"
-"Mom, do you think we are boyfriend and girlfriend?"
-"Aren't you?"
At this point, Barry was laughing so hard that he dropped his knitting needles and was snorting his signature contagious laugh.
-"Mom, we are just best friends. Barry is gay."
-"Oh." (long pause) "How long have you been gay?"
-Barry stops laughing long enough to answer, "my whole life."
Then all three of us are losing it and it is just perfect.

I am not sure Barry's dad ever accepted who he was. His dad

was a working class bowling fanatic with a shirt embroidered with his name *Randy*. The only slightly edgy, out of the box thing I ever saw Randy do was collecting dandelion greens each spring and eating mixing bowl size salads of the stuff.

Barry was such a foreign kind of person to me. He was so confident and comfortable with who he was. That was both inspiring and intimidating to me. Here he was a gay kid with scars and an incredibly talented artist and he just lived so authentically. I was more the type who was trying to fit in, unsuccessfully of course.

Lazer really laid the groundwork for me not judging someone who is different. He was outspoken about rights for all people, including the gay/lesbian community.

I was probably about 13 years old and I was sitting on the sofa at the Jackson's house. They were an incredible smart and talented black family and I was friends with the three kids. I was downstairs in the living room waiting for Bruce to finish his piano lessons. I had met the piano teacher, Kevin, many times, but hadn't seen him in months, maybe more than a year. This time he came down the stairs and he was in a dress and had breasts and make-up and long hair all done up. At first I didn't know it was Kevin. But then I saw it really was Kevin in there. He came and sat right next to me and I must have been wide-eyed with my mouth hanging open. He explained to me that he was not Kevin anymore and never had really been Kevin. He told me his name was now Jennifer and that she had finally gotten comfortable in her own skin. I loved that idea. I was never comfortable in my own skin, so it was totally inspiring to me. I asked Jennifer if she thought I could get comfortable in my own skin and how I could do that. She was so sweet in her response, "Honey, it is different for everyone. For you it may not be about having to get surgery and hormone shots. For you it may just take time. You be patient. You are beautiful and fun and kind and maybe once you see that is enough in this unkind world, you will feel at home in your skin." I just never forgot that message. And eventually it was true."

"That is so beautiful. How magical that she came into your life like so many people you attracted who helped form you. You said that being in the black communities was not necessarily a safe place for you, even though it felt like home. Say more about that."

"There is so much. It was a constant minefield. I probably should have stuck with just hanging out with Barry. Sure, we did drugs, but other than that, he was a good influence. I could have made safer smarter choices in the black community. I could have hung out with the good kids. I could have just glued myself to Muna's side. She never went toward danger. The majority of the black and brown kids were good kids and I was attracted to the dangerous kids like a moth to a flame. I had a lot of close calls that make me wonder now why I am still alive. There is the rape and drug stuff I already shared. But there were so many hairy situations, it would make a list a mile long.

Like this one night in about 10th grade, I was hanging out alone at home. The phone rang and Jimmy Brown said he needed a ride from the movie theater to his house. My parent's red AMC Javelin was there and the keys were hanging in the doorway. I figured it couldn't hurt to just quickly go give him a ride. Halfway to his house, he grabbed my arm. "What is going on with you and Curtis?"
I didn't know what he was talking about. "What do you mean?" He was squeezing my arm harder. "You know what I mean. I don't want you seeing him no more."
"I'm not seeing him."
"You lying bitch." Then I felt it. A full fisted punch to my right cheek and eye. His giant gold ring tore my cheek skin and blood was pouring down my face. My eyes filled with tears and blood and I couldn't see to drive. I swung the car to the side of the road, pulled out the keys and ran as fast as I could to

the nearest building yelling for help the whole time. Jimmy was running behind me and I pounded on the first door yelling "Help me!!!". I could hear someone running down the stairs and the door opened. A man in a thin robe and pajamas pulled me into the door and locked it behind me. He told me to wait right there. I stood shaking at the bottom of the wooden stairs that led up to their apartment. The man reappeared fast. He was carrying a rifle or a shotgun....I don't know the difference. It was just a long gun. Two little blonde girls were at the top of the stairs in nightgowns yelling "No Daddy!!"
This man swung the door open and cocked the gun and as fast as Jimmy saw that rifle, he was running into the dark night. The man shot toward him and missed. He fired a few more shots when Jimmy was under a streetlight and totally exposed. The whole time, me and his little girls were yelling, "No! Please No!" I remember hearing the sound of Jimmy's feet running on the pavement after those last shots and I was grateful he made it alive.
The man told the little girls to go get a wet washcloth. The barefoot girls ran in their nighties and got the washcloth. Their dad gently dabbed the blood at the wounds.
-"You probably need stitches."
-"No, I'm ok."
-I can take you to the hospital."
-"No, I'm ok."
-"I think I should at least call the police."
-"No, please don't. It's ok. Thank you for helping me. I am going to go home now."
-"Did you know him? Know his name? I wasn't going to shoot him, just scare the living daylights out of him."
-I lied, "No, I don't know him."
Even in that moment of extreme pain in my face, my only thought was to protect Jimmy from the police.

The dad told the girls to wait there and walked with me to the car, still in his robe and holding the rifle and looking around to

make sure Jimmy was not anywhere nearby.
"You gonna be ok?"
"Yes"
"You should tell the police."

He stood holding his rifle in the middle of the road while I drove off, barely able to see out of my one eye. I remember being grateful that the man with the gun didn't know my name or Jimmy's name and it would just be over with. At home, I washed the blood off the driver's seat, cleaned the wound and put a butterfly bandage on it to keep it closed and sat on the sofa trying to stop my shaking shivery body. I needed to make things look normal before anyone got home. I turned on the TV and pretended to be interested in what was on the screen.

When my parents got home that night and asked what the hell had happened, I told them I had just had a bad fall off the back stairs. They kept asking me to tell the truth. And I kept telling them that was the truth. Never did tell them what happened. Jimmy and I never spoke again and we both looked away when we saw each other at school or in the neighborhood near Grover Jr.

I am sure it freaked my parents out. Just another scary disappointing moment with their troubled kid. I think disappointing our parents is what teenagers do best.

It is only the rare ones who are concert pianists or math whizzes. We are mostly floundering around trying to figure out which way is up. Some do better than others. I was one of those who floundered longer than the average teen and I am still not sure I figured out what I am supposed to be doing or which way is up. Did you ever get dashed about in the ocean when the waves and current are coming from all directions and you're not even sure where the surface is? Somehow I am still in the ocean without having a clue about things."

"You sure don't seem clueless to me. I think most people feel like

they don't know what they are supposed to be doing or feel like they are doing life well. The ones who seem to have it figured out have just found a way to live that fits the culture and helps them get by in life. But I don't think they have it figured out any more than any of us. You said you were a disappointment to your parents. How do you think you disappointed your parents? I know most of us feel that we have. But, what are some ways you think you have?"

"Hmmmm, maybe one of the biggest ones is not being a real Jew. Not being a religious person. I didn't marry a Jewish guy. Aside from the fact that I didn't know any Jewish guys other than my brother and my cousins, I know this was a disappointment. My sister married a Roman Catholic and my brother married a Christian Chinese woman and I think I was the last hope. Turns out that when I married a white person they were somewhat relieved. Not in a racist way, but in a "we don't want you to struggle too much in life" way.

For a short time I was in the BBYO. Geezo, what did that stand for? I think it was Bnai Brith Youth Organization. A Jewish kids organization that did social things. I went to a few events. Kids came from all over the Midwest. Those kids were all so foreign to me. Well-behaved white kids. I hooked up with a beautiful African American Jewish guy in the group. He was adopted by white Jews. Figures, one black guy in the whole crowd and I nab him. We dated for a bit, but I think I was too "black" for him. He was from an upper class well-educated family and I was a dope smoking little hippie who hung out with pimps and dealers. Exotic at first and then I guess he could see the writing on the wall. I was sure to take him down a bad road.

After that, I went on a date with a Jewish guy once. It was a set-up. A blind date with the visiting nephew of Pearl, my mom's friend from the synagogue. His name was Phillip. I was 16 and he was in his twenties and I didn't want to go. But I decided it was a small thing I could do to make Pessy feel like I was at least trying.

Phillip picked me up and asked where I wanted to go. "Hmm," I thought, "I could make the most of this, take advantage of the situation." I told him I wanted to go to eat Chinese food. So we did just that. Then on the way back home, about an hour drive, he said, "Do you want to see my uncle's boat?" Figuring I had nothing to lose, I said, "Sure". I didn't like Phillip. We had zero in common. I was a raggle-taggle girl with long braids and hippie clothes and he was a starched guy with a life-plan going to business school. Yin and yang. Oil and water. We walked to the end of the dock on the lake to his uncle's boat. He unlocked the door to the cabin and when we got inside, he threw me on the bed and leaned his arm across my chest while he forced a kiss on me and started to pull at my skirt. I yelled "NO!". But he didn't get it. By then I had learned the concept of rape and knew I didn't have to go along with this. (I learned the word when I was raped by Lester and had to figure out what had happened by talking to my pimp/drug dealer friends)

I was also physically super-powered from being on swim teams. Mix that with adrenaline and I was a force to contend with. I punched his nose with my fist, and when he leaned back in pain I kneed him in the balls. He screamed at me that I was fucking crazy while I ran out of the boat and back up the dock. When he appeared at the car, his nose was bleeding and his shirt was blood-stained. I was pissed. He was pissed. I said, "Get in the fucking car and drive me home NOW. And don't say a word to me, just drive."

At home, Pessy was waiting up.

-"How did it go, Sweetie?"

-"Phillip is an ass and he tried to rape me."

-Pessy looked upset..."Oh no. I am so sorry. Are you OK honey?"

-"Yep, I am ok, I am going to bed."

In the morning Phillip's aunt Pearl called and asked my mother what kind of barbarian she had raised. Phillip was bruised from me punching him and his shirt was ruined.

Pessy responded perfectly. "Phillip tried to rape my daughter

and he got what he deserved. Be happy we aren't pressing charges."
She hung up on her friend. I am not sure they ever spoke again. I loved how Pessy stood up for me.

I think I always disappointed Lazer and Pessy by not taking on the Jewish thing. I never connected with any religion and I actually became an anti-Semitic Jew at some point in my teens. I figured it was religion that was causing all the problems on earth and the issues with Jews were much more clear because of their proximity to me. I saw all the stereotypes acted out in my Jewish family and the people at the synagogue. I hated the fur coats, long red fingernails, shallow materialism, loud opinionated voices, focus on money and status, Cadillacs, overdone hairdos, and anything else associated with the Jews I met. One night at a long table of relatives eating Chinese food at the Peking House, I shouted to one of my aunts, "You are such a JEW!" because she was haggling about the price of something. I said it with venom. She reached across the table and slapped me full force. I continued to hate Jews into my twenties. At about twenty two-years-old I was invited to a Passover seder hosted by some friends where I was living in Minneapolis. They said it would be an alternative seder. They were a bunch of progressive artists and musicians. These friends did not even know I was from a Jewish family. If a discussion turned to religion, I had always backed out of it. When we went around the table and I could read the Hebrew, they all got quiet. Then, Lynne said, "Are you Jewish?"
"No, but I was born into a Jewish family," I responded.
"Then you are Jewish!"
"No, I am not any religion."
"Not as a religion, but as a culture and a tribe, you are Jewish. If you deny that, you are being a self-hating Jew. You are denying a big chunk of who you are."
I was quiet. I knew on some level she was right. I also had to really look at all MY stereotypes of Jews. Lynn's friends did not

fit the image I had of Jews. They were not about make-up, big cars, cigars, materialism, money, or any of my preconceived ideas about Jews. They were artists, musicians, writers, outdoorsy, environmentalists and all working on social change issues. They shifted my whole notion of what Jews were. I got un-anti-Semitic. If that's even a word.

I knew I had changed when I was with three couples the following spring and we were going kayaking in northern Minnesota. On our way north, we stopped for a picnic lunch. Sitting under the trees at picnic tables, I was seated next to a woman named Kara and her husband Knut Lambrini. Knut said, "I have a good Jew joke." I knew that they weren't Jewish, but they didn't know I was. I jumped in, "Oh, Knut, I will tell that joke for you. Jews can tell Jewish jokes, Italians can tell Italian jokes and Germans can tell German jokes. You and Kara can tell Italian and German jokes."
Everything got quiet for a second or two.
Kara turned toward me and said, "You aren't Jewish are you?" At the same time, she and Knut moved far away from me on the picnic bench as if I was contagious.
"I am Jewish," I said smiling.
Kara didn't hesitate for a moment, "Why are you people so sensitive?"
"Well, Kara, I guess we are sensitive because so many other people aren't."
This rolled right over her blonde permed hair.
She just kept going, "I mean, the other day I was at the university and put money in the coke machine and didn't get my can of coke. I hit the machine and said 'It Jewed me' and these two women told me that what I said was offensive. You people are so overly sensitive."
I stayed pretty clear of Knut and Kara on that trip. What they didn't know was that I was also very aware of their love for their son who was a macho jock and their distaste and disapproval of their other son who was in the theater. They were

homophobic and pushing away their own child. I got to benefit from their dislike of their own son by getting family tickets to his plays, when his own parents refused to go see him perform.
The moment I had told them I was Jewish, was a first for me. I had never said those words. I always figured they would only bring trouble. When I finally said those words out loud, it was like saying, "trouble? who the hell cares? bring it on!" The trouble came for my entire life before that without ever identifying as Jewish, so what more could happen?"

"Wow, what a high intensity life you've had. I am not used to living where the Jewish thing is a big deal. We have synagogues in Stockholm and we never think about religion as a reason to judge someone. Even our churches are really more like community centers. Although I did hear that now there are armed security guards at the main synagogue in Stockholm and you have to show your passport to get in. Sad. Can you share other ways you think you disappointed your parents?"

"I know they are bummed that I didn't open my own business. Especially my dad, Lazer. He used to try to get at least one of us to open a business. He loved Italian beef sandwiches and Italian ices. There was a shop called Karm's. When we visited family in Chicago we would go there and eat Italian beef and lemon ices and on the drive home, he would try to infuse us kids with the dream of opening a place like that. When we hit our teens, he formulated a plan. One or all of us kids would work at Karm's and figure out the secret recipes. Then, in Lazer's dream we would open our own carry-out in our town, 60 miles away. I figured I had the perfect excuse to not work at Karm's since I was a vegetarian. The pressure was on Ronny and Karen.
Lazer always lit up when he laid out the plans. None of us kids lit up, and in the end, we kids never worked as an Italian beef spy or opened our own business. We told him HE should

do it himself. Instead, he analyzed every business we visited for ways it could improve or what worked well, but he never opened his own. He would have been a great success at his own business. He knew how to handle the public perfectly.

So picture sitting there with your family waiting for your food to come to the table at any restaurant. You are a kid, maybe fourth grade or even younger.... and you are getting quizzed about every aspect of the business. "What could that waitress do differently? What do you think of the traffic flow between the kitchen and the dining room? What is wrong with the signs near the cash register? Do these plates seem like the right color to use for food? What about the music and lighting?" Then, after using the bathroom, we got to rate it on a one to ten scale for cleanliness and general appearance.

There are things you are part of as a kid that you swear you can't wait to get away from when you leave home. Then, like some strange underground sludge it seeps up throughout your life and you realize it has become part of you....it is knit into your bones. You actually enjoy it. You can't stop yourself. The business analyzing started bubbling up when I was in my twenties and it hasn't gone away yet. I analyze every business I walk into. Like Lazer, I never opened my own business, but I have retail dreams and redesign every store I enter. I redo the atmosphere right down to the music and light and colors. If people come into an art gallery and leave quickly without lingering, I carefully figure out if it is the art or the music or the smells or the lighting in the gallery. It is rarely because of the art. Music, lighting, and smells are the usual culprits for lingering or bolting.

When you come from an analytical family you are never bored. I don't know what bored is. I guess that's a positive thing. But, as Lazer says, "There is nothing you can slice so thin that it doesn't have two sides." And the other side of analytical is that your mind is always doing it. Meditation and the analytical mind are opposites and that could explain why I have been meditating since 1984 and still feel like I have just begun the practice.

So many bigger disappointments for Lazer and Pessy, I am sure. Like the baby thing. Me not having kids. I look back at the major decisions I made on my own, they seem to have been made by a person who is mentally unfit to make her own decisions. I should have been assigned someone as power of attorney from birth. Just someone to use a bit of mindfulness and common sense for making life decisions. I would have been a perfect twin sister. My twin would have been the one with common sense who would have taken my hand and dragged me away from danger and stupidity.

With no option for a life-long side-kick attorney or professional decision maker or a twin, I was forced to fly by the seat of my own pants.

At 25 I was volunteering for the nuclear-freeze campaign and other world social justice and peace issues. I was also reading everything I could get my hands on about the state of the world.

The good news is that I was opening my mind to the realities on earth. The bad news is that I was freaking out. We were going to hell in a handbasket and there was very little that one person could do to stop it. One good way to not think about the state of the world was to do a lot of drinking or drugs. Since I didn't like alcohol and had stopped doing all drugs at the age of 18, that was not my way out. Instead, I was a sex junkie.

Before I tell you about the sex junkie and the stupid decisions I made because of that, let me tell you about the sudden shift away from drugs. Here is how it went: A friend found a military backpack in a dumpster at an army base where she worked in the mess hall. She gave me that backpack and I started to research backpacking. I didn't research too deeply. This was pre-internet and the first library book I found on the topic was about Yosemite National Park. I took that book home, read it cover to cover (skipping the important details) and decided to be a backpacker. I rolled up my huge flannel Girl Scout sleeping bag and tied it to the backpack with clothesline. Inside the backpack was some canned food and a can opener, a toothbrush, a bar of soap in a bread bag, a hair brush, a few tee shirts, an extra pair of sox and some underwear. I had skipped the part in the book about the importance of lightweight foods and items that would dry quickly if they got wet. I had a yard sale to raise money for the trip out west. My hiking shoes were my bright red Converse high tops. I had no tent.

The other important item in my backpack was a ziplock of weed, matches and some papers and a little pipe. My little drug stash.
I hitchhiked from Wisconsin to Yosemite and started hiking from mountain to mountain without a map. At one point I hiked out of the woods into a wildflower-covered meadow that spread out for miles. It was my moment. It just so happened I hadn't smoked that morning and I saw it with fresh alert eyes. From that moment on, I was done with drugs. There were no mirrors in the back-country, so I wasn't thinking at all about how I looked....it was a non-issue. No one was telling me I was fat, ugly, stupid or a loser. All I felt was completely at HOME and like I was "good enough". I was strong enough to hike mountains and I was getting a taste of what it was like to actually be ok with who I was. Other hikers laughed at my canned food and gave me enough lightweight foods to make it for weeks. People leaving the backcountry always wanted to get rid of their food and I was one of the lucky recipients. A father and son even gave me their lightweight cooking pots utensils. When I ran out of food, I would come into Yosemite Valley and restock at the little grocery. I mostly lived on oatmeal and cornmeal mush. They would fill me up and were easy to make with just some water and salt or sugar. When I ran out of money, I dug through the trash in the touristy valley

area for the returnable cans and bottles that people would just throw away. Each one was worth a nickel at the redemption center right there in the park. With an hour of trash picking, I would have enough deposit refunds to buy groceries for another week or two in the backcountry. I gave away all my drugs and paraphernalia to a guy I named The Bear King (because he kept losing his pack and food to the bears) and never looked back. The Bear King couldn't believe his luck.

I had no experience with bears, but my first one was magical. I had eaten my dinner on top of a boulder on one of the backcountry trails. Then, because I didn't have a tent, I slept with my back to the boulder. It felt a little safer to have my back to something each night. I was snugged into my Girl Scout sleeping bag with my whole backside against the boulder, when I popped awake because of a scratching noise. The moon was huge and illuminating everything and when I looked up on the top of the boulder there was a huge bear scratching at the crumbs I must have dropped during my dinner up there. She kept leaning over to the side where I was sleeping and sniffing the air. She must have smelled my stinky hiker body down there on the ground. I had tied my food in a tree, so it wasn't that. I can't tell you why I wasn't scared of that bear. I just kept watching her up on that rock and thinking I was the luckiest person in the whole world. I have loved bears ever since. It was my luck to be an exhibit writer on the bears exhibit for the Science Museum I worked at years later. I traveled around the country interviewing people who had bear encounters, both positive and negative, as part of that job. Everything from a woman who had a bear eat both her arms to a woman who watched her husband being killed by a grizzly and a guy who lost his whole ass to a bear when he was trying to get up a tree to escape it.

The wilderness healed so much in me. Totally stopped doing all drugs.

With my drug days behind me, I was just left with that one pesky addiction, sex.

The combination of wanting to have sex all the time with knowing the human world was a violent destructive place meant I needed to deal with the baby issue. I knew I didn't want to have kids...ever. I figured if I wanted to have kids one day I could adopt. But, my crazy sex life was like playing baby roulette. After my illegal abortion at 15, I was not willing to take the chance of getting pregnant again. I went to the University of Minnesota Hospital and asked to have my tubes tied. I had just turned 25 and they said I was too young. I asked how I could officially dispute that and began the process. After filling out numerous forms, I was given a hearing date. The hearing consisted of 6 "experts". The six experts had to unanimously agree that I would not change my mind later and want kids.

I walked into a brightly lit room with 2 women and 4 men at a long table. There was one chair across from them. It was like the set-up for the judges in the movie Flashdance, only I didn't get to dance and there was no music. I sat in the chair across from the long table. They introduced themselves. There were psychologists, a social worker, a doctor, and one psychiatrist. The first one started by holding up a large black and white photo of a beautiful baby. She asked me what I felt when I looked at the photo.

"I can see that it is a beautiful baby, but it doesn't make me feel anything beyond that."

The next one asked me about my childhood. "Were you abused physically, mentally or sexually?"

By the time we got to the fourth "expert" I stopped them.

"I know you have your process, but not one of you has asked me why I want to do this. That seems like the most logical place to start. So I will explain it to you and then if you still have questions you can ask them."

The room went silent and they looked up and down the table

at each other. Obviously I was straying from protocol.
Finally, the psychologist said, "OK".
I explained my many reasons for not wanting to get pregnant and bring another child into the world. I told them about the human population issues and the impact that was having on the environment and animals. I explained that I was not attached to the birthing process and would be happy to adopt a child if I changed my mind one day. I also said that I did not trust myself to be a non-violent parent and my chances were better if I did not accidentally get pregnant at a young age. I had tried an IUD and my body rejected it in a very painful way. I told them about the nasty abortion experience and not wanting to go through anything like that again.
Then, I asked them if they had any further questions.
They all replied "no".
They told me that I could wait in the reception area and they would have their response within an hour. Less than ten minutes later, I had their response. I could schedule the tubal ligation. At 25 I had the operation and have never regretted it for a moment. Oh, that isn't true. I regretted it when I woke up in horrible pain from a glitch in the surgery. What should have been outpatient turned into three days of painkillers and doctor observation. The entire three days my friend Wendy was knitting on the end of the hospital bed. Every time I woke up a bit from the painkillers, I would hear the comforting click-click of her needles. I didn't tell my parents about the surgery for 8 years. When I saw piles of boxes in their closet marked LU'S KIDS, I knew I had to tell them. They both cried when I told them. I assumed it was because I would be childless. Turns out they were upset that it took me 8 years to tell them and that they couldn't be there for me during the surgery. That's love, eh?"

"For sure"

"What might disappoint parents the most is when their kids

turn out to be like them. I was raised by independent thinkers. I am not a real Jew. I guess I would be called an Ethnic Jew or a non-practicing Jew. You could say I was Jew-ish. I was raised in a Jewish house, went to synagogue every Friday and for all the holidays and celebrated everything my parents did. I attended Sunday school at the temple. But, religion is not part of me. I have never found a reason to follow a religion. I had no choice on the whole temple attendance thing growing up. At 16 years old you sort of graduate from Sunday school with what is called a confirmation. Some real practicing Jews have Bar or Bat Mitzvah. That happens at 13 years old and is apparently when you become an adult. My parents never even suggested that I do that at 13 because I was too much of a wild animal to even sit through Sunday school without getting in trouble. At 16 Rabbi Rosen started training us for our confirmation. We were told to write two speeches that we would give on our confirmation day. There was one other girl being confirmed. Her name was Carol Goldmann and she was a private school kid, a good girl, and the yin to my yang. Complete opposites. She was a real Jew. A good Jew. I wrote my speeches. One was on the war in Vietnam. The other was on interracial marriage. When I handed them in to the Rabbi for his approval, he was steaming. He threw them on his desk and told me that the speeches had to be about Judaism. "Oh," I said, "I thought they were supposed to be about something we feel strongly about or something we care about."

"Yes," he said through tight jaw teeth, "that something is Judaism."

I went home and wrote two more speeches. Both related to Jewish stuff. I can't remember now what they were. I got them approved by the Rabbi and my parents. I told my parents what had happened with the other two speeches. They didn't have much to say. I knew and they knew that the Rabbi was the boss.

On the day of our confirmation, relatives and friends came to the temple to be part of the ceremony. It was a full house of

Carol's people and my people.

When it was my time to go to the pulpit and read my speech, I pulled out the one on the Vietnam war. I read the whole speech. There was not much the Rabbi could do at this point. We were in full public display mode. I remember looking out and seeing people crying in the congregation. I loved that. They understood what I was trying to say. For speech number two the Rabbi whispered in my ear that it better be the one he approved. I had left the one he approved of at home. I read the one on interracial marriage. It was full of painful true stories of the racial oppression in our country.

After the ceremony we all met with the Rabbi in his office. There Carol and I would each get one of those diploma folders saying we were confirmed. Carol's parents beamed as the Rabbi told them how proud he was of her dedication. Then he turned to me and told me to open my folder. I opened it and saw it was empty.

He addressed me and my parents, "You will not be receiving your certificate until you make up for what you did today. You can come up with some way that you can show me you are dedicated to your Jewish studies." My parents were silent, I was silent. We left the office and drove to the celebration dinner without speaking. At the restaurant with all my relatives and my parent's friends, there was nothing said about what happened in the Rabbi's office. Instead, my Dad leaned over and said quietly in my ear, "I am disappointed about what happened today. You are the most idealistic, rebellious and stubborn person I know. You are a little like me. It drives me crazy. Keep doing it. Keep being strong. I love you."

"Boy, you were so damn strong at such a young age. I think I would have had a hard time if you were my kid."

"Yep, I would not want to raise a kid like me."

"Did you ever do anything to make the Rabbi happy so you could get

the certificate?"

"No, I figured it wasn't really something I needed and probably was nothing I would look at again after that day."

"Did you go to college? You don't seem like you would have been the type to think that was important."

"I did go. Mostly to just be near my brother and because I didn't have another plan. It would just be another experience in life. I wasn't really college material. It is more for people who have a long-term plan. I never had one. Without a long-term plan, you might as well just spend days in the library learning about everything you can until something grabs you. I decided on University of Wisconsin just because my brother was there. Not much thought went into it.

For the first year or some number of credits, you have no choice but to live in the dorms. I was on the 9th floor of a 10 story high rise dorm with a roommate. I got there before her on day one, chose my bed by the window and started decorating. I had a giant poster of Chief Seattle on the wall with the quote: "Humankind has not woven the web of life. We are but one thread within it. Whatever we do to the web, we do to ourselves. All things are bound together. All things connect."

Sally, my roommate walked in while I was in my bed reading. She didn't introduce herself or say hello. Just charged in and shouted at me,"Get that fucking Indian off the wall."

I didn't say hello either, I just said, "This is my side of the room, so he stays."

"I hate Indians. I worked at McDonald's and every time an Indian came in, I spit on their food before bagging it. Once I even poured cayenne on a kid's burger. And, if I wanted that side of the room, I would take it. Just so you know." Sally and I never even introduced ourselves to each other.

She joined a sorority and was gone pledging and drinking most of the time. The problem was she did come home to our room every night and vomited in our shared trash can. The phone rang all day and night for her. I worked full time in addition to carrying a full load of classes and I was kept up by her friends and partying almost every night.

Sally went home during winter break and I used that time to rescue 60 rabbits from a biology lab. They had been through horrible experiments already and were scheduled for more torture after the winter break. It is ridiculous. The whole dissection and experimentation tradition. Most of these students would not go on to save lives and they did not need to be injecting and cutting up innocent beings. Even those who would go on to save lives, could learn so much more without doing experiments on live animals or specimens from the biological supply houses. I have researched this a lot. It is a waste of money and other resources because most of the results obtained from other species can't be extrapolated to humans and often when they claim results, it is misinformation. Drugs and products are often recalled because animal tests couldn't predict important issues. A dog or rabbit or mouse or rat cannot tell you "I have tingling in my arms and legs, I have a headache, I can't remember anything, I feel nauseous. It is such flawed science. Uggh, don't get me started…I could go on all day about that nasty business. Anyway, I knew those poor rabbits at the university were living in hell and about to go through more hell. In the large corporate product and medical labs, the animals are recycled through as many experiments as possible. So that may go through weeks of having toxic chemicals dropped in their eyes to having fur and layers of skin removed and toxic substances applied to their skin for irritancy tests."

"I had no idea. It sounds so horrible. Gives me a bit more understanding when a product says "No Animal Testing" on it. I really should learn more about it before I buy anything."

"Yep, it is a good idea if you believe in non-violence for all living beings. It is hard to navigate it all. You may see that a company claims that they do not test on animals, but they may use ingredients that have been tested on animals or they may contract it out to a testing facility, so they technically do not test themselves. It is just marketing.

I really wanted to get those rabbits out of there. I didn't have a car, so I organized some folks with bicycles and some with cars to help me get the rabbits. I outfitted bikes with boxes on back carriers and found people to donate kennels for transporting in cars. It was a major thing to organize. Some of the rabbits would go immediately to their new homes in farm areas outside of town. Some would be picked up within a few days. The ones waiting for pick up lived in the dorm room with me for that time. There were about twenty of them in there. It was a gamble. If the nasty roommate came back, I was busted. If the school began investigating and found them in my room I was big time busted. I tried to keep them from destroying any of Sally's stuff. It was total chaos in the room. Newspapers and tarps lining the floors and beds, as well as little fencing to keep them contained barely helped. They were so happy to be out of the tiny metal cages in the lab, that they were in party mode. They were finally out of the lab with it's constant electrical buzzing and no windows and the smells of bleach and chemicals and feces all combined. And they were finally able to socialize rather than each being isolated and lonely and bored.

When the rabbits finally all got to their homes, friends and I cleaned up the room as best we could.

Sally returned from break and must have noticed that things were not the same in the room, but for once, us not talking worked in my favor.

The day she got back from winter break, the three friends who had helped me clean were sitting on my bed. One was East Indian, one was African American and the other was from Kenya. When they left, she said, "No fucking niggers in here. Ever again. Keep the niggers and the curry people out of here."

I had to wake up at 4 am for work and the sleep deprivation from the constant all night calls from Sally's sorority friends were starting to make me crazy. One night when the phone rang, I ripped it off the wall and threw it in the trashcan in my crazed sleep deprived state of mind. When Sally got back at 2 am she saw the wires hanging out of the wall and had a fit. I went the next day to the student medical center. I told them if I didn't get out of the dorms I would kill myself. I left the clinic with a formal permission note to live off campus.

That day I found the house on Cherry Street and moved in the next day. It was perfect. An old house that needed work....a lot of work. I got a door for the bathroom and hung it. There were holes in the wooden floors, holes in the walls, leaking plumbing and missing front steps. I loved doing the repairs. And, the location was perfect and the price was right.

The whole college thing was tough for me. But, to keep my sanity, I ran over six miles a day and still had time to work and do school. I even did my first canoeing there. I had multiple boyfriends. Even one white guy, named Chas, which was pretty foreign territory for me, but he taught me how to whitewater canoe. We almost lost our lives a few times, but looking back, I think it was worth it."

"I am so glad you saved those rabbits and I am really glad you got away from Sally the roommate. She sounds like a total nightmare. Tell me about almost losing your life with Chas."

"The first time we had a close call was actually my first time canoeing. We had just finished canoeing a 30 mile, calm section of the Embarrass River. It is called that because in French it means *obstruction*. I was pretty exhausted from canoeing 30 miles on my first experience. Chas and I were driving back in his car with the borrowed canoe tied on top and he stopped on a bridge. We looked down at a massive canyon with another section of the river crashing through it. It was huge boulders and whitewater for as far as I could see. Chas said, "Let's do it." I told him I wasn't ready to take on that kind of whitewater. Not to mention that we would get soaking wet and it was the beginning of March with deep snow still all around us and really cold temperatures. All I had on was long underwear and a sweater under a cheap rain suit. He pushed and pushed to do it until I caved and said, "OK". I was terrified. We parked above up river from the canyon. We made it through the first two major vertical drops. Then we came to what looked like a waterfall to me. The drop was so steep and there were constant chutes through boulders. I was freezing from already being wet and Chas was constantly shouting at me to paddle harder. Then, in an instant, we capsized. I was pinned between the canoe and a boulder and the force of the river was too much for me to push the boat off me. I looked around for Chas and saw the paddles racing down river in the huge waves and then I saw Chas' head come up and him trying to get air. Then I saw his head go back under a wave. I was sure he was dead. To the left and right there were sheer cliffs and no way to get out of there. I couldn't feel my body it was so frozen in the water and breathing was hard. Then out of nowhere, I heard Chas shout. He had managed to get back up river to me and had the rope from the front of the canoe. He was holding tight to a boulder and pulling on the rope. Between his pulling the rope and me pushing, we got the canoe off me and somehow Chas untied the rope while clinging to the rock on the side of the canyon. Looking back I don't know how he was functioning in that icy water. Probably pure adrenaline. He threw the rope to me and after a few tries, I caught it. I remember hearing the canoe crashing along the rocks downriver. Chas pulled me to the boulder he was on at the edge of the river. Then he somehow managed to rock climb up that solid icy rock wall and pulled me along with the rope. We were both digging our fingernails in to get a grip in some places. We got to the top and saw a house in the distance. We trudged through the snow in our wet clothes, walking like zombies because we couldn't bend our joints anymore. When we got to the house, we knocked and a man came to the door. We were too frozen and in shock to even say anything. The guy and his wife pulled us in and closed the door behind us. They worked fast and got all our wet clothes off and wrapped us in multiple blankets in chairs by their woodstove. It was a long time before anyone spoke. The wife kept giving me hot chocolate that she had to spoon feed to me because I couldn't hold the cup. The husband was doing the same with Chas. I remember my first real thought, when my mind started working again, was, "I can't believe we are alive."

"Shit Lu. That is absolutely crazy. I was thinking the same thing while you were telling it, "I can't believe you are alive." Did you stay with that couple?"

"No, once we were warmed up and functioning, which took hours, they drove us in the dark to Chas' car. We got in the car and drove home. We went back a few days later to try to find the canoe. We did find one half of it. The canoe had cracked completely in half and we found the bow of the boat about 15 miles further down river from where we had capsized. Chas and I split the cost and bought his friend a new canoe."

"You could have easily died that day, Lu. I'm glad you didn't. OK, We got so much recorded today. It's great. I am ready for a hike. Want to?"

"You said the word and now the dogs are going bananas! They totally know the words "hike" and "walk". Lets go, I will show you another new hike you haven't done."

KARINA

So, I did what Lu suggested. I wrote on a piece of paper that I wanted clarity about what to do with my life choices. I folded the paper and put it under my pillow last night. During the night I had a dream that I was a Native American woman and I had three kids who were all around me in a strange round dome structure with a fire lit in the middle. I didn't know what to make of the dream other than it feeling like I visited an old home of mine and I was so happy there.

Lu told me that Elan called this morning and he and Winnie want us to come to dinner tonight. All Lu has to do is say his name and I feel an adrenaline rush. She is plenty perceptive and I am sure she notices. I am excited to see him again and I am terrified. My reactions to him feel too out of control and foreign. I am also worried that I am so boring compared to these people. They are creative and unusual and interesting. I am an east coast journalist with an apartment, a job and no hobbies or talents. Even if Elan is interested in me, eventually he would probably get bored with me. Anyway, I am thinking it too far ahead. I don't even know what his feelings are and I shouldn't be guessing. I am a mix of wanting to get the interviews done and hurry back to my old life and wanting to give all that up and start fresh here. Uggh, crazy thoughts. I need to just calm down and focus on what I came here to do.

DOWN TO EARTH

"Lu, the last place we left off yesterday was the canoe accident. But before that, you talked about getting the house on Cherry Street in college. How did you pay the rent and your other expenses? I mean, you had rent, college tuition, food, and other things you must have had to cover."

"I always did good at finding jobs and making ends meet. During my first year at college, I worked at a natural foods restaurant called Down to Earth. Merry, the owner, was a brilliant woman with a Ph.D. in chemistry. She had previously worked as a chemist for Kimberly-Clark and left there to go into the restaurant business.

The ad for the job was very clear: Only those over 25 years old need apply. I was 18, but that didn't stop me. She and I sat at a table in the restaurant and talked for a long time. We got along great. She agreed to hire me. I was told I could start the next day. As I was gathering my jacket to leave, she said, "How old are you?"

"It doesn't really matter, right? We have a good connection, I am a hard worker and my age doesn't affect that. I am 18."

"Sorry, you are officially NOT hired. I was clear about the minimum age. I have tried hiring younger students and it is always a disaster."

"I know you were clear about the age, but I really want this job. Please, Merry, let's do it on a trial basis. I will be on trial for 6 months and if I do anything, even something small, that you don't like, you can fire me. No questions asked, no argument, I will leave."

She hesitated for quite a while. Just giving me the stare down.
"Ok. But one screw up and you are out."
"Absolutely. Thank you so much!"
I started work the next day.
On day four, Merry asked me to wash the giant picture window in front of the restaurant. She said to use ammonia. I had never used ammonia for anything. I poured some in the bucket and then ran hot water into the bucket. Moments later the restaurant was filled with a toxic gas and had to be evacuated. Merry screamed at me. "What is wrong with you? Don't you know anything about ammonia? You are an idiot. You put cool water in the bucket and then add a small amount of ammonia! You can't put steaming hot water over ammonia!! I knew I never should have hired you. Get out now!!"
I took off my apron and left out the back door.
That night, Merry called me and apologized for getting so angry. I told her I understood her being angry, "You have a Ph.D. in chemistry...I must seem like the most ignorant person you ever met."
"I want you to come back to work. You have been so good to work with....this incident aside."
"Are you sure? We had the trial period deal."
"The trial period is over. Just come back to work."

I returned to work the next day.

Merry had a system. New workers always start out as dishwashers and then move on to prep cooks, then to cooks and bakers. She told me I was too young to move to the other positions. Unbeknownst to Merry, during any lulls in the dishwashing and table clearing, I worked on learning the prep cook job. Whenever she wasn't there I worked on learning that job inside out. When I knew I had it down, I asked her if I could start doing some shifts in prep. I showed her all I had learned. She agreed to my doing some prep shifts. Eventually she hired a dishwasher and I was doing all prep shifts. From

that I learned the baking skills and routine and soon moved on to that. The hours were crazy, but worked for me. I would get there in the wee hours of the morning and crank the music and work until just before the restaurant opened.
Some days, I stayed and worked the counter."

"Wow, you sure weaseled your way into the job and then up the ladder there. Sneaky but clever. Did you like the job? Since you are more of an introvert, the baking job sounds perfect for you, but what about the counter work with people?"

"Well, I am sort of both. I can do the people thing, it just doesn't nourish me as much as solo work. The counter was more entertaining, for sure. The eclectic bunch of customers.
One day, a young dark haired couple came to the counter. They were definitely the most memorable.
They walked straight up to me at the counter and introduced themselves, "Hello, we are called Bud and Blossom and we are traveling the world to bring a message to people. We have nothing material, no money or things and are looking for a place to stay."
I didn't hesitate. It was weird. I wrote down the address to my house on Cherry Street and handed them my key.
I easily told them, "You can stay with me. I have classes until evening, so I'll see you there later. Help yourself to any food, the shower and anything else you need."
When I got home later that day, Bud and Blossom and I drank tea on the floor of the living room and they explained their mission.
"We have given up all our material goods and our attachments to anyone or anything. We gave up our names, too. We choose different names. Now we are Bud and Blossom. We are preparing for a harvest of followers that is going to happen soon. We are connected to The Two. The Two provide whatever we need when we just mentally ask for it. We connect with The Two by getting still and just thinking about what we need.

There will soon be a harvest and everyone who is prepared will be moved to the next place after earth. We would like to share our message with the community here and answer their questions. Can you help us find a place to hold the session?"

I said, "You could do it here at my house."
They shook their heads, "No, we need a really big space. There will be a lot of people."
Without thinking, I said, "Well, I am on the student council and I can get us a room in the Union building. Will that work?"
They smiled, "Perfect, thank you."
I was a bit confused about how they would do this, so I asked them, "How will you let people know about it?"
Totally confident, they told me, "We will walk around town tomorrow and let people know. Let's have it Wednesday night."
I was skeptical, "Hmm, that is not much time to get the word out. That is the day after tomorrow."
Blossom said, "Don't worry, the room will be full. Everyone will tell someone and they will all come."
I reserved the room in the Union for 6 pm Wednesday as Bud and Blossom requested.
I didn't expect more than about 10 people, so the room seemed way too big. But there was something so believable about Bud and Blossom, so solid. I just trusted them.
On Wednesday night, I went to the room early to make sure it was all set up. There was a long table at the front of the room with two chairs. Bud and Blossom arrived early, too and sat in the chairs with their eyes closed.
Soon people started arriving. A lot of people. They just kept coming. The room was beyond capacity. Over 200 people showed up by the start time and more people were in the hallway trying to get in.
Bud and Blossom opened their eyes and just waited silently looking around the room.
Then, without any prompting, people started asking ques-

tions.

Two hours later they were still asking questions.

The questions were all so different and everyone in the room was transfixed. No one left early. Some questions were personal, like: "Is my sister who died in a good place now, a place with no suffering?" And some questions were more about the world, the universe, like, "Is everything I experience with my senses an illusion? Is it all just something in my mind?" or things like, "What is it like after this? Where will we all be when we die?"

Bud and Blossom had calm solid answers to every question. They told people that the answers were not actually from them and that they were just the conduit.

Finally, three hours later, we all had to leave the room so it could be locked up.

I walked home with Bud and Blossom.

Back home, I was all stirred up. I asked more questions of them.

I felt like this was my opportunity for something bigger, the next step in my life.

I left them sleeping at my house and went to work at 4 am. I was baking and crying. I was conflicted. A part of me was afraid to just leap into this new life, this big unknown, with Bud and Blossom. And a part of me felt like if I didn't, I was missing a huge opportunity.

At about 4:30 the phone rang in the restaurant. It made me jump. The quiet at that time of morning was just part of my routine and the phone never rang while I was baking.

It was my mom.

Pessy sounded calm, "Honey, I just woke up and felt like I needed to call you. I thought you were upset about something."

Right then, on the phone, I told my mom the whole story of Bud and Blossom.

She listened quietly. Then when I finished telling her, she said, "Don't worry. If there is a harvest now, there will be another

one someday. If you are this upset, it is not a clear "yes" for you. Don't pressure yourself. Calm down. I will talk to you soon. I love you. Good night Honey."
I had never heard Pessy sound so clear and confident. It was like listening to a different person using her voice.
It calmed me right down. I went back to baking with a joyful heart.
After my shift, I went home to say goodbye to Bud and Blossom.
I gave them some gas money and some food. Someone in town had given them an old Volvo.
They hugged me and Blossom said, "If you ever need anything, anytime, just get still and think about us and we will take care of it."
With that, they got in the car and were gone.
As I am telling you this, I am thinking about how ironic it was that the place I worked at was called Down to Earth. Here I was saying goodbye to the two people who were probably moving on to the next phase of life after Earth and I was staying behind, down to Earth.

One day at Down to Earth, I was chopping up veggies in the back, and one of the art professors from the university came back there to talk to me. He asked if I would be willing to cater the Art Ball and said I would be paid well. When he told me it would be 500 people, I should have said, "Sorry I'm not a caterer". But, instead, I said, "I will need to hire a few other cooks and servers". And that is when Nature's Bakers was born. Sarah and Ruthie worked at Down to Earth with me and we made all the food in my little rented house. Merry was super supportive and loaned us all the cooking supplies and a boatload of serving stuff she had in storage. It was crazy and impossible and we did it. Just the three of us cooking and baking and a few friends for serving the food. First we sat down and created a completely unrealistic menu. But we made everything on that list and made it beautiful. I mean who makes stuffed sugar snap peas for 500 people? And who the hell is crazy enough to create chocolate cabbages filled with chocolate mousse for each table's edible centerpiece? We did. If any recipe could be labeled as labor intensive, we chose it for that event. It turns out that would be the only giant event we would ever cater. But, 500 impressed people created a word of mouth buzz that meant we were too busy catering to work at Down to Earth. And still, no health department, no commercial kitchen. Everything out of my little house. We called our biz Nature's Bakers. The three of us were able to continue the catering biz and go to college debt-free. It was perfect. Flexible hours that we could keep and still do well in classes. When it was finals week, we just told folks we were booked up and couldn't cater their party. We had complete control of when we worked and when we didn't. The gigs were intense and required all three of us to kick into high gear. But then, we could have a lull afterward. I think all caterers need to be adrenaline junkies to succeed.

"That is so crazy and amazing. How did you deal with being a vegetarian and doing the catering?"

"That is what is so nuts. That entire art ball was vegetarian, but we never even mentioned it to the professor who hired us. We gave the committee the potential menu and they approved it and said what they could pay us per attendee. To the three of us it was a fortune. So, the business was born and Nature's Bakers was a vegetarian catering service. But, we didn't advertise as vegetarian. No one would have hired us. Instead we called it ethnic foods. One night at Joan and Gary's house, catering their party, Gary approached me. He was a philosophy professor. He said to me, "Hey, how come no meat tonight?"
-"Gary, we have never served meat at your parties. We only do vegetarian food."
-"No, I think you had meat at the last party."

-"No Gary, we have really never served meat at any event we've done."
-"Are you sure?"
-"Yep, I am sure."
-"What about those samosas last time? They had meat, right?"
-"No, they had some tofu, but no meat. I freeze the tofu first and then squeeze the water out and crumble it and sauté it and spice it and it seems like meat."
At that point he yells to his wife and motions her over, "Joan, come here." Joan comes over to us. "Joan, did you realize you hired a vegetarian caterer?" Joan laughs because she realizes we have been there three times before he even noticed. She says,"Gary, you are so slow. Of course I realized it." And she just walks away shaking her head.

College was not about the classes for me. It was about all the experiences that came my way.
I was clueless about the actual college system. In fact, it wasn't until my third college year that I went into the records office to find out how soon I would graduate and got a really shocking reply.
"You have more than enough credits, but you have not taken your required courses."
"Required courses?"
"Yes, there are required core classes you need to take to graduate. Who is your advisor?"
"Advisor? I don't think I have one."
Somehow I had slipped through the cracks. No advisor. No plan.
That day I also learned that I could get scholarships because of my grade point average, which was 4.0. I could have had every class, every year paid for by scholarships. The same woman who asked who my advisor was, handed me booklets and forms to apply for scholarships. It wasn't until my final year that I had a full scholarship and took all my required courses. I had enough credits for two degrees.

And still, no plan."

"It seems like having no plan has mostly worked for you. I mean here you are, doing fine. It is hard for me to relate to not having a plan or a future dream. I picture my future a lot. I am hoping to get married to a well educated man and have kids and take a few years off from work to be with the kids and then go back to work. I dream a lot about it. I can even picture the guy. And he is my soulmate. And maybe we will move back to Sweden and he will fit right in to the culture. Did you ever dream about your future and just picture what you wanted it to be?"

"Wow, I never thought about that until you asked. I guess most people do that. That is what gives them drive or incentive. Like a life carrot waving in front of them that keeps them going. Weird I guess, but I have never had a picture of what my future would be. That doesn't mean I am a Zen in-the-moment person all the time. I think about the past sometimes and wish I had done things differently and there are times I miss something from my past. You must be starting to think I am some sort of alien."

"Not at all. Just so different than anyone else I have encountered in my life.
Did you ever have a relationship with someone that felt like "the one"? That would be sort of like seeing a future for yourself."

"Oh yeah. For sure. But, I didn't know how special it was at the time. Looking back, it is one of my biggest regrets that I didn't do everything I could to keep it going. I threw it away.

I was biking to the university one day when I was 19 and a guy with flowing long bright red hair and a huge smile passed me. He recognized me and I recognized him. We had been in a class together in high school. Home Appliance Repair was a class we both took when he was a senior and I was a junior. We learned everything from wiring a house to fixing a toaster. I was the only girl in the class and had to fight to be allowed to take it. Those were the days of girls being allowed in classes that taught them how to sew and cook and clean, but not any shop classes that might teach them to repair and build things and be independent.

Devon was one of the popular boys. So I didn't know him very well, because the popular boys match up with the beautiful popular girls. He was also part of the white culture at our school and I was still not familiar with any of that. I was the girl with two long braids, denim overalls and work boots who rode her bike to school when other kids were driving their parent's cars. I stuck close to my black buddies from junior high and a few misfits at the school. But, Devon was an eccentric artist type rather than the popular football player type. So we both knew how to think and live outside the box. Well, I think Devon actually knew there was a box and chose not to get in, and I never actually found the box. He talked to me a few times in Home Appliance Repair class. Once, he told me he was going to a Jethro Tull concert. I only knew Motown, but I wanted to impress Devon. So I answered, "Yeah, I like him." Devon said, "It's a group, not one guy." I turned away embarrassed. I had a crush on him and was sure I blew it right then and there.

Then, two years later, there he was biking to the university next to me. He was the most interesting person I had ever met. He knew about art, history, gardening, music, pop culture and humor. We became best buds hanging out together all the time. He taught me so much more than all my years in school had ever taught me. He was also my intro to at least some of the white culture stuff I had missed in junior high and high school. We were together constantly. It was total bliss for me. Laughter, joy, great sex, and just totally alive. I don't think I dreamed details of a future with him, I just assumed we would always be together. I couldn't imagine life without him. They say that you shouldn't count on another person to make you feel whole, but with Devon I felt complete and whole. I had never been so happy.

We were pretty wild and free. We both had long thick hair and on a whim, we took the electric trimmers in his parent's basement and buzzed our hair Sinead O'Connor style. Total buzz. We were prepping for a trip to Florida and thought it would keep us cooler. I found out I didn't have a very nicely shaped head and Devon, of course, did. My mom cried when she saw my nearly shaved head. It must have been reminiscent of the holocaust images for her. My hair really was my best physical feature and I am guessing I had already given her plenty to be embarrassed about with me. I kept reassuring her it would grow back quickly, but there was no comforting her. It was weird how people felt compelled to tell me I had an odd head shape. I mean total strangers would remark about my ugly shaped scalp. And some people assumed we were in a cult and we were shunned for that. And it was the time of KD Lange the singer and more LGBT people coming out of the closet, so people had all kinds of ideas about a woman with no hair. So many times when I was at a checkout counter, they wouldn't serve me, they would go to the person behind me like I was invisible. Or they would tell me to put my stuff down on the counter and leave because they couldn't serve "my kind". But when Devon and I were together with our buzzed heads they always assumed cult. We got picked up hitchhiking one time by military guys who assumed we were two men from the military. When we got in the jeep and they saw that I was a woman they freaked out and pulled over and told us they couldn't give civilians a ride and definitely not cult people. We hitchhiked to California one time and we didn't have much money. Certainly not enough to get a hotel. So, in San Francisco we slept at the top of a parking ramp. The bright lights stayed on all night and there were other people up there sleeping. When we walked down the concrete stairs in the morning after a night of very little sleep, we had to walk over bodies....maybe sleeping maybe dead, we didn't check any of them. The next night we rolled out our sleeping bags in

Golden Gate Park. Again, lots of other people had the same idea. All night eucalyptus pods were dropping off the giant trees onto the crispy leaves around us and sounded like people walking and again I couldn't sleep all night. Finally in the early hours of the morning I fell asleep with my head inside the sleeping bag that was pushed against Devon. We woke up to a guy standing there looking down on us repeating over and over, "Good morning, good morning, good morning." I peeked out of my sleeping bag and his smiling face was right above me. He was holding a pad of paper and a pen and said, way too loud, "My name is Curt and I work for Newsweek. I was doing a story on homeless people living in the park and before finishing the story I was moved on to another story. But, since two people have been killed sleeping in the park this week, we are bringing the story back. Can I interview you about living in the park?" Devon and I had no idea people had been killed in the park. It totally gave me the willies. I told the reporter that we didn't live in the park, we were just passing through. He wanted to interview us anyway. I remember a moment there when I was wishing Devon and I were people with money who could have paid for a hotel. But, not an hour later, we were walking through Haight Ashbury neighborhood and a produce truck was driving down the road past us and the back door of the truck had not been latched. The driver hit a bump and an entire box of organic grapes came flying out the back. Devon ran for the box and put it on my head and we handed out free grapes through the neighborhood to lots of happy people. I thought, "Rich people might get hotel rooms, but they don't get to hand out organic grapes throughout Haight Ashbury".

For quite a while, Devon and I were ice cream bike professionals. We would ride our own bikes about 10 miles to the neighboring town and then get on ancient heavy fat tire bikes with massive coolers in front, owned by the Blue Bell Ice Cream Company. They had a row of copper bells on the long handlebar that we rang while we rode. They were so hard to pedal that we had to stand up to pedal for even the slightest incline and often we had to get completely off of them and push them like Sisyphus pushing the boulder up the hill. It was hard physical work, but we made good money. We were paid by how many bomb pops and ice cream bars we sold. We made a little extra selling our left-over dried ice to drug dealers at the end of the shift. Still not sure what they used them for, but they paid us a premium. The way we made big money was to go to the worst neighborhoods. We figured out that the poorest people had the most kids. We would bike to that neighborhood and then split up for the day. Kids would come flying off the porches with their coins and we would sell out every day. I think Devon only got robbed twice and I got robbed three times. A purple Cadillac pulled over one time and a guy got out of the passenger side and held a gun to me and told me to give him my money. He didn't get much because I kept the bulk of my cash in a plastic bag under the boxes of ice cream bars. The most humiliating robbery was after we buzzed our hair off. A huge gang of girls who were probably only about 14 years old, but still much bigger than me, approached the bike. I had a bad feeling about it from the get-go. The first giant girl grabbed me by my overalls straps and held me down with her knee in the curb grass. "Watcha gonna do about this Baldy? You ain't gonna do nothin'. That's watcha gonna do."

The other girls took all the ice cream boxes out of the bike cooler and distributed them to all the people watching from their porches and front yards. Grandparents, parents, kids and babies all watched and enjoyed the show. None of the adults were interested in saving the ass of some little bald whitey who rode an ancient ice cream bike and drove them crazy with the constant ringing of the row of bells. They not only got all the ice cream and the money in my belt pouch, but they got the plastic bag with the bulk of my day's take. I can't remember how much that was, but it was a boatload for sure. The girls all got some punches and kicks in before they finished the job. My sides ached from the kicks too much to get on the bike and ride....so I slowly pushed it up the street toward what I thought was the right direction. I was definitely dazed. When I got about three blocks from the crime scene, I saw Devon peddling his ice cream bike toward me at top speed. You gotta understand that these are bikes that are meant to go at a snail's pace. He was peddling that thing like he was in the Tour de France. I had never seen one of those things move that fast. Apparently, word was out in the neighborhood and some kids had told Devon, "You should see what they did to the bald lady who sells ice cream over there." They pointed toward where Devon knew I was. There was already no question in his mind it was me. There were no other bald ladies on ice cream bikes. Before he got any more information from the kids he was flying through the streets toward me. Being the thrifty money saving girl I was, the money being gone upset me more than my black and blue body and face. Devon, being the totally caring human he was, took me in his arms and held me tight. He was more worried about me and never even asked about the money. Our boss at Blue Bell told us to stay away from that neighborhood. But we didn't. Instead we just stayed together all day riding the same route as a team.

Devon and I biked like addicts. We couldn't get enough. Any distance and all the time...nothing stopped us. Twenty-something powerhouses. Neither of us owned a car. One summer we decided to bike from southern Wisconsin to northern Wisconsin and camp the whole way. We didn't know about panniers (bike saddle bags) so we put heavy loaded backpacks on our backs and rode for weeks. It was tornado season and one ripped through our campsite on day five and destroyed our tent while we were huddled in our sleeping bags in the damp smelly turquoise painted cinder block bathroom in the campgrounds. It was not flush toilets, just big pits, and the smell kept us from sleeping. But it was a good thing we were in there because the path of the tornado was easy to follow by the fallen trees and shreds of our tent. It had passed right over the knoll we were set up on. We bought a tarp at some mom and pop store and used that as a makeshift shelter for the rest of the trip. On the way back home, a guy passed us going the other way and he had panniers on his bike that carried his gear. We both stopped in our tracks and watched him with our mouths open and in what seemed like slow motion. It was like we were seeing a mirage. When we turned to each other, we just shook our heads and said, "oh shit". Right then I showed Devon the dents and bruises in my shoulders from carrying the backpack the whole way. We fantasized about getting some saddlebags for our bikes. About a mile further down the road, a panel station wagon filled with kids and their mom and dad pulled over next to us and the father told us there was a tornado coming and we better get off the road. We pulled into the long driveway of the next farm we came to with a plan to ask if we could camp there. We had already experienced the other tornado two weeks before... and we did not want to get pummeled and ripped up. Neither of us had any interest in fucking around with another tornado. We rode up to the farmhouse and when we looked to our right, there was an old guy in overalls peeing in the grass. He kept peeing and smiled and waved to us. We looked the other way and waited. When he got to us, we were greeted with a bright light smile and a huge sausage fingers calloused handshake. This was the meeting of us and Alex Maurer. He became family almost immediately. He was the grandfather neither of us had. He set up a giant canvas tent for us in a field and we ate blueberry bread in his house with him and his wife Alyce until the tornado passed. He was retired CIA and was so old and sick now that he couldn't even sleep at night. He used the awake time reading stacks of books and in the coming years taught us everything from the iChing to real-world history. He and Howard Zinn would have been great buddies if they had met. He wrote long detailed letters each night and sent them to me while I was at the university. His barn was full of wacky auction items like antique dental office chairs and tools and multiple tractors. Turns out Alex was a little addicted to going to auctions. I have small regrets and big regrets. One of the big regrets is that I didn't save the hundreds of letters he wrote me. They were treasures. But, I am so unsentimental that I didn't save even one of them.

Life was rich with Devon. He was the smartest funniest person I ever met. He could make me pee my pants laughing on a daily basis. One time he had me laughing on the streets of Madison for so long that I just gave up....I was on the ground soaked in my own pee laughing til my sides ached. We couldn't stop ourselves. Our connection was pure joy. Lucky for Devon, he could laugh hard without peeing his pants.

One day Devon's mother, Ann Marie, asked me over for coffee. She took a long drag off her red lipstick stained cigarette and begged me to marry Devon so he wouldn't go to hell. She was very Catholic. When I told Devon that his mom proposed to me, we figured "Why not?" since we assumed we would be friends and lovers forever anyway. When we told my parents, they begged us not to get married. "Live together, even have kids if you want to, but don't get married....please." This was the exact opposite of Devon's parents.

A few months before we got married, we were offered a job as live-in caretakers at the Jewish temple. The same one I had spent my childhood attending. The same one that my father was president of. We would get an apartment in the basement of the temple and a small stipend. We would also get extra pay for any large events. Our jobs were to keep the giant old stone building clean and to set up the tables and place settings for any events. Every Friday our job was to set up for the "Oneg Shabbat" (the social that took place after every Shabbat service.) Living in the temple meant that everyone thought that we were on duty 24/7. They also all thought they were person-

ally our boss. They would either knock on our door or walk right in for anything they wanted to ask for. It was often small things. "There is a fork missing on the table settings." "There is a stained napkin on one of the tables." "25 more people are coming, can you set up another table?" Sometimes it was big stuff. "There is no hot water." "The toilet in the men's bathroom is clogged and has flooded the bathroom and hallway."
The job was strange from the very beginning. When they offered us the job, they told us that they first had to get rid of the guy, Gene, who was currently holding the job. He was not doing any of the work and had sort of riff-raff shady stuff going on with the apartment as his base. It took a team of temple member lawyers to get the guy out. Before he left, Gene trashed his own stuff and took photos and sued me and Devon claiming we had broken in and destroyed his place. He was pissed that we were taking his place. We waited months for the trial that he never actually showed up for. During those months Gene would pull his big Lincoln up to the windows of our basement apartment and shine his brights in our bedroom at all hours of the night. Each day he would follow me when I biked to work...driving real slow and close to my bike. He would call our landline and hang up the phone all day and night. We were freaked out by it. The guy was such a predator. We called him Mean Gene. One day, a year later, we got a call. It was our friend Bill. Bill said, "Who is your worst enemy?" We couldn't think of an enemy. Then he told us that Gene did a bad drug deal with a Turkish gang in town and they burned down his house and beat him so bad he was in the hospital. Bill sniggered, "Karma, right?"
Yep, karma.

Once that creep was out of our lives we settled into temple life. Devon set up a darkroom in one of the temple closets and I set up a batik studio in another one...mine had a little window, his didn't. It was perfect. The temple had a music room with a piano in the basement, just down the hall from our apartment. We loved playing in the music room when no one else was using the temple for any events or services. In yet another unused basement closet we grew our own gourmet mushrooms in bags of manure. The mushrooms were so prolific that we were giving away pounds of them every week. Devon was able to do his photography and his other art and still take care of the temple. We had a good gig with lots of freedom. After a lot of hilarious trial and error, we learned to use the enormous floor buffer without having it whip us into the wall or drag us in the wrong direction. The temple had replaced the not-nice rabbi, Rabbi Rosen, with a new younger guy with a family. Rabbi Adelberg was a soft spoken pretty shy guy. With the congregation leaders he was definitely a "Yes" man. He didn't have a sense of humor. You really have to have a sense of humor if you are going to work in a synagogue and it would have helped me and Devon be more comfortable with him. So we tried to be on our best behavior around him. In a way he seemed like another one of our bosses.

We got married in a small civil ceremony at my parent's house with only our parents and siblings, and Alex and Alyce Maurer. After that, we had a giant party in the hall at the synagogue. It was free for us because we worked there. The only catch was that, since we were the custodians, we would have to do all the setup and then clean up after our own wedding. We made all the food for the wedding in advance and froze everything from 500 felafel balls to buckets of refried beans. The big vegetarian feast was heated up and served by caterers who charged us a fraction of what it would have cost to have them do the whole thing with the food included. There was plenty of refereeing to do between his parents and mine before the big day. Mine insisted on champagne and his insisted on beer kegs. Mine insisted no beer kegs and his insisted on having them in the center of the giant hall. Mine wanted smoked fish because you couldn't have people travel all that distance for a wedding that didn't reward them with meat or fish. His parents begged for bratwurst for the same reason. The biggest expense was hiring our favorite band, Big City Bob and the Ballroom Gliders. They had a bubble machine and played music like R. Crumb and His Cheap Suit Serenaders. Have you ever heard that group?"

"I have never heard of them, but it sounds totally fun. I will look them up and listen."

"You are probably too young to know the same bands as me. Well, that and you growing up in Sweden. Devon and I loved dancing and planned to do nothing else through the whole celebration. Lazer kept coming out to the dance floor and yelling at me to go greet the guests. I kept telling him that anyone who wanted to talk to me had to come out and dance. He was enraged. Following Devon and I around the dance floor yelling, "Get your ass off this dance floor and go say hello to your aunts and cousins!" I yelled back, "It is MY wedding, you get YOUR ass off the dance floor!"

Looking back, I understand that he was just trying to get me to do the right thing and it makes sense from my current perspective....but I never responded to someone yelling or telling me what to do in a nasty way. So, his methods didn't work.

As my sister says to me now that we are old adults ourselves, "Dad would say 'jump' and Ronny and I would ask 'how high?'... you would say, 'I am not jumping for you, I could never jump high enough to satisfy you anyway.'"

After the wedding party, Devon and I and a few relatives worked for hours cleaning up the hall and doing dishes. Hmmm, this must be a theme in my life because when I got married decades later, in my fifties, I was doing the wedding dishes in my wedding dress for hours with the help of a few friends.

At some point in that short career, we grew weary of the many synagogue bosses. Hundreds of Jewish women telling us what to do. Just imagine. All of them determined to have us do things their 100 different ways. We were both frustrated.

There was a huge sale in the basement banquet hall of the temple (the same one we got married in) to raise money for Hadassah which is a Jewish women's organization. The ladies called it the Country Sale. Some was used junk and some was valuable stuff. The community came and they raised a lot of money, but there were truckloads of unsold leftover items that they wanted us to sort through and deal with. It was overwhelming. We were already frustrated with them and now this. On one of the tables, there were two stacks of yellow ceramic dishes. About 30 dishes per stack. Devon picked one up and frisbeed it across the giant hall. It crashed and broke into shards and Devon got giddy. Then I grabbed one, flung it, and felt the same exhilaration and tension release. We couldn't stop flinging them across the hall and celebrating each crash. Then, the unthinkable happened. We heard footsteps coming quickly down the staircase toward the hall. We froze. Shit, we thought we were alone in the building. The Rabbi appeared at the bottom of the stairs and shouted, "What is going on here!?" I told him, "I am so sorry. We are just getting our frustrations out. It isn't easy having a hundred Jewish ladies who all think they are our boss."

He walked over to us and the remaining stacks of plates. We expected the worst. I assumed he was going to tell the board and get us fired. Instead, he picked up one of the plates and turned to us as he frisbeed it across the hall, "Remember, I have the same bosses!" The three of us were laughing crazy hysterical and tossed the plates until every single one was part of the pile at the other end of the hall. Then all three of us sat on the floor, all relaxed and self-satisfied. The Rabbi was still laughing, but softly now. He gave us each a hug and whispered, "Thank you, I really needed that", then headed back up the stairs to his office.

Devon and I looked at each other with big happy disbelief faces.

He was definitely our kind of Rabbi. Who knew that was going to happen? Our cat, Gingko, escaped from the apartment once and left a big shit on the pulpit three floors up. On Shabbat!! This might have made most rabbis angry. I mean, this giant pile of cat turds was between the place the rabbi stands and the revered place they keep the Torah! The Rabbi told us about it with no anger, just laughter."

KARINA

Lu and I walked to the canoe with the three dogs. We brought some of her homemade apricot jam and homemade dog biscuits to give to Elan and Winnie. Somehow Lu's dogs knew they were coming with us and they hopped into the canoe that was tied to the dock. Other times they just sat on the dock and watched us leave, but this time they really knew. We all piled in the truck to drive the couple miles to Winnie's place. A short tree-lined driveway took us to the house. It was on the opposite side of the river from Lu's and that meant no paddling across. The dogs leaped over my lap to get out the second I opened the truck door. Two other dogs raced over to greet them. It was a pure delight dog party. Lu and I were laughing at the dogs and I was glad for the distraction. I was so nervous to see Elan again. While we were in the yard laughing at the dogs, Elan came over to us with three goats following him. We hugged and he introduced me to the goats and the dogs. The dogs, Honey and Scooter had been rescued from a horrible situation where they were tied to trees in an apple orchard. No food or water for years. They had just been living on rotten apples for at least three years. The goats had been rescued from an abuse and neglect situation. Elan told the story of going to get them and seeing their faces in the top of a two-story building. He thought they had gotten up the stairs of the building and were standing on a floor. It turns out they were locked into the place and they were standing on a mountain of feces that was tall enough for them to be staring out the second story windows, there was no second floor. Elan had tears and was holding his hands on the goat's backs while he was telling me the story. They had all been very sick and emaciated and the three who survived had been eating the bodies of the dead goats and eating feces. When he brought them home one of them had her first poo and it was nylon rope that she had eaten. Elan sort of shook his head to shake the memory and said, "I shouldn't welcome you here with that story, I'm sorry. They are here now and we love them like family. They follow me everywhere." Then he gave me another hug and said, "I am so happy you are here. Come on, I will show you around. Dinner is in the oven." Lu had already gone into the house to see Winnie.

We walked around the beautiful land with the sound of the river rushing as a constant background. It was magical. There are about 20 rescued chickens in their chicken coop. Some had been rescued blind or with missing feet or other issues from their previous situations. There was a donkey named Rosie and a pig named Sully. We finally went into the house as the sun was starting to set and I was blown away by the house. Elan's father had started using the adobe walls as a canvas and every wall was covered in the most incredible artwork. Winnie heard us come in and came right over to hug me. She moved quickly and confidently in her familiar surroundings. I had not seen her move like that in Lu's house. When I mentioned it to Elan, he remembered to tell me not to move anything to a new spot. All the chairs and other furniture spots had been memorized by Winnie.

We ate a totally delicious meal of shepard's pie and fresh homemade bread all made by Elan. Then chocolate mousse which he had made with avocados whipped up with cocoa.

After dinner Lu asked Winnie if she wanted to play music and they both left for a back room with a piano and other instruments. Elan told me they always raced through dinner to go and play music together and that it was Winnie on piano and Lu on flute or vocals. Moments after they had gone to the piano room, there was piano with two beautiful harmonizing voices floating out of there into the kitchen. Elan and I did dishes together and cleaned up, then we went to the back room and sat next to each other in a hammock and watched and listened to those two. Our thighs were touching in the hammock. Even with thick winter pants on, I could feel electricity between our thighs. I couldn't tell if Elan felt it too….After a few songs, Elan got up and picked up a clarinet and joined Winnie and

Lu. They were doing songs that I knew, but I just stayed quiet. After a bit, Lu motioned for me to come join them. I was shy about singing in front of others, but for whatever reason I did it. We actually sounded great together. We were all totally into it and after a few hours, Winnie said she was tired and was heading to bed. She told Lu and I to just stay the night, "Lu, you know where the extra stuff is, make sure Karina is comfortable."
Elan helped Lu and I make up a guest bed and he showed me where towels and other things were. I wondered later where Lu was going to sleep, but I kept forgetting to ask.

Elan asked if I wanted to join him to put all the animals in their shelters for the night and feed the dogs. We did the rounds to the different buildings and came back and fed the dogs who were all exhausted from playing in the snow. They ate and passed out in front of the woodstove. I was petting them while Elan added wood to the fire. Then he took my hand and walked me back to the hammock. We sat in the hammock and talked and laughed and time was pretty much non-existent. Then he put his arms around me and slid me down next to him. I got nervous. He could feel it and asked me, "Are you ok?" I explained that I was scared and that I was not an interesting person with an amazing life and talents like him and Winnie and Lu. "I am just a boring journalist with an apartment and a few friends. I am not like the rest of you. You are creative and unusual and talented and such a different world from mine. I can watch all of you and write about all of you, but I am not interesting like all of you." Elan laughed, "That is crazy talk. You do realize that we are not all that interesting to each other, don't you? We have been talking about how funny it is that you think Lu or any of us are interesting enough to write about. We are so used to ourselves that we seem pretty boring to each other. Don't get me wrong, we totally love getting together and hiking and making music and seeing each other's projects, but we don't think we are story worthy or journalist worthy. I just think you don't see yourself clearly. You don't see your beauty and your specialness. You can't see what we see. When Winnie asked to touch your face after dinner, she could feel every *bit of your beauty. She was obviously blown away by you. You do know that this community is ready to welcome you, right?"*

I couldn't even say anything after that. I breathed in the smell of him...a mixture of sage and wood smoke and his smell. We melted with our arms around each other in the hammock. He gave me a gentle kiss on my forehead and we fell asleep wrapped around each other. Lu found us there in the morning. She had a big smile and winked at me. It was just total sweetness.

GET THE JEW OFF THE BUS!

"I keep thinking about you having to deal with the Jew-haters as a kid. And then some as an adult. Did you ever feel like it was finally in the past and people would just see you for who you are and not as the representative of all Jews?"

"I don't think that stuff ever leaves society. I can't imagine it will in my lifetime. People and their stereotypes and hate for groups. My grandma Franny experienced that kind of judgment and hate directed at her for her whole life, but that didn't stop her from hating certain groups of people. Lazer used to want her to watch Martin Luther King Junior whenever he came on the television. He would make her sit with all of us and watch his hero. She hated it. She hated my black friends, too. She would insult them in Yiddish whenever they came over. We would parade past her and the kids were so nice to her. But she would call them "schvartze" and fake spit on the ground. It was the equivalent of her saying "nigger" and she would never have done it in front of Lazer because he would have gone ballistic. My black school friends would ask what she was saying and I would make something up and pretend she was being nice. Grandma Franny died during our synagogue era. She never did like Devon and I have no idea what she thought of me. When she met Devon the first time it was in her apartment in Miami. It was the trip that we had prepped for by buzzing our hair to a quarter inch. Devon and I hitchhiked from Wisconsin to Miami with some Greyhound bus rides mixed in. One of the bus rides, somewhere in the south, I was sitting next to a guy from Chicago. He and I were chatting away, when we realized he lived near where my uncle worked.

"Oh, my uncle works at the liquor store near your place."
"What's your uncle's name?"
"Lefty Horowitz"
(I said this assuming that he would be all excited that we had my uncle in common. Lefty knew everyone and he was a funny guy who made everyone laugh. His right arm had been cut off by machinery in an awful factory accident. But, he even rolled along with that and loved being called Lefty. I was barely in first grade when Lefty took me and my cousin, Lisa, to the basement and taught us to give anyone the middle finger who gave us trouble. I had never seen the middle finger, or any finger, used to communicate something. Oh, I guess I knew about thumbs up, but that was about it. While he was teaching this important communication tool to me and my cousin, his wife, Maxine, busted us and told him to cut it out and made us go back upstairs.)
Anyway, the Chicago guy on the bus turned right toward me, but leaned his body away, "Lefty, the Jew?"
"Uhhh, yes, he is Jewish"
"Well, that means you are a god damned Jew! I am a proud member of the Nazi party. So get your Jew ass off this bus. Driver, get this Jew off the bus! She is stinking up the whole bus with her Jew stink."
The guy went completely bonkers, "Driver, stop the bus now, get the Jew off the bus!! I won't ride on a bus with a Jew!! Stop the bus right now!!"
He was shrieking at the driver and at the same time pushed me out of my seat into the aisle and then wiped his hands on his pants. The passengers were me, Devon, the Nazi guy and all the others, who were all African American. I looked for an empty seat somewhere and there were none. Devon was way back in the bus and I was on my way back there when an older black

woman moved over in her seat and had me sit with her with our butts squished together. She put her arm around me and kept gently patting my arm with her right arm and my chest with her left hand. The Nazi kept screaming at the driver to pull over and get me off the bus and the driver kept nervously looking in the rearview mirror and asking the guy to please stop shouting and to calm down. I just stayed there in the peace of the black woman's arms. Again, in this crazy world it was the blacks who provided comfort.

The Nazi (I never did get his name) couldn't calm down. He was absolutely frantic and crazed.

The black woman kept patting my arm and chest and saying, "Don't worry, you ok. Don't worry, we here for you. Don't worry, just relax."

She was some kind of good medicine angel because I closed my eyes and was able to almost relax in the midst of the Nazi screamathon.

Then, I felt the bus pull off to the side of the road and opened my eyes. I figured the driver was going to ask me to get off the bus. That is about how much faith I had that anyone who wasn't black would stick up for me. Instead, the driver came back to the Nazi and told him to either calm down or get off the bus. I couldn't watch. I closed my eyes again. Then I heard a siren and a state patrol car pulled over in front of the bus. The bus driver opened the door and told the black state patrol officer what was going on. He didn't really have to explain because now the Nazi was screaming and pleading with the state patrol officer to get the smelly Jew off the bus. The state patrol guy surveyed the scene and then walked slowly to the Nazi.

"Sir, please come with me."

He was gently taking the elbow of the Nazi, who would have none of that.

"Get your goddamn filthy nigger hands off me!"

The officer, took his hand off the Nazi's elbow and asked him calmly, "Do you have any luggage in the lower compartment?"

"None of your goddamn business."

"Sir, you are leaving the bus now and if you want your luggage, I need to know where it is."
The driver was waiting by the luggage compartment and I heard it open. The Nazi and the officer walked off the bus with the Nazi yelling and pointing at me, "It is her you should be taking off the bus! Get the Jew off the bus! I am not the one you should be taking off the bus! Get the goddamn smelly Jew, not me." The officer put the Nazi in the patrol car, the bus driver put the Nazi's luggage in the trunk of the squad car and returned to the driver's seat. The driver talked to me while looking up at me through the rearview mirror, "You ok?"
"Yep, I am ok"
We drove off while the Nazi and the officer were still sitting on the side of the road in the patrol car.
There were now two empty seats for me on the bus, but I stayed there with the black woman patting my chest and closed my eyes. Devon moved up to what had been my seat with the Nazi, just to be closer to me. For the next hour, the black woman kept up her mesmerizing comforting and no one spoke in the whole bus. I opened my eyes when we got to our stop in Miami. I thanked the black woman for taking care of me and we hugged for a long time. And I finally got her name. Pearl. I never did forget Pearl and her kind heart. I wish there was some way to thank her again, now, at this age. Other people from the bus hugged me, too. Older black folks who knew what it was liked to be treated like you are some nasty contagious filthy vermin.
Devon and I walked slowly with our backpacks on toward my Grandma Franny's apartment. He asked about what had happened in detail. I told him about the Nazi knowing my uncle Lefty. Then I changed the subject to lighten things up and told Devon about Lefty and my other uncles wanting me to memorize a book of jokes when I was about 8 years old. Lefty knew I was smart enough to memorize it and gave me the little book all wrapped up and said not to tell my mom. I easily memorized all the jokes, but understood none of them. It wasn't until

a year later that I found out it was a book of adult jokes and they thought it was funny to hear a kid say them. At family events, the women would gather in the kitchen and the men would gather in the living room with pipes and cigars. I loved the smoky room best. Lefty would ask me to tell one of the jokes from the book. I would pick one from my head randomly because none of them made any sense to me. I would tell the joke and the guys would howl with laughter. I wish I still remembered them because I could tell you one. I just remember one of the jokes that always made me laugh: "Guy walks into the doctor's office with a frog on his head. The doc asks the guy what he can do for him. The frog says, "get this wart off my ass." There was probably more to it, but that one always stuck with me.

I knew I was a hit with the uncles, but I sure didn't know why. At least a year into this, my Aunt Sophie caught me telling them one of the jokes. She grabbed my hand, scolded the men, brought me to the women in the kitchen, and told me to never tell a joke to my uncles again. I explained that Lefty had given me the little joke book. She told me to throw the book away and forget the jokes. She explained that they were "not nice". Then she looked me straight in the eye, "Never do anything your Uncle Lefty asks you to do. Ok? Promise me?"

I promised.

Devon liked the story about my uncles and it made us laugh and forget the nasty Nazi on the bus for a few moments.

Devon and I camped in some absurd noisy Miami campground under a highway overpass, but went to see my Grandma Franny every day in the city. When we first arrived, she asked Devon if he was Jewish. When he told her he wasn't Jewish, she gave a pthewie pthewie spit toward the ground. It is a thing old Jews do that I think is supposed to either curse someone or ward off the evil in the room. I never figured out which one. I am guessing Pessy would have known for sure since she knew all about warding off evil spirits and curses. But, I think the spitting thing is not so nice because remember it was what Franny did when she insulted my black friends in Yiddish?

Devon and I took Grandma Franny to Jewish delis for lunch a few times during our Florida trip. We should have figured out right away that it was best to bring food to her place rather than take her out the second time. She had intimidated the waiter at Itzie's Deli and pretty much freaked out all the other diners. Franny ordered her favorite, small curd cottage cheese with canned peaches on top. She would say, "I vont de cling peaches", (I am not even sure what cling peaches means). And that is exactly how she ordered it in her thick Russian accent, "I vont a dish of small curd cottage cheese vit cling peaches on top..no large curd, just small." When the bowl arrived, it was large curd cottage cheese and she flipped. Grandma Franny was shouting at the Cuban waiter who barely spoke English and who was trying to move past her flailing hands to grab the dish of offending curd size. He finally, and impressively, got the dish and was heading back to the kitchen, but she was still going off about the curd size. Everyone in the restaurant was staring at us and looked pretty horrified, but she didn't notice a thing.

To me, it seemed like nothing short of a miracle that the waiter re-appeared some time later with the right curd size. She got small curds and cling peaches and without so much as a thank-you, she was slurping it up.

The second day, we took her to Levy's Kosher Deli because I couldn't bear to face the staff at Itzie's after the scene we caused. At Levy's she complained loudly about the small portions. The waiter there avoided our table and we couldn't even get his attention for more water. I gave him a huge tip for his great survival skills and to help with my embarrassment.

After lunch at Levy's, we were shuffling back to her apartment (she wore giant brick sized white orthopedic shoes that made her walk like a slow-motion Frankenstein) when she announced she was going to stop in the grocery for some Postum (not-coffee sort-of coffee made from barley or beets, I can't remember). She was very clear that she wanted to go into the store alone and we should wait outside. You didn't argue with Franny. So we waited in front of the store. I sat on the edge of a huge concrete planter with a massive tree in it. Devon stood next to me. Suddenly, my ass was on fire. A mob of fire ants had decided to go up my shorts and take a million bites out of me. The not-single-file line of waiting ants in the planter was like people waiting to buy a new Harry Potter novel before the bookstore opens. They were anxious and excited consumers. I jumped off the planter and without thinking about who might be watching, I pulled my shorts and undies down to my ankles and Devon and I swept off the ants we could and pulled the embedded ones out of my butt cheeks. This was the scene awaiting Franny when she emerged from the automatic doors of the grocery. She came out to see me with my pants down, in full frontal public pubes show, Devon and I worked furiously to un-ant me. The crowd of people outside the store were watching and laughing or turning away embarrassed, but didn't seem to want to help. Without a word, Franny pretended she didn't know us and did a Frankenstein shuffle beeline toward her apartment.

When we finally finished ant removal, I pulled up my shorts and hobbled, tear-streaked face and burning butt, back to Franny's apartment. She had just gotten in the door with her Postum and was putting in the cupboard. When she turned around toward us, she told us it was time for us to leave Miami. I tried to explain the ants to her. But she had decided our visit had gone on too long. I told her we would leave the next day, but that we would bring her dinner that night. She just shook her head and pushed us out the door and locked it behind us. When we got to her apartment with dinner that night, she must have looked through the peephole and decided not to answer. I had heard her Frankensteining to the door and then nothing, silence. I yelled through the closed door, "Gram, we have Chinese. Let us in." Just silence. I wrote her a note saying it was good to see her, signed it with a heart, and slid it under the door. Still it was silent. We took the carry out Chinese food and sat in the lobby of her apartment building eating with chopsticks and trying not to breathe in the mothball smell coming from the sofa pillows. I think if she had known we had Chinese food from her favorite place, she would have opened the door and told us to give her the food and leave.

The second time Grandma Franny saw Devon, it was when we were going to get married. By then, she had been moved from her apartment in Miami to the Jewish nursing home in Chicago near her boys and their families. Devon had let his red bristly beard grow to his chest. We drove to Chicago to tell her the news of our upcoming marriage. The moment we walked in, she grabbed his red beard, yanking it hard, and shouted, "You are a filthy pig! Get this filthy pig out of my room!" Beards were not her thing. She was married to a clean-shaven barber and was not in the habit of keeping her opinions to herself. I guess the beard reminded her of lice filled hair in the old country.

She did not come to our wedding. I think she had lots of good reasons, but I am sure the top reason was that I was marrying a Goy (non-Jew) and that he had a beard she could only picture swimming with lice.

When she died, I inherited her black and white television. Devon and I actually liked not having a TV, but everyone felt sorry for us like we were deprived of something essential to life. Truth be told, we were anti-TV. On her TV, the picture was crooked and the numbers on the dial didn't correspond to the station numbers. Devon was vehemently opposed to having a TV in our home, even a half-assed one. We agreed to take it up to the roof of the three-story synagogue and throw it to the ground in a rejection ceremony. The thing exploded when it hit the gravel parking lot. We hooped and hollered and danced like fiddlers on the roof.

Our synagogue apartment was in the basement and that meant when the water main broke one autumn, the place filled about halfway up the wall with water. We came home, opened the front door and our shoes came pouring out with the river of brown gritty water. I remember seeing my wooden clogs float by me while I grappled with what was going on. With the water pouring out the front door we went in and found our cat, Mugi, wet and crying on one of the upper window sills. As our furniture started to appear in the receding water, she leaped across it and out the door. It was a month before she returned looking much worse for wear with bloody worn out paws and crusty eyes.

We had renters insurance that replaced everything that could be replaced. They did not give us a check. They actually brought the items to us as they replaced them. Devon had 400 vinyl record albums that had all been ruined along with their covers because of the gritty mucky water. The insurance company had Devon list all the albums. He wrote up the list for them. Three weeks later, the insurance guy appeared at our door with a van load of boxes with brand new records for Devon. Since most of our possessions were from yard sales and thrift stores, there was no replacing most of it. I really didn't care about that stuff. I only cared about Mugi. When she finally returned, life could get back to normal. She was my everything buddy. She hiked, rode in my jacket when I biked and even went cross-country skiing with me.

Devon and I had a smooth easy life with a lot of joy. We hitchhiked all over the country, dressed in wild clothes, worked any jobs we wanted to, and didn't worry about the future.

We didn't own a car or anything of real value. At some point we ended up with an old sewing machine and I was determined to sew us all custom designed and sewn clothes. This is Pessy's forte and not mine. After I made Devon a patchwork shirt that looked like a misshaped costume from a high school play, he politely asked me to please stop making his clothes. He said he felt obligated to wear them, but they always made him feel embarrassed. That was the end of making our clothes, but not the end of my wanting to sew things. I got this bright idea to make a magician's robe out of blue satin. It was a sort of Dumbledore meets Merlin outfit with yellow stars and sparkles all over. I had gotten a magicians starter kit at a yard sale and thought maybe I could become a magician. I sewed a sparkly hat to go with it. I would put on the outfit and practice my tricks for Devon. Then, Devon announced one day that he may have a new job. His new potential boss was going to come for dinner with his wife. I wasn't sure how that would work, having them for dinner in the temple basement with our rickety old table. It was a table I had gotten at a yard sale when I was in elementary school and it was my first refinishing project. That tells you everything you need to know about it. I borrowed a tablecloth from the synagogue collection to cover it up. So this potential boss and his wife come for veggie lasagna and a dessert that Devon made that he called Mayan Sun Temple Cream Lush Delight. I still remember that giant thing with towering layers of cake and frosting and fruit. After dinner, Devon said, "Why don't you do your magic show for Craig and Pam?" I froze for a moment. I had never done the show for anyone but Devon and me. And, on top of that, I knew he wanted to impress these people. It was high anxiety, but I decided to do it. I changed into my magician's robe and hat. For my first trick, I asked Craig to please give me a dollar. I put the dollar into my fist. Inside my fist was a little holder on the end of a long elastic cord. The other end of the cord was attached to the inside of the robe behind my right shoulder. I said my magic words and showed my outstretched hands to Craig. The dollar had mysteriously vanished. What I didn't realize is that I had a rip in my robe under my arm and the dollar was dangling in the holder under my armpit. When the three of them started laughing, I knew something was wrong and spotted the dollar hanging there. I started laughing with them, but unlike the three of them, I couldn't laugh without peeing. I had dropped to the ground laughing and now was peeing all over my satin robe. Devon was looking mortified and was motioning for me to get to the bathroom. I was still laughing so hard I couldn't stand up and I crawled to the bathroom in my pee soaked robe. That was it. End of my sewing stuff, end of my magician hobby, end of his potential new job."

"That is so funny and so sad. It wasn't your fault. Devon asked you to do the show. And I love that your laughter was so big you couldn't stand up or not pee. That is big wonderful laughter. I hope Devon appreciated that on some level."

"Oh he totally appreciated it, just preferred that we were alone when it happened. "

"You and Devon had amazing times. What a unique and magical relationship. Tell me more about you two."

" Well, this is a memory I will never forget. One winter we drove his dad's panel station wagon to the farthest reaches of northern Wisconsin. I don't remember where we were going or why we borrowed the car. Must have been some adventure we thought up. It was well below zero with a howling wind and snow deeper than the top of the car. There were walls of white we were driving through where the snow had been plowed up high. We got to the area that was just forest, no homes. It was called Chequamegon National Forest. At some point on the road that had so much snow the front bumper was pushing it like a snow plow, the car just stopped. It was already dark out. Everything got very quiet. Just a deep low "shit" came out of Devon's mouth. He kept turning the key in the ignition. Nothing. The first few times a little cough, but then absolutely nothing. He wrapped his arms around me and whispered "This is it."
-"What do you mean by "it"?"
-"We will either freeze here in the car or freeze walking the road, but we will not live either way. We are about 30 miles from the last house I saw."
I couldn't say a word. My mind was racing with what we could do and then it would jump to wanting to be peaceful about

dying and being happy I would be with my favorite person in the world when I died. I could feel the temperature already dropping in the car. I thought about Devon's mom and how her life would be over if Devon was dead. He was the light of her life. Then I thought about how weird it was that I couldn't picture Lazer or Pessy being sad about my being gone. I stopped thinking about my family after that. Then I remembered Bud and Blossom. Remember them? The couple who had stayed with me and told me if I ever needed anything to just think of them and they would take care of me. It had been a year before and I hadn't used that offer. I somehow thought it had to be something really important to ask for help. I got all quiet inside and pictured Bud and Blossom. My toes and fingers were frozen and I had to concentrate on connecting to Bud and Blossom and not on the painful numbness. At some point I felt warmth coming back to my toes and I turned to Devon.
"Devon, try starting the car."
-"It is pointless, the car is dead and now it is cold and dead."
-"Devon, please just try one more time."
Devon reached for the key in the ignition and turned it. It was trying to start. After a few pumps on the gas pedal, it turned over and the car was running. Devon quickly did a U turn and drove as fast as he could through our old tracks. I was smiling and feeling filled with gratitude for Bud and Blossom. It was one of my first direct experiences of things beyond our knowledge happening in the world...the power of our thoughts and connections. After about a half hour we could see the lights of a house in the distance. We had made it the 30 miles back to that place. We both pointed toward it and at that moment the car died again.
We trudged through the snow to the small house. The couple who answered the door were both smoking cigarettes. They coughed pretty constantly and the short haired wife's voice was a deep smoker voice so you couldn't tell if she was a man or woman at first. They let us stay there overnight on their orange flowered sofa. Her name was Lee, which I imagined

only added to the gender confusion when she was out in the world. In the morning the car was towed to a garage with us in the tow truck smelling like cigarette smoke and cooked bacon from our night and morning at Lee and Carl's. They had asked if we wanted breakfast while Carl was frying up the bacon. I explained that we were vegetarian and they looked at each other like I had said we were from another planet. Carl asked if we could eat toast and gave us each a piece of white bread toast without the lard spread on it. At the mechanic's garage, we found out the engine block had cracked. The mechanic couldn't understand why it started up and made it the 30 miles back. It was then that Devon finally asked me why I had asked him to try again. And it was then that I told him about Bud and Blossom.

I figured my magical life with Devon would go on forever, but it came to a screeching painful end when my insecurities met his attraction to another woman. I remember the moment it all broke apart. Devon was watering plants on the high window sills of our basement apartment. He had been acting strange for about a month. His back was to me. I asked him, "Is there something wrong? You seem different this past month." He said quietly, " I really like Lesley." I was confused. I said, "I really like Lesley, too." She was a friend of ours and I knew we both liked her. Then silence. I asked, "Oh, do you love Lesley? Do you want to be with her?" His back was still to me and he kept watering plants. "Yes, I think so." I couldn't bear it. He told me that he was attracted to her because she was intelligent and he was tired of always being the teacher in our relationship. I couldn't argue with that part. I was not the smartest and had little experience with textbook learning. I would have had limited categories I would excel at on Jeopardy. My best categories would have been food, Motown stars, bicycle parts and repair, trees, dumpster-diving and...hmmm, maybe that was it.

I could not imagine life without Devon and I did not want to stay around there and stew in the pain of it. I begged him to talk to me about it all, but he said he couldn't. After reacting by sobbing and throwing breakable things against the wall of our synagogue apartment, I started planning my escape. I called my boss. I was the art teacher at a private school a few blocks from our apartment. When I reached the headmaster, she told me not to worry, when I came back, my job would be waiting for me. I was so sad because I would miss the kids. This would just add more pain to having to leave. When I tried to figure out where to go, the first thing that popped into my head was "Taos, New Mexico". A friend who was in my international folk dancing group had once told me I would love it there. I got out the atlas and looked at where it was. I packed my backpack and Mugi the cat and left. It was the 70s and hitching was still part of life for a lot of us. OK, enough of me talking for today. Getting to Taos is a long story. Let's do it tomorrow. I have to go check on something in town. I got a call this morning about some fish in a tank. Being the "animal person" in this area means I get some weird calls. This person called and said, "Go check on the fish at this address, but be careful. She said the address and then hung up. Anyway, I am going to drive down there and see what is going on. I will see you later."

KARINA

Just after we finished our session today, Lu's landline rang. She called upstairs for me, "Karina, the phone is for you, its Elan." And like clockwork, there were the stomach butterflies again. I came downstairs and took the phone from Lu. Elan sounded less calm than usual. He reminded me that we had talked about me getting the rental car back to Albuquerque so I wouldn't keep paying to just have it sit there being useless. "Today is a good day to drive it up the driveway since everything is dry and the ice is gone. I have to be in Albuquerque, so I can pick you up at the airport after you drop it off. A semi-truck filled with sheep headed to slaughter was in a huge accident in Albuquerque. I got a call this morning. They were going to just kill the two surviving sheep....the rest were killed in the crash. Over 50 of them died in what must have been absolute terror. Anyway, I told the rescue folks to get the wounded ones to the vet and I have to go and get them there today and hopefully they will be ok. I know I sound a little rushed. Just have a lot to tell you. Can you be ready to leave there in less than an hour?" I told him I would just drive to the airport and I would have phone reception once I drove out of the gorge and we could just coordinate him picking me up. I told him to just go straight to the sheep right away and he seemed grateful.

I talked to Lu and she said just go and take the canoe across to the car. She was planning to be home all day and wouldn't need the canoe on her side of the river.

After easily getting the rental car up the hill, I drove to the airport and called Elan. While I waited for him to come and pick me up, I listened to 19 voicemails. It had been two weeks and my boss and friends were getting concerned. I called my boss and gave her Lu's landline for emergencies only. I let her know I still didn't know when I would be back. I called a few friends and told them not to worry about me, that I was doing great. I should have emailed them with an update, but there was way too much to share. And, I am not sure I have the words yet to describe what is happening in my life.

When Elan pulled up, I looked for the two sheep in the back of the truck, but they weren't there. I climbed into the cab and there in the back seat of the cab were two skinny sheep wrapped up in blankets. Elan said they needed to be kept warm. He seemed so relieved to have them in his care.

On the two hour drive back to Lu's, Elan turned my world upside down, again. He told me that his neighbors, two properties over from him, were leaving for California for two to four years. One was going to go back to school there and the other one had a job offer for a building project. They needed someone to stay at their house and just be there for security. They had someone all set to be there who just had to back out last minute because of a family emergency. The housesitter would just pay utilities and if that person wanted to use their truck for the two or more years, they could pay the insurance. Elan told me it was a wonderful well-built house right on the river with fruit trees and easy access from the road. He recommended me to his neighbors. I was getting tingling skin all over my whole body. Excitement mixed with panic. Elan kept going with his idea. He said he had talked to Lu because the housesit would not start for two more weeks and he wanted to make sure Lu was ok with me sticking around for that long. Apparently she was more than happy to have me stay longer. Elan was so excited for me because all the pieces were coming together. I would have a vehicle and a home that would cost very little.
I told Elan that it seemed perfect and I was so grateful he put in the good word for me, but I would have to think about it. It would be a huge change for me and a major decision I couldn't take lightly. The house part would be taken care of, but my work is in Scranton. I had

pushed so hard to get into the media world in the USA and my job was a dream job in so many ways. I realized right then that I hadn't totally let go of that part of my life yet. I'm not sure I ever could.

He said he understood my not wanting to give up my work and needing to really think about this. About 10 minutes before we would have reached Lu's turn off, Elan said, "Before I drop you off at Lu's do you want to visit Andrew and Celeste's place? You could meet them and have a look at it, but no commitment to taking the housesitting. You would just have more information about it all. Would that work for you? I am not pressuring you to do this. It has to feel right."

I figured there was no harm in just checking their place out. So we drove to the road to Elan and Winnie's and then just past their place to Andrew and Celeste's driveway. It is winter here, so the archways we drove under that were usually covered in flowers were brown and dormant....and still, the drive in was like a fairy land. It was so perfect. Again, I got the skin tingle and I couldn't stop smiling. Andrew and Celeste greeted us at the walkway gate. They were beaming when they saw Elan. Elan showed them the sheep in the back of the cab. The entire drive, the two sheep had just slept and didn't make a peep. We all hugged and went into the house. I can't describe it any other way...it was home. Like home with a capital H, like nowhere else had ever been. We didn't stay long because Elan was worried about getting the sheep home and settled, but I didn't want to leave. Before we left, without thinking, I told Celeste and Andrew I would be happy to take care of their place while they were gone. I could tell Elan was excited about me saying I would stay, but he tried to hide it from all three of us. I will have to work out so many details. I am not sure what I have done. All I know is that it feels right. It feels right in my whole body and some other part of me that is not my planning brain. Is that my heart? Not even sure what that means... making a decision from my heart not my head. But I think that is what I did today.

SURPRISE FLIGHT

"Lu, we ended our last session with you remembering Taos, New Mexico when someone in your folk dancing group happened to mention you would like it there. Your relationship with Devon was blowing up and it sounds like New Mexico was offering you a lifeline....is that true?"

"Absolutely. It was all I could focus on in my pain. Within a day of finding out about Devon and Lesley, I hitchhiked from Wisconsin to New Mexico. Back then I was unwilling to hang out in any painful situation. I know those painful things can be powerful teachers if you are willing to sit with them, but I wasn't there yet in my life. So at 2 am on a Saturday I arrived in the Taos area. I had my last ride drop me off at a field outside of town. It's always easier to get to a new place in the daylight. I rolled out my sleeping bag and Mugi and I climbed in and slept. In the morning we walked into town. It smelled like what I would later learn was burning piñon wood. To me, it smelled like something I wanted to be surrounded by for the rest of my life. I noticed you comment on it, too, when you stop and breathe in that smell. Then, I saw a sign for a Sufi Dancing group meeting that morning at 10. I had never heard of Sufi anything, but I loved dancing, so I found the building and went in.

Mugi slept in the corner of the big hall on my sleeping bag while I did the strange Sufi dance routines with the other people. If you've never done that Sufi dancing...it goes like this: You sort of chant these sweet little phrases and the circle goes around and around and you look in the eyes of each person and sometimes you do hand motions like putting your hand on their heart. You know it is a little woo woo for someone like me, but it felt good anyway and it was part of my new adventure in a new place. Doing things out of my comfort zone. I only remember one of the chants. *May the blessings of god rest upon you, may his peace abide in you, may his presence illuminate your heart...now and forever more.* I am not a god person or a blessings person, but it really did feel like a heart opening thing to do. Haven't done it since, though.

After dancing, we sat in a circle and people made announcements. One couple announced that they were going to school in Santa Cruz and needed a house-sitter for a few years. Without hesitation, I blurted out, "I can do that!" That is part of what is so weird with you getting the housesitting for Andrew and Celeste. It is eerily like history repeating itself. Mine was in Taos and yours is here, but still the parallels are there.

Anyway, during the community announcements at the end, a guy named Robert says that the Millicent Rogers Museum needed someone who could lead tours and work on exhibits. He was the person doing the hiring. Turns out he was the director of the museum.

Again, no hesitation on my part, "I would LOVE to do that!"

By Monday I had a home and a job. This is really the New Mexico magic. It either pulls you right in or it spits you out fast. New Mexico is not for everyone. Two people can visit and one sees a brown dry dustbowl and the other one sees paradise. I saw paradise.

It seems to be pulling you right in, too. Things are lining up for you so quickly."

"I know. Honestly, Lu, it is freaking me out a bit. And I am a bit high with the excitement of it. My life had gotten predictable, but calm, out east. I feel like a chapter of my life is over and a new, completely unfamiliar, but totally exhilarating part of my life is beginning. It is pretty intense for me. I am terrified and excited mixed together in some strange internal recipe. I need to figure out the work thing

and how to deal with my apartment and my housemate there. I just have a feeling it will all come together...and that is SO not like me."

"Yep, it will all decide itself. Feels like there is not much you need to do. Any big effort on your part will probably just get in the way. I am loving watching you opening up to new possibilities. And, Winnie called me and was telling me that Elan is happier than he has been for a long time. He is always a content and pretty happy positive guy, but he gave up a lot to come and live with his mom. She is loving seeing him excited about something. And, wherever things go with you two, it is pretty sweet to watch you connecting with each other, even if you will just be good friends."

"I have no idea where it is going with Elan, but it is waking up something in me that I didn't even know was in there sleeping. I was just doing my day to day life and not thinking that there could be something more. I was just focused on my work. But, it also makes me think about listening to tugs, pulls to do things. I was being so strongly pulled to do the interviews with you. It was like coming out here was something I just had to do that I couldn't explain to anyone, not even myself. Not sure why it took me years to follow up on it, but maybe that had to happen, too. I guess there are no mistakes in it all. The timing had to be what it is."

"I agree totally. If you had come years earlier, Elan would have still been up in Taos and Andrew and Celeste wouldn't even be living up the road. Things would have been very different."

"Yep, I see that. Whew, what a wild ride this life on Earth is. OK, back to you. So, there you are in Taos with your cat. What was life like for you there?"

"It all happened fast. I arrived on a Saturday, got a job and house on Monday and by Tuesday, I was hitchhiking down the road and 4 pick-up trucks pulled over. They were filled with women in the truck cabs and enormous hairy dogs and toboggans in the back of the trucks. The woman driving the first truck rolled down the window and asked if I wanted to go sledding in the mountains. I went for it. This was beyond sledding. It was flirting with death. These mountains were meant for skiing and not tobogganing as far as I could tell. We can take a day trip up to Taos and you will see what I mean. This is the southern tip of the Rockies and up there you can really see it…those are serious mountains.

There were about 10 women and maybe 12 dogs. The happy dogs pulled the toboggans back up the mountain and we trudged in the deep snow next to them. Then we would fly down the deep snow for long runs. If I think about it, I am not sure why none of us crashed into a tree or got hurt that day. When we took a break they told me they had a lesbian theatre group and asked if I wanted to join it. I told them I wasn't a lesbian. You know what they said then? "You can be our token hetero!!"

I joined the Magic Mirror Players right then and there.

What we all soon discovered is that I couldn't act, so I was given all non-speaking parts and always the ones that required wearing a dress or girly uniform like a nurse's outfit. They told me to get tap shoes and taught me to Shuffle Off To Buffalo and other great tap moves for one of our plays. I loved these women and I still have tap dancing skills in my repertoire if I ever need them! We mostly got along great and my heteroness didn't bother them except one time. One evening I arrived for practice on the back of Frank's horse. He was a guy I met in town and we were friends. Frank was in front of me on the horse and we rode up through the snow with me holding my arms around his waist. Vern was sort of the alpha of the theater group and she was frowning when I walked into the practice space. She crossed her arms on her chest and everyone got real quiet.

"What are you doing with Frank?"
"I'm just hanging out with him, why?"
"He is trouble, that's why."

"He doesn't seem like trouble to me. And we are just friends, nothing more."

"He will use you."

"Use me how?"

"Probably make you fall in love and then have his way with you and then move on to someone else."

"Vern, no worries, I am more likely to be the one who does that to him and bolts first. I am a bolter"

"Well, just be careful. You really need to try women. Frank is not someone you want to get close to. You using protection?"

"Yep, got it all covered, don't worry about me. And, I have no intention of having sex with Frank. Not my type."

"Well I guess this is what we have to deal with if we are going to have a token hetero. But, you just say the word and I know a couple of us who would be willing to train you in the ways of women."

Looking back, I wish I had taken Vern up on that offer. I didn't know about being with women back then. I didn't even know about myself. Had never given myself a flight and sure didn't know how I would give another woman one. It was years before I had a relationship with a woman. There was so much that was more a fit for me with women.

I was 23 before I accidentally learned that I could give myself a flight, an orgasm. I know some very young children who discover how to give themselves flights. I was not one of those young body explorers. My body was foreign territory to me. Anyway, it was a weeknight and I lived in a coop house. Five men and women sharing a house in Minneapolis. I had just come home from work and everyone was making dinner. I had forgotten that we were interviewing a young woman who wanted to live with us and she was coming for dinner. I was upstairs taking a bath and using the cheap rubber hand-held sprayer that attached to the faucet. The end of it popped off and I was using the hose with a strong warm stream of water coming out of it. When I was rinsing between my legs, it started to feel too good. Next thing I knew, I had given myself the best flight ever. I could not have been more excited. It was a life changer. I pulled a towel around my waist and ran soaking wet downstairs shouting "I did it! I don't need guys anymore! I gave myself a flight!" We were all so close and knew everything about each other in that house, so I thought nothing of it. When I got to the bottom of the stairs everyone was looking up from the dinner table real quiet. It was then that I noticed little blonde Marcie. She was looking at me bug eyed from the table. My housemates gave me a stink-eye that made me turn on my heels and race up the stairs to get dressed. I joined everyone for dinner, but there was no discussion of my triumph over my pleasure button. After Marcie left, the housemates filled me in on what I missed. Marcie was a very sheltered born again Christian. It was pretty unlikely she would be joining our little family after my display. But, to everyone's shock, she called the next day and wanted to move in. Marcie went from Christian to Pagan within a month of living with us. Guess she had just been waiting for another option to show up. My appearance and orgasm announcement might have been what sealed the deal for her! That cheap little hose became a best friend. I even took it when I was traveling. I remember going to Northern California with my friend Yvonne to go to a wedding of a close friend of hers. I packed the hose in my backpack. We stayed with Yvonne's sister. Her sister was in a lesbian trapeze troupe, called Fly By Night, that performed at concerts before the musicians came on. They lived on this beautiful Sonoma County property and there was a trapeze studio and a music studio where some of the best women's music was recorded. Chris Williamson and Tret Fure recorded there and lived there part of the year. You have probably never heard of them. You ought to look them up. They were pioneers in feminist womens music. It was so popular back then. Anyway, all these lesbians just loved that I traveled with my little hose. I think they all wanted to teach me how to get the same results without the hose, but I never took any of them up on that. I do remember feeling so free there that I took a long walk down the road without my shirt on and they had to give me a good talking to. Their neighbors were already just tolerating their unusual lifestyle, and I was not helping their relations with them."

"I love that you traveled with the little hose. I wonder why you weren't more comfortable with your body and why it took you so long to give yourself pleasure. Oh well, at least you figured it out. Back to Devon and New Mexico. Was there any part of you that wanted to really work on getting back together?"

"I was not mature in my twenties. If I had been, I would have jumped on the opportunity to reconnect with Devon, leave New Mexico and go home to Wisconsin and work things out. Instead, when he came to New Mexico to talk me into coming back home, I left him alone at my place and went and had sex with a beautiful one-legged Latino guy named Daniel who I had the hots for. Should I share how he lost his leg or is that too much information?"

"Oh definitely NOT too much information. I don't think anything is."

"Ok, I will share it. A month before Daniel lost his leg, he was at a crystal healing woman's studio. She ran a crystal pendulum over him while he was on a massage table. She told him that he needed to be very careful about his left leg. He asked why. She told him it was in danger. A month later, on a hot summer day, he was in the backseat of a friend's car cruising down the highway. He had both his legs hanging out the window of the car and was on his back cooling off. A Trailways bus passed them and sideswiped the car and took his left leg right off."

"Oh shit, that is too much. Just took his leg right off?"

"Yep. He had a stump on the left side and wore a prosthetic leg that he strapped on over a silk sock on the stump. Thinking back on it, I am guessing I was just trying to torture Devon. And I was in so much pain about how our relationship ended that I couldn't open up to him again. I remember him putting his hand on my arm when he came to New Mexico and I couldn't feel it. I mean physically I couldn't feel his hand. That is how protected I was from opening up to him again.

I can't tell you how often I have looked back wishing I had done things differently. I just didn't know that there would never be another relationship like me and Devon. There never was. That relationship raised the bar so high and no one else ever came close to it. Ever. Here I am in my sixties, and still, nothing has come close."

"Did you ever find someone who you wanted to be with for life after that? Even if they weren't another magical Devon, did anyone come close?"

"I have never really thought about that. I am guessing not. I think if someone had come along who was even close to what Devon and I had, I would have stayed put. Instead, I have tried on more relationships than I can even remember. Remember the other day I told you about trying to list all the people I have had sex with? I really did try to make a list. I was almost 60 years old when I tried to do this. After two full pages of handwritten names, I just broke down and cried. I realized for the first time that I had been a sex addict all of my adult life. I also realized how little self awareness I have. It is sex that got me into each relationship, not a mindful exploration of what I had in common with the person. Even the marriage I am in now. Sex drew me in and even though we have a common values system, we are not ideal for each other in many ways. Our daily passions are not matched well. And, I got married before realizing that I am such an introvert, I am happiest being alone. So living with another person full-time doesn't really work for me. I keep craving quiet and alone time. He is retired so he is not even going to work. We found an arrangement and a way to work it out that is comfortable for us and I am guessing, at this age, we will be together for the rest of our lives. And I am totally content with that."

"Lu, what the hell? You are married? How did I not know this?"

"It just hasn't come up yet I guess.."

"Wait wait wait…that is crazy. Where is he? Where is his stuff? I don't see any sign of another person living here."

"Right now, he is in Africa traveling with a friend for two months. He isn't living here anymore because he wanted more city life, more connection with people and he started to hate the paddle across the river every time he wanted to go somewhere. He has a condo in Santa Fe and we see each other a lot in the nicer months, but he gets the hell out of New Mexico in the winter. Since you will be living at Celeste and Andrew's place, you will meet him when he comes back in a month. You will like him. His name is Ben. He is a gentle, quiet person. Passionate about animal rights and all social justice issues. That is what brought us together. We were both speaking at a conference and I wanted sex with him and he refused to have sex with me. He wanted a real relationship. I fought it for a while. I thought we were too different. And I just wanted a no-commitment thing. Then on a whim, during a road trip, when we were talking about who would make each other's medical decisions if something happened, we parked in front of a town hall in Maine and got married."

"I am pretty shocked that this never came up before. Wow. OK, more on that later. Lets get back to that sex addiction and the list of names you wrote out. Two pages of handwritten names is a lot of people. Did you ever question what you were doing or try to get help?"

"I didn't question it because it was so unconscious. I never really looked at it closely until I was in my late fifties. Maybe everyone has things that they do to run from the pain of life, but some people are better at catching the unhealthy things and nipping them in the bud and changing course. I couldn't even see what I was doing, so I never sought help. It was just too normal for me. I think other people tried to point it out to me occasionally. Some more subtly than others. When I was first in Taos, I was walking through the pueblo where the Native American population live in a beautiful adobe village. As I was passing an open door, an ancient looking native woman caught my eye and waggled her finger for me to come in. The place was empty except for her sitting on a stool and another little wooden stool. She told me to sit down. I sat on the stool and she looked at me straight in the eyes. She was silent for at least a minute. Which is a long time to sit silent with someone you don't know staring in each other's eyes. Then very firmly she said, "Stop having sex with so many people. The spirit of everyone you have sex with stays inside you for at least seven years. You have too many spirits inside you. It is chaos in you. Quiet your life down. Face your demons. You cannot do that when you keep having sex with everyone."

I was about to ask her how she knew that about me, when she said, "Don't ask me how I know about you. Just go now and do what I say. Stop having sex with everyone you are attracted to. It will ruin your life."

So I just left. A little dazed for sure. And I could feel the crossroads I was at. I could really hear what she said and take it seriously or I could blow it off and continue my destructive ways. It gave me a headache because I think it was my old habitual ways battling with healthy wisdom. Sadly my old habitual ways won and I didn't change my pattern at all."

"I just have to say that nothing like that has ever happened to me. Strangers just telling you things. I don't think I am that approach-

able. You attract such incredible experiences. I wonder what brings those things to your life."

"I have no idea. Maybe it is just carelessness. You are probably more careful. And not all of the experiences are good. They are big Technicolor things, but not always easy or comfortable or safe. And maybe that is changing in your life. You are definitely approachable, you are just more subtle. I like that. I wouldn't have you staying here this long if you were like me. I am a bit too much for even myself sometimes.

The unplanned stuff can put me into situations that last a moment or last for years. The relationships stuff is some of my biggest mistakes and then there are little oops moments sprinkled throughout my life.

When I was biking the long distance back from the Pueblo to my place, I had time to mull over some of the relationships that were a mistake, that I hung with until something better came along. Well not better, but more exciting or interesting to me. I had completely forgotten so many of them. I remember on that bike ride a few of them popped into my head.

One of those situations came up with a high-powered wealthy black man named Robert Tellington III.. We met when I worked at public radio and he was actively pursuing me. I really could tell he wasn't my type, but since my decisions were made with my yoni, I finally gave in and said yes to him. The first thing he wanted me to do was meet his mother. Usually mothers of partners didn't like me. I was not the type of woman who would be an asset to any guys career and I had zero class. He took me to dinner at his mother's place. Well, first of all, I was white. He let me know she wasn't so keen on that. Secondly, I was vegan. She had to research it to give her cook recipes to make. I was high maintenance before we even met. The housekeeper answered the door and we walked into the mansion entry. She looked me up and down and then took my ripped up jean jacket in her arms with Robert's trench coat.

I was in over my head already, but I decided to just enjoy the experience. I loved that this jet black family had all white servants. A perfect cultural turn around. It gave me a flashback to my Aunt Minnie who was wealthy and had a housekeeper and cook. The cook was a beautiful older black woman, named Mable, who always wore bright red lipstick and at any family gatherings at Minnie's place, I would sit on the kitchen counter and talk to Mable the whole time instead of hanging out with the family. She was fun and we made each other laugh and I just loved touching her black skin. I learned all about her family and her history and her life. She would laugh and tell me that I knew more about her than my Aunt Minnie who she had worked for and known for 30 years. Anyway, I did like seeing that the Tellingtons had white servants. Just felt like a bit of racial balance. I get that it is still the haves and the have-nots. Class issues. Anyway, Mrs. Tellington, walked tall and proud and a bit full of herself into the entryway. She was wearing a silky long dashiki and her hair was up in a matching turban. They were an intellectual family that was very much into their African roots. She looked at me in a way that made me feel like I was sort of polluting their tidy life and their perfect home. The disapproval was instant. She air kissed Robert on each cheek, and then took my hand in hers and gently patted it a few times and said, "Welcome." I responded by being as formal as I thought I needed to be, "Nice to meet you Angelina." She frowned and snapped a bit, "You will call me Mrs. Tellington." That was screw up number one. I don't think I took a single deep breath during that meal. It was so tense. Robert and Angelina mostly chatted about nothing important and I just tried to stay invisible. She would ask me a question and I would give the shortest answer possible. These were not my people. So I am not sure why I agreed to get together with Robert a second time. Not really sure why he asked me to do something again after the disastrous meal with his mother. A few days after the mother meal, he picked me up to take me to his lake house three hours north of Minneapolis. There were two tall blonde women there when we arrived. He introduced them and said that he paid them to come from Denmark to live with him so he could become fluent in Danish. The four of us went out on his pontoon boat and while we were crossing the big lake, he kept coming on to me while the Danish women just watched. I realized at that point that I was not even slightly physically attracted to him. I think there was the lure of the money and security of that and I was trying to force myself to be open to it. I asked him to please give me space, but he didn't listen. When the boat was anchored on the opposite side of the lake from his house, I said I was going for a swim. I just kept swimming until I had crossed the 2 miles and was around enough little bays that he couldn't see me from the boat. I ran into his house, grabbed my clothes, dressed over my wet swimsuit, and wrote a quick note saying I was heading back to Minneapolis. I sprinted the mile to the highway and hitchhiked back home. He tried calling many times that evening, but I didn't answer. Just had to erase the whole mistake."

"Oh my. Being judged by the guy's mother is so cliché, just classic. But it sounds like you were just from a totally different culture. Working class meets aristocrat. That is fantastic that you swam across the lake to escape...love that. I have a note here to ask you about the relationship you had with a woman. Can you say a bit about that before we end for today?"

"Sure. Her name was Emma. I met her when a mutual friend of ours, Tracy, hired both of us to sort through her parents stuff. Tracy's parents had died and she brought all their stuff back east without going through it at all. So it was a giant basement full of stuff. The job was going to take a long time. Turns out Emma had been through a bad relationship with a woman named Sig. Emma and Sig opened a cafe together and Emma worked her ass off on every aspect of making the place beautiful and inviting. Right after the cafe opened, Sig fell in love with someone else and stole everything from Emma. She was a wreck. Tracy told me she was suicidal and had purchased a gun. Emma and I instantly clicked and had a blast doing the work. After a few weeks of working together we were pretty tight friends. Then, I will never forget this conversation, we were walking down a dirt road together and she said, "Hey, we should try being in a relationship. We can take it slow. But wouldn't that be great if we could have it all? Best friends and lovers?" That was the start of one of the most incredible connections. Emma was like no one I had ever met. She could do anything and do it well. She was an artist, massage therapist, carpenter, dancer, you name it. And on top of all that, she was hilarious. It was really heaven. We lived together and she would even pack my bags when I was working out of town....and I always had the perfect stuff to wear when she packed my stuff. On my own, I always packed the wrong things and dressed horribly and always had the wrong stuff for whatever the local weather was. Lazer and Pessy came to visit us and they just loved her. It was beautiful to see how they didn't skip a beat about me being with a woman. They said they just wanted me to be happy. Pessy said that people who reject their gay children are sick. She said it was about love and that was nothing to judge. At some point in Emma's and my relationship, she started to be angry more often. She got mad at me for caring too much about the dogs and just started getting upset with me more and more about little things. It felt like there was a chemical switch in her brain. Even with that, I knew she loved me a lot. So it was strange. Then I started to understand why her anger was surfacing when she started having lots of major health issues. She had three surgeries in our second year together. The first surgery was gall bladder and I was shocked at how the hospital treated me. They would not let me be with her in the recovery room because they said I was "not family". I had to be pushy and almost threatening to get into that room. When it was good with me and Emma, it was GREAT. But when the health issues started popping up, she got resentful and was pushing me away from her emotionally.

I would suggest things like her going swimming after she had knee surgery, because she couldn't walk far. And, she shouted at me, "get the fuck away from me Suzie Sunshine." It was pretty hurtful. But looking back I know it was just the pain she was in both physically and emotionally from not being the strong one in the relationship who could take care of any and everything. We grew distant and she moved back to the midwest. It was really a sad time. After that I heard she had cancer and it was serious. I wanted to visit, but her cousin, who was her caretaker, said I shouldn't come because she didn't want me there. I should have ignored Emma's cousin and flown out there to be with her. It is one of my biggest regrets in life. Emma died and I wasn't there. And she was someone I loved so deeply."

"Oh, that is so sad. I am so sorry. Sounds like when she was still healthy you had such a beautiful thing."

"Yep, we sure did."

"Lu, just want to ask you about one more thing before we stop for the day. You and Lazer had a lot of friction in your younger years, but it sounds like it got better later in life. Can you say a bit about your relationship with him?"

"Oh sure. Well, Lazer and I were in a pretty constant power struggle for many years. I wanted him to be kinder and he wanted me to be more of who he thought I should be. When I was about 30 or so, we got together with the intention of being friends. All we did was talk. We were honest with each other, but not attacking or criticizing. There were a lot of tears. I asked him if he understood that I had been raped but didn't even know the word. He felt terrible. Told me he had no idea how to handle the situations I kept getting myself into. He felt helpless in trying to make me safe and helping me fit in better in society. It was such sweet sharing. We have been good friends since then. It is really a beautiful thing. A psychic told me that I had done my soul work with Lazer and that he had done his with me. She said we did what we came to the planet to do with each other. It sounded so right to me. He is still one of my closest friends to this day. He is my go to person when I need practical advice. You have probably figured out that I am not the most practical person."

"Oh Lu, I just love that you two became friends. What a fabulous full circle. I want you to dig up some photos of the whole family and you with Lazer. Would love to see those."

"You got it. We will look at a few over tea one evening."

"Lu, I meant to ask you about the fish situation. What happened?"

"Oh, it was a bad scene. I knocked on the door, and a drunk guy answered and the house was filled with smoke. I looked past the guy and there was a huge sectional sofa with a bunch of drunk men and women watching TV and smoking. I said my name and asked the guy his name. He said, "Who the fuck are you?" I said, I am here to see the fish you have. A woman from the sofa said, "Who the fuck is that?" The guy turned to her and said, "It's the fuckin' fish lady." I walked in and asked where the fish were. He pointed to the kitchen and I went in and there was a tank in there that looked like it was filled with mud. It was filthy. I saw a fish body occasionally swim against the glass. I reached in and felt three fishes in there. They were huge Koi fish and were almost as long as the tank. I walked back through the living room and told the guy I would be back in two days to take the fish to a better place. He got really mad and screamed at me, "They are MY fish!!" I just calmly told him that they are not anybody's fish. They are their own beings. I told him that nobody owns them and that I would be back to get them. I already found a beautiful enormous Koi pond where they can go live with other Koi. It is at the vegetarian restaurant in Taos. You could help me in a few days if you want to. We will take three coolers and fill them with fresh water and transport them to the pond."

"I would love to help with that. Do you think the guy will let you take them?"

"I am not really going to give him a choice. If you are worried about going there, you don't have to. Only do it if you really want to."

"I am totally up for it, count me IN."

KARINA

Went on a long solo hike today. I just needed to clear my head out. Tried meditating this morning and my head wanted to explode from thinking about all the details and crazy changes. Work is the biggest fear I have. I am in the states because of my job. So, without that, what am I doing here? Anyway, the hike helped a lot. An hour into it, I was able to actually look around and see where I was. My crazy mind switched off a bit.

When I got back from the hike, three hours later, Lu was busy in the art room but she yelled that I had a message on the kitchen table. There were two messages. One from my boss, Claire, and one from a local number I didn't recognize. The one from Claire just said to call her. I called Claire right away. I really need to figure out this job thing. Lu said not to worry about it all, that it would sort itself out and decide me rather than me deciding it.

I made some tea, settled into the sofa in the warm sun and called Claire. Here is how the conversation went (I recorded it, assuming I might need to revisit it all):

-Hi Claire, it's Karina

-Karina, I am so happy to hear from you.

-I am sorry I have been so out of touch. But you are getting my emails, right?

-Yep, got them. I just wanted to connect by phone and talk about how things are for you and what our options are at this point. Do you know when you are coming back, yet?

-Well Claire, that is what I need to talk to you about. Do you have some time for a longer conversation right now?

-Absolutely Karina, this is perfect timing.

-Honestly Claire, I will have a hard time explaining how things are

going because it is so out of my norm. But I will try to explain it all as briefly as I can.

Then I told Claire everything. I told her about the house sit and Lu and Elan and Winnie and the dance and the community and the land and my needing to leap into the unknown of it all. And I told her about my fear about work. And who am I without that work? I explained everything as best I could. I sort of assumed she would just say that I was no longer working for the paper and I should find work out here. But she surprised me.

She sounded excited, "Wow Karina, that is an incredible story. And it sounds like one that is just beginning. It also sounds like too much of a life opportunity to turn your back on just for this job. I want to work with you on this. I want to find a way that you can still keep working for us remotely. This just came to me. I have been tossing around an idea in my head for a few months about a new column. I don't have an exact description or name for it yet, but I want it to be about survival skills or life skills. Helping people navigate these crazy times in our country and on earth. Kind of a mix of spirituality and practical ways to be a positive force on earth. While you were telling your story of being in New Mexico, I was thinking that you might be the perfect person to write that column. It sounds like you are crossing paths with a lot of inspiring people and you are growing in ways that you didn't expect. I wouldn't have picked you for this column when you were here. But, my gut is telling me that you are the perfect fit for it now that you are out there experiencing this new openness and meeting a lot of new people. You could work remotely. The phone thing is a bit of an issue. You not having cell service there. But, we can figure that out. What do you think? Would you be interested in doing that column?
-Claire, that sounds amazing. I would love to do that. I know I will have a landline at my new place, but not sure about a cell phone. I am guessing no reception there. But I might have strong enough wifi to use it for my phone. I will work that out.
-Fantastic. Let's really try to come up with a good name for the

column and maybe a bit more thought into what it will cover and length. We could also think about it having a write-in section for readers. They could ask about some life question or decision they want input on and you could answer it or run it by your new wise counsel out there. Lets each let this incubate a bit and check in on Wednesday, does that work for you?"
-That would be so perfect Claire. Oh my god, I don't know how to thank you. I am so relieved and so grateful.
-I will really miss you being here in person with us, but I am so happy for you. You sound more alive and happy than I have ever heard you.
-Thanks so much Claire. I have no idea what is ahead for me here, I just know that for now, this is where I am meant to be.
-I think so too, Karina. You are answering a call of sorts. Your life is shifting. OK, have a sweet day there and give me a ring on Wednesday at about 10 my time, 8 your time.
-Will do, thanks again Claire.

So, I got off the phone and just sat there wondering what just happened. My greatest fear about staying in New Mexico just floated away like it never existed. Trying to sort out how I would work here kept me up worrying most of last night and now, poof, gone. I love the idea of the new column and the creative freedom I will have with it.

Next, I called the local number that was on the message Lu left on the table. An older man answered the phone and said his name was Richard. He explained that Winnie was a good friend of his and they had been talking over the weekend and she told him about me. Richard told me he was interested in starting a local paper for the communities along the gorge. He said that many of the people were not computer savvy and needed a paper to connect to neighbors and what was going on in the community. He explained it would be a sort of newsletter. He wanted it to be both email and snail mail versions and people would choose. He already has a dozen businesses willing to pay for a little ad in it. He asked if I would be interested in

putting something like that together. Then he went on:
"I will give you lots of support in it since you are new to the community. People would be able to call you or email you with announcements or ideas. There is a printer in Espanola who will do the printing and mailing and organize the addresses and mailing lists. Your job would just be to write up the newsletter with any events and special interest stuff. There is room for it to grow if it is popular. I will tell you up front that it won't pay much to start. But the ads will bring in some revenue and I think it will catch on with businesses from Taos down to Espanola. When Winnie told me about you, I thought that you might be just the person for the job because you will see everyone and everything here with fresh eyes. And, people won't have any history with you and they will probably be more open with you."

Richard and I had a great conversation about it and I accepted the job. We decided to meet in person next week to sort out details and timing.
So, I started today thinking I had no work here. And, I am ending the day with two jobs.

When I told Lu about the jobs, she beamed at me, "That is New Mexico welcoming you with open arms. Like I said, things either flow smoothly and almost miraculously for people here or New Mexico spits them out. I love watching the magic swoop you up."

I want to tell Elan and Winnie right away about everything. But, I am going to make myself wait until tomorrow to tell them.

THE BOOK OF ETIQUETTE

"OK, Lu, last session we ended with guys and their protective mothers. Any others that stand out?"

"Yep, guys and their mothers...it wasn't the only time I dealt with that. There were so many. One guy was from a Christian family and somehow they learned that I was from a Jewish family. They were also extremely wealthy. I was only at their home once, even though I was with their son, Claude, for two years. The one time I was at their house was on Christmas Eve and I didn't know some of the hymns or caroles they were singing and the mother handed me the hymnal and told me to "at least try to sing along." It was awful. She had a plate of Christmas cookies and she was walking around the room offering them to everyone and when she got to me, she suddenly pulled the tray back and said, "Oh, sorry, I am sure your people don't eat Christmas cookies." I thought, "ignorant bitch".

Had another memorable mother-of-guy experience. Chas was the guy I met in college who taught me how to canoe. The one I told you about having a near death experience with. He was in business school and hated it. What he really wanted to do was build sailboats. His family was pressuring him to stay in business school. I was pressuring him to do what he loved. We went on a short road trip because he wanted to visit his mom and dad in Chicago and he wanted them to meet me. When we got to the door, his mom answered and scowled at us, and shouted at him, "What are you doing here? I have told you to give me at least two weeks notice when you are coming to visit." I was pretty shocked by that. I come from a family that welcomes anyone without notice...and this was her son! She reluctantly let us in the house and Chas introduced us. She was super cold toward me. At dinner that night, they had a little television on the table that was playing the news pretty loud. I guess they didn't want to have to have a conversation. After dinner, Chas and I were sitting on the sofa and his mom walked into the room with a huge book and put it on my lap. It was the Emily Post Book of Etiquette. She said, "You need to read this cover to cover. You buttered your bread in the air at dinner and made so many other mistakes. If my son is at a business dinner with wives included and you do that, he has lost any deal he might have made." I didn't hesitate for a moment. I looked her straight in the eye and said, "First of all, I have no intention of marrying your son, so I wont be at any business dinner. Second of all, what page in this book explains how rude it is to hand the book to a guest? And third, I am sure that having a television blaring at dinner is not part of polite etiquette." Oh boy. She stormed out of that room and Chas just sat there in shock. The next day we went on a tour of his old stomping grounds. I had a skateboard in the back of the car because I loved skateboarding. We were on a quiet road on top of a hill and the road ahead was so steep down to a crossroad and then steep back up. I told Chas I wanted to skateboard it and he could wait for me on the other side of the intersection. I didn't see any cross traffic, so I was going at top speed on the way down and, before I realized that the crossroad was all sharp gravel, the skateboard came to a halt on it. I flew in the air and landed on one leg so badly that my jeans were shredded and blood was flowing pretty fast out of the wounds. We got me back to his moms and were so happy she wasn't home. I was sitting on the edge of the tub in the bathroom and we were cleaning wounds and putting on butterfly bandages to stop the bleeding. In the midst of all that, his mother walked in on us. She went off on me, "Why don't you grow up? You have no business being with my son. He will never get anywhere in life with an immature, uncultured person like you. I want you two to leave today." Happily, I never saw her again. And, I am also happy to say that Chas dropped out of business school and became a sailboat builder. He made his dream come true. I don't know for sure, but I am guessing his mom always blamed me."

"You were sure a wild and free spirit. It would take a very open minded parent to welcome you into the family. My family is pretty rigid about who they think is perfect for me. No one has matched up to their standards yet. My siblings and aunt and uncles rarely get to meet the people I date and that's for the best I think."

"You may just have to turn your back on their standards and find the person who nourishes you and is a fit for you, not them. They, like most families, can learn with time to love and welcome whoever you choose."

"You are probably right. I mean just the fact that you hitchhiked and you are vegan would make my family judge you as crazy."

"In the seventies, I hitchhiked a lot. Back then, when I was in my twenties, hitchhiking was a common type of public transportation. It was my preferred transportation for going anywhere I didn't bike to.
It mostly worked out ok, but sometimes it was as dangerous as roulette.
On a summer afternoon, I was hitchhiking just north of Minneapolis when a yellow Cadillac pulled over. A guy who looked a lot like how Donald Trump looks now, was driving. His yellow golf pants matched the car color and he had on a white golf sweater and white shoes. He had a bad hair comb-over going on, like I said, Trump style. The car smelled like aftershave. I held my pack on my lap and told him my name and where I

was heading. He didn't share his name, just said, "I can take you there." I was jazzed because it was two hours further to my destination. About 10 minutes into the drive, he put his hand on my thigh. I told him to get his hand off me. "You take it off," he replied with a big sinister smile.
It was all I could do not to hit him. I was pissed. "I am not going to touch you. You just get your fucking hand off my thigh."
His grip got tighter. We were going about 70 on the freeway. His hand moved further up toward my crotch. I looked up and saw pictures paper clipped to his visor of what must have been his daughter and son.
"Would you do this if your daughter was in the car? Would you want someone to do this to your daughter?"
Again, the grip got tighter.
"Shut up bitch."
He started telling me what he was going to do to me. I won't repeat that to you. But, it was not good.
I decided I would rather die than have this guy do what he was planning on doing. So, I opened the passenger door and started to dive head first.
With some kind of adrenaline superpower, he jerked me back up into the car by my pants leg and swerved to the shoulder of the highway.
He was shouting like a madman, "You crazy fucking bitch, get outta my car!! Get the fuck out!! What the fuck is wrong with you? Crazy fucking bitch, I should have let you die. Get the fuck out of my car."
He didn't have to invite me twice. I was out of there.
I didn't have the mental strength to continue hitchhiking. I walked miles to the nearest town and waited for a Greyhound bus that would take me to meet my friends.

Another ride that picked me up was in Arizona. A man and woman who never told me their names, but who had an open bucket about a quarter full of gasoline in the back seat. They were both of some Spanish background...I couldn't tell exactly where. The guy spoke perfect English with an accent. He had rotten teeth and Florida plates on the car. I must have been desperate for the ride to accept that sloshing stink bomb (or we were already moving down the highway before I realized what it was.) As we rode, the guy told me I was going to Panama with them. It was then I leaned forward and saw the gun between them and the terrified look on the woman's face. I had landed in the middle of some damn shit storm for sure. I started trying to figure out what to do. I now understood the gasoline bucket. This asshole was not going to stop at any gas station unless he had to. Long story short. The guy eventually used up what was in the bucket of gas when we were near Joshua Tree, California. He stopped at a gas station and told the woman to get out and pump the gas and to fill the bucket. I wondered what he planned to do at the Mexican border and how he thought this was the route to Panama. He held his hand over the gun. I saw my escape route and waited until another car was pulled up next to us to get gas on the other side of the tanks. If I didn't make a move now, we would be across the border into Mexico soon. I silently pulled on the left passenger door handle and when he looked distracted by what the woman was doing on the other side of the car, I pushed that door open and did a squat run keeping low until I was on the other side of the other car getting gas. I didn't look back toward the car at all...but I heard his door open and he screamed at the woman, "Vuelve al auto, ahora, date prisa", which is basically, "Get back in the car NOW, hurry up." I ran low and zig zaggy into the station and hid behind the counter telling them to call the police. I was shaking so hard I could barely get the words out. The guy behind the counter looked as freaked out as me. I stayed on the floor and the station guy hit the floor with me and was calling the police when we heard the squeal of the car taking off. The crazy guy didn't pay for the gas and that poor woman was still in the car with him. I never did find out what happened. I told the gas station guy I had to get out of there and gave him as much detail as I could for the police. One customer shouted that he got the license number of the car. I hope they got that guy and saved the woman.

A nice semi-driver had pulled up to the station and seen some of what happened. He gave me a ride to the next town. He fed me Oreos and orange soda and lectured me about hitchhiking. "I seen some bad stuff", he said while we bounced along the potholed road, "ain't no place for a girl alone. Ain't no place for anybody out here hitchhiking. You can't trust nobody." I think it was years before I would hitchhike again. That one gave me the total willies.

I am not a person who thinks things through. I have tried to re-train myself to think before I act or speak, but I really haven't made much progress in all these decades of life on Earth. The positive side of not thinking things through is the joy of often being in the moment and having some wonderful unexpected magical adventures and experiences. The negative side of that is getting myself into a lot of "oops" situations. Most of the situations I find myself in are a combination of oops and joy."

"That is crazy stuff...I can't believe you survived all that. Tell me about some other oops situations you were in if you can think of any right now."

"Well, quite honestly, there are so many of them that it is easy to think of them. OK, here's an example. I love biking on long trips and decided I wanted to bicycle from Los Angeles to Vancouver, BC. Since it was pre-internet days, I did very little research. Well, I can't honestly remember doing any research. All I did was get a good map. I prepped by dehydrating many pounds of veggies and fruits and loading up on some ramen noodle packages. The day before the trip, I packed my bright orange 10-speed Peugeot into a bike box and the next day flew to L.A. When I arrived I dragged my bike box into the terminal and started re-assembling it. I had to adjust the handlebars and re-attach the pedals. A guy leaned against a pole and watched me for a few minutes before coming over.

"What are you doing?"

"I am putting my bike together and then biking up to Vancouver!"

"Do you plan on biking out of the airport?"

"Yep."

"Well, guess what? That is impossible. There is no place for you to bike out of here. This airport and most of L.A is built for cars. You will never get out of here."

"Oh shit. I just assumed I could bike out to the highway."

"Don't worry. I have a pickup truck and you are welcome to put your bike in the back and I can drive you to the highway."

"Really? You don't mind?"

"Nope, don't mind at all."

"What's your name?"

"Jim."

"My name is Lu. Thanks for the kind offer, Jim."

Jim drove me and my panniers and my bike for an hour in traffic to get me to highway 101. The whole way I noticed that there was definitely no place for me to ride my bike safely.

"Jim, I am so grateful for the ride. What a great start to my trip!"

We hugged and he waited in his truck while I got prepped for the ride. He rolled down his window as I pedaled away, "Be safe out there! Take care of yourself!"

"Thanks so much, Jim!!"

It was early June and I just started working my way north.

There were special bike sections of every campground that were established during the Bikecentennial of '76. I would see other bikers during the day who were always going south. By the second day, I figured out why. The predominant winds were out of the north. The people at my first Bikecentennial campsite were shocked I was going north and informed me that I would have a headwind the entire way. I actually didn't believe that would be possible and I figured I didn't have much choice now, so I just kept slowly creeping north. Had I done my research, I would have started in Vancouver and cruised south with a tailwind the whole way. I was in my twenties and strong as a horse, but that wasn't enough for some of the weather and hills I encountered. I spent many hours off my bike trudging and pushing it up hills and mountains. One 90 degree day, I was slowly pushing the bike up a small mountain. I came across a construction crew working on the road. One of the workers was a woman holding the stop/slow sign and she asked what I was doing. When I told her, she filled me in on a local secret.
"About 1/2 a mile up the road, you will see a curve sign. A few feet past that sign there is a trail that takes you just a few minutes into the forest to a waterfall with a deep swimming hole with ice cold water. You can rest and cool off there."

"That would be fantastic! Thank you!"

I found the trail and did not emerge from the magical spot until the next day. I had no tight schedule. Actually, I had no schedule at all. So, I set up camp and skinny dipped and sunbathed for the rest of the day.

Not having a plan comes in pretty handy when you are doing a long bike trip, because unexpected stuff pops up a lot. People see you munching on a cantaloupe outside a grocery and invite you home for a "real meal". Everyone wants to know what you are up to when you are a woman alone with a bike piled high with equipment. I did not travel light. I would hit the occasional yard sale and at one point my bike had vinyl LPs and a ceramic flower vase hanging from the back rack.

There were three weeks in a row of cold rain on the coast highway and without realizing it, I had gotten myself into a hypothermia situation. I don't remember the road into Berkeley, but I was there. An older woman saw me and my bike sitting at the bus stop in the morning when she got on the bus. I was hanging out on one of the benches. When she got off the bus at the same bus stop 9 hours later, I was still there. Hadn't moved. She tried to talk to me. I didn't answer. Apparently, I was very white and glassy-eyed. She searched in my pannier and found my tiny address book in the side pocket. She found one local contact. It was my friend Lena's mom, Ruth. When I re-joined the world, I was in Ruth's guest room under a lot of blankets. Ruth had picked me and my bike up at the bus stop after getting a call from the woman. Ruth called the doctor and was told I must have hypothermia. She gave me high-calorie foods and hot drinks to raise my temperature. I had no memory of any of that. Not the highway into Berkeley, not the bus stop, not the woman, not the hot drinks, none of it. I stayed with Ruth a few days and then took off for the rest of my journey. Never knew who the woman was who called Ruth and probably saved my life. I always wished I could thank her.

I was rolling along highway 99 in Oregon when I saw the sign for Burley Bike Trailers. I was passing the factory that made the best bike trailers in the world! I stopped and went inside to see if I could get a tour. I was shocked at how tiny the factory was. Everything was done right there by a handful of workers. David was the first one to greet me and take me on a tour. I was in bike equipment heaven. Some of the owners/workers lived in a co-op house in Eugene. They invited me to stay there with them. I stayed for days. They would go to work and I would go to the co-op grocery and get food and bake bread and make dinner while they were at Burley making trailers. On that first day, they weighed my bike. I think it was 80 pounds with my equipment. Looking back I wonder why they didn't give me a prototype trailer to test. They said I was crazy to carry that much weight and definitely crazy to be traveling north instead of south. They offered for me to move in and be another housemate. Life was fun in Eugene: dancing, great vegan food everywhere, wonderful community and sweet weather. (It was summer after all, not a realistic time to decide to move to Oregon...) I was tempted to stay but decided to get to my Vancouver goal. I left my new friends, not knowing that I would be moving there by fall.

The trip ended at the University of British Columbia. I set up my tent on the forested berry bush covered university land and lived on berries for a week. People would come by who were hiking and running the trails and say hello, but no one told me to leave. Every day I would leave my little tent home with all my stuff in it and bike to the Museum of Anthropology at UBC with my sketchbook and pens. When the museum closed, I would be the last one out the door. About 5 days into this routine, the guard started asking me questions. He wanted to know what I was doing there all day every day. I told him I just loved learning about the local indigenous culture.

"I can see that. I want to invite you to something on Friday evening."

He then told me that in the building behind the museum there would be a potlatch ceremony between two tribes starting at sunset. He also told me I would be the only non-native person there and that I would be welcomed by everyone.

"I would love that. I will definitely be there. Is there anything special I should bring or wear?"

"No, there will be food and lots of dancing and salmon roasted over a pit fire"

I chose to not share that I was vegan.

The ceremony was one of the most beautiful things I have ever been to. The tribes shared dances, food, and gifts with each other. I sat way up in the back bleachers and watched it all, hoping I was somewhat invisible. About halfway through a young girl came and asked me to join the dance. I told her I didn't think that was a good idea but thanked her for the invitation. Then, the guard who had invited me to the ceremony came up to the top bleacher and said I should join her for the dance.

I joined the circle dance, but I felt pretty awkward and very white. Everyone laughed at my dancing, but not in a mocking way. I guess I was bringing them a lot of joy with my wacky dance style. I must not have an ounce of native blood in me or I would have figured out those steps.

After my bike trip, I quit my job in Minneapolis and in October hauled a rickety trailer loaded with my stuff to Cottage Grove, OR. I didn't own a car, so I signed up to deliver someone's car to them in Oregon with one of those drive-away companies. I mounted a hitch and towed the trailer. I dropped off the trailer at my new rental and then I delivered the car to the owner in Portland. I thought he would be excited to have the hitch on the car (I was young and naive), so I left it on the car. When the guy saw the hitch on the back and my cat's hair inside the car, he kept my $300 deposit. That was a boatload of money in those days. It was so disappointing. My housemate at the rental was also the owner of the house, so he had the final word on everything. He had told me he was fine with my cat, but failed to tell me she wouldn't be allowed inside. I kept sneaking her in and he kept busting us. When the rain started, I couldn't bear that sweet Mugi was out in the cold rain. And that cold rain was going to supposedly keep drizzling on her for months. I lasted one month before I hauled my butt back to Minneapolis. Give me 10 below zero, snow and the periodic sunshine any day over the constant drip drip and everything turning to rust and mildew in Oregon."

KARINA

I called Elan first thing this morning and told him everything about the whole work miracle. We talked on the phone for a long time. I have never been a phone talker, but Elan is one of the easiest people to talk to that I have ever met. There is some kind of ease about it that is brand new for me. After talking to him, I emailed friends and family letting them know what was going on. Then I called my housemate, Lorna, in Scranton. I wasn't looking forward to telling her that I wasn't coming back. Again, I was surprised. Lorna was so excited for me. Without any judgment, she just offered to pack up anything I wanted sent and even offered to ship it. I told her I would send her a list of what I wanted. She agreed to either keep the other stuff or give it to thrift. It was just another piece of the puzzle falling into place. Lorna said she would come out to visit me and could bring anything too fragile to ship. It was just so easy....all of it.

Well, not all of it was easy. When Lu and I meditated together this evening, I fell asleep. The ending chimes rang and I woke up with my chin down on my chest and tears pouring out of my eyes. Lu reached over and put her hand on my knee and asked if everything was ok. When she asked that, it all came back to me. I was dreaming during the meditation sleep. I dreamed that I was crossing a really wide river, wider than the Rio Grande. I was alone in a canoe and the canoe tipped, I went under the water and the current was taking me. I couldn't breathe. I kept rising to the surface struggling and then I would sink again. Each time I rose to the surface I could see across the river that Elan was there waiting for me, but he didn't try to help me. He stood there with no emotion, no expression. Just stone faced, watching me sink over and over. Eventually I didn't come back up for air and I was gone. I told Lu about the dream. Every detail.

Lu asked me what I was afraid of with Elan. Then, what she said jolted me, "Karina, I don't think it is about Elan. I think it is about your father. You haven't told me about your mother and father, but I know you haven't had any serious relationships, so I assume it relates to your mother and father."

I was quiet for a bit before I told Lu the truth, "Lu, I have never shared this with anyone. I just stowed it away inside me somewhere. Like a storage locker you forget you even have. When I was 10 years old, my mother died in a car accident in Stockholm. It was horrible. A guy ran a red light and hit my mom and two of her friends in the car. My mom was killed instantly and her two friends lived, but were permanently injured. Neither one ever went back to their old life as runners, distance skaters or hikers. All three of the friends shared that love of sports and outdoors. When my mom died, my father never cried. He never looked at my face again. Everyone said I looked exactly like her. He never talked to me and my sister about what happened. It is like he died that day, too. He started drinking a lot and by the time I hit 20 years old, he was dying of liver cancer. But, like I said, he was already dead. He had no friends and never left the little cottage we used to have on the island. He would have the neighbor bring him alcohol and go deposit his welfare checks for him. My sister and I tried to help him, but he didn't want help and he certainly didn't want us around. My sister, Elsa, is a bit like me. She has never had a deep love relationship. She has been with a few women, but never anything serious. We are both so stunted in the emotions and relationships world. But I think you are right, the dream has more to do with my father than with Elan. And it has a lot to do with my fear that there is no one who will really be there for me."

I told Lu all of it. And my shirt was soaked with tears that kept flowing out while I told her.

Lu didn't say anything, she just moved her meditation cushion closer to mine and held me tight. That act of love and caring only made me cry harder. I don't know how long we stayed like that. Lu hugging me and me sobbing. When I finally opened my eyes, the sun was setting, so I knew we had been there for at least a few hours. I felt so embarrassed. No one but me and Elsa and a few close relatives knew all the details of our parents' painful endings. And now I had taken up so much of Lu's time telling her everything. I apologized to Lu and she said, "Never apologize for having feelings and being real with me or anyone. I am grateful you shared it with me. I am so sorry you had to experience those painful times. I cannot even imagine." And then she hugged me more and I cried more. Maybe it sounds crazy because I haven't known Lu very long, but it feels like she is like a mother to me. Like a mother I never had.

TRUCK DRIVING WOMAN

"Lu, we ended the last session with you talking about it not working out in Oregon. What did you do after that?"

"I was lucky that my job was still waiting for me in Minneapolis. It was the truck driver and warehouse worker job I mentioned when we were talking about the suicide attempts. It was a wholesale organic produce collective. I got that job in an off chance way. I had been in one of the food co-ops in Minneapolis shopping and heard a woman talking about the produce collective she worked for needing a truck driver. I planted myself right into the conversation and got more info. That night I called Sam, the person in charge of hiring. After a long conversation, he told me to come in Monday morning at 4 am for an interview. Yep, 4 am. That's produce world start-up time.

I rode my bike in the dark on Monday morning to the address he gave me. I got in the door and was immediately handed a two-wheeler, you know a loading dolly, and told to get 4 boxes of size 32 pink grapefruit. The tall blonde guy in charge of loading the truck was smoking a pipe and pointed to a corner of the warehouse,"32's not 48's!"

I had no idea what that meant. I finally found the 32's and stacked them on the two-wheeler and pushed them to the truck. All he said was, "load em." I got the stack into the truck but wasn't sure how to release the dolly plate from under the boxes. He came in and inserted his foot under the bar between

the wheels while he pushed on the top of the dolly and pulled it right out. "That's how you do it," he mono-toned at me without making eye contact. Next, he told me to get 4 one hundred pound reds.
"What exactly is that?"
"Potatoes, over there."
I was struggling with loading a one hundred pound burlap sack onto the dolly when Sam showed up. He was already laughing at my potato wrestling match when he introduced himself and shook my hand.
"Don't worry, you will get used to heavy loads in no time."
He helped me load the potatoes onto the dolly.
I managed to do the other three with my drop and drag method. Pull them off the top and let them fall to the ground then drag it by a corner of the sack onto the dolly.
After about 3 hours of continuous loading of delivery trucks, I was exhausted and my arms ached.
Sam was so kind and connectable and made me feel more welcome there. I asked him if we were going to do the interview now.
"That was your interview. You survived the truck loading! You're hired."
Eventually, it was Sam who taught me to drive all the trucks. Some a whole lot bigger than others. Some with split axles. I had told him I could drive a truck when we talked on the phone that first night. But, I was talking about a pickup truck, not a 25-foot delivery truck. I was the first woman driver at our warehouse and in the entire city. This made it tough out there. At the end of the day when I took the empty truck to the other produce warehouses to pick up extra things we needed, there was no warm welcome. The places would be buzzing with pallet jacks and forklifts loading everyone else's trucks with produce. I would hand my order in and wait and wait and wait. Finally, I would have to go to the owners of the produce companies or to the floor managers and complain that they weren't getting my order. Eventually, I got tired of

being treated like shit because I was a woman. One afternoon, I backed my truck up to the loading dock and handed my order to the guy in the forklift. He took it and then proceeded to load up three other trucks that had pulled in after me. He had no intention of filling an order for a woman who thought she could drive a truck. I spotted an empty forklift and got in and took off into the giant coolers to fill my own order. Soon I had warehouse guys running at me and screaming, "You can't do that, get out of there," "That is union-only get the hell off of there," "That's a liability, only our guys can use the forklifts!"
I ignored them and kept grabbing the boxes and bags for my order. Finally, the owner came down and asked me to come upstairs to his office. He had seen the whole thing from his office window up there. Before he had a chance to reprimand me, I told him that I was tired of coming there and being ignored or disrespected by his workers because I am a woman.
"I know you are right, but these guys really don't like a girl doing a man's job."
"First of all, I am a woman doing a job that pretty much anyone can do. Second, I waste hours waiting while they ignore me and load every other truck. I want you to tell them to start treating me like the other customers."
"Ok, I will talk to them. Just don't get into the forklift again."
"If they fill my order when I get here, I won't use your forklift again. If they don't fill my order, I have no choice."

I never had an issue at that warehouse again.

I had no accidents for the first 7 or so years of driving the truck. I was out on deliveries one day and was reaching down to get something that had dropped on the passenger side floor and hit a parked car. When a huge truck going slowly hits a parked car, the car gets smashed, and in this case, pushed up onto the sidewalk.
I had someone call the police to do a report.
when the police got there, I climbed down from the truck cab

and one officer started immediately shaking his head.
"Oh come on, you gotta be kidding....what is a little girl like you doing this job for? No wonder you had a wreck. Why don't you get a different job?"
The other officer told him to cut it out. But, he was on a roll and kept going.
I went to the cab, got my clipboard and pen and wrote his badge number and name.
I turned my back to them and announced, "I am done with you. You can leave now. I will get another officer to come."
His partner tried to smooth things over. "He didn't mean anything by it. Let's just get the report filled out."
The sexist officer was not giving up so easily. "I mean come on, you know you are too small to drive this truck. This is not a woman's job. That's all I am saying."
I didn't hide my anger. "I would say that I am in the right job and you are in the wrong job. Nobody needs a sexist biased cop. You might want to find another job. Just leave, I will call for two other officers."
The partner tried to get his buddy to stop and finally succeeded. I was back in the truck cab trying to get calm when the partner came and tapped on the door. I rolled the window down.
"What?"
"I can just do this with you and my partner will wait in the squad car."
"Your partner is a jerk."
"Yep, sometimes he is. But he is pretty harmless."
We filled out the paperwork and I drove back to the warehouse.
There was no damage to the truck. I was wishing I had just left the scene of the accident. Getting harassed for being a woman in that job got old fast. Luckily, other women joined the collective and I was not the only one out there.
We would have semi's pulling up to the warehouse many times a day with deliveries for us. Pallets of boxes and bags of

produce.

One of our regular deliveries was driven by a woman trucker. She was from California and wore all sequined pink clothes and pink high heels. She weighed about 100 pounds at most. None of that stopped her from climbing up over mountains of produce in her trailer to see how far back our pallets were. Things were changing in the produce world.

I called the lieutenant and the chief of police to report the sexist cop who wouldn't stop harassing me. He said they would speak to him and take action. I doubt if any of that happened.

Sometimes the assumptions that truck driving was a man's job made my job amusing. One really cold ass day in Minneapolis, I was delivering to the Seward Cafe. I had now gotten strong and could slide two one hundred pound sacks of potatoes off the back of the truck, one on each shoulder, and carry them into the restaurant. Seward had ordered 400 pounds, so I did it twice into their side door. It was actually easier to carry the huge burlap sacks on my shoulders than to wrestle even one onto the two-wheeler and wheel it in. I was carrying the second 200-pound load across the sidewalk and an old man stopped me and said, "That's a mighty heavy load for a little fella like you." When I turned toward him, he could see the earrings I was wearing inside my winter hood. He literally jumped back a bit. (I wonder if that is where the expression "Taken aback" comes from) He roared, loud enough for everyone around to hear, "Why, you're no fella at all! I can't believe my eyes! Good for you little lady!"

"Wow, you were sure a tough one. Well, you still are. You are a pretty tiny woman and I have seen you haul stuff here that most big twenty-year-olds couldn't carry. When we were out cutting wood the other day, I didn't want to admit to you that I was exhausted and ready to quit about an hour into it. I figured we wouldn't be out there that long. You know we were cutting and hauling and splitting wood for 5 hours? I was amazed. Then you didn't come back

and pass out like I did. You came back here and ate a little and went right into the art room to paint. Where do you get that strength and energy?"

"I just don't have a good stop button. I imagine at some point I will. Lazer and Pessy were strong and active well into their 90's, so some must be genetic. I am either sleeping, meditating or busy. Nothing in-between. It is probably not very balanced. Never could just sit and do nothing."

"What just came to me is that you have had a lot of experiences with people and places. Some good and some really bad or disappointing. It is surprising that you came out of all this not hating people or that you can still trust any of them."

"It is a mix for me. I prefer to be alone, but I can function with people. I am one of those introverts who does the social thing when I have to and can be around a bunch of people, but then I need to recuperate because it drains me. I have met quite a few speakers and performers or famous people who are great on stage presenting and then have no social skills or are painfully shy once they are off the stage. They can't have a conversation once they are out of that public role. I am not one of those. I can get off the stage and connect with pretty much anyone. But it is not energizing or nourishing for me. I am glad that I have had so many experiences of being judged or mistreated in society because it has given me more empathy for people who are not at the top of the heap. So relating to a diverse population comes easy for me. That said, I am often shocked at how humans treat other humans. I don't really understand it. I think I got that from Lazer. He could be a raging hellion at home, but he treated everyone with equal care and respect in his life out in the world. But most people can be so cruel to others who they may not understand or want to understand. Here I am asking people to care about other species when we can barely care about our own species. Whether it is someone's race or religion or gender or weight or age…we just can't seem to get over seeing differences."

"You included weight in that list of things we judge people for. Is that a sensitive issue for you?"

"I think it is an issue for everyone. I did grow up with Lazer wanting Pessy to be slim and giving her shit for it. But, it feels bigger than my personal experience. We just don't know who lives inside a person's body and we often don't want to know. It is easier to judge.

I was in a small church thrift shop some years ago and out of nowhere, I hear this woman loudly asking if someone can help her get home. There were lots of customers and she was the one near the door who weighed at least 300 pounds...probably more. She didn't even have the courage to just approach an individual and ask for a ride. She stared at the floor and almost shouted, "Can someone please give me a ride home?" I went to her and offered her a ride. It was hard for her to walk and I helped her to the end of the walkway and went to bring my car over while she waited. She could not have made it to where I was parked. I got out of the car and opened the passenger door of my Toyota Corolla and realized she was not going to fit in my car. As gently as I could, I said, "Deborah, I am not sure my car is going to work for you."
"No, it will work, but we will need someone else to help."
I called to another person leaving the thrift store to help. She pretended not to hear me. That is how fearful we are of people who look different. She couldn't handle being near the fat woman. I told her to wait and I got one of the thrift store staff to help. I pulled her in from the driver's seat while the other person pushed her blobs of fat into any spots left in my car and we were finally, after several minutes, able to close the door. Deborah gave me directions to get her home. When we pulled up in front of it, it was a nursing home. Here is how the conversation went and she was sobbing the whole time.
I said, "You live here?"

She said, "Yes, now I do"
-"But Deborah, you are only about my age, about 30 right?"
-"Yes"
-"Well, why are you here?"
She said, "Do you really want to know?"
I really did want to know, so I told her, "Yes"
Then she told me the background story and it was horrifying.
"Three years ago I was home and my kids were at school. They were just 7 and 8 years old. Their father was a horrible man and he would get a lot of joy out of beating me up and making the kids watch. I let it go on too long. I didn't know how to get help. On this one morning, the kids had gone to school, it was close so they walked there. I made breakfast for their father. I can't say his name, it makes me feel sick. He didn't like the breakfast I made. It was just toast and eggs. Even now I can't bear the smell of either one cooking. He grabbed me by my hair and brought me out to the tree where he hangs dead deer after killing them. The bloody rope was always hanging from that tree. He tied the rope tight around my ankles and then pulled the other end of the rope so I was hanging upside down. I was skinny then and it was easy for him to do. He took a stick and beat my whole body while I was upside down. My body was swinging all over every time the stick hit me. I smashed into the huge trunk of the tree a few times. I remember the blood pounding in my head from being upside down and then I remember wet blood dripping down my face and my arms and legs. Then he just got in his truck and left me there. I tried everything to get untied, but he had tied my hands up behind my back and I was too weak and in pain because he had hit my arms and shoulders so hard that he broke bones and smashed my shoulders. I was screaming at the top of my lungs for anyone to help me, but the neighbors' houses were too far away to hear me. Eventually I went unconscious and 6 hours later, my kids came home and found me hanging in the tree by my ankles. I don't remember a lot of what happened during or after that, I was too out of it. But I found out later that my son,

Trevor, ran to a neighbor down the road and an ambulance took me to the hospital. Trevor and Chloe were already with social services when I woke up in the hospital. I was released from the hospital after two months of surgeries and therapy and they brought me here. I just want my kids back. I get to see them in a supervised visit every week. I want my life back. They won't let me have the kids until I am physically and mentally stable. I just kept eating my pain away and now I am this. I am this mess and no one wants to be around me. I am not sure my kids will even want to be with me. But they are both so kind and loving when I see them for our visits. One of my greatest fears is that one of them will turn out like their father. The only good thing is that he will not be torturing anyone else. He was charged with attempted murder and sent to prison. He hung himself with an extension cord he found in the prison after only two months there. Weird and ironic that he hung himself after what he did to me. I am working so hard on getting better. I know it doesn't look like it, but I am slowly losing the weight I put on. I want to be with my kids and that is the only incentive I need."

After she told me that story, I reached over her formidable body and hugged her for a long time. She was sobbing through the whole telling of the story and my shoulder was wet from her tears. I just kept holding her. She told me no one had touched her in three years other than doctors and nurses and her kids holding her hands. She said she didn't want to hug the kids when she saw them because she knew she was disgusting. We held hands and looked in each other's eyes for what seemed like an hour. I don't know how long it was. All I could feel was love for her. And I could tell she was receiving that love. I wrote my phone number down and told her to call if she ever needed anything, even just to talk. That made her cry even more.

I waited a month and was surprised I hadn't heard from her, so

I called the nursing home. I figured I could go visit her. The receptionist told me that Deborah had passed away that month. I asked what happened and she told me her heart gave out.

I had a good cry about her dying. But, I was also grateful for being able to give her love before she left earth. I planned on trying to find out what happened with her two kids, but I never did.

There are just so many people out there who are lonely or rejected by society and we don't know their stories. They are just like us and some bad luck or life circumstances left them in desperate situations with no support. One small turn in someone's path can send them down a rough road."

"Oh my god, that is the most intense story. I am so glad you reached out to her. You are right though, we judge people by their exterior and we do not know who is inside. Wow, I just need to take a little break after that story. I could just picture the whole thing. Makes me feel a little sick to my stomach."

"I so get it Karina. Let's take a break. Come on, we can walk down to the river with the dogs. That is the best healing there is. They have sure taken to you. This whole time Noodles and Olive have been next to you on the sofa and Pip had his head on your foot. When you started to get upset about the story, look what Noodles did."

"I barely noticed that Noodles did that. She put her head right on my chest. They are so perceptive. I have gotten so used to them being right next to me that I really don't think about it anymore."

"I love how they are with you. Come on, let's take a walk and then start again."

"Lu, why do you think we judge other people so harshly?"

"It is not even that we just judge others. We also harshly judge ourselves. I am my own worst critic. Most people are. I haven't been much of the type to go to a counselor or therapist. But I did reach out to some recommended therapists a few times. One therapist was pretty tough on me. I was in my twenties and I sort of fought the process of looking at my shit. One week, he must have been getting too close to something sensitive and I called in sick to cancel my appointment. About half an hour before my appointment I got a call from him. He said he knew I wasn't sick and I should hurry up and get over there and he refused to accept my not coming or my being late. I got there almost on time. We were talking about body image stuff. He had me draw myself with one of the crayons in the box on his desk. I drew this elaborate self-portrait from the neck up. He asked me, "Why just the head? Draw your whole body." I told him, "I am not a good drawer, I can't draw bodies very well." He said, "You didn't do such a perfect job with the head, so go ahead and add the body." I drew the whole body and he was talking to me the whole time. Then he said, "What are you doing?" I didn't even know I had taken the black crayon and was drawing a huge line back and forth between the head and body. I said, "I'm just doodling, scribbling." He took the crayon from my hand and said quietly, "You are not doodling, you just cut the head off from the body." Then he asked me if I had a full-length mirror. I told him "no way." I realized at the same time he did that I had never looked at my body. I refused to look down at it.

He asked me, "When did you last look at your body?"
I couldn't remember the last time and I told him so.

He gave me homework for that week. I was instructed to go and buy a full length mirror and stand naked in front of it and look at my body at least once a day. I bought the mirror at a thrift store and then set it in the closet, thinking I would pull it out and do my homework each day. But instead, I never looked at it. It never came out of the closet. I felt so ashamed when I went to the session the next week and hadn't done what he asked me to. We worked hard on getting me to just accept my physical self. When we dug deep in those sessions it came back to when I was raped. I had not thought that I was at all affected by the violence of the rape. I just thought, "Oh, that is ancient history." But I found out I couldn't even say my rapist's name without laughing hysterically, which is an intense emotional reaction. It was a lot of work to even accept my body a little. I now realize this is the case with most women. We only see what we label as flaws with our physical selves. We can't see the beauty of our bodies. It would be great if we could at least be neutral about our bodies, but we are so hypercritical. The fact is that at every age, I look at photos from about a decade ago and I am shocked to see that I wasn't so ugly as I thought. There are even moments where I can look at one of the photos and think I look beautiful. It will probably happen with the age I am now. In ten years I will look back at photos of me from this time and think I looked fine. But, I just can't see it in the here and now. Instead of dwelling on it much, I just keep reminding myself that we are all just a mass of subatomic particles and any idea of beauty or ugliness is just a made up story. That works well for me and I don't get all obsessed with how this physical self should look.

It really is just a cultural story, like so many that we have. When I was hanging out with the Kenyan's in Minneapolis, they thought that me and my girlfriends were too skinny and that was not beautiful to them. I had one friend, Shelly, who was very full bodied. I guess, fat by American standards. They thought she was the most beautiful of my friends. There was this time when I got tired of hiding the fact that Shelly was a lesbian. We couldn't talk about it in front of the Kenyan buddies because they were so vehemently anti-gay and homophobic. I was heading over to the Kenyan's apartment one afternoon and asked Shelly if I could tell them that she is a lesbian. She said I could tell them, but she understood that she would most likely never be able to hang out with them again.

We were all sitting at their table eating. They would make me some amazing vegan food. They would, of course, have chicken with their food. Oh, that reminds me of an aside. When they first came to the USA, they had never been outside of their village in Kenya. Their first escalator was Nairobi, their first woman bus driver was in Minneapolis. It was all foreign and crazy to them. I met them on their first day in the states and I took three of them to the grocery. They walked through the grocery and asked me why all the food was "sick". Everything from tomatoes to onions to chicken meat all looked unhealthy to them. The first time they cooked a chicken, the older brother Enoch broke a bone of the chicken before he would let them eat it. He broke the bone and shook his head "no". The chicken was too unhealthy and he didn't want any of them to eat it. The first meal I had with them, they made me such great food from cornmeal and greens and beans. I went to go help with the dishes and reached under the sink for the dish soap and saw dozens of products under there. There were many products that did the same thing. I asked one of the sisters, Zawadi, why they had all those products under the sink. She said, "We want to be a real American home. This is what real American homes have." When I asked Zawadi if she knew what the products were for, she said "no".
"Zawadi, nobody looks under your sink. You don't need those things to be an American."
"But Lu, YOU looked under the sink."
The first thing they had gotten when they arrived in America was a television. So, they took all their cues about being an American from what they saw on the television. This means that the five brothers all got big white cowboy hats because they were watching shows like Dallas. And they got dirt bikes and would ride the motorized dirt bikes all over Minneapolis with their giant cowboy hats snugged right down on their heads. It was hilarious. I will get back to the lesbian story, but now I remembered the horrible thing that happened their first

week in the USA. They were all riding in their uncle Caleb's car with the windows down. They were stopped at a stoplight and the guys in the car next to them yelled, "Nigger go home." And they threw something wet at Mokamba and his uncle on that side of the car. It hit them in the face. It turns out it was some kind of acid and it burned their facial skin and took the paint off that side of the car. They were hospitalized and layers of their skin peeled off. It was just horrible. It is pretty amazing they stayed after that incident. I think that would have been enough to send me packing. But they were a strong family and had each other for support.

Anyway, back to that lunch talk. We were all sitting and eating and I asked them, "Who is your favorite of my friends?"

They did not hesitate. They all answered that Shelly was their favorite because she was the most beautiful and funny and smart. All of them, the brothers and sisters and the uncle said they loved her.

I then told them, "Shelly is a lesbian. I asked if I could tell you and she said I could."

They all started laughing hysterically. That is, until they looked at me and I wasn't laughing. There was a long silence. Enoch, the oldest, broke the silence.

"Shelly is NOT a lesbian. She can't be."

I asked, "Why not?"

Enoch answered, "Because we love her."

I explained that Shelly was afraid to tell them because they were very clear that the gay people were the sick ones in the species and should all be put on an island or killed so that the human species wouldn't be weakened.

That moment was really powerful for all of us. Just meeting and loving this one person and finding out she was a lesbian changed their whole attitude about gay people. They became outspoken gay rights advocates in the Kenyan community. It was amazing to see the power of knowing and caring about one individual in a group and how it can change the entire perception of that group. And I carried that with me for life.

It helped me understand the importance of seeing beyond the group and relating to and getting to know the individual. And it carries over beyond our own species. When someone gets to know an individual cow or pig or chicken, they have the opportunity to stop treating the whole group like they are nothing, unworthy of care and respect. I think the only disappointment that lingered for the Kenyan family was that the guys were all hoping to marry Shelly one day and now she was not an option.

The family was treated horribly at their various jobs. They were working illegally until they got their green cards from immigration. That meant they basically had no rights. They would be verbally and physically abused at their jobs as dishwashers and cleaning people. We realized we needed to get them all their green cards so they could choose other employment. A bunch of us friends agreed that we would marry each of the brothers and sisters. All seven of them. We would do whatever it took to get them their green cards. It was illegal, of course. But, we didn't care. I have never believed in boundaries and immigration was tough on black and brown people and much more lenient with whites trying to enter the country. We paired up with the siblings. I married Mokamba. We staged wedding photos and hung them in his apartment. I changed my drivers license to his address. I put my stuff all over his house and in his closet. None of us took money for marrying them. There are people who take large sums of money to marry someone so they can get their citizenship, but we were doing it out of principle. Once Mokamba applied for his green card, the challenges started. Immigration would do surprise visits to his apartment. I didn't live there, so I was very rarely there when they came. Mokamba would always say the same thing, "She is at work." I had warned my co-workers about what was happening and if I wasn't at the warehouse when immigration got there, they would say, "She is out on her truck run." This is when I was delivering produce.

Some days they would come to the apartment and we would be required to appear at their offices within 24 hours. They would put us in separate rooms and ask questions, then they would bring us back together and tell us what didn't add up. We had practiced every question we thought they would ask. We had looked at each other naked to see what birthmarks or moles or scars we each had. We memorized all we could. But, there was no way to anticipate all they would ask us. The first appointment, they brought us back together and the immigration guy said, "He says he met your parents and you say he hasn't met them. He says you get along great and you say that the two of you argue a lot."

I had to think fast to reply, "Do you see how nervous he is? He is here sweating and shaking." This was true, he was a wreck and sweat was dripping down Mokamba's face and his legs were shaking uncontrollably. "I told him to just tell the truth, but he is just saying what he thinks you want to hear. I will make sure that in the future he just tells the truth. This whole process is foreign to him and is really stressful for both of us."

It worked. We had to live with this process for one year and then he got his green card. We had to stay legally married for a few years before we could get divorced without suspicion. I think the family was all grateful. Mokamba was able to bring his girlfriend from Kenya and they got married and had three children. Ironically, they moved back to Kenya because they felt that the USA was too violent a culture to raise children in. I am still glad that we took care of that family so that they could get safer jobs and feel a bit of peace in their lives.

Hey what happened to our break? Come on, let's end for the day and take the dogs on a nice long hike. We can start and end at the river. It is so nice out right now. And at 4 we are going to get Elan and go rescue the fish."

KARINA

OK, first I have to write about this fish rescue. It was epic. We had three coolers full of water in the back of Lu's truck. We picked up Elan and all sat tight in the cab. When we pulled up to the house the yard was full of trash and broken cars and appliances. The porch looked like it was about to fall over. Elan and I grabbed one of the coolers and followed Lu. She knocked on the door and a guy answered with torn jeans, no shirt and a cigarette hanging from his mouth. He seemed drunk. I saw the sofa was still full of his drunk friends, just like Lu described it. Lu said, "We are here for the fish." The guy had totally forgotten that Lu was there before and said, "Who the fuck are you?" Lu didn't hesitate, "I am the fuckin fish lady and you and I already agreed two days ago that I would take the fish to a pond nearby." Lu didn't even give him time to compute it all. She told us to come on in and we went straight back to the tank. Someone had been apparently jabbing a pen into the tank and one of the fishes was bleeding. Lu reached in and lifted on fish out and put him in the cooler. Elan and I carried the cooler out and Lu told a big woman on the sofa to come outside and help. The woman looked pissed, but did it anyway. She helped Lu carry a cooler and Elan and I got the other one. We got the other two fish and were heading out the door with the coolers when the drunk guy got right in Lu's face. "You can't take my fish." Lu got right back in his face, "We already agreed to this. You can't change your mind now. Those fish were going to die a miserable death in there and now they will have a good life. So, go back to your friends and be happy you did the right thing letting them go. And, never get any other animals who need your care. Your chained up dog out there is miserable and needs a new life, too." At that we just walked out and loaded the coolers and drove away. Elan was laughing, "Welcome to Lu's world, Karina".

When we got to the restaurant in Taos there was a jazz band playing and it was a mellow scene. We walked through with our coolers and the band stopped playing and all the customers and the band came and watched the release of the fish. Lu stepped right into the shallow part of the pond to release the injured one who was bleeding. There was still ice on the edge of the pond, so I know that water was freezing cold. I couldn't believe what I was seeing. She gently lowered the fish into the water and kept her hands on both sides of him. Not even touching him, but just her hands about an inch off his body on both sides. She kept talking to him and the other two fish wouldn't leave him. They hovered real close. Then after at least five minutes, Lu stood up straight and smiled and the three fish swam off together in the clear water. The pond was the biggest I had ever seen. Elan and I both had happy tears and the customers and the jazz band were all cheering and applauding. It was such a high. That feeling of giving someone their life back. The whole drive home I was buzzing. Elan said I had caught the bug and now was an official member of their rescue team. Lu laughed and said, "Oh, our team of two just became three?"

My head was just stirring with Lu's stories from yesterday and the fish rescue. I was up and down all night just feeling unsettled. So many thoughts about my life. I have never had a very serious partner relationship. Never been in love. I have always taken the safe route. Maybe I have been lonely sometimes, but I have never really let myself go there and think about it much. I don't even know if I could do a real relationship with someone. Maybe I am just too damaged from all the stuff with my mom and dad. I am not sure how much I could open up to another person. Elan is so relaxed in the world. He is kind and open and clear. It would probably be better to just be his friend so he can find a person who really meets him where he is, a better fit. There is something so different about him. We spent that entire night in the hammock together and he didn't even try to kiss me. I know I wanted to kiss him, but I was too scared to go down that road or be the one initiating it. Maybe he just wants to be friends. I have no idea how to figure all this out.

ONE WAY TICKET

"Good morning Lu. I was wondering if I could ask you about something personal before we start our session today. I am going to record it because you may really be able to help me here."

"Sure thing, Karina. I will help if I can."

"I have never had a really serious relationship and I don't think I have ever been in love. I don't know exactly what love is or how it should feel. I am pretty sure I would want something more than friendship with Elan, but this is all new for me. How do I know what he wants? And how do I deal with the fact that he is much more open and creative and just better at living at ease in the world? I mean, I keep thinking I want to move toward him but I shouldn't because I am not a good fit for him. He could find someone so much better to be in a relationship with. Does that all make sense? I am just confused."

"Karina, my first thought is that you are overthinking this. You and Elan have a wonderful connection and you don't need to decide what it is. You sure don't need to figure out if you are good enough for him or not or a good fit. Let it decide itself. He is one of the most honest and kind people I know. Ask him about it. Ask him how he is feeling about you. I think it is time you two had that talk anyway. You will be his neighbor soon and it would be good for you both to have a good understanding of how you are feeling about each other. But, once you have talked about it and been direct with each other….you know, talking about the elephant in the room…then just let it go. Just be together without analyzing it all. Just live in those wonderful times you have together."

"OK, I will talk to him about it. We are going to a movie at the community center tonight. Are you going? We could paddle across together."

"Yep, I am going, too. I am actually in charge of providing the popcorn for the movies, so I will pop up a giant bag of popcorn before we go. Ready to head into our interview for today?"

"Absolutely. Thanks for talking about the Elan stuff. I feel better about it all. So, I woke up today thinking about all your stories. You have lived so many lifetimes. Somehow you fit in working and lots of adventures. How did you pay for the trips? How did you manage to fit everything into your days and weeks and years?"

"I never needed much to travel. I am a better saver than a spender. Sometimes just a yard sale paid for a trip. Sometimes it was just being frugal. One year I had saved up $2,000 and decided to get a one-way ticket to Europe to bike as long as my money held out. I left my apartment in Minneapolis with my Australian friend Helena staying there. Last I had heard from her, she would be heading back to Australia within a month.
The cheapest ticket I found was to Athens. This worked for me because I wanted to visit Katarina, the Greek exchange student who lived with our family when I was in high school. I spent time with Katarina and her family at their city house in Patras and at the village house where they grew olives. That is where the "feed the vegan" program began. Everyone I met in Greece and all of Europe wanted to feed me. They worried that a biking vegan would be hungry all the time and made it their mission to feed me every vegan dish they could make or get their hands on. I gained so much weight on that trip. I mean, who bikes all over Europe for months and gains weight?
After a few weeks, I left Katarina's family and biked to the ferry that would take me from Greece to Naples, Italy.
I biked a lot, but occasionally, I would pop my bike onto a

train and cheat during dangerous or long difficult lonely sections of road.

I was riding from Naples to.... I can't remember where, in a train compartment with 5 other people. They were obviously all Italian. One old woman with a genuine babushka, a middle-aged couple dressed like they were going to a fancy event like a wedding, a guy who must have been about 40 and a teenager I assumed was his niece. They didn't have that friend energy or immediate family communication or tone. The uncle was smoking and no one, except me, was bothered by the smoke-filled space.

I didn't have a lot of food with me, but I had been taught by my Kenyan friend in Minneapolis, Mokamba, that you always share the food you have. He taught me this important lesson one evening when I chowed down in front of him and didn't offer him a thing. I was so embarrassed when he asked me what kind of family I was raised in that didn't teach me to share my food.

On the Italian train, I had a giant bag of whole carrots in my pack. I pulled it out and offered carrots to all my train car mates. I just held the bag out to each of them and smiled, since I don't speak Italian. Everyone took a giant carrot. Lucky for me, the smoker put out his cigarette so he could focus on the carrot. We all starting chomping noisily on our carrots. It looked and sounded so funny seeing all of us eating the same thing. I took out my Italian dictionary and said in Italian, "We look and sound like a bunch of rabbits!" Every one of them stopped biting their carrots. They looked at each other puzzled. They shook their heads and rolled their eyes, but no one looked at me again. "Oh shit," I thought, "What have I just done?"

I opened my dictionary again and saw that rabbi is just above rabbit on that page. Uggh. I had just called us a bunch of rabbis. I tried to show each of them the dictionary page and the source of my mistake. They all humored me by glancing at the page, but I am not sure they got it because they avoided eye contact for the next hour on the train. When I got off at my stop, they all stayed on the train and I gave them a cheery, "Addio, Ciao!" The teenager gave me a half-hearted little waive and the others pretended not to hear me.

When I told the story to my new friend Luisa at the hostel that night, she was next to me on my little bunk. I told her no one said anything when I said "bye" to them. Luisa was howling about me calling everyone rabbis and then leaned in and whispered, "you didn't really say ciao, did you?"
"Um, yeah, I did."
Then she giggled more and finally told me that in Italy, I could only use ciao for people I am familiar with and that its literal meaning is "I am your slave."
Geezo, who knew? I think it is used more loosely these days than it was back then.
I officially labeled myself a bumbling American traveler at that point. But, at least I wasn't intentionally rude. I saw so many rude Americans. I started saying I was from Canada because I couldn't be associated with those people. In a plaza in Rome, I heard a middle aged man shouting at a newspaper vendor. The guy selling the paper looked to be about 90 years old and was shorter than me. I rode my bike over and asked the man what the problem was. He shouted at me in a thick Texas accent, "This guy is ripping me off. He is charging me 10 dollars for a newspaper!"
I turned to the now shaken newspaper vendor and asked him in my not-so-great Italian how much the paper was. He told me and it was about $1.50 U.S for an American newspaper.

I turned back to the irate Texan, "He is only charging you $1.50. How long have you been in Italy?"
"Three weeks, why?" he barked at me.
"Because it would make sense to learn a bit of the language. At least learn the money system and "please" and "thank-you."
Now the Texan went crazy on me....arms flailing all over the

place, "He is the one who should learn something. He needs to learn English if he is going to work in a place with tourists!!"
All this time the little Italian guy and all his waiting customers watched the show of me and Mr. Rude Texas.
"Why should he learn English? You are visiting HIS country. How many people in the U.S. who work in the tourist industry speak any other language but English? Almost NONE!!"
"This is none of your business."
"This is everyone's business because you represent all Americans and not very well."

At this, Mr. Texas threw some coins at the vendor and stomped away, not looking back. Some coins hit the ground behind the little wooden counter. I went behind the counter and picked up the coins that had dropped and apologized for all Americans to the little Italian guy. He patted my shoulders with both hands and then held my shoulders and looked me right in the eye and nodded his head with a smile. He had not understood a word of the exchange between me and Mr. Texas, but he had understood it all.

I biked and trained from Greece to Italy and then to France. I was camped with my little tent in a regular campground in Italy. It was mostly giant rv's and it was next to a very fancy resort hotel in the same complex. I had been camping in the rain for a few weeks and when the campground finally flooded and waves were coming into the door of the tent, I had had enough. I left my tent and walked to the resort hotel in the middle of the night. Everything I owned was soaked and cold. I arrived at the reception desk shivering and wet. I explained that I was camped in the orange tent in the campground. They stopped my explanation midway. They said everyone knew I was out there and they were all worried about me for the weeks I was camped there. I asked if they had a tiny room that I might be able to afford for one night because I hadn't slept in weeks. They smiled and the night manager said to wait there.

He came back with a thick white luxurious robe and fat fluffy fresh towels. He told me to go into the showers by the pool and take a hot shower and they would have a bed ready when I came back. While I was showering, one of the sweet staff grabbed my soaked clothes off the chair and yelled into the shower that she was going to wash and dry the clothes. She left a pair of fresh clean slippers there. It was heaven. After weeks of being wet and freezing, I was in a hot shower with lots of water pressure and there was a fancy robe waiting on the hook. When I walked back to the reception desk in the robe and slippers, the manager took me over to a big wide sofa that had been made up into a bed. He told me that there were no vacant rooms, but I could just sleep on the sofa. I was a bit shocked. This kind of thing would never happen at a fancy resort in the U.S. I told him to wake me up before any of the guests came down in the morning and then I passed out. I was buried in the warm blankets and slept all night. When I peeled back the blanket in the morning, a British guy was sitting in the chair of the conversation pit I was sleeping in. He chirped, "Good morning Sunshine!" He was not the only person up to greet me. The whole lobby was full of wealthy guests reading papers and drinking coffee. I was so embarrassed. I slinked over to the reception desk and asked the night manager why he didn't wake me. He just laughed and handed me the stack of my clean dry clothes and dry shoes. I was just blown away. No one was judgmental or upset by me being there. It made me cry grateful tears....it was just so caring. Italy was like that. Everyone was super kind and caring.

I had a bike accident there. Someone ran a red light and hit me on the bike. I was pretty scraped up and had to go to a hospital and get stitches. When I went to the desk to pay, they said they had no system for me to pay. All healthcare is free there. It was really amazing. Here in the U.S.A you have to pay or prove insurance before they will take care of you."

"I know. I really don't understand why the richest nation doesn't have universal health care. Seems crazy. Where did you go after Italy?"

"I rarely spent time in cities, but after Italy I went to Paris to visit some art museums and flea markets. In Paris, I was biking down the road and I saw a woman with a scarf like my Australian friend, Helena's, and a backpack like Helena's and she was short like Helena. I stopped my bike and saw she was reading a menu posted on a cafe window. I couldn't believe it. Helena was supposed to be back in Australia by then. I figured I had seen the last of her when I left my apartment in Minneapolis. I crossed the street with my bike and whispered in her ear, "You can't afford it." She whipped around and we hugged and laughed and jumped a happy dance.

I asked her what the hell she was doing in Paris. Apparently she had decided to travel a bit more before heading back to Australia. But, she never imagined bumping into me on my bike trip. Here is the really odd thing, not only did we bump into each other, but we each had in our pockets tickets for the same ferry to the UK for the next morning. It was really more magical considering there was no internet and no cell phones then....she and I were just meant to cross paths. I think that is an issue with the internet and cell phones. It doesn't allow for as much synchronicity, the magic stuff. People these days can't even figure out how to pick each other up at the airport without a cell phone.

We traveled together through Scotland for a few weeks and then she left for Australia....leaving me to bumble through more crazy no-plan adventures. in Edinburgh, I lived with Brazilians, danced at the Goambe Club to African music until all hours and slept with African men who wooed me on the dance floor. Finally, I got back on my bike and made my way down to Spain and Portugal.

The three generations of women who ran a little pension in Bom Jesus, Portugal, were out of a storybook. They made me a vegan lunch and while I was eating my lunch in their kitchen with them, the grandma dragged a struggling goat in and kept chatting with me while slitting his throat and butchering him on a table. Nothing in her thought it odd to be smiling and chatting with a vegan woman while killing a goat. They tried to convince me to stay and live there and work with them at the inn. They didn't understand why I would want to keep biking and not just settle down in the most beautiful place they had ever known. Actually, none of them had ever left Bom Jesus in their lives. But, they were right, it was definitely one of the most beautiful places on the planet.

After a few days, I made my way down to Sagres in the south. There I rented a little house on the beach for $3 a week and walked all day on cliffs above the ocean with my new friend, George, an 85 year old Swiss man. We spoke in Spanish, which was our only common language. We would walk for hours carrying baskets and filling them with firewood twigs and branches we found on the ground for him to use in his fireplace. Somehow we managed to talk about everything under the sun even though neither of us spoke perfect Spanish. We talked about everything from abortion to animal rights and told each other all about our past and how we got to where we were. George was so not-Swiss in many ways and so Swiss in other ways. He was floored that I had traveled for months and never owned a watch. He pulled open a drawer in his living room bureau and it was filled with fancy Swiss watches. He picked one for me and put it on my wrist. I told him that not having a watch was a way to meet people when I asked them the time. He insisted that I knew enough people and I needed to have the time accessible on my arm.

About a month into my Sagres life, I left George's at sunset and walked along the cliffs to my little house. It was getting dark, but I knew the path so well, I wasn't worried. Way in the distance I saw some flickering candle light and I walked toward it. It was an abandoned clay shack that George and I had passed many times. When I got to the doorway, I saw four people in there in the candle light. A man and a woman and two kids. They were sitting on the floor on thin blankets. I backed out saying "sorry" in Portuguese. The woman came out and took my arm and smiled wide and brought me back in. She was probably about my age, but life had obviously been rough on her. She had lost most of her teeth and her skin was leathering and had deep wrinkles. She motioned for me to sit down. The only possessions I saw was a worn out cloth bag and a handmade basket with a towel in it and a partially eaten loaf of bread. The woman kept patting my arm and smiling. Then she reached in the basket and took out a second loaf of bread. It looked like these two loaves were the only food the family had. She carefully wrapped up the full loaf in an old newspaper and handed it to me. Then she stood up and had me stand up and walked me to the door. I tried to explain that I couldn't take their food. But, she insisted and the kids and the man were all smiling and laughing and seemed happy about me leaving with the bread. I didn't get it. I hugged the woman and said goodbye and walked home in a bit of moonlight. When I got home, I sliced the bread and there was a hard-boiled egg baked into the center of it. The next day I brought the loaf to George. He was able to explain it all. He said that the family were Romas (what Americans called Gypsies) and it is tradition at Easter time to bake bread with an egg in it. Part of the culture of the Romas was to share what you have and that makes life full and rich and brings a lot of contentment and joy. He explained that the act of giving was more nourishing for them than having more food to eat. I loved this whole idea, but my experience of Romas in big cities on my trip had been very different. I told George about seeing a family in Florence begging for money in a plaza. I went and bought them a bag of oranges and came back with it and gave it to one of the little kids approaching people for money. He took the bag to his mother who was sitting on a piece of cardboard next to a statue. She said something to him and he and his little sister came back and kicked me hard and repeatedly in the shins. She obviously wanted money and not a bag of oranges. I just hadn't experienced a lot of grace in the Roma culture. George just said that every culture has all kinds of people. I treasured the friendship with George and his three dogs, Cuckoo, Mini and Rebs. I couldn't see any reason to end my sweet little life in Sagres. But, sadly, it got decided for me.

One evening I came home and found the police at my little house, standing with the landlady. It turns out someone had planted drugs at my place and then called the police to search the house. George got the full story from someone at the market the next day. I had turned down going on a date with a young guy who turned out to be the police chief's son. So the son got back at me. George and I both tried to explain it to my landlady, but she said it was bad luck for me and bad business for her. She needed to kick me out or the police would come after her. The police had let me go with a warning, but told me I had to leave town that week.

It was a sad morning when I left George and Cuckoo, Mini and Rebs at the front gate of his house and biked down the road toward Lisbon.

I arrived in Lisbon with 120 dollars left. After 9 months of biking and camping I had almost used up my $2,000. I went into the student travel agency and told them I had 120 dollars and had to get a ticket to the USA. They said they had a ticket for me, but I had to be at the airport and ready to go in two hours. I scrambled to find a bike box to ship my bike on the plane. I found a young guy who had a bike repair shop that consisted of a few wooden boxes on a street corner and a few tools. He helped me construct a box to go around the bike and I gave him the last spare coins I had. I managed to pack up my bike and be at the airport just in time for a flight to New York. Just more crazy seat-of-the-pants stuff for me, right?"

"That really is insane. I couldn't handle all that chaotic travel stuff. It would stress me out big time. I am more of a planner. I have advance reservations at motels and a complete itinerary when I travel. We could never travel together. Either you would go crazy from the lack of unknown adventures or I would go crazy from the lack of known elements."

"For sure, we would kill each other or last about two hours before we split up and went our separate ways. But, I must say, as I get older, it is kind of nice to have some creature comforts and know that I will have a solid roof over my head each night."

"Yep, that is me for sure….and I am decades younger than you. I hate being uncomfortable or out of control."

"That is why you will probably always have a plan and a real career. As long as that is in your control. I think I always thought, and really still do think, that the rug can get pulled out from under us at any moment. We actually don't have any control. Just a bit of influence on our lives and a bit more influence on how we handle what is tossed at us. I think on some level I never wanted to get used to any comforts because I want to be ready for any shit that hits the fan. Maybe all those years of learning about the holocaust as a kid pushed me in the direction. So, I trained myself to be ok with no running water, no electricity, being cold, not having money, sleeping in all weather outdoors with no tent, going without food, and anything else I might need if I lose everything. But, somehow I also always had jobs. I never did go hungry for very long."

"That makes sense. I am not at all trained for losing everything. I would have to learn on the spot. Can you tell me a bit more about some of the jobs you've had?"

"Let's start there tomorrow. I have a bunch to do here today. That work for you? I know that was a short recording."

"Sure, let's end here for today. Oh, wait, one quick question I keep forgetting to ask you. Lu, are you a Buddhist? You have Buddha statues in the garden and in the house and I thought you weren't a religious person. Is that too much to answer before we break for the day?"

"No, that's not too much. I can answer that one pretty easily. I am not at all religious. I guess I like having the Buddhas around because they make the space feel calm for me. They just sit there with closed eyes, meditating and it feels good when I look at them. But I have to laugh when I think about one of the statues that isn't here. I was traveling a few years ago with my friend, Spencer. We took a few weeks to travel up the California coast in his van.. I found a huge concrete Buddha statue at a little shop. I bought it for a song, couldn't resist the bargain. I strapped that Buddha in one of the van seats with a seat belt. I kept telling Spencer to be careful on curves or bumps. I was driving him nuts with my constant, "Careful of the Buddha!!" I babied that Buddha as tender cargo. On the last day of our trip we were coming through Santa Fe. We were parked above the Santa Fe River and the deep arroyo on Alameda. I was in the back of the van and a skinny old guy with a white beard down to his waist stood in the open door of the van. He was in ragged clothes and had a huge smile and he said to me, "What are you doing?" I said, "I'm adjusting the seatbelt on the Buddha." He stared at the giant concrete statue. Then really quietly he said to me, "Don't you know that the Buddha is inside of you?" It made me stop what I was doing and sit there silently for a bit thinking about my attachment to the statue. I asked the old man his name and he wrote it on the notebook I had at my feet. Then I unbuckled the Buddha and picked it up. Me and Spencer and the old man walked to the edge of the deep arroyo and I tossed Buddha in. The statue slammed on the rocks and broke completely apart. We were all howling with laughter watching the statue turn to dust. When I turned to the old man, he was gone. Vanished. Spencer and I looked up and down the road and couldn't see him. He had disappeared. Poof, just like the statue. I asked Spencer if he'd seen the old man, too, because I started to think I imagined him. Spencer was as baffled as me. We walked back to the van and I picked up the notebook to see what name the old man had written down. It was all consonants. It said in capital letters: NGZVTLX. Spencer and I just kept shaking our heads and saying, "What the fuck just happened there?"

"Geezo Lu, the stuff that happens to you...that you attract to your life! I love all these Buddhas around, but, I guess you weren't meant to have that big concrete one."

"Yep, the lesson was bigger than the statue."

KARINA

I did it. Had the talk with Elan. I should have known it would go easily with him, but I was still nervous. Lu and I met Elan at the movie at the community center last night. Andrew and Celeste were there and told me there was a chance they might leave a bit earlier. They asked if I could come by today and they could show me around to all the quirks and to-dos of their place. Elan offered that I could stay over at his and Winnie's place and walk over in the morning if that was easier for me.

The movie was an old Humphrey Bogart film, so I didn't expect there to be a lot of people attending. I was shocked that over 100 people showed up. I grabbed a chair in the back row as soon as we got there and helped Lu and Elan fill little paper bags with the popcorn. We got there early and I really couldn't figure out why we were filling over a hundred little bags, but I didn't ask. When the people started filing in and taking their popcorn bags I was amazed that we actually ran out of popcorn. I asked Elan why everyone was there. He told me it was the only thing going on in town, "Just like African Dance, whenever there is any event in town pretty much everyone comes. Winnie might be the only one who doesn't come to the films. She only goes to films she hasn't heard before." I looked around and saw that it was the same diverse crowd who had come to the dance. All ages, races, bodies, genders. I sat in my chair in the back row and realized I had saved a seat for Lu but not Elan. He seemed just fine to stand up in the back with about 20 other people who had to stand. He stood right behind my seat and for the entire hour and twenty minutes of the film, he gave me a neck, head and back rub. It was a mix of absolute heaven and felt like electricity was running up and down my body. I thought of telling him he could stop, but I never did. I was also throbbing between my thighs, which has never happened from just a back rub. I decided to take Lu's advice and not analyze it, just go with it.

After the film, we helped clean up the community center and I told Lu I was going to stay at Winnie and Elan's place because I had to meet with Celeste and Andrew at their house in the morning. She smiled, "Ok, let me know if I need to pick you up in the morning or if Elan is driving you over." That reminds me what I forgot to share here. Someone gave Elan an older canoe a few days ago and he gave it to Lu to have an extra one at the dock. So, she doesn't need to paddle over to get people as often.

When Elan and I got to his place, the dogs went crazy on us, like Elan had been away for weeks. The tan one, Honey, literally jumped into my arms and I held her little 12 pound body all the way to the house. The house was dark, so I figured Winnie was sleeping. Elan flipped the entry light on when we got to the door and Winnie was still awake and sitting in the kitchen. Elan explained to her that I was staying over so I could go to the neighbors in the morning. Winnie just smiled and offered us tea. Then she came over and gave me one of those wonderful Winnie hugs. She whispered in my ear, "I am so happy you are here."

The woodstove was going and Elan lit a few candles and explained, "It is always dark in here when I get home at night, since mom doesn't need any lights."

I have never spent a lot of time with a blind person, so it hadn't even occurred to me that she wouldn't have lights on in there, even when she is awake at night.

Winnie finished her tea and kissed each of us on the forehead and went to bed.

Elan and I sat in front of the woodstove. Flames were jumping around in the stove door window and the light danced all over us and the walls of the living room. It made the murals that Elan's dad had painted look even more alive.

We talked and laughed quietly in front of the stove. Our chairs were close to each other and Elan kept reaching out and touching my hand with his hand. Every time he did it, I got that whole body electricity.

He added wood to the fire and matter-of-factly said to me: "I think you should just sleep in my bed instead of us making up the guest bed. You ok with that?" I couldn't even speak, I just nodded my head "yes". My first thought was that I didn't have any pajamas, but I didn't say it outloud. Elan took my hand and blew out the candles and led me to his room. It smelled like the rest of the house. A mix of sage and woodsmoke. But his room had an added smell of him. The closest I can come to describing that smell is that it is like freshly sharpened pencils. It is a really good smell that you want to bury your nose into. Like he read my mind, he handed me a nice flannel pajama top and the toothbrush I had used the last time I was staying there with Lu. He had put a little label on my toothbrush. It was the letter K with a heart. It was a small thing, but it made me think he had hoped I would visit again.

We brushed our teeth at the same time in the beautiful mosaic bathroom and it felt intimate and I couldn't even look at him while we were doing it.

Then he took my hand again and we went to his bed and like we had planned it, we both sat on top of the bed and just looked at each other. Then Elan took my face in his hands and kissed me. There is a look that people get in their eyes that says, "I want to kiss you." And I know I was giving that look and I know that he read the look. From there we melted into each other and slid under the covers. We made love for hours and when the sun finally came up through the window, we woke up completely naked and wrapped around each other. When I opened my eyes, Elan was looking at me from over on his pillow. When I looked at him, he got watery eyes, "Nizhóni, that was the most beautiful night I have ever experienced. I have had sex, but that was not sex. That was absolutely love making." I was thinking the exact same thing and he said it out loud. I just said, "Me too. It was that for me, too. What is Nizhóni?" Elan explained that in the Navajo language it means "beautiful" but not just about appearances or external beauty. I heard Winnie was up and about in the kitchen and adding wood to the woodstove. Elan didn't seem concerned and just kept me tied up with his warm long legs and arms. It took a while for us to finally come out of our blanket cocoon. Both dogs were sleeping at the foot of the bed. When we finally got up, he wrapped me in a thick robe and put fat winter socks on my feet. He actually put the socks on like you would do with a child. I had not had someone do that for me since I was a toddler. It was such a sweet loving thing, it made me teary. We walked into the warm kitchen and Winnie was sitting with tea and porridge, "Good morning sleepyheads. There is hot porridge and tea water ready for you on the stove. Did you sleep ok?" Elan and I answered in unison, "We slept great." It was so comfortable. That kind of comfort, between us and between us and his mom felt so new for me. I grew up in a house, but I never realized until that moment that it hadn't been a HOME. This felt like being at home.

Elan went out to take care of all the animals and I walked to the neighbor's house and they showed me everything. It was pretty simple and there is not going to be much for me to do there in terms of chores.

Elan drove me back to Lu's and I canoed across and walked the path smiling, and feeling high. She and the dogs were in the sunroom. Lu was reading and drinking tea and she looked up when I came in the door. "How was your night?"

I sank into the seat next to her, "Oh Lu, it was the best night ever. Just magical."

I told her almost everything. And for some reason I am not terrified that I am falling completely in love with that amazing person. I did tell Lu that.

SERIAL MONOGAMIST

"Lu, we ended yesterday talking about your jobs."

"I have been a serial monogamist for most of my life. Both in relationships and in jobs. I don't stick with things. I flit from one shiny thing to another and get easily tired of the same routine or distracted. As long as things are going smoothly and there is no drama and it is pretty fun, I stick with it. As soon as it gets tough, I am outta there. My friend Bella calls every one of my new jobs "a career". Even if it lasts only a few days, she celebrates the beginning and end of each "career" with a party. I don't really like working for people or with people. I am fine to be in a service-oriented job where I am caring for others, but I don't want bosses or co-workers. I wasn't always like this, but it grew on me after some unpleasant jobs.

Here is how my job searches would go from the time I was about twelve years old. I would ride my bike from place to place picking any business that looked it might be somewhere I could tolerate. Most were not even hiring and I would just judge by the outside of the place. The majority of places would let me fill out an application even if they weren't currently hiring. I could do about 15 to 20 in a day. At least 3 or 4 always called me to schedule an interview. I would go through the interviews and choose the one I liked the best. By 18 years old, I had already gone through many "careers". I served giant cone creations at Dairy Queen and made the boss mad because we were supposed to weigh each cone precisely. I made tacos and burritos at Taco Bell, but the manager screamed at me for not being willing to cook the ground beef (even though I had told him that was one thing I wouldn't do). I worked at Silver Nickel Pants Store with giant ladders on pulleys and floor to ceiling cubbies of pants. Some people weren't buying pants and would come right to the register and tell me a name. I would hand them labeled brown packages with the name they said. Then they would give me sealed envelopes that went into a special lock box. Word around town was that it was just a front for some sort of illegal activity and one day I came to work and it was closed up, shut down for good. Never did find out why.

When I was 19, I biked up to Earl Thompson's Fine Dining. Turns out Earl was gone on a cruise, but his son, Harry, was running the place in his absence. He sat down with me and hired me on the spot to be a waitress. I was required to purchase big clunky white waitress shoes and a polyester white uniform and apron. I was told to wear nylons and make-up. I skipped the make-up part, but I bought some awful pantyhose. Always hated those things since they don't let your crotch breathe. Earl's had 5 waitresses on staff who had all been there 20 years or more. They were big tough eastern European women with names like Helga and Olga. Harry introduced me to one of the waitresses who said, "You won't have an easy time here." And she walked away. Harry told me that the waitresses were very territorial, but that I should be able to hold my own. "My dad, Earl, lives in the penthouse upstairs. If you have any issues, you talk to him once he is back."

My first day on the job, Marta, who was apparently the alpha of the wait staff, sat me down to train me. "We have our regular customers who request us individually. You will get a few of the newer customers, but never our regulars. We will pool our tips at the end of the shift and divide them equally. You will give half your final tips to the busboy. You fold napkins and set up tables when you are not waiting on anyone. You will do what I tell you. They have not hired a new waitress here in twenty years. Earl will not be happy when he gets back. You are too young and don't have enough experience. You won't be here long."

I didn't say a word. I somehow knew that anything I said to her would have no impact and these women were not going to be my friends.

I folded napkins at a separate little table set up just for me. The other waitresses, all at least 30 years older than me, sat together at another table drinking coffee and chatting with each other. After my first 2 hours of napkin folding, I was given a table to wait on. It was a totally tailored looking woman on her own. I brought her water and a menu and told her my name. I also told her it was my first day and that she was my first table. She had a huge smile, perfect red thick hair and told me she was honored to be my first. I had waitressed in little diners before where you get a quarter tip stuck under the saucer if you are lucky. Base pay for waitresses is next to nothing and the tips are supposed to pay your wage. I had a great time with my first table at Earl's. Her name was Jennifer and she was a flight attendant. I guessed that the other waitresses gave me that table because they figured a single woman wouldn't have a very high tab and wouldn't leave much of a tip. After her dinner, Jennifer left the table and I went over to clean it up. I found a 10 dollar bill under the water glass and grabbed it and ran out to the parking lot to catch her. She was across the huge parking lot so I shouted, "Hey, you left this on the table!!"

She laughed and turned to me, "That's yours! It's your tip!"

I stopped in my tracks, "Ten dollars? That's too much!!"

Still laughing, she yelled, "Get used to it, you were great!" as she got into her car. That was the high point of my Earl's career. It went downhill from there.

Turns out that the waitress who said I would have a hard time working there was a prophet.

I got a bunch of tables that first night and the other waitresses waited on their regulars. But, mostly sat around at their party table spot. None of them talked to me or wanted to help me with anything. I was a vegetarian then and didn't know the different types of meat and fish and finally got help from one of the cooks so I could put people's food in order on the tray. Same thing with the mixed drinks. I couldn't tell the difference between a Manhattan, a Martini and a Whiskey Sour. The bartender helped me put them in order on the tray.

At the end of the first night, I had a lot of money in tips. But, when we all pooled our tips together and divided them, I lost 40 dollars because the other waitresses put in less. I ran around all night and they got my tips. 40 dollars was a lot back then. Then after I got my share, they told me to give half to the busboy. But I noticed that they only gave a dollar each to the busboy. Harry was still running things while Earl was gone and I decided I would ask him about it the next day. When I asked him, he said, "I can't get involved in all that. You waitresses have to work that out."

I told the other waitresses that I was not going to be pooling tips anymore. I said, "You are all welcome to do that, but I don't want to do it anymore."

The alpha waitress, Marta, told me I had no choice. She said, "You WILL be pooling tips"

At the end of our shift that second night, they called me over to hand in my tips. I said, "No thank you." Then I gave the busboy a huge chunk of my wad of tips.

Marta was pissed, and shouted to me, "You will be sorry."

The next day, day three, Earl returned. We met in his penthouse and he sat me down to ask how it was going. He was an older guy who looked like the KFC Colonel Sanders, white hair, goatee, and glasses.

I told him it was not easy with the other waitresses and that I had a lot to learn. "I really like all the customers, but the other waitresses all hate me". I didn't want to overwhelm him with details on his first day back from his cruise. He smiled back, "Yep, those waitresses are a tough bunch. Hang in there. I understand why Harry wanted to hire you, but it probably wasn't a good idea. You just take care of yourself."

That night, there was an obviously well-planned ambush. The other waitresses would pass me closely and elbow me full strength in my sides. They would try to knock over my tray when it was full and would push me into the wall when they could. Earl came through the dining room once and they behaved like angels for the short time he was there. He visited the tables of each of the regulars and walked through the kitchen and then back up to his penthouse. When he passed the other waitresses they all smiled sweetly and welcomed him back with chipper little voices I had never heard them use before.

I didn't pool tips with them that night. I biked home with aching sides. When I pulled off my uniform and saw my body in the mirror, I was shocked to see how bruised I was. Solid black and blue up and down my sides and parts of my back.

The next day, I biked to work in pants and shirt and changed into my uniform there. I knocked on Earl's penthouse door and asked if I could speak with him. He let me into the fancy golden penthouse. Everything was brocade and crystal and like a prince's palace.

"I don't want to bother you long Mr. Thompson."

"Please, call me Earl."

"Ok. I just wanted to show you what happened. The other waitresses did this to me yesterday."

I lifted my shirt to show him my bruised torso.

"Oh no, that is horrible. Why did they do that? Did they tell you why they did that?"

"I think it is because I am not pooling tips with them. I take care of most of the tables and help the customers at all of the other waitresses' tables while they sit and talk in the waitress station. Then if I pool tips, I lose most of mine and they make me give half to the busboy. I am fine to give a lot to the busboy because he works hard. But, I don't see why they should get my tips when they hardly wait on anyone or do anything."

"I am so sorry you are going through that. Unfortunately, I don't really run things with the waitresses. Marta mostly runs the dining room. You better just do what she says. I had no idea they could be that cruel. I'm sorry I can't do more."

"Earl, can't you talk to Marta and just ask her to be kinder to me?"

"No, I'm sorry. That is really not my role here. I am really really sorry. Just do what they say and stay out of their way. I am guessing they are not happy that my son hired someone so young and pretty. He shouldn't have done that. But, I hope you stay. The customers like you. I have been hearing wonderful feedback about you."

"Ok, thanks."

I walked down the carpeted steps into the kitchen and told the cooks what happened. They weren't surprised.

That evening, one of the regulars came in and asked to have me as their waitress instead of Carla, their usual waitress. This only made Marta and the others more furious. The customer insisted. This regular customer had brought a huge group of diners that night. The whole family. Twelve of them at a long table. They ordered a few bottles of a high-end wine. The bartender unlocked a cabinet in the basement and pulled out the bottles. He told me to be careful with them.

I had been taught the whole wine routine with letting the head of the table examine the wine bottle, smell and taste the partial glass of wine and then pouring the full glass. I was still nervous. This wine was worth hundreds of dollars.

Then the unthinkable happened. I was removing the cork and I messed up and pieces of it crumbled down into the wine. I was sure that the guy would call Earl over to have me fired. I was also sure that all the money I had made working there so far would go toward paying for that bottle of wine.

Instead, the man laughed and told me to go to the kitchen and get a small strainer.

"Really? You're ok with this?"

"Of course. It's only wine. You're new at this. You'll get better at it."

I went to the kitchen and got the strainer from the nice cook.

The guy strained the wine into his glass and had me bring the other's wine glasses over. When he emptied that bottle, he showed me the best way to open the other one so I wouldn't have a cork fiasco again. I thanked him profusely for being so kind about it. His wife said, "That is the way he is. And lucky me to have lived with that for the past 30 years!" Everyone at the table laughed and all was well.
Almost.
Unfortunately, Marta, the other waitress, had witnessed the whole thing and had called Earl over. He had been downstairs talking to the bartender. She told Earl what happened and that he should fire me immediately. I was sure he would, but instead, he told her, "Marta, let me go talk to Mr. Berrin and make sure he is ok."

When Earl got to the Berrin's table, Mr, Berrin got up and gave him a hug. They laughed and talked for a bit and then Earl returned. "Marta, we all make mistakes. The Berrins are just fine. Lu can stay."

This only made Marta angrier and I spent that evening trying harder to keep a distance from her and the other waitresses. It was like roller derby without the skates or rules. I only got one elbow in the side that night, but it was more painful sinking into my already black and blue flesh.

I got a gigantic tip from the Berrins that night, even with the wine issue. I was clearing their table with the busboy and Marta came over and asked me how much they had given me. I didn't answer. She then went right in my face, "I said, how much?" Again, I said nothing. She walked away. When I came through the kitchen door with the dishes from the Berrin's table, she was waiting. She stood close and spewed, "You little shit, I will destroy you." The cooks and everyone else heard it. They all looked at me with pity. I decided then and there that I would stay for two months and make a bunch of money and then get the hell out of there. On the one hand, I was being abused and I hated serving meat and fish because I didn't want to support that kind of violence to animals. On the other hand, I wanted to make a lot of money. I also didn't like serving alcohol. Especially to people who I could tell were alcoholics. One of the local, well-known doctors came in every Friday with his wife and requested me as their waitress. They would order food and barely touch it and then spend hours ordering and drinking hard liquor. Their tab was huge because of all the alcohol and they tipped beyond generously. But, I didn't really like being part of that destructive dance of theirs.

Jennifer, the flight attendant came in whenever she was in town and would request me. We got to know each other better and better. The tips got larger and larger. At the end of my two months, I told her I was leaving and it would be my last time waiting on her. She asked why I was leaving.
"I don't really want to say why, Jennifer, because you love eating here and I want you to keep enjoying it."
"Well, I won't enjoy it nearly as much without you as my waitress. I'm sorry to see you go."
"I'll miss you, too. Thanks for being so kind and generous with me."

Some of my "careers" were only one day or one night. And some of them never got beyond the interview. In my early twenties, I answered a want ad that read: HIRING FEMALE SPECIAL OCCASION MESSAGE DELIVERY PERSON. IF YOU ARE HEALTHY, FUN AND CREATIVE, APPLY TODAY!"
I pictured myself in various costumes singing at people's doorways and making them happy on their birthdays. I figured I would be dressed as everything from Spiderman to Obi-Wan Kenobi or Princess Leia or maybe a court jester with bells on my shoes. I should have known to just turn around when I got to the address. Actually, I should have known to never go when the address was a suite number. Suite numbers, from my experience, are rarely legitimate businesses. The suite for

this interview was number 351 with no name on the door. Another bad sign. The door had places where it was kicked in through the cheap hollow core fake wood. Obviously, a sign I should have turned right around.
I knocked on the door and after quite a wait (another missed opportunity for me to do a 360 and bolt) the door opened. In front of me stood a massive guy in zebra print Zubaz and a dirty white t-shirt. You might be too young to know what Zubaz are. They were this weird fashion for a while. Big flouncy print pants with elastic waist and ankles. Men and women were wearing them. This guy was about mid-sixties with a slimy comb-over hair mistake trying to cover his bald head. He reached out to shake my hand, "You must be Lu. I'm Bud. Come on in."
The first room was pretty bare except for a black desk with an office phone and overflowing ashtray on it and a black mesh office chair that was totally broken from Big Bud sitting in it. There was a putty colored folding chair in front of the desk. The phone was the kind with a bunch of lights for all the extensions or lines, but I guessed none of them blinked with calls holding. Not exactly a bustling place. The thin carpet was worn through to concrete in lots of places with stains all over. The fluorescent lights were flickering and that combined with the old cigarette ashtray smell made me feel nauseous. I had the willies, but I thought I was in too far to back out now.
I pointed to the metal folding chair and asked Bud if I should sit there. "Sure. You can sit there."
"So, Lu, what kind of experience do you have in entertainment?"
"Well, I don't really. But I like singing and I can always make my family and friends laugh if that counts. And I am super friendly and get along with people."
"Ok, that's a good start."
"Bud, can you tell me how much the job pays? Is it by the job or by the hour?"
"Oh, I wouldn't worry about that right now. You will be well

compensated for your work."

"Oh, ok."

"Lu, let's get the interview going. Here is what we do. You go into that room and put on the costume you see on the table in there. Then come out here and let me see you."

He pointed toward another cheap hollow core door with a brass knob.

I got up and went into the room and closed the door behind me. The only things in the room were a folding banquet table and a black and red lace, very tiny, costume. it was like the kind the Zigfield Follies women would wear or the saloon dancers in the wild west. It was nothing like the Spiderman or Obi-Wan Kenobi outfit I hoped for.

I stood in the room biting my thumbnail, trying to decide if I should go through with this.

I looked around the room to make sure there were no peepholes or cameras. Then I peeled off my own clothes and stuffed myself into the lacey thing. It was ridiculous. I have always had more of a boy body than a girl body. My waist and breasts and hips have always been close to the same measurement. I never understood that 36-24-36 thing. I was more like 31-31-31. My back fat oozed over the top and the leg holes were cutting off my circulation.

I nervously shuffled through the door back into Lou's office.

He looked me up and down.

"Not bad, Lu, not bad."

He spun his pointer finger in circles and told me to turn around so he could see the back. Then he asked me to do a complete turn two more times. I felt like an idiot. It was even worse than when my mom would tell me to "Go show your dad what he bought you." after we would shop for school clothes and I had to model them. I despised that ritual.

After I had turned, Bud calmly told me, "Now take the outfit off."

I started toward the other room.

"No Lu, take it off right here. You have to practice what you will be doing for the customers."

I froze.

My mind was reeling, "He was looking for a fucking stripper. Or, maybe he wasn't hiring anyone at all and he just gets his jollies this way."

"Sorry Bud, I thought I was going to be singing and wearing costumes from popular movies."

"You are welcome to sing if you want to, Lu. But our customers want more."

"I guess I am not the right person for the job. I will go put my clothes on."

"Oh come on Lu. Don't be such a prude. You will make good money. The tips are great. Customers are very generous."

"No thanks."

I ran into the room and put my clothes on as fast as I could. I was praying that Bud would not block my way out of the place. "Please, please, please, just let me get out of here!" I pleaded to the stained popcorn plaster ceiling, hoping somebody 'up there' would hear me.

When I opened the door, I didn't see Bud at his desk. I panicked. What if he was outside the suite door, waiting to push me back inside?

I was reaching for the knob to leave the suite when I heard a toilet flush and a door open behind me. I spun around to see Bud emerging from the bathroom pulling up his pants and wiping his hands with a paper towel.

I didn't wait for any goodbyes, I blasted out of there and levitated down the stairs three at a time and out to my bike. I got the lock combination wrong the first spin, because of my shaking hands. Finally, it clicked and I whipped it off and into my basket. I only turned back one time to make sure Bud wasn't following me as I rode down the middle of the deserted street. The cool wind felt like it was washing me clean of the whole thing. I didn't bike straight home. Unconsciously I must have known that I needed to ride until I had completely erased all traces of Bud and the black-lace outfit. I biked three times around Lake Calhoun and finally raised my head up to the autumn trees and the wind. Out loud, I expressed my gratitude to the powers that be, my guardian angels (who must work overtime), "Thank you, Thank you, Thank you."

Most of my early jobs started with the understanding that I would not be there long and would not hesitate to leave on a long backpacking or bicycle trip when the urge came along. I was always clear up front with any boss. They would go into the arrangement knowing my lack of long-term commitment.

I mostly landed in the jobs accidently. I graduated from college with a degree in Cultural Anthropology. Before I even graduated, I was offered a job at the Science Museum of Minnesota as an exhibit writer and developer. There were parts of the job I loved, but exhibit departments are in the basement of most museums and this one took up the entire dark basement. I wasn't built to spend my days in a basement without windows, so I knew I wouldn't be long for that job. I would come in at 9 sharp and leave at 4:30 sharp. My boss called me in one day and told me he could set his watch by when I arrive and leave. He let me know that to really get ahead in the museum world you had to give more than expected and he asked if I noticed that the other staff came in early and stayed late. I told him I did notice and that I would never do that. I reminded him that he was already getting my best hours of the day. On some of my days off I was volunteering for a program with at risk teens. I had this idea that I could help them get to their dreams in life by really focusing on what they wanted. I love working with them. I was spending a day with the teens and noticed a guy in a suit standing at the back of the room watching and listening. He spoke to one of my co-volunteers and then left. The next day while working at the museum, I got a call and it turned out to be that guy who had been observing us. He told me he worked for Minnesota Public Radio and could I walk over and talk to some of them about an idea they had. I went there on my lunch hour and was in a board room with a bunch of guys in suits. They wanted me to produce a radio show. So, just like that we came to an agreement and I was producing and hosting a show called Welcome Home. It was such a great job. I would decide the theme of each show and drive around the Midwest interviewing people on the theme. It would be topics like fathers, holidays, and anything I thought would get people talking. I started calling the people I interviewed the "extraordinary ordinary" because I would find these amazing people in the most unexpected places.

One show had the theme "community". I drove to northern Wisconsin and stepped into a barbershop and interviewed some of the people in there. Then I asked them who I should interview next. This was sort of my system for finding folks to interview. I would go into a café or small grocery or beauty salon or barbershop and ask their advice. So one of these guys in the barbershop tells me to go visit the Cass sisters. When I asked for their phone number, the guy told me they don't have a phone. But he gave me directions to their place. When I pulled up to their double-wide trailer I figured this might not go anywhere. Boy was I wrong. I knocked on the door and the most beautiful Native American woman answered. She was probably about 60 years old and lived there with her sisters. She invited me in and made a tea I had never tasted before. The sisters joined us and they started telling stories. Then, Jo, the one who had answered the door, started playing this big beautiful flute. I was recording the whole thing, the conversation and the flute playing. I was mesmerized by the music. After she played she handed me the flute and told me this story. "I was a little girl and would visit the home of the man who always played flute at our ceremonies. I wanted to learn flute, but the tribe said it was only for the boys and men. I spent years visiting Big Carl, the flute player, and watching and listening and longing to learn. One visit, I went to their kitchen to sit with Big Carl and Lucille, his wife. I noticed the table had only three legs. I asked what happened to the other leg.

Big Carl smiled and reached into a hand sewn cloth bag on the table and pulled out the most beautiful flute. He had carved me a flute from that table leg and then moved the other legs around so the table would still stand up. I held the flute and cried happy tears. All Big Carl said to me was, "today you begin learning to play your flute."

Then Jo reached over and took the flute back from me. She started another song and that mix of the music and the smell of the tea and the warmth in that room made me totally forget I was in a trailer and that I was working, getting an interview. It was unbelievably magical....what a gift for me."

"I love that story. Just too beautiful. Why did you ever leave that wonderful job?"

"I didn't really choose to leave. Although it wasn't a perfect job, I was pretty happy doing it. It is a pretty corporate place. My bosses, the guys in the suits asked me to do a Christmas special. I said I couldn't do that because there were already Christmas specials and that left out a huge segment of the population. I finally convinced them to let me do a holiday time special that was more diverse. They claimed people weren't interested in that, but I told them it was that or nothing. I produced the show and included people from the homeless shelter telling me what the holidays felt like for them and some sang and played guitar and cried about missing their old life. And, you will like this, I had a Swedish woman sing the Santa Lucia song and tell about how she celebrates the holidays. And I went to a family's Kwanzaa celebration and recorded that. Do you know about Kwanzaa?"

"Not really."

"Well each night represents a principle or quality and they make food that is traditional African food and they have a discussion and activity about that quality. The holiday was created by a man named Dr, Maulana Karenga who taught Black

Studies at California State University. After the Watts Riots he wanted to bring African Americans together and decided they needed their own holiday to celebrate their African roots. It was 1966 when he introduced the holiday. Seven candles are lit in a kinara, which is like a Jewish menorah, and they symbolize the seven principles. I love the seven principles. The seven principles are in the language Kiswahili. Unity (umoja), Self-determination (kujichagulia), Collective work and responsibility (ujima), Cooperative economics (ujamaa), Purpose (nia), Creativity (kuumba), and Faith (imani). The family I celebrated with all wore African cloth on their head wraps and outfits and there was only candlelight. It was beautiful.
I was able to produce that holiday show and it was one of the most popular.

This is becoming another really long answer to your question of why I left that job. I was actually on a sort of working vacation in Australia when it happened. I was writing a story on Australia for Northwest Airlines when they started flying there for the first time. So, I flew there and hitchhiked around so I could meet lots of locals. One ride was with a guy who did explosives for road work and I was riding on top of the explosives in the truck. It was a great trip. Got into a borrowed 4 wheel drive with Tina, a Chinese-Australian, and we drove up to Cooktown on what should have been roads, but were really boulder strewn paths. One night we came to a tidal river that was too high to cross and waited there with the local Aboriginals who were also trying to cross to their village. They made a big fire to keep away the salties, which is what they call alligators. When I had to pee, they sent a boy with me who had a torch with a giant flame and he swung that stick around me to keep the salties away. I could see the eyeballs of the gators just past his swinging. They told us stories for hours. I so wish I had recorded those stories. At 3 am the tide went out and the river was crossable and we all made our way across.

When I got back to my job after Australia, my boss called me in to tell me that my show was being replaced by a more sellable show about sports. That was it. End of that job. I knew this guy never liked my out-of-the-box ideas. So it was just a matter of time."

"No worries on the long answers, that is what we are here for, hearing it all. The Australia time sounds great. Did the airlines print your story?"

"Sadly, no. I thought it was a brilliant idea to hitchhike around and meet people. But the airline said they couldn't include something so risky in an inflight magazine that families would be reading."

"That's too bad they couldn't be a bit more open minded.."

"My real work found me eventually. It found me while I was working at the MN/WI Boundary Area Commission. MWBAC was not my real work, but it was there that the chain of events began.

My job was to keep the peace between everyone who had an interest in the river or bordered or lived on the river. That included: 2 states, multiple counties, and cities, private homes, various businesses, motor boaters, jet skiers, kayakers, hikers, swimmers, politicians. At public meetings, I was the facilitator (or more like a referee). The kayakers wanted quiet and no wake, the homeowners wanted no motorboats, the motorboaters wanted freedom to go any speed, each business owner and county along the river wanted their specific demands met, and on and on it went. My number one priority was the wildlife and the water quality and that bias did not go over too well with the people who wanted it just for their profit or recreation.

I worked full time at the MWBAC and used all my sick days and vacation days to go to schools and teach about our relation-

ship with other species and the environment. I had critical thinking programs I had developed and a brochure with what I had to offer. I labeled myself as an organization called Bridges (bridging the gap between humans and other species.)
I straddled life between my paid work and the Bridges work and a new relationship.

I had met Andrew when I had yet another part-time job cleaning offices. He was a high-powered attorney and I was finishing college and cleaning offices. Weird mix. I better not get into all that now. It went on for years that included living with his kids and finding out he wasn't capable of not having affairs. I gave some of my best years to that guy, unfortunately. When we broke up, I moved into all I could afford, a nasty old farmhouse. I was in rough shape mentally from the breakup. The basement had stone walls and the windows would fill with solid flies from my landlord's dairy operation. I scrubbed all the walls in the basement with a bleach solution, thinking it would smell better down there. The next morning I was going down the tottering wooden stairs to the washing machine and it looked like someone had dumped hundreds of pounds of rice all over the floor. Then I saw the rice wiggling and realized it was maggots. Two inches deep covering the entire basement floor. I am not generally squeamish about anything, but I screamed and ran upstairs and called Dave, the landlord.
"Oh, you found where the fly babies live. You ruined their home. Don't worry, I will take care of it while you are at work today." (He shop vac'ed them for hours while I led my first public meeting for the MWBAC.) I blamed Andrew for the maggots and any other hardships I faced after our break up.
One well below zero winter day with snow up to the windows, I stepped out onto the porch naked to give my dog, Blondie, her breakfast. She insisted on sleeping outside and wouldn't use the double wall insulated dog house I had built for her. It was deluxe with windows and a breezeway, but she snubbed it and preferred to sleep in the deep snow. The door

blew closed behind me and locked. The commuter traffic was cruising along the road and I was running around naked in the snow trying to get into my house. I finally ran back to the shed and grabbed a screwdriver and some window putty. I got in by rigging the screwdriver with some putty on the end and flipping the interior cellar door latch. All the while, cars honking their joy at the naked woman in the snow. I blamed Andrew for that, too.

I didn't make much at the MWBAC, so I took a related side job. I became the photographer for the river use research team. I was outfitted with a fancy Hasselblad camera and a plane and pilot. Mary Dodson (Mad Dog) was my pilot. She and I spent months flying up and down the St. Croix River with me bent over a huge hole in the bottom of the plane taking photos. It was precision work, so I had a metronome ticking in my ear and would take a photo every 14 seconds or so, depending on our altitude. I had to watch the altimeter and adjust the timing based on the altitude. If I ran out of film, I had less than 14 seconds to change rolls. I practiced this in the dark of my bedroom closet until I got it down to a science. So, Mad Dog and I were in this tiny Piper plane with me staring through a camera I held over a hole cut in the belly of the plane. Imagine that with a little bit of turbulence. Some days, a LOT of turbulence and I would feel like a kernel of popcorn in an air popper. I was nauseous about 90 percent of the time. When we stopped to refuel, I would do handstands and drink ginger ale thinking it would help. And it always did for a few minutes.

Greg was in charge of analyzing the data in the film. He developed the film, counted boats, gave reports. He was also one of my serial monogamy relationships. Brief, but fantastic relationship. He was one of those people who could have been anything he wanted to be. I always thought he was the reincarnation of Thoreau because of his writing and lifestyle. Just a brilliant and creative guy.

The other related job I took at the time was zebra mussel mitigation. Sounds like an important position, but here is the reality. I would hang out at the boat launches along the river with a pressure washer. When boats got pulled out of the water, I would fill out a questionnaire with the boat owner and find out where they had been. I would inspect the boat for the invasive zebra mussels and just for good measure, I would power wash all the orifices of the boat.

Weekends, I was the enemy. Boats would be lined up waiting to get their trailer backed up so they could load and leave. But, I couldn't let them leave without washing their boat and filling out the questionnaire. The government guys actually thought I was doing something useful. I knew that I was about as effective at stopping the zebra mussel as TSA is at stopping terrorism. It was all for show. I guess there was a little education work to it, but I figured it was just a way to get funding for the office and a little pay for me.

The MWBAC job was ok, but very government-y for me. Lots of guys who sat at desks and liked to tell me to get them coffee, until I jogged their memory that I was actually not their Girl Friday. On the other hand, with my non-MWBAC days, I loved going into schools and leading programs I had designed, like, "Lifestyles of the Eco-Friendly". They were all interactive and got the kids thinking about their role as a caretaker of the planet and all life on it. I got paid nothing for the school programs. As Andrew's kids pointed out to me, I loved my unpaid work more than my paid work.

One day I came into the MWBAC office with my personal mail. On my lunch break, I was looking through the mail, which included an animal rights magazine, a utility bill, a bunch of junk mail and a free airline ticket for anywhere in the USA. This was the pre-e-ticket era and if you got enough points the airlines sent you a paper ticket in the mail. I read through everything and tossed most of it into the recycling box next to the copy machine. When I glanced down, I saw the back of the animal rights magazine. I picked it back up and read the ad for a humane education conference called Open Hearts, Open Minds being held at Harvard. It sounded like people who were doing similar programs to mine. They were on the east coast and I called the number to get more info. The person who answered the phone started asking me a lot of questions. Then she asked who paid for the programs I was doing in schools. I told her no one paid for them. I used my sick and vacation days and paid for the materials myself. She put me on hold and then came back and asked if I would present at the conference. I was pretty stunned. I had never met other people working educating kids the way I was and I was sure not a public speaker.

I responded without having to think about it, "I don't think so. I know how to present this stuff to kids, but I would be too nervous to present at Harvard."

She said, "Please think about it. You would be our only presenter who is doing this on her own without large organization funding."

I lied, "Ok, I will think about it."

I actually had no intention of thinking about it or presenting to people who knew what they were doing.

I registered for the conference and a month later I was flying to the east coast for the first time in my life with my free airline ticket.

I brought a bunch of my brochures and set them on a table in the information area. When she saw my brochures, one of the organizers introduced herself and asked if I was ready for my presentation.

"Presentation?"

"Yes, you are on the program. Look, right here."

She pointed to the time slot with my name on it.

I immediately looked down at what I was wearing. I was in old jeans and a pilly pink sweater and red high top tennis shoes. I was not in any position to present and I told her it was a mistake.

She was not going to let go of it, "You are fine. You can do this.

Just share what you do in Minnesota and Wisconsin with the schools"

I decided I could just relax and handle it.

When my time came, I told the large lecture hall full of people that I was going to pretend that they were junior high students and just show them what I do. I had none of my props with me, but I somehow made it work. I was pretty surprised at how engaged they all were. When I finished my presentation, I took questions. Then, they started clapping. Lots of clapping. And many of them made their way down the steps of the lecture hall and handed me cash and checks. I had tears. I wasn't sure what was happening. I had been just on my own doing this education work. When I asked people why they were giving me money, they told me they wanted to make sure I kept doing what I was doing. I flew home from there with a wad of money in my pocket that was more than I would make in my paid job that year.

I had found my work path and my people.

One thing led to another and I found myself living on the east coast doing full-time humane education and co-running humane ed departments. And it only grew from there. I ended up starting a humane education training program with a co-worker and we opened a center called Center for Compassionate Living. I left the center after some years, but the powerhouse woman I started it with kept it rolling and it is a great success now."

"How would you describe the humane education work in a nutshell? It is not a familiar term for most people. I am not sure we even have that in Sweden."

"For sure you have it in Sweden. The animal rights group Djurens Ratt has a huge education program. Humane education is about teaching people of all ages to align their deepest core values, their most caring values with their daily choices. It covers all issues of social justice, non-violence and caring for the Earth. The critical thinking aspect is key, because we are not raised to question the status quo that humans can destroy anything and anyone for their own profit and power. There are now schools and programs around the world embracing this idea of caring for each other and all life on Earth."

"I love that whole concept. I wish I had been taught about caring for all life as a priority when I was growing up. We claim to be so environmentally aware in Sweden...but the reality is quite different. You should see our landfills. It is so horrible. The island where I grew up had its own transfer station with huge dumpsters. Each was labeled for what you could throw in there. So there was a giant one filled with bicycles. Perfectly good bicycles. And another filled with electronics like stereos and computers. We were made to think that all would be recycled. It was a crime, really, because this stuff was almost all perfectly good and should have been given to people who really needed it or couldn't afford it. I had a friend, Lysette, coming to visit from France and I wanted to get a bike for her to use so she could get around with me. I asked her what color and type of frame she wanted. That is how many bikes were being thrown away. I had my choice of color and type. I stopped at the transfer station and climbed over the edge of the dumpsters and was pulling out a purple bike for her when the workers came storming out of the little building there. They were all in orange jumpsuits, the sanitation worker uniforms. They shouted at me to put it back and get away from the dumpster. Four of them coming toward me. The thing with us Swedes is that it doesn't take much for us to back off when someone is confrontational or even just strong willed. So I just shouted back at them to stay away from me and to go back into the building. And they did. So I loaded the bike in the back of my car and got one more for Lysette so she could choose her favorite. My dad asked me to get him a new stereo receiver one time when I was going by the transfer station. I laughed because he told me what brand and model he wanted and I actually found it!

But, I think it is such a waste. We create so much trash with our crazy consumer and throw away habits."

"Yep, and we also cause so much suffering to other species. It is one thing to destroy our own home, Earth, and make it uninhabitable for our species, but we are destroying everyone, every species', home. We are taking so many down with us.

The humane education work has been my path, but it has not always been an easy path. When you decide that, whenever possible, you want to make compassionate choices, you have to look at some hard realities of what is happening on Earth. It means facing injustice and violence and not turning away. There are so many times I wanted to just quit doing the work. I wanted to be a regular American who just does all those self-centered things and dives into distractions. Those choices, those diversions keep people from seeing what is happening around them. They don't have to look at the cruelty and destruction. The flip side is that those distractions also divert folks from seeing the beauty. The more you are willing to look at what is behind closed doors and gates in many of these industries we support with our dollars, the more you wake up and that also includes the balance of it, you really appreciate the beauty around us and the things we have not yet destroyed.

I have had to see some horrible violence. I was treated for PTSD because of it. There are times I have had to steal animals and do other illegal actions because the people in charge of these animals' lives would not do what was legal or caring. One horse stands out. She was a brilliant white horse and she had laminitis. All four hooves were totally bent upward and had grown about a foot in this position. She was walking on bone for who knows how long before she just dropped to the ground and couldn't walk. When I found her, I was out for a walk with my translator while working in another country. I came across her in a giant green field. She had eaten all that she could reach in her collapsed position. So there was a circle around her head and neck of totally eaten grass and it was just dirt. That told me she had been there a long time. She was skin on bones and I could see her entire skeleton. Through the translator, I asked some boys whose horse this was and they pointed to a man standing near a barn below me. We went to the man and I offered to have the vet come and treat the horse. I explained that she could be walking again in three months or so. I also explained that if he did nothing, she would be dead within a few days. He refused my offer and got very angry and started shouting wildly. Then I offered to buy the horse. I told him he could name his price, any price. He refused again. The translator explained that the guy could easily get another horse for very little money in that region and that because I was a woman, there was no way he would do what I wanted. I then asked the guy what I could do for that horse that he would be comfortable with. At that point he pulled out a gun and held it 6 inches from my face. He said if he ever saw me on his land again, I would be dead. But I couldn't leave it at that. I always try to keep the translators safe in any country where I work, so I told this particular woman that there was nothing we could do and we left the guys land and walked back to the car. Back at my hotel I contacted Emma, a horse rescue person from the Netherlands who speaks English and has a farm about two hours from where we were. She offered to bring a trailer and straps and her strong son and his friend and the four of us would steal the horse and get her to the rescue farm. We met that night at an intersection and I hopped in the truck with them. I explained that the guy would shoot us if he heard or saw us on his land. We had to do this totally silently. So we planned exactly how we would put the straps and where each of us would be standing and how we would carry her over the rocky field to the trailer. We couldn't use flashlights, so we stood next to the trailer until our eyes adjusted enough to walk the uneven ground. The friend of Emma's son tripped on a rock while we were making our way to the horse. I heard him land next to me and I immediately reached down and covered his mouth with my hand. We could not make any noise. I whispered in his ear, "I know you are in pain, but if you make any sound, we are all dead. Just breathe. We will take care of you as soon as we are back in the truck. Breathe deep." Poor kid was really hurt, but I couldn't chance him getting us all killed. We managed to get to the horse and by some miracle, and not very gracefully, we got her in the trailer. We drove about a mile to where my car was. I turned on the overhead light in her truck and saw that the kid who had fallen was bleeding badly from his knee where he had hit a boulder. His pants were torn and I asked if I could tear them a bit more. Emma had a first aid kit in her truck and I cleaned and bandaged him and asked how he was doing. The adrenaline of the rescue had kicked in and Emma's son and this kid were high as kites from succeeding with our mission. I flew back to the States a few days later and Emma emailed me that the horse was doing better and was eating and drinking and the vet had already started treatment. Six months later I got a video from Emma of this horse totally filled out and running. It just made my heart sing. Here is the crazy part."

"Wait, you haven't already told me the crazy part?"

"No, that was the routine part. So, about two years later, I was back working in that village with their schools. I was walking with the same translator through the center of the little town and a guy I didn't recognize at first comes running toward us and is shouting and grabbing at me. The translator told me that the guy was saying I stole his horse. Then I remember who he is. The guy who had the dying white horse with laminitis. When he stops shouting, I tell him through the translator, "I am glad someone stole your horse. I wish it had been me. But, I am just one tiny American woman and I am not capable of lifting up a horse and where would I have put the horse if I had stolen it? I don't live here, I have no place to put a horse. I just hope whoever stole your horse is taking better care of it than you did." The guy kept shouting and now he was shouting to anyone around who would listen, "This woman is a horse thief, she will steal all the horses in our town. Help me stop her. She is a criminal. She stole my horse. I will kill her." We just kept walking and the translator kept translating what he was shouting. People on the street looked at us, but they looked at the guy like he was nuts. The story was too far fetched for anyone to believe. When we were a few blocks away from the guy, the translator asked me if I had stolen the horse. Remember, I keep them out of any danger and definitely don't share info that would put them in danger. So I just said, "How would I have stolen the horse? I don't even have a car, let alone a truck and horse trailer." I kept the info from her without lying. It is really tough work when you have to witness violence everyday and in many of these places that is exactly how it is. A few days after we bumped into the guy who accused me of stealing the horse, we were walking through the same village and saw a man with no legs on a wooden cart with four wheels low to the ground. He was propped up on this wooden thing. It is like the gizmo that people use to work on cars and they can easily slide in and out from under the car. Anyway this guy used his hands to move along. It just looked grueling. We watched him cross the street just ahead of us. We stopped to make sure he didn't need help. It took him forever. He kept looking left and right until the road was totally clear and then he crossed. He got down the curb and up the curb. The moment he finally got up the curb on the other side, a big guy who was walking past kicked him and the cart back into the street. He tumbled away from his cart, but quickly made his way back to it. The cart had started rolling back into the road, but stopped in some gravel. The guy who had kicked him was laughing and shouting awful things to this poor man while he just walked away. No one on the street was paying attention or helping this guy. I grabbed the translator's hand and we ran across to help. We helped him back on the cart and up on the curb with both of us holding his arms. I asked him if he was okay. He couldn't understand why I would think he wasn't okay. I explained that we saw the guy kick him off the curb. So then he told us, "I have been doing this for 40 years. Did you see how I have to look down the road and can't cross until there are no cars? That is because cars try to hit me. I have been kicked off the curb more times than I can remember. It means nothing to me anymore. To them I am just like a piece of trash or some animal. They would rather not have to see me in their world. I just remind them that life isn't perfect. Thank you for helping me, but don't worry, I am fine. This is my life."

"Oh god, I can't believe that people would do that. It is making me feel sick. How have you lived with decades of witnessing things like this? I don't think I could do it. I just can't bear that kind of suffering."

"It is not easy. But, on the flip side, there are a few lives that have been improved from my education and rescue work and that makes it worth it. There are so many times that I have wanted to walk away from it. Just quit. One time, I was flying to California. I had just come from the Middle East. I had been asked to help in a region where a security camera had witnessed some boys with a dog on a long rope. The boys drenched the dog in gasoline and lit him on fire and laughed about it. The same night, another security camera caught the same boys q a dog and the dog hid in a huge concrete pipe at a construction site. The boys tried to get the terrified dog out of the pipe. When they couldn't get the dog out because the pipe was too long, they filled it with cardboard and paper on both ends and used the rest of their gasoline to light a fire on both ends and kill the dog. Then they played with the charred dead body of the dog. The authorities showed me both security tapes. They had the boys in custody, but they couldn't keep them because they were minors and the parents were fine with what the boys had done. I was asked to work with the community on compassionate living education work. But, seeing those films haunted me. I couldn't get them out of my head.

So, on the flight to California, I decided to quit doing the humane education work and the rescue work. I made a firm choice to find work that did not involve witnessing violence. I would do this one last workshop in Monterey California and then be done with this work.

While I was in Monterey, I went running each morning. I kept trying to get to the water, but it was all private property and I couldn't get past the fences. Finally, I got to a park on the water. I was squatting down on a rock at the water's edge when I suddenly saw the roll of kelp next to me moving. I saw eyes. Then I saw the kelp unroll and there was a sea otter not even 5 feet from me. She was so beautiful. She rubbed her eyes and stared at me. I had apparently woken her up from a nice sleep. I learned later that they roll in the kelp to sleep so they don't drift out to sea. Then for the next 30 minutes she dove into the water next to me and came up with urchins and cracked them open and ate. I can't put it any other way, I fell in love. I also got a message loud and clear from her, "If you stop doing this work, who will speak up for us?" That day I figured I was saved by an otter. I ran back to my hotel and I'm sure people thought I was on my honeymoon because I had that stupid smile on my face that people have when they are in love. I obviously didn't quit the work after that workshop."

"That is so amazing. I have never even seen an otter in the wild. They are one of my favorite animals on the planet. Wow, she was so close to you. I love that. Lu, you really have experienced the beauty and the ugliness of this Earth. And somehow you keep going after decades of looking at it head on."

"Yep, like I said, I never planned to do it this long. I cannot imagine being your age and what you will witness in your remaining years. I am old enough that I will see a lot of the demise of us in the next decade or two, but you will see more. I don't know how you even decide what you want to do with your life. It is like a ship is sinking and you have to decide if it is too late to help keep it afloat or if you want to do something to slow down the process or if you want to just party and enjoy life until it is all sunk. You are about 27 or so?"

"29 actually. And, you are right, it is a confusing time. I cannot see a future for humans and somehow I need to still live life and feel enthusiasm for my work. But, I often wonder what the point is. Even us spending these days together and me interviewing you. I have no idea what I will do with all of this information. I will put so much time into creating an article or a short story or a book from it, but when there are no humans and the planet is whatever it will be without us, what difference will any books make or any creations? I have also really loved painting in your art studio. It is one of my favorite things to do here.... But, I think about how pointless it is in the face of how doomed we are. This full speed ahead path to destroying the earth and humans. I mean really what is the point of all we create?"

"Even with the huge age difference between us, our questions are the same. I guess it is no accident we are connecting like this. I look back at all I have created and done and tried and wonder what the point was. And even now, I also paint and write and create gardens and wonder what the point is. Here is what I have come to understand through meditation and exploring life: There is no point. There is only right now and what is right in front of us, in this moment. There is no past, that is over with. There is no future, that is yet to be. When you create art or any other thing you do, it is how you show up in that process. It is not the product you are creating. You are being created and re-created with everything you do. So right now I get to sit here with you and make the most of this connection right now. And when we are done with today's interviews, we will walk together and take it all in. The sky and the sound of the river. And that is enough. We can find gratitude in every moment.

I once read a true story about these Jewish men who were in a Nazi concentration camp. I can't remember who was telling the story. The men were taken to an area and made to dig a giant hole that would be the grave of other prisoners. They dug for days and then they were made to stand and watch as fellow prisoners were lined up along the hole they dug and were shot dead and the dead bodies fell into the hole. When they got back to the barracks, one of the guys kneeled down next to the hard wooden shelves they were forced to sleep on and started praying the Hebrew prayer for gratitude. The other men watched and listened and then confronted him. They said, "How could you say that prayer when we just witnessed what we did? How could you? What is wrong with you?" The man got up from his knees and calmly answered them, "I am so grateful that I am not capable of the kind of barbaric things that those soldiers do." I love that story because I really think we are at forks in the road every day, all day. And we can choose gratitude as what we focus on or we can choose the other road, which is sadness and misery.

There is another great story about the Cherokee activist and tribal leader, Wilma Mankiller. She wore a necklace with the heads of two wolves. A boy asked her what the wolves meant. She said, "One represents fear and one represents love." So the boy asked which one was the strongest, and she replied, "Whichever one I feed the most." I think about this a lot. What am I feeding? Fear or Love?"

"That is beautiful. And so true. Whatever I give the most attention to and choose to "feed" is what determines my life."

"It is not always easy. I think it is why we are here on Earth. All these opportunities to choose love and connection rather than hate and fear. They are presented to us all the time.
I lived in a remote cabin on a river in Minnesota for many years. I planted gardens and apple orchards. The apple trees grew huge. When they started getting a lot of fruit, the deer

would come and eat the apples. I could sit on the porch and watch them stretch on their hind legs and eat all the apples they could reach. I got a special fruit-picking ladder so I could get the highest apples and leave the lower ones for the deer. Over the years, I got so used to the deer that I knew who each individual was and when there were new deer born I could recognize their unique markings and scars and size. There was one huge male with giant antlers and I loved seeing him in all seasons. I owned that land and marked it with no hunting signs. The signs welcomed hikers and swimmers, but clearly and legally said no hunting. One autumn there was a banging on my door and when I opened the door there was a guy with a large bow for hunting. He started shouting at me, "My family has been hunting here for generations. You have no right to post the land and push us out. We are bow hunters. We don't use rifles and we respect the animals and the land." He was so upset with me. When he finished shouting, I asked him if he wanted to sit with some tea with me and we could talk about why I had posted the land. Surprisingly, he said "yes". We sat on my front porch in the sun and I explained my relationship with the deer. I pointed to the apple orchard and told him about my arrangement with the deer who came and ate apples. I told him about my special friend, the large male with the antlers. Then I told him about the previous winter when I was in the yard and heard labored breathing and that special friend was passing on the edge of the meadow with an arrow through his back, under his spine. He was walking slowly and breathing hard and I knew the arrow must have pierced a lung. I tried going to him to somehow help him, even though I didn't know how I could help. When I was about 20 feet from him, he panicked and ran toward the forest and I never saw him again. It was one of the most helpless feelings I have ever had in my life. The bow hunter listened to my story. I explained that I had lost a close friend and that most of the state was open to hunting and I wanted this little piece of land to be a sanctuary for wildlife. A place they could relax and live without being hunted. After I finished talking, the hunter sat there silently for a while holding his steaming tea with both hands and looking toward the orchard. I saw that his face wasn't angry any more. He closed his eyes and the sun was hitting his face. Then he turned to me and said, "I understand. I totally understand. I will make sure my family honors your signs and your wishes. Sorry I was so angry and I am sorry you had to go through that experience."

I think our reactions to things are the only thing we can control and work on. It is a way we can grow. So, we can slow down and rather than react in our habitual ways, we can ask the question I love to ask before speaking or acting, "What would Love do?" It changes everything."

"That is so perfect. Wow. Thanks for that story. I have never thought about reaching out to anyone who is very different from me and trying to create an understanding."

"You can practice it. I think you will love what it shifts in your life. In that instance, I was wanting the hunter to understand my perspective. But, most of the time I think it is more important to try to understand the other person's perspective than trying to be understood. People want to be heard and understood.

There is an incredible American woman named Fran Peavy. She traveled around the world with a banner that read AMERICAN WILLING TO LISTEN. She would unroll the banner in a public place like a park, and place it on the ground next to her. In every country, people would line up to tell their stories, that is how much people want to be heard. She later started an organization teaching strategic questioning and I am sure it is still going today. It is all about the power of understanding others and how we can personally grow from it and create important social change. Before I had even heard of her, I was learning about the power of asking questions and understanding others.

In my years of being vegan, many people have not understood that it is a choice based on my core values of compassion. Many people think it is a fad or diet and they can be pretty cruel in their comments and actions. When people make jokes or tease me or insult me about my choice, I have learned to ask them, "What would make you say that to me knowing that it will most likely hurt me?" It is a way of addressing the reality of what is happening without a huge conflict or walking away silently and wishing I had said something.

I was on a long flight across the U.S. years ago and I had rushed to the airport straight from the garden. I had on Teva sandals and my feet were totally muddy. The woman to my right was all dressed up. I mean the works. High heels, fancy hair and clothes and long shimmery fingernails. Tons of make-up. I noticed her staring at my muddy feet. I figured we had 7 hours together and I might as well get to know her. So I asked her, "Are you staring at my feet?" She looked stunned that I caught her. She said to me, "I think you are the bravest woman I have ever met." I asked her, "What about my feet makes you think I am brave?" She said that she did not know anyone who would leave the house without polished toenails. I laughed and said to her, " Wow, bravery looks so different in my world." We had a laugh. Then I said to her, "I have an idea. We have hours together. Let's learn about each other's world. You can ask me anything and I can ask you anything. I never get to connect to someone who is living such a different life. What do you think?" And she was excited about it and said she would love to do that. So, she started by saying she would never live more than 5 minutes from a spa. I didn't know what she meant because I just thought a spa was the machine you can put on the edge of the bathtub that makes the water swirl and bubble. She explained what a spa was and then looked at me and said, "Who does your skin?" I didn't understand. So, I said, "Is someone supposed to do my skin?" And she said, "Who is your esthetician?" I didn't have a clue what that even meant....never heard of it. So she explained it all to me. The trip went so fast because we were both loving hearing about each other's foreign world. Her name is Sue Ann Clark and we are still friends to this day. I think it has been almost twenty years now. Our worlds are still totally different and we mostly laugh about it when we talk on the phone.

The first time I realized the power of just asking questions or trying to understand the other person, I was about 18 years old. I had set up a table at a mall during some event. The table had information about how animals are treated in society and ways people could change their lifestyles to stop harming them. I had written and printed up some of the information and others were from organizations that promoted spay/neuter and other animal welfare issues. It was the first time I was doing this kind of tabling. In the first hour of my being there, a man came up to the table and pounded his fists on it and started shouting at me, "You goddamn animal lovers have no idea what you are talking about. I treat my animals better than most people treat their kids. I hate you people." I was pretty shocked by his anger and I couldn't understand why he hated me when he didn't even know me, so I just said, "Why? Why do you hate me?" I saw everything in his face change. The color, the expression, everything changed. And he unballed his fists. We had a long conversation about his work as a farmer and I mostly listened to him. All I remember saying to him was, "Oh, this is your livelihood and all you have done your entire life and you are worried aren't you?"

After our talk, we shook hands, and he took some literature and left. I had to really think about what had happened there. It seemed magical, but it was really just focusing on understanding him rather than him needing to understand me. You and I are doing that in our interview time and our hiking time. We are learning about each other and it is so rich, isn't it?"

"*Oh my god Lu, it has been SO rich. My life feels totally changed. What is inside my head and heart is all brand new right now. Really,*

I barely recognize myself and I haven't even been here that long. And the time with Elan is so incredible. I thought I would be too boring for him. I figured his life is so much more interesting than mine ever will be. He laughed about that. He explained to me that his life is just his familiar life and not all that interesting. He compared it to people not knowing they have an accent when they speak. So I don't think I have an accent and your accent sounds exotic to me and Elan's accent is over the top exotic to me. And it goes beyond our accents. It is our lives. Mine seems boring when I am sharing with you or with him, but to the two of you it is not your everyday familiar and you both seem interested when I am sharing."

"Exactly. I love to hear about your life and your path and, watching your openness to all that is happening to you here is so inspiring. You have definitely made my life here more interesting. I was pretty much just in my routine with a few friends and occasional visits from my partner. But, just having you stay with me was such a stretch. And now, so quickly, you feel like family. I will miss you when you move to your house sit. And I know the dogs will be sad. They just think of you as part of our pack now. We will have to come visit you and go hiking over there. You will love some of the trails that will be right in your backyard. And in a month or so the river will be perfect for rafting and long canoe trips. Elan and Winnie always join me for some day trips and overnights, so you will have to join us, too."

"That sounds so fun, I would love to. Does Winnie do ok in the boat? Don't you go through rapids?"

"Ha, Winnie will surprise you. She may not have her sight, but her other senses are amazing. I tease her about being one with the river. She can read the current better than most of us. It's like she just surrenders to it. Similar to what we are talking about with being right here right now. Winnie is not looking ahead at the scary crazy rapids in front of her and she cannot see the boulder in the water or the dead tree stump way ahead of us, but she just does what the water does. She flows right around the obstacles just like the water. You will love watching her in action. She is an incredible woman."

"I can't wait to see that. Yep, she is special. Did you know she taught Elan both his native language and English growing up? So they are both fluent in each language?"

"Of course I knew. She will sometimes sing native songs while Elan plays flute or he sings when she plays and it is the kind of music that stirs up your soul. Winnie and I are like sisters now. I spend more time with her than anyone else and it is the same for her. Other than Elan, she spends more time with me than anyone. It is beautiful. When I have the dogs with me and visit them I often just stay over and Winnie and I sleep in the same bed and spoon and giggle and talk into the night. It is not sexual, it is just intimate. We never had any discomfort with it. I think I would feel a little lost without her. She is so grounding for me."

"I love that. I thought at first that Elan and I would just be close and intimate friends like that. I just sort of felt like the electricity sexual thing was just what I was feeling. Turns out that wasn't so. He feels it, too. I have to make myself not think too much about where it is going and just enjoy it each time we are together. That's not easy for me. I keep dreaming about the future and getting ahead of where we are at. But, I am practicing just enjoying being in the moment with him."

"That is a good practice. I am always practicing that. Something in us wants to daydream the future, or dwell on the past. But, whenever I do that , or any of us do that, we are missing what is happening in front of us right now."

KARINA

After our interview session Tuesday, Lu wanted some space to just be on her own. We had lunch together and then I went across the river and took Lu's truck to the co-op for groceries. On the way back I was going to just find a place to hike along the way on my own. But, without even thinking about it, I ended up driving down Elan's road. I got out of the truck and Honey and Scooter ran from the porch to greet me. They were so excited that I ended up getting pushed to the ground and they were licking my face and I was laughing and trying to get up. We were there on the ground awhile and then I heard someone else laughing. When I looked up I saw Winnie above me with her big white smile in the middle of her brown face.
I was still laughing hard, "Winnie, save me. I am being loved to death."
This made her laugh even harder and she put her hand out and pulled me up. I was surprised at how strong she is. She kept holding my hand and we went into the house. She told me Elan had gone to get some supplies for fixing his tractor, but he would be home soon. The house smelled so good, like spices cooking. She had just made some soup and scooped me a bowl of it without even asking. Then she moved her own bowl of soup next to where I was sitting and she sat so close to me that I could feel her knee next to mine. Normally this would have made me so uncomfortable, but for some reason it felt right.

She ate her soup with some of the noisiest slurps I have ever heard. Then she asked me, "You don't like the soup do you?"
"No Winnie, I love the soup."

"Then why are you eating so quietly?"
"I just eat quietly."
"In Navajo culture if you eat with no noise it means you don't like the food. More sound means more enjoyment of the food."
"Winnie, that is the exact opposite of Swedish culture. We were taught that you don't make noise when you eat because it is not polite to make slurpy sounds or chewing sounds."
Winnie and I had a good laugh about it and she told me to try making sounds with my soup. I was so bad at making the sounds that we were just cracking up from my lame efforts. Then we started comparing cultural differences and norms. We had a blast. We discovered that when you say "uh huh" in English and in Navajo language (called Dine') it means yes. But in Swedish the same thing means "no". And in Swedish "uh uh" means yes and in English and Dine' it means "no". We practiced doing the opposite of our familiar and both Winnie and I were so bad at it that we laughed even harder. I had come there hoping to see Elan. But, being with Winnie was so joyful I forgot all about why I had come there, until about an hour later. Elan appeared at the door while Winnie and I were so busy laughing at ourselves, we didn't hear him. I don't know how long he was standing there smiling and watching us. He came over and kissed us both on the top of the head. I can't explain the feeling. But, when he kissed the top of my head with his hand on my shoulder, tears rolled down my cheeks. It was just all this gratitude and joy I felt in me and it was too much to hold and it came pouring out my eyes. I just love being with them and in their home.

Elan and I grabbed the groceries that needed to stay cool out of Lu's truck and put them in his refrigerator. Then we did chores together and he asked if I wanted to help him fix the tractor. I am so not-mechanical, but said "yes". I warned him that I would be no help. He just said, "Well, I am not so sure about that. Anyway, it is high time you learned to fix a tractor. I am sure that was on your bucket list of things to learn before you die, right?" We were walking to the tractor and he gave me a kiss that sent a shockwave all the way to my thighs. I have to say that being in that state did not help me *focus on my tractor-fixing lesson. While we were deep into the tractor project, we heard a whistle greeting from the front gate. Elan knew immediately who it was, "That's Andrew's whistle". We put down the tools and walked together to the gate. I didn't say anything to Elan, but us walking together to greet Andrew and Celeste felt like we were a couple. Usually that would have made me feel embarrassed. But this time I was really relishing it. Andrew was holding two loaves of bread he had baked and he went right inside to Winnie. Celeste had a tool bag hanging off her shoulder and gave Elan a hug and a pop on top of his head, "Winnie told me you were trying to fix the old tractor. You should have called me. You know I know that thing like my own child." Then she turned to me, hugged me and told me, "Elan bought that old thing from us. What a sucker." The three of us went back to the tractor and Celeste knew exactly what to do. I watched her easily install the new parts Elan had brought and then she just hopped up on the tractor and started it right up. She motioned for me and Elan to get on the tractor with her and we stood on the bar behind her while she tooled around the land. The goats started following us. Elan said the tractor is like a dinner bell for them. Celeste drove the tractor to the river's edge and turned the motor off and all three of us hopped down. It smelled so good by the river. The snow had all melted from the sun and the grasses were still wet and smelling like spring. I bent down to touch the water and it still felt like freshly melted ice, it was freezing cold. While I was crouched by the river, I heard a splash and when I looked up, Celeste was stark naked, in the river, hooping and hollering from the cold. She was swimming at hyper speed to stay warm. Elan and I looked at each other and he winked and nodded at me, "come on, let's do it." I was already cold the moment I got my clothes off and the mud on the edge of the river was making my feet numb. I was rethinking this crazy idea when Elan grabbed my hand and yelled, "Don't think", and jumped in pulling me with him. I am from Sweden, I thought I had experienced the coldest water on earth, but I have never felt anything that cold. And no sauna before jumping in! I didn't last long..well none of us did. We were out on the shore jumping around like wild chimps to try to get warm and* dry....and crazy laughing. Then all three of us hugged in a bundle trying to warm up and we were jumping like that...all three of us as one big jumping trio. And it worked. We got warm enough to drop down in the wet grass in the sunshine. Celeste gave me a high five and we all got dressed and hopped back on the tractor. On the ride back to the house, I told them we were going to have to build a sauna if jumping in freezing water was going to become a regular thing. Elan didn't hesitate, "One sauna, coming right up. I will get on that." I felt more alive than I have felt in years, maybe in my whole life.

I ate some of Andrew's fresh bread with everyone. The stuff we were spreading on it was all unfamiliar to me. Elan pulled jars out of the fridge and we were all devouring this fabulous fresh bread and these mystery spreads. I asked Elan what these were and he pointed to each jar, "This is homemade almond cream cheese that I make with probiotics, this is a pesto spread I make that is Winnies favorite on everything, and this one is a cheesy chipotle spread I make from sunflower seeds." I had a mouthful of the cheesy chipotle on bread, "Elan, you could sell these and make a fortune!" Elan winked at me and Winnie said, "He already has too much money". This made everyone crack up. The sun was starting to set, so I loaded my groceries back up and headed home to Lu's. The happy alive feeling is still with me, hours later. I will admit, though, that I have a part of me that doesn't trust this happiness. I keep thinking that something will come along and squash it and the reality of life without happiness will raise its ugly head. Wish I could just bask in the yummy feeling without looking around for the other shoe to drop. That is such a weird saying. It looks weird as I write it. Maybe it is not really a thing people say. I can't remember if we have something like that in Swedish. I am actually losing some of my Swedish from being here so long. My brain is starting to think and dream in English.

LITTLE BRUCE THE GURU

"Karina, you had a special day yesterday, didn't you?"

"Lu, it was just amazing in every way. Celeste and Elan and I jumped in the icy river. It was wild and crazy and I felt totally alive. Everything about being there with them feels right. I hope I am not getting too attached to it all, only to be hurt and let down later."

"Oh Karina, just love it and let it be wonderful in real time, in this time, right now. Don't sabotage it with any negative thoughts. This is such a magical time in your life. Let yourself just enjoy it."

"It is all just so new for me. I have never felt this happy."

"Good. Just soak it up. The only thing you can count on is change. Remember things will ebb and flow and nothing stays the same. But, you can enjoy it all right now without being fearful about it changing. It will definitely change, but not in any ways you can predict, so it is pointless to obsess about that unknowable."

"You're right, Lu. Thanks for that. I may need your support and advice a lot in this whole thing."

"You got it, anytime"

"OK, back to work. Let's get back to talking about you. You spoke at one point about doing volunteer work for at risk teens. What drew you to doing that work and what other volunteer work did you do in *your life?"*

"Wow, that could be a book in itself. The work with the teens was a total fluke. I was in a week-long workshop experience at a Unity Church. They are kind of new-age spiritual churches and I saw there was a workshop there called Leap Into the Void. Something attracted me to it. The week was so intense. We were literally locked in this room and when something difficult came up, we couldn't just get up and leave. It was basically a week of letting go of anything we were clinging to. Old thoughts, old habits, material things. Any attachments. On the last day and last hour of the workshop, the leader told us it was time to pay for the week. She did a guided meditation and told us to trust whatever number came up. I closed my eyes and the number 4,000 showed up. I kept my eyes closed and tried to mentally at least erase part of the 4 to make it a 1. I only had 5,000 dollars to my name. If I gave them 4,000 I would be dangerously low for making rent and other expenses. No matter how hard I tried, I couldn't make that 4 into a 1. So I opened my eyes and wrote a check for 4,000 dollars. At the moment I signed the check, the door to the room opened. It sort of shocked everyone because this person wasn't in our workshop and the door had accidently been left unlocked. We had not been around anyone outside of that workshop room for a week. Then I realized I knew the person who had opened the door and started coming in. It was Mary and we had met at a party about a month earlier. I jumped up and started toward her. I was asking her while I was walking toward the door, "Mary, what are you doing here? This is a closed workshop." She said she was looking for the Course in Miracles group. I told her that was one flight up from us. She reached into her purse and pulled out a card and said, "Rae, so glad I am seeing you. I have been trying to find your contact info. I have a project I want you to work on with me." I took the card and was a little stunned that right at the moment I signed the check, she had appeared.

The day after the workshop, I called her and she told me she wanted me to volunteer with at risk teens helping them to create the lives they wanted instead of being stuck in their own and their family's patterns. The interesting thing is that the volunteer job then led to the work with public radio. And all that happened when I let go of the money and the fear of not having enough. The same day, the day after the workshop, my Uncle Lenny called. He told me he had a Jeep Grand Wagoneer in his driveway and it wouldn't start. He said if I would come get it started and take it away, I could have it. I got the Jeep going and put it in my driveway with a For Sale sign and it sold for 4,000 dollars. No coincidence, for sure. So you would have thought I would have banked that money, right?"

"*For sure.*"

"Well, the thing is Uncle Lenny was a homophobic, racist, classist guy who hated anyone who wasn't white, Jewish and wealthy. So I took the money I got from his Jeep and donated it all to groups working on gay rights and social justice issues. It felt like balancing things out a bit. The whole family learned just how homophobic he was when we were at a family event. There were 50 of us hanging out in a room. Little kids all the way to older folks. Uncle Lenny was Lazer's younger brother. So, somehow we get on the topic of gay rights. Uncle Lenny says, "Gay people shouldn't be allowed to teach in the schools or any job with kids and they shouldn't be allowed to buy houses in any neighborhood they want to." The rest of us jump on his ass. Lazer says, "I am ashamed to call you my brother. What is wrong with you?" Aunt Sophie says, "Lenny, were you fucking dropped on your head as a baby?" This is hilarious because at that time Sophie was 94 years old and she just lets the F word fly. Turns out, Lenny is the only conservative homophobic one in the bunch. Then one of the kids, Bruce, who was about 6 at the time, says, "Uncle Lenny, would you still love me if I was gay?" Lenny doesn't skip a beat, "Of course I would still love you Brucey". So everyone goes crazy at this point and Lazer says, "Stop lying to the kid. You are telling us he shouldn't be able to do any job he wants to or live anywhere he wants to and you call that love? You are full of shit. Tell the kid the truth." Lenny is so outnumbered that he refuses to continue the conversation. That was really the day we all realized just how deep his hate ran. I left that conversation feeling grateful that most of my relatives were open-minded liberals. And I watched little Bruce on the floor looking up at Lenny with soulful eyes and thought he was such a little Guru. With one question he said it all."

"I cannot imagine any conversation like that in our family. We never had anything close to that real. We never talked about stuff like that so honestly. Well, we never even talked about controversial subjects at all. I would have loved hanging out with your family."

"Yep, they are mostly passed away now, and the few that are left don't get together anymore. But you would have loved those family reunions and you would have been totally welcomed with open arms."

"Do any of your other volunteer jobs stand out?"

"Whew, so many to choose from. There was one that was really creative and fun. I traveled part of the Mississippi River with a puppet theater called In the Heart of the Beast. They are still around. The puppet shows they do include giant street sized puppets that take two or more people to hold and little puppets that one person works. All of their shows are eye open cultural and social change themes. For many people, those plays are the first time they learn the truth about historical events like Columbus coming to the Americas. The play about that was called Grim Reaper. The one I was involved in was called Circle of Water and told the whole story of the history of the Mississippi River, including the human and non-human history of the river. The show went on the road and toured down the entire river from north in Minnesota to the south in New Orleans. I joined the southern part of the tour and was in the show as various characters from a buffalo to the prairie. The group worked with local schools along the route and the students would make puppets, learn about the river and be part of the plays that were performed. They would also have a big parade in each town with the student's puppets included. It was so fantastic for each community. We slept in churches and school gymnasiums. I also helped with shopping for groceries and cooking for the cast and crew. One day I was taking one of the group's bikes to the farmers market in New Orleans. It was a Monday morning and I was speeding down the road when this guy opened his car door and the rusty corner of the door sliced right into my foot. This guy was so drunk. That is how it is in New Orleans. Lots of partying and drinking at all hours. We both looked down at my foot and the amount of blood pouring out freaked us both out. The drunk guy told me to get in the car and he would take me to the hospital. I told him he was too drunk to drive. He told me that seeing all that blood had sobered him right up. I didn't see any other option, so he took me to the big public hospital and I got in the long line with people who had gunshot wounds and other emergency issues. I asked how long it would be before someone would be able to see me and was told it was about a two hour wait. My jacket was wrapped around my foot and was soaked in blood that was dripping on the floor of the hospital. No one seemed alarmed at all. "This is Monday in New Orleans.", I was told by a nurse who went by us. The drunk guy told me to just come with him again, "You will die by the time they see you. Lets go to a different hospital." We crossed the river to a very different suburban scene and a private hospital. There was no one in line. The receptionist told us that we would have to put a 250 dollar deposit down to be seen since I didn't have insurance. I was blown away when the drunk guy pulled out a wad of cash and gave her the 250 dollars. He looked like he wouldn't have a dime to his name. I got a line of stitches that

went around the top and bottom of my foot and between my toes. Twenty stitches in all. The doctor told me to find anyone to take out the stitches in a few weeks. They wrapped the foot in a giant cast-like bandage. Turns out that two weeks later we were in Mississippi still doing some shows. We were all traveling in a bus and I was hobbling around checking out a new town with a few of the other cast members. I saw a doctor's office and told them I was going to go get my stitches out and would meet them back at the bus. The receptionist told me to have a seat and she would call me in soon. I sat next to an old black woman and a boy who looked like he was probably her grandson. She patted my arm and said, "You ain't from around here, are you?"
I said, "No, I am from Minnesota."
She smiled and patted my arm again, "You ok. Just sit here. But folks might not like it too much."
I looked around and saw that there was a white folks area of the waiting room and a black folks area. I thought, "What the hell is going on? This is 1985, not 1920." The receptionist eventually called all the white folks in for their appointments. Then she came to me. I reminded her that the woman and her grandson were there before me and probably had appointments. She kind of nervously chuckled and told me to just "come along now". The black grandma patted my arm again, "You go on now. It's ok."
So racism was alive and kicking in the south and this grandma was so used to it that she didn't even seem disturbed with it all."

"That is awful. I wonder if it is still like that down there?"

"I imagine it is, just not quite so blatant."

"The puppet theater sounds so wonderful. I am going to have to look them up, maybe there are some YouTubes of them."

"I imagine there are."

"Ok, tell me about another volunteer job."

"Well, you know, there were lots of ongoing volunteer things at animal sanctuaries and shelters. Those were always the dirtiest and, of course, my favorites. I still volunteer at the sanctuary up in Taos. I go once a month and do cleaning and building projects. Elan and Celeste and Andrew go with me most months. We have a blast working our asses off."

"Oh, I so want to do that with you next time. When are you going next?"

"We will go a week from tomorrow. You will love it there. It is called Finally Home Sanctuary and it is one of the best I have ever seen in all my years of visiting rescues and sanctuaries. But, let's see, other volunteer jobs. One was really tough for my heart. I volunteered with a group that takes people with disabilities on wilderness trips like canoeing the Boundary Waters in Minnesota. I started as a volunteer and then worked as hired staff. The first trip I did as a volunteer should have made me just call that the last trip with them. Instead I loved so much of it that I kept doing it. But it was hard. That first trip was all guys. Nine men who were all severely disabled. Turns out, all but one had been in motorcycle accidents. 4 of them were paraplegics and the others had major mobility issues, too. We were canoeing in the Boundary Waters and that involves portaging long distances between lakes. It was a weeklong trip. At night we would sit around and process the day. I'd hear all of their stories and they were heartbreaking. Most of them were on the trip to regain a sense of confidence and strength. All 9 of them had gotten divorced or broken up with partners after their accidents. One guy said his wife told him that he wasn't the man she had married and she couldn't live the rest of her life taking care of him. He was the one in the group who hadn't been on a motorcycle when his accident occurred. He was driving a car and came to the railroad tracks and a train was coming so the guardrails were down and the flashing stop lights were going. He looked one way and saw the train and knew he could make it, so he drove around the guardrails. What he didn't see was that there was a second train coming from the other direction. That one hit his car and nearly killed him. He wished it had killed him. He did not have use of his legs at all. We had one wheelchair on the trip for a guy who couldn't hold himself up without it, and we carried that guy on portages. But the ones with no use of their legs could either get a piggy back ride or make their way on their own. The guy who was hit by the train, his name was Corey. I will never forget him. He chose to do every portage by dragging himself with his arms while his legs and feet would get dragged along behind him. His shoes got worn down to almost nothing and I had to invent a sort of sling with my bandanas to hold him up a bit at the knees so his pants wouldn't get shredded. I used my other hand to try to swat mosquitoes away from his face. It was like watching a self-induced torture session. Corey was covered with mosquito bites and cried much of the way on the portages. The worst one was a long portage that took him over 8 hours to do. Over rocks and mud and tree roots. Just awful. But, at the end of that day when we gathered around the fire to process together, he was victorious. He was beaming. He just kept saying, "I did it. I can't believe I did it." He was truly happy and proud of himself. That first trip, I would go into my own tent at night and cry my eyes out about what these guys were going through. I never did that in front of them. I just wanted to support them, but it was really tearing at my heart."

"Geez Lu, why couldn't you choose volunteer jobs that were not so hard on you? That just sounds way too intense. You could have done tutoring or some other easy volunteer stuff."

"Where were you when I was deciding what to do with my life? I could have used that advice! Actually, I never chose these, they definitely chose me. Like almost everything in my life, I just stumbled into them and didn't walk away."

KARINA

Well, today is the day I moved into Celeste and Andrew's place. It has felt bigger than leaving Sweden to come to the USA. I stood hugging Lu on the dock and glanced across the river to see Elan waiting on the other side sitting on a rock smiling. Lu saw my tears and hugged me again, "You are right down the road and the dogs and I will come visit you and you can come here anytime. It is your home now." I didn't tell her my tears were grateful tears, not sad tears. I told her I would miss our regular interview sessions and that I might be back with more questions and my recorder. She said, "Oh my god, Karina, if you aren't bored out of your mind when you write up the sessions, there is something wrong with you." We had a good laugh at that. It was our ongoing thing....Lu assuming she was boring as hell and me wanting more and more info. I looked down in the canoe and there was a big box. When I asked Lu what it was, she just said, "A few housewarming ditties." I canoed over to Elan. The moment I left Lu on the dock, she must have pulled her clarinet out of her daypack. She was playing the Happy Trails song and it was both funny and sweet. The sound of it over the roaring Rio Grande River was a moment I wanted to keep forever. I got to the other side and Elan grabbed the front of the canoe and gave me a hand up on the rocks. He tied off the boat and then pulled me in for a hug. While we hugged we both started singing Happy Trails. We turned toward Lu and sang with her playing. She stopped playing and blew me a kiss from across the river. I went from one loving set of arms to another one. How did I get so lucky? It felt like some sort of birth and the river crossing was the birth canal. I yelled across the river to Lu, "Thank you for everything Lu, I love you." I surprised even myself. I do not easily say those words to anyone. Elan loaded the box into his truck and we drove away with me and Lu waiving non-stop until we couldn't see each other anymore. Elan took me straight over here to Celeste and Andrew's place and after bringing the big box in for me, he hugged me and said, "I will leave you to get settled in. Come to me and Winnie if you need anything. We would both be happy if we saw you everyday. Winnie told me to tell you that she made a wonderful curry and you can come for dinner tonight if you like. Here is a bag of stuff we put together as a little "welcome to the neighborhood". He handed me a heavy canvas bag and took off in his truck. I came in the house and just stood for a moment listening. There was absolutely no sound, just silence. But as I stood longer I could hear the river rushing in the distance. I opened the canvas bag and it was filled with jars of food. Soup, almond cream cheese, fruits and veggies and little notes on everything. Some were in Winnies odd blind person handwriting. I love this one, "Karina, eat the soup even if you don't feel hungry. It will help this place feel like home". Then I opened the box from Lu. There was a brand new pair of rubber boots with a note that said, "practical shoes for the new you". She had also packed cozy socks and sweaters and a winter hat that I had seen her crocheting in my last days there. Then, at the bottom of the box was a beautiful meditation cushion and next to it a collection of art supplies. Lu had been more aware of what I was doing in that art room than I thought. The items she packed are the exact things I had been using to make drawings and paintings at her place. I sat at the kitchen table and looked around. The sun coming through the window was heating up my body and I felt as content as I had ever felt in my life. I am home.

ACKNOWLEDGEMENT

I am grateful to Hy and Hanc who never gave up on loving and supporting me through all the crazy times. Sue Shepanek, couldn't have moved forward without your critical eye on the manuscript. For the moments of peace I feel, I am indebted to my teachers, SN Goenka and Byron Katie and all the non-humans around me. To the trees and the wildlife and domestic animals, thank you for keeping my life somewhat balanced and I am so sorry that we humans have not figured out how to care for you. Thanks to my amazing huge chosen family of compassionate people. And, to JC, for being by my side through all the ups and downs and unplanned chaos and for understanding who I am.

Made in the USA
Las Vegas, NV
31 May 2021